ASK FOR IT

Jo had never kissed an aristocrat. Her driving goal hadn't been to kiss one, but to kill one. If she wanted to kiss him, now was her chance. There was nothing to stop her.

"I'm going to kiss you, Nathan," she said in barely a whisper, sitting beside him and bending close.

She kept her eyes focused on his, watching for signs that he might wake. Her heart began to race, beating wildly. She held her breath and touched her mouth to his. He was warm against her, but he didn't open his mouth, or respond the way she imagined he would—hungry, hard, demanding. She didn't know what she'd hoped for—he was unconscious, after all. But she wanted more, his heat and temper.

She wanted the fire that had burned in his eyes.

But there was nothing.

She drew back slightly and sighed, disappointed. Frowning, she looked down—and met a pair of cold gray eyes.

A gasp lodged in her throat. Nathan's icy gaze was clear and sharp and focused on her.

She pushed away. He gripped her neck with a strong hand and flipped her onto her back, pinning her to the mattress with his body.

"If you want me to kiss you," he said in a growl, "all you had to do was ask."

Dear Romance Reader,

In July we launched the Ballad line with four new series, and each month we'll present both new and continuing stories set everywhere from medieval England to the American West—the kind of passionate, romantic stories you love best, written by the most gifted authors. At the back of each book, we'll tell you when you can find subsequent books in the series that have captured your heart.

Martha Schroeder's atmospheric *Angels of Mercy* debuts this month, chronicling the dreams and desires of three women stubborn enough to join Florence Nightingale on the battlefields of the Crimean War. In **More Than a Dream,** a young woman of privilege wants nothing more than a life as a healer—until a brooding physician tempts her wish for love. Next, Corinne Everett begins the *Daughters of Liberty* series, in which three young women chart their own passionate courses in the wake of the War for Independence. An ardent Patriot meets her match in a dangerously attractive man who may be Loyalist—and who threatens to steal her heart—in **Loving Lily.**

Next, rising star Tammy Hilz continues her breathtaking *Jewels of the Sea* trilogy with **Once a Rebel.** When a woman who despises the nobility's arrogance encounters a handsome aristocrat, she never imagines the adventure that awaits them on the high sea—or the thrilling fulfillment she finds in his arms. Finally, the second book in Kate Donovan's *Happily Ever After Co.* series presents a Boston society beauty and a widowed sea captain marooned on a tropical island—and the once-in-a-lifetime love that results when they are **Carried Away.**

Kate Duffy
Editorial Director

Jewels of the Sea

ONCE A REBEL

Tammy Hilz

ZEBRA BOOKS
Kensington Publishing Corp.
http://www.zebrabooks.com

ZEBRA BOOKS are published by

Kensington Publishing Corp.
850 Third Avenue
New York, NY 10022

All Kensington titles, imprints, and distributed lines are available at special quantity discounts for bulk purchases for sales promotions, premiums, fund raising, educational, or institutional use.

Special book excerpts or customized printings can also be created to fit specific needs. For details, write or phone the office of the Kensington Special Sales Manager: Kensington Publishing Corp., 850 Third Avenue, New York, NY, 10022. Attn. Special Sales Department. Phone: 1-800-221-2647.

Zebra and the Z logo Reg. U.S. Pat. & TM Off.

First Printing: February, 2001
10 9 8 7 6 5 4 3 2 1

Printed in the United States of America

*For Sherrel Congemi, mother, teacher, friend.
If only you knew how many lives you
touch, and how deeply.
Thank you.*

Prologue

Wind tore at her hair, pulling pins loose, setting the braided and coiled length flying out behind her. Joanna Fisk shook her head and lifted her face toward the sun. For the first time in weeks, brilliant sunshine had replaced black, thunderous clouds. Freak April storms had unleashed freezing rain and stinging sleet on the city of London, turning dirt roads into muddy rivers, and rivers into gushing rapids. She'd been trapped indoors for too long, trapped with no way to escape the ludicrous folly her life had become. Another day and she would have surely gone insane.

Daring to wear her thick wool pants, boots and a man's overcoat, she sat her gelding astride. She touched the *Sea Queen* blade sheathed at her waist, more out of habit than for the need of protection. Tightening her knees against her horse's sides, she felt him stretch his legs, lengthening his gait. It was still early morning, the wet streets nearly empty as she and her mount flew down one cobblestone street after another, dodging the few men and women who were caught in their path. Brick-terraced town houses lined her way like a row of towering cliffs. The ring of hoofbeats echoed off the walls, making her think she was being pursued. A quick glance behind her confirmed that her fear was unfounded—she was free, at least for a while.

Free and uncaring of where she went, so long as she

didn't stop. For over a year, she'd endured one hated etiquette class after another. She had tolerated the lessons only for her older sister Morgan's sake—not for the loathsome aristocrats Morgan was trying to impress. Jo shuddered, feeling her joyful mood turn black. There was another reason she suffered being among the nobles: revenge—for the lives they'd ruined, the countless deaths she held them responsible for, deaths that had crushed her heart like an eggshell. And all because of the needless Seven Years' War, fueled by the aristocrats' greed.

Jo took in a deep breath, pushing the bleak past away, though not too far, and wished for the scent of the ocean. She caught only the smell of mildew, damp with rain, the underlying stench of sewage that even the stiffest wind failed to lift away. What she wouldn't give to feel the salt spray of the sea on her face, feel the deck of a ship loll beneath her feet.

She hated the city. She'd leave London if not for her sisters. But this was where they wanted to live, and so this was where she'd stay—for now.

Jo looked around, surprised that she'd not only left the prominent residences of the West End behind, where she lived with her sisters and brother-in-law, Daniel; she'd also passed through the Royal Exchange, where the banks and merchants were housed. Without realizing it, she'd entered the slums of the East End—an area synonymous with poverty and grief. She slowed the gelding to a walk and frowned at the timbered buildings, brown with age and layers of soot. Lean-tos littered the street fronts and wrapped around dark alleyways that even the sun seemed unable to reach.

Jo felt a scowl steal over her face, knew people were watching her as she rode past, taking note of her aversion to their filthy homes and desperate lives, but she couldn't help it.

Because I came close to living among them. She suppressed a shiver. Her horse must have sensed her shift in mood; he tossed his head and pranced to the side.

A group of children, barefoot and wearing rags for clothes, darted past. One boy had a squawking chicken trapped in his arms; another clutched a loaf of bread. Two small girls chased after them, glancing back to see if they were being followed. Their eyes widened, and one of them made a startled squeak.

Jo followed their gaze and saw a shopkeeper, as wide as a solid oak door, in pursuit, yelling for a constable. Without hesitating, Jo shifted her mount and cut him off.

"Out of my way!" The man raised a meat mallet and tried to dart around her. Jo turned the gelding, blocking the men's path again.

"Is there trouble, sir?" she asked when he glared up at her.

"Those guttersnipes have stolen from me for the last time!" he yelled, spittle flying from his mouth. "They're going tae be locked up this time. I'll have their filthy hands chopped off."

Looking in the direction the children ran, Jo caught a glimpse of the last one disappearing around a corner. Something inside her tightened, loathing the thought of the shopkeeper running them down. She drew a shilling from her pocket and tossed it to him. "That should cover what they took."

"They 'ave tae be stopped." Eyeing the coin, probably to make sure it was real, he clutched it in his heavy fist.

"I'll see to them."

"See that ye do, or I'll make sure they regret ever steal'n from me."

Jo put her heels to the gelding's sides and followed the path the thieves had taken. She wandered up and down alleyways crowded with wattle-and-daub huts, scraps of rotting food and things she couldn't identify.

The stink that rose from the ground made her stomach turn sour and begin to heave.

Babies were crying, men were shouting and women could be heard selling fresh vegetables and flowers to passersby. Then she heard it—the chattering of young voices, and the distinct cluck of a chicken.

Dismounting, she eased her way into a lean-to that, to her surprise, led into another room of packed straw and mud, a small hole in the wall the only source of light. Dark and gloomy, the room was cold despite the crowding of wooden crates and piles of rubbish. With the ceiling too low for her to stand, she crouched down and peered around a makeshift wall of stacked barrels. In the far corner, gathered around a battered pot, were four children and one hysterical hen. From their conversation, she gathered they were trying to decide the best way to cook their dinner. Jo arched a brow, not knowing who to feel more sorry for, the children or the chicken.

"You might consider keeping her alive," Jo suggested, smiling when the startled group spun to face her.

"If you find some grain for her," she said, not venturing any closer, "she could lay enough eggs to feed you for months to come."

"Who are you?" a boy she guessed to be twelve or thirteen demanded.

"My name's Jo." Seeing one of the little girls shiver, she took off her coat and held it out, wishing she had one for each of them. "Go on, take it."

The girl looked at the older boy. He compressed his mouth into a tight line, but nodded his approval. Taking two tentative steps, the girl took the coat and slipped it on.

"Is this where you live?" Jo asked.

"It might be."

"What's your name?" None of them answered. "I'm not going to hurt you. But I might be able to help."

"Why would you?" the younger boy with dark, stringy hair asked warily, clearly not trusting her any more than his older friend did.

Jo started to answer, but a deep, wrenching cough erupted from beneath a pile of trash beside her. Moving a box aside, she discovered a small boy no more than four years old, his eyes glazed and his cheeks flushed. "My God, he's sick."

"Leave 'im alone!" The older boy started forward, but the girl wearing Jo's coat gripped his shirt, stopping him.

"That's why we need the chicken," she said. "Sammy hasn't eaten in days. I'm Amy." She pointed to the oldest boy. " 'E's Peter and that's 'is brother Farley. She's Chelsea."

"Do any of you have parents?" Jo asked, laying her hand over Sammy's brow. She sucked in a breath. He was on fire, burning from the inside. "He needs a doctor."

"We ain't got no parents or no money for a doctor," Peter spat.

How well Jo knew the emotions behind those words. But things were different now. She could help this child, where she hadn't been able to before. . . .

"I have money," Jo said with such anger the other children stepped back. She started to rise, but Sammy reached out, surprising her, catching her leather necklace. His thin fingers gripped the toy soldier dangling from the end. On reflex, she almost took the soldier out of his grip, but hesitated. She'd worn the toy for the last twelve years, never once taking it off—not since the day her baby brother had died. Seeing the child's small, grubby hand, the pleasure in his eyes, her chest clamped around her heart.

He looks like Robby. Pale blond hair, a small button nose, a face made for laughter. She squeezed her eyes shut.

"You're too big for a toy," Sammy said in a reedy

voice. He doubled over coughing, hoarse, ragged gasps that jarred his thin body. With every shudder he made, every wheezing gulp of air he tried to take, never fully succeeding, panic balled into a tighter fist against Jo's chest.

Once the attack ended and the bright red spots faded from his cheeks, she realized he'd kept his grip on her necklace.

Her eyes stung with tears, but she forced them back. "Do you like it?"

He nodded. "I never had a toy."

Drawing the leather cord and painted soldier from around her neck, she pressed it into the boy's hand. "It used to belong to my little brother, but I think he'd like it if you kept it for me. Will you?"

Sammy smiled as Jo pulled away. She scanned the squalid shack, the other children's solemn faces, and felt a surge of fury that made her want to lash out and scream. They were without their parents, without any means to survive, yet they were desperately trying—the same way she had not so long ago. Because no one had cared. Not the wealthy who had taken everything from her, or the king whose duty it had been to protect her.

She held her anger in, though it nearly killed her to do so. She'd already learned that shouting at injustice didn't do any good. But something had to be done, or Sammy wouldn't survive.

"You don't need to kill the chicken," she told them, already making plans. She needed a carriage, a way to move the boy without doing him more harm.

"He needs tae eat," Peter said, clutching the chicken.

"I'll be back." She touched Sammy's fevered brow once more. Her heart lurched against her chest. She didn't have much time. *He* didn't have much time. Meeting Sammy's hopeful gaze, she smiled when she wanted to cry. "I'll be back for you. I promise. I'll be back."

One

"The dance has begun," Jackson Brodie announced with a devil's grin.

Joanna Fisk tossed her *Sea Queen* dagger from hand to hand, the jeweled hilt a blaze of steel and gold. Candlelight framed her opponent's chiseled face, the sheen of sweat on his brow, the gleam of anticipation in his whiskey brown eyes. Jackson topped her by a foot, outweighed her by four stone, and beneath his white, long-sleeved shirt of crisp linen, he possessed enough muscle to best ten men. Clearly he had the advantage.

Jo smiled and waved her friend toward her. "Shall we dance then?"

Music floated up the stairs, down the hall and into her bedroom, announcing the first minuet of the evening. Briefly, she wondered what the guests would think if they saw her sparring with Jackson. The men would most likely glare down their arrogant noses; the women would undoubtedly faint. She should be downstairs among them, smiling and curtsying, showing off her newly acquired skill of conducting mindless conversation. She'd practiced for the occasion; she shouldn't let her time go to waste.

Instead she shifted her weight onto the balls of her feet, thinking she should have kicked off her satin slippers. She circled Jackson, keeping an eye on the eight-inch dagger he gripped in his hand.

He lunged, his arm whipping toward her. Jo leaped back, tripping over the train of her gown. His blade arched in a silver streak, slicing her sleeve with a whisper of sound. Emerald green silk sagged halfway down her arm.

Jo muttered a curse. "Your aim is true tonight, Jackson. And rather close, but you'll not be so lucky next time."

He chuckled, used to her admonishing tone. "I've heard your warnings before, Jo. This time I have you."

"We'll see about that." Before the words were out of her mouth she dodged left, only to counter with a surprising move to her right, slashing Jackson's shirt at his waist in the process.

He sucked in a breath and leaped back. Touching the rip with his fingers, he eyed her with an arched brow. "Grace gave me this shirt so I wouldn't look like a pauper tonight when I dance with her."

"You don't like to dance." Jo examined the long tear and grinned. She'd aimed well. There wasn't a scratch on his muscled stomach, but only because she hadn't wanted to put one there. It had been weeks since they'd practiced dueling with knives. They could have delayed until morning, but swordplay held much more interest for her than what awaited below. "Besides, Jack, my little sister won't notice what you're wearing. Unless you decide to shock her and attend the ball like a new-born babe."

"Joanna!" Morgan's outraged voice clapped like thunder, rattling the framed pictures along the walls.

Jo winced and hid her knife in the folds of her skirt, though she knew the effort was too late. Her older sister entered the room looking as if she intended to box Jo's ears.

"You're supposed to be downstairs." With her silver eyes flashing, Lady Morgan Tremayne included Jackson in her reprimand.

Jackson straightened his stance, but he had the good

sense to appear abashed. Then he ruined the contrite look by pursing his mouth to hide a rueful grin.

"Yes, I know." Jo fluttered her eyelashes and sighed exactly the way Madame Fournier had instructed her during her hated etiquette class. Even now she could hear Madame's voice: *Make a small sound of distress, like a forlorn kitten, lifting your chest as you do, but not overly much. You don't want a gentleman thinking wanton thoughts about your person.*

"What was I thinking?" Jo asked with feigned alarm. "Your masked ball will fail utterly unless I'm there to smile, giggle and engage in trivial chatter."

Morgan folded her hands at her waist. Jo clenched her jaw, disgusted with the lady her sister had become. What she wouldn't give to see Morgan scream, shout, throw a vase across the room. But that wasn't her sister's way. It never had been. Morgan was calm and observant, sensible and strong. So sure of herself. Everything Jo wasn't.

Crossing the room in a sweep of russet satin, Morgan opened a sewing box and began threading a needle. "Grace is looking for you, Jackson. You promised her the first dance, which will soon end."

Jackson ran his fingers through his blond hair, the ends curling over his collar. He glared at Jo as if his lingering were her fault. "Is Angel disappointed?"

Morgan sliced him a look that didn't need to be voiced. "Your coat should cover the cut in your shirt. Go find her."

Sliding his knife into his waistband at the back of his pants and gathering his coat, Jackson left, leaving Jo to face her sister's anger alone. *The traitor.*

"You don't have to stay," Jo said. "You have guests waiting."

"I can still sew, and my guests can wait a little longer."

Jo wasn't about to give up, not wanting to hear the

lecture that was sure to come. "I'll call a maid to repair my gown."

"I'm going to tack the rip, Joanna, and you're going to stand still and let me." Morgan gathered the rich fabric and jabbed the needle through. Jo tensed, expecting to feel a sharp stab.

"How could you do this?" The strain in Morgan's voice pricked Jo's conscience. "You know how much tonight means to me."

Jo started to defend herself, but her mouth had suddenly gone dry. She looked away, feeling shame press against her neck. She did know, all too well.

"I'm counting on tonight to secure my place in Daniel's world."

"Daniel doesn't care what his blue-blooded friends think."

"I care, Jo," Morgan said, her voice trembling. "I'm not the only one they've ostracized these last four years. They turned their backs on my husband. I won't stand for it, not any longer."

"You can't change the opinions of people who are pigheaded and blind to the world around them," Jo argued, incensed at how truly blind and heartless the wealthy could be when they chose.

"I will," Morgan said with resolve. "Or I'll die trying."

Her sister had set herself up for defeat, Jo thought, biting her tongue to keep from saying something that might deepen her sister's hurt. Morgan was not only a fisherman's daughter, poor and of common birth, but worse yet, she'd been a pirate. One wanted for murder.

Being cleared of her crimes by King George III hadn't mattered. England's elite had ostracized Morgan since the day of her wedding to Daniel. The crowning blow, declaring just how far aristocrats would go to shun her, had occurred on the night of Morgan's first ball. Only a handful of Daniel's closest friends had arrived. The three hundred other guests hadn't bothered to send word of apology, giving Jo another reason to hate England's wealthy. Not that she needed another reason.

She touched the pocket inside her skirt and felt the bulky wooden shape of her toy soldier. Grief—hot, boiling grief—churned inside her, filling her with a need for urgency. It was time to act. England's nobles had harmed too many people she loved, ruined too many lives.

Like Robby's. And Sammy's. The pain of Robby's death lingered like a festering sore, but when she thought of Sammy, envisioned his small face, so still, so thin . . . so quiet . . . *I was too late. Even though I promised him. . . .* She clenched her hand around the soldier, not caring that she crushed her gown. She'd given the toy to Sammy, but he hadn't been able to keep it; life hadn't let him.

And for what reason? she asked herself for the thousandth time. So the rich could become richer? She clenched her teeth and would have hissed out a curse if not for her sister's presence.

They won't get away with it, she vowed. She'd make them pay. And she knew just how.

She shook herself from the past and the purpose that drove her. For the moment she had to think about Morgan. Since that disastrous ball, years before, Morgan had performed charity work, attended teas, perfected the art of dressing, shopping and decorating, everything within her power to gain society's nod of approval. Tonight was Lord and Lady Tremayne's first ball since that horrible night. The least Jo could have done was support her, instead of sparring with Jackson.

"I saw a long line of carriages waiting to arrive," she said as a way of making amends. "The ballroom must be full to bursting by now. Everyone in London must be here."

"Which is why I need you downstairs." Her sister made her last stitch and tied off the thread.

"You don't need—"

Morgan gripped Jo's free hand and squeezed. "I do need you. Everyone claiming a tie to England's society is here. Do you think they've finally accepted me, Jo?" She glared at the doorway, her chin coming up. "Or do they expect the mask to be a sorry event, and they want to be present only to see me fail? To put me in my place for good?"

"You'll amaze them all," Jo reassured her, trying to sound as if she believed the words, though she doubted them, and she sensed Morgan did, too. The wealthy ruthlessly guarded the gates into their world, and were selective about who they allowed to enter. "I don't know why you're so determined to gain their approval. They're nothing but selfish, greedy, arrogant—"

"Let it go, Joanna."

Jo sucked in a breath and started to pretend she didn't know what her sister meant, but their argument was an old one. "I hate them, Morgan, and I always will. For what they've done—"

"They're not to blame for Robby's death, any more than you are."

Jo didn't reply. Her sister didn't understand; no one did, and she was beyond trying to explain her feelings.

"Besides, you can't hate all of them," Morgan said, smiling for the first time that night.

"I concede," Jo added with a reluctant smirk. "You married the only English aristocrat in possession of a heart."

"Daniel is why I'm trying so hard." Morgan handed Jo her mask of gold beads framed with ostrich feathers in a deep jewel green that matched Jo's eyes. "But I'm afraid he's a man of little patience when it comes to entertaining. Come now. All of my acquaintances have met Grace before tonight, but they're curious about the elusive Joanna."

"Why don't we let the mystery continue?" She'd visited Morgan and Daniel at their London town house countless times, but so far she'd managed to avoid meeting any of their friends. It seemed that her luck had run out. She lifted her gown and slipped the *Sea Queen* blade into the sheath strapped to her thigh.

"Must you wear the knife?"

"As I recall"—Jo straightened her gown and led the way into the hall—"before you gave it to me, you never went anywhere without it." Besides, she added silently, it reminded her of the other reason she had to attend the ball. She might loathe the aristocrats, but she knew enough about them to know that when they danced and drank themselves into slobbering fools, they became a fountain of information.

Morgan released a thoughtful sigh. "Sometimes I wish for the return of those days."

"Only sometimes?" Jo scoffed. "Every day when I awake and remember I'm in London, I wish I were on the deck of the *Sea Queen* instead. Sailing wherever I chose, wearing whatever clothes suited my mood. Instead I'm pretending to be a lady with manners and sensibilities."

"You know what they call you, don't you?" Morgan laughed, a deep, smoky sound, as she wound her arm through Jo's and led them toward the stairs. "The Emerald of London."

"Don't you mean the *curse* of London?"

Morgan's eyes sparkled as she tried to suppress her mirth.

"I'm an emerald and you're a pirate?" Jo rolled her eyes. "The wealthy are more dim-witted than I thought."

Morgan shrugged. "Perhaps it has something to do with the fact that everyone knows about my past as the pirate captain of the *Sea Queen,* whereas no one has yet caught a glimpse of you. You've refused to attend any balls or the theater or . . ." She sighed. "You've made them curious. No one purposefully shuns their society."

"They know I'm your sister and a pirate as well. What else is there?"

"They want proof you exist."

So they can rip me to shreds, as they've done to Morgan.

"The Emerald of London." Jo snorted at the absurd description of herself, and earned a disapproving look from her sister. "Who started this rumor?"

"I believe my husband had a hand in it."

Jo should have guessed. Daniel Tremayne, once a narrow-minded nobleman, now loved to mock his opinionated peers. The Emerald of London, he'd called her. It was a fitting description, she decided, because when it came to the lords and ladies of England, her heart was as cold and hard as stone.

With her mask covering all but her lips, the line of her jaw and her chin, Jo moved among the crowd, nodding to those who caught her eye, loving the anonymity the mask gave her. She could hear them whisper among themselves.

"Does anyone know what she looks like?"

"Has anyone received an introduction?"

"Does she have a sensible mind?"

"Is she a duchess or a countess?"

Twin chandeliers drizzled soft light over the guests' satin gowns and silk formal wear. Most everyone wore wigs, Jo realized: curled blue ones, short gray ones, pink or white, all greased, then powdered until they were stiff. Half the guests had powdered their faces as well, giving them a pasty, unnatural appearance. Like the walking dead, she thought with a grimace.

Jewels in every size and color glittered from women's throats, ears and wrists, the cost of which could feed every impoverished soul in England for a year, solving Jo's dilemma. If she were a pickpocket, her prayers would have been answered and she'd be in heaven.

But outright thievery during her sister's ball was out of the question. That didn't mean the evening would prove to be unprofitable. She touched the soldier in her pocket. *Sammy.* She briefly closed her eyes. *I won't lose any more children. I won't!*

Jo studied the room for a pigeon. She needed money—large sums of money, and quickly. She smiled, but the effort felt tight with strain. Where better to find a treasure chest than in a roomful of wealthy nobles?

"You're going to ruin the ball." Grace's hushed warning stopped Jo. Behind her ivory-and-pearl mask, suspicion glittered in her young sister's blue eyes, making her seem far older than her seventeen years. Candlelight shimmered in her upswept blond hair, turning it to liquid gold.

None of the Fisk sisters had donned a fashionable wig that weighed more than a small child, for which Jo was certain they'd be criticized. With Morgan's sable hair twisted with pearls, Jo's russet curls laced with a string of jade beads and Grace's blond locks finished with miniature pink roses, the sisters were like spring flowers growing in the snow.

Dressed in beaded white lace, and without makeup, Grace seemed more ethereal than human—an angel cast down to earth to lead the sinners to salvation.

"Has Morgan told you of my decision?" Grace asked, cooling herself with her fan with slow, elegant movements that amazed Jo. She couldn't have managed anything so willowy if her life had depended on it.

"She told me. Why on earth would you want to go to a boarding school?"

"Wilmouth is highly respected. I can learn things there that Madame Fournier can't teach me."

"What things?"

Grace tilted her chin with as much defiance as her gentle nature would allow. "I want to be a lady."

Jo snickered, but cut off the sound when Grace gasped with disapproval. "If you were any more of a

lady, I'd have to curtsy whenever you entered a room.
Besides, you're too old to attend Wilmouth."

"I don't care. I'm going."

Jo sighed, wanting to argue until she changed her
sister's mind, but she let the issue drop. "Why aren't
you dancing with Jackson?"

"I'm not speaking to him at the moment." The defiant tilt vanished as Grace dropped her gaze to the
floor. "And I shouldn't be speaking to you either. How
could you spar with him? Tonight of all nights?"

Jo grimaced, knowing how tender her sister's heart
was. "It was my fault he was late for your dance."

"It doesn't matter." Grace shrugged and glanced
across the crowded room, where Jackson stood in his
new evening clothes, leaning against a pillar, the scowl
marring his brow evidence that he wanted to escape. It
also served as a deterrent to keep everyone else away.

Jo started to contradict her sister, knowing it mattered
a great deal. Grace had harbored a crush for Jackson
since the moment he'd joined their crew, nearly eight
years ago. Everyone thought she'd outgrow her infatu-
ation for the orphaned boy, but Grace still wore her
heart on her sleeve, letting everyone know just how she
felt—Jackson included.

"Why don't you ask *him* to dance?" Jo suggested.

"I will not!" Grace sputtered, appalled. "If he wishes
to make amends and dance with me he has to do the
asking."

Of the three of them, Grace had been the only one
who'd welcomed their lessons in decorum. Like a
parched flower, she'd soaked in the rules of etiquette,
the dos and don'ts. She'd been determined to change,
as if she'd wanted to erase the memory of her days as
a pirate and begin anew.

Morgan had viewed their time aboard the *Sea Queen*
as a necessity; Jo had loved the challenge. Grace had
seen only the danger.

Because of that Grace wanted security, a life that

was constant, predictable. Something she'd never have with Jackson—a man who loved only the sea.

"Perhaps it's for the best," Jo mused out loud. "There are several fine young men here tonight. Perhaps Daniel will introduce you to them."

She scanned the crowd and spotted her brother-in-law speaking with two men. One was a short, obese man who looked like a keg of ale with arms and legs. The other . . . Jo arched a brow. The other was tall, lean and, she sensed, well honed. Not overly muscled, but still powerful, like a panther, tense from prowling. Though richly attired, he wasn't dressed in evening clothes, a faux pas for certain. Yet he didn't seem entirely out of place in his deep brown coat, cream pants and black riding boots, as if *he* were the one to set fashion trends. His raven black hair was tied in a negligent queue. Apparently he didn't care for social decorum any more than she did. Jo smiled, intrigued.

"I don't want to talk about Jackson," Grace said, clearly exasperated. "I've been watching you, Jo. I've seen the way you've studied the guests. You used to do the same thing when we were going to attack a ship."

"Really?" Jo gave her sister her full attention. "And how is that?"

"Like it's your birthday and you've been given a present to unwrap."

Jo laughed at the comparison, yet her gaze slid back to Daniel's friends. Could the tall one be the surprise of the evening? The pigeon she'd been looking for? Or the shorter man?

The dark-haired gentleman crossed his arms over his chest and shook his head adamantly. The squatty gentleman threw his hands up in frustration. Her brother-in-law frowned. She recognized Daniel's look—he was worried. But why?

She took Grace by the arm and began walking. Her sister pulled back. "What are you doing?"

"I need to speak with Daniel."

"You're up to something, Jo," Grace whispered as she removed her mask. "I see it in your eyes."

"I simply want him to introduce us to his friends."

Grace looked at the group of men, then at Jo. "Since when do you take an interest in our brother-in-law's acquaintances?"

"Since you became in need of a dance partner," she lied.

Jo tugged Grace's arm, giving her a choice of following or creating a scene. As Jo knew she would, her sister relented.

"Please, Joanna, don't embarrass us."

Closing the distance, she strained to hear the men's debate, but the music was too loud, the guests' chattering voices too shrill and boisterous. As soon as the portly man realized they were approaching them, he touched Daniel's arm and nodded, upsetting his double chin.

"Lord Tremayne," she said when she reached them.

Daniel narrowed his gaze, as if he too were suspicious of her sudden appearance. *Bloody hell, am I that transparent?* "My lord, Grace is in need of a dance partner for the minuet."

Grace stiffened beside her. Jo knew she was mortified, but her sister's well-learned manners wouldn't allow her to scream at Jo in public.

"I'd be happy to oblige," Daniel said, smiling with true affection. "There are two sets before the next minuet, I believe. I'll see you then, Grace."

The three men stared at them, conveying a silent message for the women to leave. Daniel's gaze was quiet, authoritative; the plump man's small eyes darted between them with alarming speed.

But the tall stranger's—Jo sucked in a breath—his eyes were piercing, rigid. She felt the strength of his annoyance, like a burning heat gathering at the base of her neck. Whether it was unease or anticipation she felt, she couldn't say for certain, but she wasn't about to leave until she knew what was going on.

"Are you going to introduce us to your friends, Lord Tremayne?" She turned to the taller man and met his gaze. His eyes were gray, like frozen metal, cold and brittle. They were the eyes of a hunter, merciless and shrewd, she thought, suppressing a shiver—like the panther she'd imagined him to be.

"Of course." Daniel nodded to the shorter man first. "May I present Byron Fitzhugh, and Marquess Darvill of Winstone Castle. Sirs, this is my youngest sister-in-law, Grace Fisk. And this is—"

"The Emerald of London," Jo interrupted, wanting to continue the charade. It worked so well with her plans. So this was Marquess Darvill, she mused, the unapproachable Nathan Alcott. She'd heard Morgan mention something about him, but since the conversation had revolved around a hunting party, she'd assumed Lord Darvill to be a stuffy old boar. Perhaps it had been his title that had given her that impression. Whatever the reason, she'd been wrong.

Daniel frowned at her, while Grace looked puzzled. Mr. Fitzhugh bowed like a bobbing cork; Lord Darvill bent at the waist, a slow, controlled motion. Anger sizzled the air around him, singeing Jo, making her wonder if lightning had struck the room. She stopped herself from stepping back. Had everyone felt the dangerous jolt, or just her?

A muscle pulsed in Nathan Alcott's jaw. A cold fire flared in his eyes, and he turned that fire on her. Because she'd interrupted them? she wondered. Because he didn't like women, or was his mood caused by something else entirely? Jo remembered to curtsy. The *Sea Queen* blade in its leather sheath dug into her thigh.

"So you are the Emerald everyone is talking about," Mr. Fitzhugh said, his small brown eyes roaming over her, but it was Nathan Alcott's intense gaze she felt move from her face to her shoulders and lower. Her skin tightened over her breasts, a rippling sensation that could only be a warning.

Mr. Fitzhugh smiled then, not unkindly. Dust fell from his wig, dotting his black coat like tiny gnats. "Are you not going to reveal your face? I would love to be the first one to see you. Imagine the bit of news I could deliver to the other guests."

"And remove their fodder for gossip?" She forced a smile. "I wouldn't dream of being so cruel."

Everyone laughed—everyone except Lord Darvill. His hard mouth twitched, but the movement could have turned into a sneer as easily as a smile. She should find another pigeon for gathering the information she needed. There were plenty of popinjays in attendance who would preen if she fed their egos. He might be sinfully handsome with his aquiline nose, squared jaw and angular cheeks, but he was dangerous as well. Jo sensed it as surely as she felt the hairs rise on the nape of her neck. But the mysterious man beside her kept her feet rooted to the floor.

She recognized Mr. Fitzhugh's name, as well. He was Daniel's banker. So what did that make Lord Darvill? A friend? A businessman? A rival of some sort? And why had Daniel and the banker looked like they'd wanted to throttle the man?

Something had happened, she reasoned; she could smell it in the air, see it in the guarded looks they exchanged. They shared a secret. And she intended to learn what it was. She thought Darvill would sooner cut her in half than reveal any pertinent information. But the banker, on the other hand . . .

"Are you familiar with the minuet, Mr. Fitzhugh?" Jo asked, seeing an opportunity and grabbing it.

The banker stammered, his face flushing beneath a layer of powder. Before he could manage a response, a woman who equaled his plump roundness and short stature hurried up to him.

"There you are, Mr. Fitzhugh. I've been looking everywhere for you."

"My dear, I'm in the middle of an important conversation."

The woman's shrewd eyes narrowed as her gaze raked over Jo and Grace. "I'm sure you are, but I need you to partner me in a game of whist."

"But my dear . . ." The rest of the banker's protest was lost as his wife gripped his hand and dragged him away.

Forcing her expression to remain calm, though she wanted to curse, Jo stared after the pair. She'd never be able to question the banker now. But she wasn't about to give up so easily. Squaring her shoulders with resolve, she turned to the second man and threw her misgivings to the wind. "Do you dance, Lord Darvill?"

"Rarely."

The single word rumbled through the air. She held out her hand. "The orchestra has begun another set. Would you care to join me?"

She heard Grace gasp, as well she should. Even Jo knew how scandalous it was to ask a man to dance. But she was the mysterious Emerald of London. She could do anything, could she not? Besides, she'd never learn anything about Lord Darvill if she couldn't get him away from Daniel. And for some reason she wanted to know why Nathan Alcott looked like he not only wanted to attack, but to tear his prey to shreds.

"Another time perhaps." His voice matched the edginess in his eyes. He glanced at her outstretched hand, but he didn't take it.

"We may not have another chance, my lord," she persisted. She wasn't like other silly women who would be crushed by rejection. But she didn't like being told no, either.

"Let me accompany you," Daniel said, his tone possessing a wealth of warning.

"No." Jo smiled and studied the panther from behind

her mask, knowing she couldn't back down now. Linking her hand through his arm, she shifted to his side and glanced at the three stunned faces regarding her. "I believe Lord Darvill needs a diversion."

"This isn't done. . . ." Grace insisted, but Jo began walking, giving Lord Darvill no choice but to follow.

"Do you always get your way?" he asked stoically, falling into step with her.

"Not always." She felt the heat of his skin through his coat, the tension knotting his muscles. Reaching the center of the ballroom, she released his arm and took her place opposite him.

"I find that hard to believe," he said in a near growl.

With his attention narrowed on her, she questioned her actions—and her motive. She felt the full impact of the anger burning deep inside him, churning, building bright and hot. If emotions had color, she thought, he'd be surrounded by bloodred smoke. He stood a head taller than she, with wide shoulders that seemed to be his own instead of the result of padding. She'd known taller men, stronger and better built from years of laboring the land and the sea, but none had unnerved her as this one did.

With a flash of clarity, she realized she'd made a mistake by toying with him. Whatever his secret, it wouldn't help her cause. She was wasting time. Annoyed with herself, she decided to finished the dance with the angry lord, then leave him to his secrets.

She had her own secret that needed her attention.

Nathan Alcott barely heard the music through the roar of blood in his ears. He didn't have time for this nonsense. He should leave the chit on the dance floor, only he didn't want to cause a scene. The fewer people who took note of his presence the better.

There was another reason as well, he grudgingly admitted. She was no ordinary lady. That fact had been obvious from the moment he'd turned and met her mischievous green gaze. Not impish, he amended, but sensual, with a wealth of intelligence, a shrewdness he'd never seen in a woman before. He could almost hear her mind at work, calculating, planning, but planning what? If it was marriage, he hated to disappoint her. She might prove to be attractive beneath her mask, but he wasn't interested.

The musical overture ended and the dance began. Nathan moved through the steps without thought, taking her ungloved hand in his as they turned. He felt the jolt first, then the coolness of her callused fingers. *Calluses?* He scanned her satin gown, emerald as befitting her fabricated name. Matching beads covered her snug bodice from her daring neckline to her trim waist, running down her skirts in a waterfall of green. A mask of sparkling gold beads and jade feathers hid most of her face, leaving him to focus on her full lips, the arrogant line of her jaw, the glimmer in her bewitching green eyes. He had no doubt that the rest of her would be just as lovely.

The Emerald of London appeared every inch a lady, yet something told him she wasn't. Pale freckles she hadn't bothered to powder dotted her bare shoulders. Her skin wasn't creamy white, but glowed with a vibrancy wretchedly out of fashion. He frowned, intrigued, when he didn't want to be.

Perhaps she was a courtesan? He discounted the thought, knowing Daniel Tremayne would never allow such a woman in his home. Whoever, or whatever, the Emerald of London was, didn't matter. He didn't have time for it to matter, not when his sister's life was at stake.

"You aren't a man of convention, Lord Darvill," she mused as she stepped around him in rhythm with the music, then returned to her place.

"A woman who asks a man to dance isn't concerned about convention." He copied her moves, moving behind her, catching her scent of sun and air in a room otherwise overwhelmed with cloying perfume and sweat.

"True." She smiled, a sly cat-and-mouse smile that caught him off guard. She should be embarrassed, yet she found this amusing. "I couldn't help noticing your clothes. They're . . . rather casual."

"I had not planned on attending the mask," he said, knowing his mahogany coat, tan wool pants and riding boots didn't live up to society's idea of formal wear. He didn't give a damn.

"Yet here you are." She tilted her head, waiting for him to fill in the details. He wondered if her amused smile would falter if he told her his true reason for crashing the ball—he needed fifty thousand pounds in gold and a swift ship before the sun rose on the morrow.

Instead he said, "I had business to discuss with Lord Tremayne."

"Business that couldn't wait until after the ball? What could be so important?" she asked in a voice that dripped with an innocence he didn't believe. He put his hand at her waist to guide her in a circle, feeling another jolt shoot beneath his skin and up his arm, leaving a path of sizzling warmth. She moved away again, too soon, he thought, scowling. Like a moth teasing a flame, when the fire should be burning her wings.

"A trivial matter." He almost choked on the lie. *Lauren, sweet Lauren, I promise I won't fail you this time.*

"There's nothing more tedious than men when they're consumed with their work," she said as the dance came to an end.

Though she smiled as she spoke, Nathan sensed she mocked him. He took her hand and kissed it. Her skin was warm against his lips. He breathed in her scent, musky and unique. Forbidden.

As if pulled by an invisible cord, he stepped closer

to her and heard himself demand, "Take off your mask."

She tilted her head back to keep his gaze. Her smile faded, drawing his attention to her mouth—full, lush, a mouth meant for giving pleasure—and taking it.

In a husky whisper she said, "It's not time to reveal myself, my lord."

Walk away now, he told himself. *Find Daniel and Fitzhugh and finish your business.* Saving Lauren was all that mattered. He possessed wealth, titles and power, but time had become his one weakness, his enemy. He didn't have any more to waste on a woman, even one as comely as the Emerald of London.

Whoever the hell she truly was.

TWO

A bell chimed like the voice of a bird, sweet and high-pitched, calling the dancers, drinkers and cardplayers in to dinner. Like cows to the trough, Jo mused. The guests moved like a herd through the double doors and down a hall to another set of rooms where pheasants, crab cakes, spiced summer squash and more waited to be served on gold-rimmed china.

In the ballroom, Joanna hung back among the dying candles, their light fading as wax dripped and beaded onto the marble floor. She had no desire to watch the same people who'd once snubbed her sister now stuff their faces with her food. If it were up to Jo, she'd toss them all out. Bloody hell, she amended, she never would have let them put one silk-clad toe through her front door.

"Damn it," she muttered between clenched teeth, knowing her darkening mood had less to do with the snobbish guests and more to do with the possibility that she might fail tonight. She'd eliminated Nathan Alcott from her list of possible targets. The man was too dangerous, too rough and volatile for her to trifle with. His eyes were too dark and turbulent. She'd imagined he could see through her mask, could hear her thoughts, could know she plotted against him and his kind. What would he do if he guessed the truth? The hairs at the back of her neck rose in answer. No, Lord Darvill might be as handsome as he was intriguing, but she knew it was best to avoid him.

So for the past hour, she'd danced and flirted and engaged in polite conversation—the essence of which had nearly driven her insane—and had learned nothing about any business ventures that would be of use.

She clenched her hands and fought back a wave of frustration. She had to find the money. The children were counting on her. The shanty house they lived in was to be torn down within a month so a warehouse could be built in its place. Jo felt the heat of her rising anger, knowing this was the politicians' way of taking care of the homeless problem—remove the downtrodden's shacks and hovels and the downtrodden will go away.

She had to find them a place to live that was safe—warm and clean would be an extra bonus. But that required money neither Jo nor Mira had.

At least the children had someone to look out for them until Jo could find the needed funds. When she'd returned for Sammy, only to be devastated to learn she'd arrived too late, another woman had been there holding the boy's frail hand. Mira had neither home nor family—having lost both years before during the Seven Years' War—so she'd found a new one with the orphans, bringing them whatever food she could find. Mira and Jo had joined forces that day.

Jo touched Robby's tiny toy soldier, feeling the solid shape through her gown. The vow she'd made to her baby brother and Sammy weighed her down on one side, while the *Sea Queen* dagger burdened the other. Neither were responsibilities she could forget, even if she'd wanted to. The ball should have given her countless opportunities to learn about shipments of wares or cloth or rum, all of which she could steal, then sell for coin. The food stores Jo had bought were running low, and with winter coming soon, the list of supplies they would need seemed to double and triple by the day.

Daniel owned World Quest Shipping, but Jo couldn't target his vessels and raid his supplies. She could simply ask Daniel or Morgan for the money; they'd given her a considerable amount twice before when she had asked. But she couldn't expect them to feed every homeless child in the city. Not when there were hundreds of wealthy aristocrats who, in Jo's opinion, should be sharing the burden, since it was their greed and gluttony that had created the severe poverty that now existed.

Her plan to steal valuable cargo had to be carried out on a stranger. *Like Lord Darvill?* She pushed the thought aside. The man was far more trouble than she needed. No, she'd be better off joining the other guests at dinner and trying again to pry something of value from their painted lips.

Following the last group out into the hall, she touched her mask and accidentally loosened the silk string. Everyone except Jo had removed theirs during the final dance. She'd been reluctant to shed her disguise. She rather liked being whispered about, as if she were some great mystery.

"I'm a mystery, all right," she muttered so no one could overhear. "One who intends to dip her fingers into their pockets and pull out their coin."

Once in the hallway she turned in the opposite direction of the crowd and headed for Daniel's study. She closed the door behind her and sighed, welcoming the dark and the instant hush of chattering voices. She lowered her mask. Cool air brushed her face. Silvery light from the quarter moon poured through the paned windows, spilling onto the carpets and chairs. Crossing to the desk, she lit a taper. Light flared and spread over the mahogany desk, the papers, pen and assorted mail all neatly arranged.

Setting down her mask, she withdrew the toy soldier. Her father had carved an entire set for Robby on his fourth birthday. Jo had crushed berries and painted them, adding eyes and red mouths and bright blue coats and pants, Just like real soldiers. The dye was wearing thin from her constantly handling the small scrap of wood. Her talisman—or perhaps her curse.

Hearing a pair of male voices drift through the door, she brought her head up and glanced around. One of them she recognized—Daniel. He wouldn't mind that she was in his study, but still, she ought to leave. Picking up her mask, she opened her pocket to slip the soldier inside, but dropped it instead. It bounced on the carpet, landing behind a five-foot-tall screen to her right.

"Oh, bloody hell." Would nothing go right for her tonight? She hurried behind the hand-painted Oriental partition to retrieve the toy just as the door opened.

"This way, gentlemen," she heard Daniel say. "We'll be able to talk without being interrupted."

Gentlemen? Jo leaned forward to peer through the crack in the screen. The portly Mr. Fitzhugh entered. Nathan Alcott followed next. He didn't simply walk into the room; he prowled, glaring at the plush surroundings as if he wanted to rip the legs off the chairs and the framed portraits from the walls.

Perfect, she thought, suppressing an annoyed sigh. The very man she wanted to avoid.

"I've waited long enough, Daniel." Lord Darvill came to the exact spot where Jo had stood only seconds before and stared at the candle she'd left burning. Soft light sharpened his features, his broad forehead, his lips that seemed incapable of a smile. The flame flickered as if disturbed by his presence. She could sympathize; it was impossible to be near the imposing man and not feel a skittering of nerves. Unbidden, she recalled the nerve-jarring feel of his hand at her back, his scent that was both dark and earthy.

"I didn't mean to keep you waiting, Nathan," Daniel said in the diplomatic voice Jo recognized. "But this is Morgan's first ball since our last disaster. I couldn't abandon her entirely."

Jo thought now was the time to show herself. She grimaced, knowing she was about to look the fool. They'd want to know why she was hiding behind the screen. What could she say? She'd dropped her toy?

"I apologize," Lord Darvill said, some of his gruffness fading. "I wish I'd never had to come here tonight at all. But I need to know; do I have your help or not?"

Jo stayed where she was. Lord Darvill needed Daniel's help? If she recalled Morgan's conversation, Lord Darvill's wealth and political power exceeded Daniel's.

"I want to assist you in any way I can." Daniel crossed to a side table before the cold hearth and poured three tumblers of brandy.

"We both want to lend our support," Mr. Fitzhugh confirmed, accepting his drink. He downed half of it, then hissed out a breath.

"Then have my gold ready for me in the morning, Fitzhugh. And Daniel, simply agree to loan me a ship to carry it in."

"But, my lord," Mr. Fitzhugh implored, looking as if he needed another drink, "fifty thousand pounds is an outrageous amount of money. It will take time to gather such a sum. And all in gold."

Jo gripped her mask, crushing the feathers to keep from jumping up from her hiding place. *Fifty thousand pounds? In gold?* Her heart pounded so hard, she was sure the men could hear it. That amount would be enough to buy the children a home in the country, feed and clothe them, open a school. The possibilities made her head spin.

"Then you should leave now." Nathan sent each man a dark, commanding scowl. Mr. Fitzhugh took a step back, his plump hand going to his throat as if he suddenly found it difficult to breathe. "Work through the night if you must. I don't care what it takes."

Daniel wasn't so easily intimidated. He frowned, no doubt weighing his options. "I understand what you're going though."

Daniel held out a tumbler of liquor, but Nathan waved it away. "I mean to sail for Saint-Nazaire, France, at dawn."

"In one of my ships," Daniel said. It wasn't a question, but a statement of disapproval.

"Do you doubt I'll return it to you intact?" With his hands clasped behind his back, Nathan turned, moving out of her line of sight. "If that's the case, I'll buy *Lady's Luck* from you."

"It's not the ship I'm concerned about." Daniel's tone sharpened with irritation. "There has to be another way to handle this situation. You shouldn't go alone."

"I agree," Mr. Fitzhugh voiced. Jo's view was limited, but she could tell he'd made his statement from a safe distance away, near the door, she thought. "To take such a large sum of money out of your account . . . well, it's too risky."

"In case you need reminding, Mr. Fitzhugh," Nathan said, the words so hoarse they sounded raw, "it's my money. You'll have it ready for me at dawn. I'll pick it up at the bank myself."

"This is a mistake," Daniel said as he sat at the desk, gathering pen and paper to write. "But I'll give you what you ask."

"If it's a mistake"—Nathan stepped before the screen, nearly startling a gasp out of Jo—"then it's mine to make."

She clamped her hand over her mouth to cut off her breath. She hadn't heard his approach; the man moved like a prowling cat. He stared at the screen, his eyes nothing more than shadows, his cheeks and jaw sharp angles that made him all the more stern and forbidding. Compelling, she added in a whisper in her mind. She sensed the anger in him, the danger, like an animal wounded and wanting revenge.

If he looked close, he'd be able to see her hiding behind the partition like a cowering thief. If he spotted her and announced her presence, Daniel would be furious that she'd eavesdropped on their conversation. But she didn't concern herself about that. Nathan Alcott was staring at something, his gaze focused and intense, but he wasn't looking at her. He saw something besides the screen with its painted birds and water lilies. Jo felt a shiver of warning slide down her spine. Whatever it was he saw, it was something he didn't like.

"One last thing, gentlemen," Nathan said, his eyes growing darker as his gaze seemed to bore into the wood. "I want absolute secrecy. No one is to know what I'm about to do."

Jo barely heard the other men agree. She was already planning. *He's sailing for France at dawn. With a fortune in gold!* If she pirated cargo of cloth or spices, she'd have to sell it at market to gain any coin, and then probably only a fraction of what she needed. But with fistfuls of gold the impossible could become possible. The children could have a garden, raise their own livestock. They'd have clean air to breathe during the day and real beds to sleep in at night. The potential made her chest tighten and her hands shake.

It was an opportunity she couldn't resist, even if it meant facing Nathan Alcott's fury.

She smiled into Lord Darvill's dark, unseeing eyes, and felt her stomach clench with anticipation. Fate had led her to Nathan. She prayed her luck would hold, because she knew Lord Darvill was no pigeon. If she wasn't careful, he could turn into a deadly beast.

Wind tore at Jo's hair, pulling it free and wild behind her. Cold morning air, wet with mist, coated her face, dampened her black wool coat and pants. Her hands

were chilled, her fingers stiff and numb, but she hardly
noticed. She and Jackson had ridden all night through
dark, sleepy towns and empty fields, but she'd never
felt so alive. Finally she'd found her chance to make
the orphans' lives better. Jo urged her horse faster over
the rise of a hill, knowing her mount had already given
more than it should.

"Only a little farther," she whispered, rubbing the
gelding's lathered neck. She felt the muscles in his
rump and legs tense, pushing them over the crest and
giving her a view that made her smile with relief. The
village of Chattenden waited below, a cluster of rough,
unmortared stone cottages lining a potted dirt road. Beyond, concealed by a bank of swirling fog, was a cove
that hid a treasure that was hers alone. The *Sea Witch*.
Her horse slowed to a trot. She didn't object.

"It will be dawn soon," Jackson said, reining his
mount up beside hers. This was the first time he'd spoken since they'd crept from Daniel and Morgan's home
in London, hours before the party ended, leaving a note
saying they were returning to Dunmore, the village Jo,
Morgan and Grace had been raised in. Normally she
would have felt guilty for the lie, but not this time. Too
much was at stake.

"We'll be ready," she said. As if hearing her, the
night lifted, turning the sky and lowlands into a cloud
of gray steel. "Unless the weather doesn't clear. Too
bad Grace isn't here. She could tell us what the day
will bring."

"Grace has no love for adventure, Jo. She's had her
fill," Jackson said, his voice strangely quiet. She knew
he was as anxious as she to escape the city and return
to the sea where they both belonged. But he always
seemed sullen when leaving Grace behind. Jo doubted
that he returned Grace's affections, but he cared about
her deeply, and knew she would be upset by his sudden
departure.

"She's not like us," he continued, as if trying to convince himself. "She's a lady now, and deserves more than a bunk bed on a stinking ship."

"Did she tell you that?" Jo asked, wondering for the first time if there wasn't something more to Jackson's feelings than he'd let on.

He shook his head and smiled, though it wasn't humor she saw in his eyes, but regret. "Didn't have to. I know what Grace wants from life."

She wants you, Jo thought, but opted to keep her opinion to herself. She faced front and watched as thatched roofs and struggling gardens grew larger with their approach. Everyone knew what Grace wanted— the things that were stolen from her as a child: a safe home, the comfort of her parents' arms, permanence— if there was such a thing. The kind of life Jackson couldn't give her. Hopefully another man would capture her heart, Jo thought. But only time would tell.

"Stop thinking about Grace, Jackson," Jo ordered, trying to sound encouraging. "She'll be fine. Besides, she's not the kind of woman you need. The two of you are far too different."

"And how would you be knowing what kind of woman I need?"

"I know." She grinned, wanting to tease him out of his sulky mood.

"You, I suppose?" he suggested, raising a wheat-colored brow to an arrogant tilt.

"Oh, God, no." A laugh burst from her chest. "We're too much alike!"

"With sword we meet."

"Our revenge is sweet," she said, finishing their motto that described their secret mission as pirates. She had another motto, though she rarely spoke it out loud: tears are only for broken hearts. It was a saying she lived by, ever since the day she buried her brother. A broken heart was something she never intended to suffer again.

"You know what today is," Jackson said, more as a statement than a question.

"Aye, I know." Though she'd tried not to think about it.

"Then I'm surprised you're not waiting another day to leave."

" 'Sunday sail, never fail. Friday sail, ill luck and gale,' " she quoted. Every sailor knew it was a bad omen to start a voyage on a Friday, but what choice did she have if she intended to intercept the *Lady's Luck?*

"If we delay, we might as well stay home." She nudged her mare into a trot.

As the cove came into view, she put thoughts of her sister, Jackson and troublesome omens aside. Local fishermen were awake, readying their skiffs, preparing their nets in hopes of a good day's catch. She heard cows in a barn off to her right, mooing their need to be milked. Smoke drifted on the soupy air as fires were stirred to life in soot-coated hearths.

The sounds and smells reminded her of her past—before fate had made her a pirate. What did fate have in store for her future? she wondered. Would she be allowed to fulfill her vow to save forgotten children? It meant risking her life, and her crew's. But it was a risk she had to take, because if she didn't try to help them, who would? Certainly not the wealthy noblemen, who would shudder at the thought of even wiping their shoes on the poor should they pass them in the streets.

Well, she vowed, the wealthy might prefer to turn a blind eye to the poor, but they were going to help the forgotten ones whether they wanted to or not.

She was going to make sure of it.

Reaching the stables, she handed off the reins to Little Georgy, a young boy of eight she'd rescued from the sewers of London three months ago. He'd gone by the name Imp then, because he'd known no other. So relieved was he to have a home of his own and someone to care for him, he'd taken his guardian's name, yet he had a boy's lust for the sea and dreamed of joining her crew. His guardian, Big Georgy, stepped out of his house, dragging his coat on.

"Good morning," Jo called to the pair as she dismounted, noting that the boy had put on weight since she'd last seen him.

"You've worked a sweat on your mounts," Big Georgy said, his mouth puckering with disapproval. "I take it ye're in a hurry."

"I am." She drew several coins from her pocket and pressed them into his palm, but spoke to the boy. "See they're wiped down, Little Georgy, and give them an extra scoop of oats."

"Are ye tak'n the *Sea Witch* out?" the boy asked, his cheeks flushed from the cold morning air.

"Just to stretch her sails." She ruffled his shaggy brown hair and followed Jackson toward a skiff near the shore.

"Can I come?" he pleaded, pulling her horse behind him.

"Not this time."

"How long will ye be gone?" Big Georgy asked.

"If all goes well, only a few days."

"Is it trouble you're sailing to?" he asked, the caution in his tone stopping her.

"Trouble?" She faced him. "Why would you ask such a thing?"

"You've never taken the *Sea Witch* from our cove during the day. Always at night, so as not to be seen."

She exchanged a wary glance with Jackson, then stared at the older man, worn thin with age and the recent loss of his wife. Yet little remained of the grieving man she'd first met when she'd sailed the *Sea Witch* into his cove. Adopting the boy had done much to restore Georgy's health. A new, proud light glowed in his eyes whenever he looked at the boy. But evidently his renewed vigor allowed him to see more than she wanted him to. No one in the village knew about her past or the true reason she kept her ship anchored in Chattenden. The villagers thought her a trader, like so many others who harbored their ships in the cove.

If Big Georgy suspected her real intentions . . . She shuddered to think of what the consequences could mean.

Four years ago Morgan had retired the *Sea Queen,* vowing never to sail her again. Jo had honored that vow, knowing that taking their ship to sea meant risking the king's wrath and a hanging at Executioner's Dock—a fate Morgan had barely escaped after Daniel had captured her. He'd taken her to London, not with the intent for her to stand trial, but to try to clear her of the charges against her. But Daniel's friend had betrayed him. Morgan had faced King George, but it was Daniel's determination to marry Morgan, and the king's warning that the *Sea Queen* was never to sail again or they'd all suffer the consequences, that had saved Morgan's life.

Though it went against her nature, Jo had contented herself with practicing the art of manners when she was in London and honing her skills with a sword when she returned to Dunmore. The last four years had been a peaceful time, if annoyingly dull.

Until the day I found Peter and the others. Until I promised to help Sammy, only to fail him, as I failed . . .

The sting of tears burned her eyes. Tears are only for broken hearts, she silently quoted, willing the wetness away. Things would be different now. She knew what needed to be done. The first difficult task had been accomplished. She'd refitted the *Sea Queen,* giving her new life and a new name.

The *Sea Witch.*

Her second task—relieving Nathan Alcott of his gold—would be just as easy.

She considered Georgy. He'd opened his doors to one of her homeless children, giving him food, shelter and love. She didn't want Big Georgy prying into her business; it would only cause trouble for them both if he learned how she intended to raise the money needed to care for the countless others.

Finding her voice, forcing it to be strong, she said, "If I always leave at night, it's just a coincidence."

Big Georgy stared at her without saying a word, but his eyes conveyed his thoughts. He was worried. For her? For his village? She couldn't tell which.

"I won't be bringing trouble here," she reassured him, "if that is your concern."

"Of course you won't, girl." Big Georgy put a protective hand on his ward's small shoulder. "You only bring us children in need."

Smiling hesitantly, she turned away and joined Jackson in the skiff that would take them to the *Sea Witch*. *Children in need.* The phrase circled her thoughts like a chant, a chorus that seemed never to fade from her mind. Before the day was through, she swore she would be fifty thousand pounds richer. Then there wouldn't be any more children in need.

The *Lady's Luck* cut through swells like an avenging knight, her deep bow slicing, pushing, fighting her way forward. Her solid hull seemed to growl as she battled one surging wave after another. Cold wind snapped her sails taut, drying dew that glittered like armor in the morning haze. She'd been designed for speed and maneuverability, two things Nathan valued most right now. He stood at the forward deck, gripping the balustrade as the ship rocked beneath his boots, and watched the horizon, though the shoreline he was desperate to see wouldn't appear for at least another three days.

I have time, he thought. Of the fourteen days he'd been given, he had ten left—more than enough time to reach Saint-Nazaire and fulfill the demands of the ransom letter.

He touched the breast pocket of his coat. His sister's

companion, the dowager Easterly, had neared hysteria when she'd delivered the letter he now carried. The dowager blamed herself for his sister's fate. But Nathan knew differently. If anyone was to bear the blame, it was him. The note, written in a bold, arrogant hand, detailed the instructions he was to follow if he ever wanted to see his sister, Lauren, alive again.

An unfamiliar sensation grazed the back of his neck—fear unlike anything he'd ever known. The chill prickled his skin, the cold going bone-deep. He imagined icy fingers touching his throat, circling around, tightening their grip. He closed his eyes and drew a deep breath, willing the choking pressure to ease.

It didn't work. He envisioned Lauren the last time he'd seen her, before she'd left London with dowager Easterly to tour France, her silken black hair always coiffed in the latest fashion, her soulful gray eyes that made her appear as fragile as she was gentle. Lauren had just celebrated her eighteenth birthday, but there had been little joy in the event. She'd been depressed and weepy—a condition Nathan also felt responsible for. If only he had refused her choice of husbands to begin with, she'd be safe at Winstone Castle. But since becoming her guardian two years before, after the death of their father, he'd never been able to refuse Lauren anything.

From the moment his sister had stepped foot among society, matrons, young ladies and men alike had touted her as a dove any man would be honored to marry. Yet for some reason, Lauren had never believed them. Since the day she'd understood what marriage meant, she'd been plagued with a conviction that she wasn't good enough, charming enough, pretty enough. Her lack of confidence had mushroomed into a fear that she would never marry, but would die a spinster, an old crow left on the shelf. Nathan knew her fears were groundless, but to convince her . . .

He still didn't know where her anxiety stemmed

from—an old nanny whispering tales in her ear, or perhaps it had something to do with their mother dying while giving birth to Lauren. Was it guilt that had compelled her to find a husband? he wondered. Or did she simply want to be a wife and mother, like any other young woman since the beginning of time?

Her fear, and his wish to see her happy, was what had persuaded him to accept Philip de Maurier's proposal, a devastating event that had led to another and another, Nathan thought, scowling at the rolling sea.

"Luck is with us today, Lord Darvill," Captain Perry said, stopping beside Nathan and interrupting his pensive thoughts. "With the wind in our sheets, we'll make up the time we lost navigating the Thames."

"Then we'll reach Saint-Nazaire on schedule?"

"With this vessel? That won't be a problem. She used tae be a pirate ship, ye know."

"I'd heard something about that," Nathan said absently. His hand went to the pocket of his vest and felt the gold ring forged with the Alcott family crest, a falcon with spread wings and talons outstretched to catch its prey. A lock of black hair was tucked in his pocket as well—items of Lauren's that had accompanied the letter. He withdrew the small ring and slipped it on the little finger of his right hand. The metal was cold against his skin, a chilling reminder of what still had to be done.

But he would reach his sister, he vowed. Nothing would stop him from freeing her. And once she was safe, nothing would prevent him from seeking revenge on the slave trader who'd kidnapped her.

"Used to belong to Halo Jones, before Lord Tremayne and his wife captured him."

"Excuse me?" Nathan said, only half listening to the captain.

"She went by the name *Devil's Luck* then."

"Who?" Nathan asked, frowning. "Tremayne's wife?"

"No, sir. The ship." Captain Perry burrowed short, thick fingers into his scraggly beard; the color must have been red at one time, but age and sun had faded the bushy length to rust. "The *Lady's Luck* used to be named . . . Oh, never mind. The only thing of importance is that Lady Tremayne thought it a waste to put a torch to the vessel, so she renamed her and had her husband add her to his fleet. That's one amazing woman, our Lady Tremayne."

"Yes, she is." Nathan knew about Morgan's past as a pirate captain. He'd questioned Daniel's sanity when he'd married a woman with such a notorious history. Then Nathan had met the woman in question. She was one of a kind, he thought. Strong, sensual, as decisive as she was beautiful—a worthy match for his friend.

Sunlight broke through the fog, spearing the sea, turning it to swirls of emerald and foam. A pair of eyes as different from Lauren's, or even Lady Tremayne's, appeared in his mind's eye: green and mysterious, taunting him with secrets that would never be shared. They'd been almond-shaped, and fringed by lashes as lush as her russet hair. He imagined he could hear her voice, like red wine, smoky and velvety rich. Nathan shook his head, dispelling the illusion. The woman at the mask had refused to give her name or show her face, preferring to remain in shadows and deception—elements he already had in his life; he didn't need more.

He shouldn't be thinking of the woman at all, he reminded himself, not with his sister's life at stake. But something about her, some puzzling allure, had aroused his attention and wouldn't let go. The woman had been a contradiction with her rough hands and elegant dress, her outrageous manners and compelling charm. He couldn't help thinking that if times had been different, if he weren't desperate to reach Lauren, he would have pursued the mystery lady.

Instead he had to forget she existed.

The regret he felt surprised him.

"So, ye're going on holiday in Saint-Nazaire. Seems everyone's heading tae France these days," Captain Perry said, obviously determined to make conversation when all Nathan wanted was to be left alone.

"I have business there." Nathan thought about the fifty thousand pounds in gold coins he had locked in a chest and hidden beneath his bunk. Dirty, vile business, he thought. He had to pay a ransom to a man he'd once trusted, a man he'd allowed his sister to become engaged to.

Philip de Maurier had owned his own ships, and ran a decent trading business, earning him a respectable reputation. But a twist of fate had shown Philip's true nature. Silks, spices and exotic fruits had been secondary to his real cargo: human flesh, slaves from Africa. Parliament might condone slavery, but Nathan viewed it as a legal form of piracy. He refused to have anything to do with it, and he'd die before allowing his sister to marry a man who did.

His fury and contempt had run so deep, Nathan had broken off their engagement, letting society know the reason why, and encouraging them to shun the man as well, both socially and in business dealings. They'd obviously listened, because within a year, Philip was bankrupt, losing his ships, his cargo, the tainted wealth he'd gained.

Nathan knew he'd made Philip a desperate man, and desperate men did desperate things. But if Philip de Maurier thought he'd bring Nathan to heel by kidnapping Lauren, he'd made a grave mistake. Because nothing—and no one—would harm what belonged to him.

Three

"Luck is with us and she's in the North Sea," Jackson said with a smile that seemed more fierce than cheerful. He lowered the telescope, but didn't take his gaze off the horizon. Sunlight had burned away the morning fog and now glinted off the gold hoop in his ear—an accessory he wore only while at sea.

Jo took the telescope and quickly spotted her target. The ship rode the waves like the demon she'd once been named. Wind fed the *Lady's Luck*'s sails, stretching the sheets so taut they were in danger of ripping. Salty mist sprayed the deck as the bow plunged over a swell, then reared back to take the next crest.

The captain was pushing the other vessel harder than necessary. Jo would have thought that curious if she didn't know who and what the ship carried. Nathan Alcott had been desperate to have his money and the means to reach France. *Why the hurry, Nathan? What are you after?* She pushed the questions aside. She didn't care about Alcott's intent—only his gold.

"I want eighteen knots, Jackson," she said, snapping the telescope closed. "Raise the extra canvas at the main mast's top."

Jackson bellowed the order aloft, but he didn't leave to oversee the task as he normally would have. Instead he watched her, his brown eyes contemplative, the gold specks within glittering with life. *"Lady's Luck* belongs to Daniel."

"I'm aware of that. I'm also aware that she's carrying a fortune in gold."

"You swore you'd never raid one of your brother-in-law's ships."

"It's not Daniel's gold we'll be stealing."

"What if they put up a fight?"

She shifted her stance, feeling uneasy. She didn't want to fire on her brother-in-law's ship. Daniel might be an aristocrat, but he was a good man. *Who will be furious if he ever learns what I've done.*

"So you intend to attack her?" Jackson pressed when she didn't respond.

Jo propped her hands on her hips and tilted her chin back to fully meet Jackson's disapproving stare. "We aren't going to sneak up on them during a moonless night or play any other kind of trick, the way we used to. This isn't the *Sea Queen* any longer. I'm doing things my way now."

"I understand." He pressed his lips into a firm line and gave a vague nod. "Wearing disguises to hide our identity, waiting until the other vessel's crew was asleep before we boarded were tactics for people afraid to fight in the open."

"And we aren't afraid." Though an outright battle was the last thing she wanted. She turned away and headed down the ladder toward the gun deck. She had twelve monstrous cannons lining the port side, another dozen positioned starboard, three at the bow and two at the stern, each one capable of blowing a ship to kindling if properly manned. And that was what worried her.

She trusted her crew, but they were young and green in battle, regardless that they'd survived the streets. They'd been thankful for their rescue, but more important, they'd believed in her cause, wanting to help the ones she had yet to save. The half dozen raids they'd accomplished so far had been on small trading vessels, fishing boats, excursions meant to give her men a taste of the dangers involved more than for the bounty they could steal. But they were ready now. She had the ship, the cannons, a gunner who'd trained her crew how to swab, reload, tap and fire without fault.

Now all she had to do was catch the *Lady's Luck*, without putting the crew's newly acquired skills to use.

She hadn't been aware of Jackson following her until he gripped her arm and spun her around. "What—"

"You can't openly assault a ship like the *Lady's Luck*," Jackson admonished, as if he'd read her mind. "Our crewmen are loyal and hardworking, but what do they know about battle? What do we know, for that matter?"

"Perhaps I spoke too soon," Jo said, hardly recognizing the scorn in her voice. "Perhaps you are the one who's afraid? We're going to board that ship, Jack, using any means necessary."

"Even if it means firing on them." A muscle pulsed dangerously in Jackson's jaw. "I don't like hiding behind a mask any more than you do. But Morgan's way always worked. Our crew never got hurt, nor did the men on the ships we boarded."

She jerked her arm free. "I don't recall your ever questioning Morgan's orders. I don't appreciate your questioning mine," she said, feeling the old resentments return. Morgan had always been the perfect one, the Fisk daughter the entire village had looked to for answers—and Morgan had provided the answers, saving them all from starvation and death.

While Jo had failed herself, her village—Robby.

"If you're afraid for your life, then hide below," she said, her jaw clenching.

"It's not me I'm worried about. It's you." The anger faded from his eyes and something stirred in its place, something that might have been compassion, though it looked dangerously close to pity. "You're so determined

to save the children England forgot that you don't care
if you kill yourself doing it."

"I'm not going to get anyone killed, Jackson. Now
are you with me or not?"

His features hardened and he looked like he wanted
to shake her, but he gave her a curt nod. "With sword
we meet. Joanna's revenge is sweet."

He'd changed one simple word in their motto, making the revenge hers instead of the crew's. She couldn't
agree more. She wanted revenge against the people who
had caused the near ruin of her home, the death of her
brother. She could taste her vendetta as surely as she
could taste the bitter salt air on her tongue.

"I'll take that as a yes." She moved around him,
silently vowing to break his nose if he followed her
again. Since they still had at least two hours before
they caught the *Lady's Luck,* she said, "I'm going below."

Reaching the companionway where the air was cool
and damp, she stormed down the hall and stopped as
shadows reached out from the corners and hid her from
view. She leaned against the wall and willed the sudden
racing of her heart to slow.

Jackson thought she was being reckless. But he
didn't know, didn't understand, not completely. She
wouldn't allow anyone she'd sworn to protect to be
harmed or die. She'd let that happen twice before. This
time *she* would die before letting it happen again.

She knew what she was doing; she'd been planning
it since the day they'd first raised the *Sea Queen*'s sails,
nearly eight years ago. With cannon fire, speed and a
ship as agile as a dancer, she would bring her foe to
his knees.

Pushing away from the wall, she continued through
the narrow passageway, her hand closing around the
jeweled hilt of the *Sea Queen* blade, tucked like a lover
against her side. "When I attack the *Lady's Luck,* no

one I care about will be killed. Which makes English aristocrats fair game."

"God blind me, she's flying the black flag." Captain Perry snapped the telescope closed before dropping it to the deck. The brass tube rolled away, lodging between two barrels of ale.

Nathan stared at the other ship, sleek and narrow and full of sail, as it gained on the *Lady's Luck*. He clenched the steel haft of his sword as something savage and dark crawled through his veins. Whoever thought to seize his vessel had made a grave mistake.

"Do you recognize her?" Nathan asked, accompanying the captain to the wheel.

"She's a pirate ship heading straight for us; that's all I need tae know." Captain Perry shouted to the crewmen midship: "Throw the barrels of freshwater overboard. We have tae lighten our load."

"Can we outrun her?" Nathan bit back a curse. This couldn't be happening. Not now!

The captain's green eyes narrowed on the cutlass belted at Nathan's hip. "I hope ye can swing that sword *and* swim, my lord, 'cause ye might be doing both before the day is done."

That wasn't the answer he'd wanted. Nathan glanced at the sails overhead. Every last one was raised and tight with wind, pushing the *Lady's Luck* south fast, but not fast enough.

"There has to be something we can do." His gaze swept over the deck, noting the men readying cannons and arming themselves with pistols and knives.

"Aye," Captain Perry said. "We're going to fight. But from what I can see, we're badly outgunned."

Nathan swiped his hand though his hair as he paced the deck, feeling frightened and furious and wanting to rip the pirate ship apart with his bare hands. "I have to reach Saint-Nazaire."

"No doubt ye do, Lord Darvill." Captain Perry's pale red beard flattened against his chest as the wind slapped him full in the face. "But this may not be the day."

Anger bled through Nathan's veins—for the pirates who'd chosen now to attack, for Philip de Maurier's deceit, for his own stupidity. The pirate ship was closing fast, her deep hull slicing through the sea like an ax through air, taking the swells as if she were hungry and the ocean was a feast.

"It's going tae get rough, Lord Darvill; ye'd best go below." Without waiting for an answer, Captain Perry spun away with an agility that belied his great size.

Nathan remained where he was. He refused to hide below. He had a sword, and if the pirates tried to board, he'd send them to hell before allowing them to seize his gold.

The pirate ship fired from her bow. Nathan held his breath. The warning shot cleared the deck ten feet from where he stood.

A crewman as rough and thin as a stick laughed and shouted, "Them pirates are blind. If that's all they gots for the *Lady's Luck* they best turn tail and run for their lives!"

Nathan didn't share the man's opinion. While he'd had no part in the Seven Years' War, he'd once been caught in the cross fire. While he was sailing to Africa on a merchant ship, a French military vessel had attacked. That battle had ended with bloodied men and splintered ships. Neither France nor England had declared a victory. Both had limped back to their ports to lick their wounds and bury their dead.

No, Nathan was sure the pirates' first shot had been a test—the next wouldn't miss.

The vessel pulled abreast, her gunports open, cannons filling their mouths. Captain Perry ordered his gunman to fire. A lone cannon erupted, spending one shell, but it fell short. Seconds passed in tense silence;

then the other ship's cannons detonated all at once. The
air exploded. Cannonballs flew past him, crashing into
deck and mast. They ripped through canvas, opening
them like wounds.

The ship shuddered beneath his feet. Men shouted
and cursed. In a voice that boomed with command,
Captain Perry ordered another return of fire. An answering volley roared to life. *Lady's Luck* lurched with
the force. White smoke plumed, mixing with the gray
flames that erupted not far from where he stood.

With a sense of disbelief, Nathan watched the fire
spread to a stack of coiled rope. The flames flared,
turning golden white as they climbed up the nearby
railing. Fury gathered inside him. He glared at the pirate ship, knowing there was nothing he could do to
stop the attack. He had to wait. The captain's men were
manning the cannons and overseeing the riggings. His
time would come. He could feel it, the hot spurt of
anger, the certainty that he would face the thieves who
thought to stop him.

The pirate ship had reloaded, firing another round
that ripped through man and ship alike. Screams and
shrill cries tore through the air. As if punched by an
invisible fist, Nathan was thrown back, landing against
the binnacle box. Pain sliced down his side. He
clamped his jaw, sucking in a breath. Riggings snapped,
becoming weapons as they whipped across the deck. A
yardarm broke free, crashing down, splintering, flying
through the air like a thousand spears.

Flames roared at the bow. Men left their posts to
douse the fire with their shirts and bare hands. Nathan
breathed in a lungful of smoke. His chest contracted
and his head spun. He searched the deck for something
to help put out the flames. He saw only tangled ropes,
shattered wood. They'd tossed the barrels of water overboard to lighten their weight. The ship would be consumed by fire, and with it his hope of saving Lauren.

"No!" he shouted, the word drowned by the cries of

men. It wouldn't end this way. His sister needed him, was waiting for him.

He pushed to his feet and stumbled to the railing that overlooked midship. The fire at his back was but one of a half dozen that burned from one end of the ship to the other. Fallen sails, mounds of coiled hemp rope, the deck itself—all of it smoldered, the smoke blackening as the blaze spread a devastating path.

"Helmsman," Captain Perry shouted. "Bring us hard about."

Nathan realized his intent and grinned a murderous grin. They were burning and badly damaged, but they weren't dead yet. He leaped to the lower deck, ripping off his coat and shirt, beating the flames with both. Heat singed his arms. Sweat coated his chest, dripped from his brow. His hair clung to his cheeks, and his eyes stung from smoke. Yet with the aid of another crewman, he cut a sail free and shoved the burning mass over the railing.

The ship turned in to the wind. Tackle scattered, canvas sheets snapped taut, cables strained and the hull moaned like a dying whale as she pitched leeward. Nathan grabbed hold of the capstan as the deck shifted beneath his feet. *Lady's Luck* careened, sending mast and sail hovering over the sea. It was then that Nathan saw Captain Perry's mistake. They'd turned in to the wind, but the effort had slowed their attack, giving the pirates an opening to come about for a final blow.

"Lauren . . ." He couldn't finish the plea.

The sky filled with thunder and smoke. The air shook with the force of cannonballs tearing through deck and rail, ripping through the bowsprit and shattering the top sails. Debris flew in all directions, toward the masts and out to sea. Splinters of debris stung his bare chest; another piece ripped his cheek.

The wounds bled, a warm gush of blood, but he couldn't feel them—couldn't feel anything but rage, cold and deadly and soul-deep. Wounded men struggled to pull themselves to midship, where the fire hadn't reached. A few moved to help them, but most fought fires or struggled with wreckage from bow to stern; some cried. It wouldn't end this way, he vowed. So help him God, it wouldn't!

The pirate ship circled the *Lady's Luck,* her guns strangely silent, like a vulture waiting for its prey to die.

"They're gonna board us," Captain Perry said, then spat onto the deck.

"Have your men armed. We can take them when they cross over." Nathan headed toward his cabin for his pistols, but the captain caught his arm.

"We've lost, my lord." The resignation in Captain Perry's voice hinted that he'd been through this before. "We'll let 'em board and take what they want. If luck hasn't fled us completely, they'll let us go on our way. Though I don't see how we'll get very far. The fires we can contain by hauling up water, but we lost our rudder in the last volley, and our sails are near tae useless."

Panic clenched Nathan's chest. He gripped the man's coat and hauled him close. "Then we'll fight them hand to hand and take *their* ship. We're *not* surrendering."

"I'm captain of this vessel, what's left of her, Lord Darvill." Perry pulled free of Nathan's hold. "My men won't fight if I tell 'em no. And I'll tell 'em no."

"I'll double your pay," Nathan said. Hell, he'd even hand over his title if that was what it took to save his sister.

"It's not worth the risk. You're the only cargo we're carrying. Once they learn our bays are empty, they'll leave us be."

Captain Perry couldn't be more wrong. Nathan might be the only passenger, but *he* wasn't the cargo. He wanted to believe they wouldn't search his cabin. Maybe the captain was right and the pirates would leave when they found nothing but a disabled ship and wounded men.

Leaving me stranded in the North Sea with no way to reach France.

The pirate ship pulled alongside, throwing grappling lines and shouting orders. The *Lady's Luck* crew obeyed as if they were greeting a friendly neighbor. Nathan scowled and stepped forward with the captain to meet the thieves as they boarded.

With a wide plank joining the two ships, a handful of young men scurried across, landing on the deck with the arrogance only victors could possess. With swords and pistols drawn, with chins displaying boyish beards, each one scanned the destruction they'd caused. Nathan detected neither excitement nor remorse but curiosity, which puzzled him.

Shouldn't they be laughing and calling insults? Mutilating the crew? Drinking and swearing and instilling enough fear to make a man's knees go weak? Yet the dozen who had boarded so far remained quiet and moody. They weren't behaving as pirates should, he thought. But then he'd never met a pirate—besides Morgan, and she was unique.

Urgent whispers among the *Lady's Luck* crew drew his attention to the plank. Another pirate crossed with the surefootedness of one born on the sea. Dressed in black breeches, knee-high boots and a shirt, he seemed small, yet agile. A black scarf tied behind his head covered him from cheek to hairline, hiding his identity. He didn't watch his step or glance to the sides as the ocean swelled and slapped against the ships. With one hand gripping the knife at his side, he leaped onto the deck, then crossed to Nathan and the captain.

"Ye've done ruined my ship," Captain Perry charged, his voice gruff with bottled-up anger. "We have no goods, nothing of use to ye."

"Is that so?" the pirate asked as smoke coiled over

the deck like a snake. "I'm afraid I must disagree. You do have one thing on board that I want."

"My God," Nathan blurted as a new form of outrage seized him. "You're a blasted woman!"

Green, insolent eyes met his. In a bold, rasping voice that held a trace of a smile, she said, "Through and through."

Nathan glanced over the woman, noting what he'd missed before. She was fine-boned, slender, with a waist his hands could easily span. She had a feminine curve to her hips despite the cutlass strapped there, yet her long legs were braced in an arrogant stance. His gaze slid up, and to his utter shock he realized she had breasts—full and firm, from what he could tell as the wind swirled against her shirt.

"Are you finished?" she asked, her tone hardening with derision.

When she turned aside he saw her waist-length hair, braided and so deep a red it didn't seem real. She called out to another pirate who'd boarded after her. A scarf also disguised his face, though this time Nathan was certain the second man *was* a man. Tall and muscular, with a shadow of beard and wheat-colored hair curling over his collar, he waited for the woman's orders.

"You know what to look for." She waved him and a handful of others away.

Nathan watched as they headed for the portal leading to the lower deck—which lead to his cabin and the gold. His hand went instinctively to his cutlass. From the corner of his eye, he caught Captain Perry shaking his head in warning.

Facing the woman, Nathan demanded, "What is your name?"

She regarded him with a cool gaze. "My name is none of your concern. However the cargo you're carrying concerns *me* greatly."

"I told ye, our bays are empty." Perry nodded to Nathan. "He be the only passenger we're carrying."

"Hmmm." Her gaze slipped down Nathan's bare chest, lingering on the cuts and drying blood. She showed no remorse or delight in his wounds, but continued to look at him as if he were horseflesh up for sale. Her utter brazenness made his skin tighten and his hands fist. He couldn't stand here and endure this any longer. But unless Captain Perry ordered his men to raise arms, he was outnumbered and a battle would be lost before it had begun.

The woman finished her slow perusal, meeting his gaze with one that was as bold as it was familiar. He should know those green eyes, but he was too furious to remember why or how.

"As appealing as you are, Lord Darvill, you aren't on my shopping list today."

"So you know who I am." The knowledge unsettled him. Had she also known he'd be on this ship? God, he didn't want to believe it. If that were true, she might also know about the gold. But how? Only Daniel and Fitzhugh knew about his mission to save Lauren. Neither of them would have broken his trust. But if not them, then how did this woman know where he'd be?

"You're an aristocrat." She said the last word as if it were a foul disease. "Of course I know who you are."

"Then you know who you're dealing with," he warned. "Leave this ship or suffer the consequences."

She laughed, a deep, throaty laugh that teased him and called him a fool. "You're beaten, *my lord,* and in danger of sinking, yet you have the presumption to give me orders?"

"I'll not let you take anything off this ship."

Her grin faded, the pull of her lips becoming her own brand of warning. "You aren't in a position to stop me."

He heard laughter behind him and spun to face it.

The tall pirate she'd ordered below emerged from the hatchway carrying a leather-and-iron-bound chest; the sturdy lock Nathan had used to secure it was gone from its latch.

He ground his jaw. His breath rushed through his lungs as fire burned through his veins.

The tall man heaved the burden onto his shoulder, his mouth lifting with a triumphant grin. "I believe it's time to go, Captain. We don't want to overstay our welcome."

Hot, murderous rage squeezed Nathan's chest. They were stealing Lauren's only means of freedom, leaving him helpless, with no way to reach her.

"Put the chest down," Nathan ordered, feeling the words shake through him. His palms turned clammy with sweat; his heart beat hard against his ribs.

The woman's gaze narrowed, and the corner of her mouth quirked into a mocking smile. "Trying to give orders again, Lord Darvill?" She nodded to Captain Perry. "You're heavily damaged, but I trust you can make it back to port."

She motioned to her men and began to turn away. "Across."

"No!" Nathan drew his sword from its sheath, the screech of metal against metal ripping into the air. He caught the woman beneath her chin, the cutlass's tip burrowing into her flesh. "You're not going anywhere."

Four

Steel dug into her skin, where her jaw met her throat. Jo froze, holding her breath. Her gaze locked with a pair of eyes the color and strength of iron. They were cold and unyielding, the fury hammered deep into their core making them as lethal as the sword poised to take her life.

She heard Jackson drop the chest with a loud bang, draw his cutlass and move close, as did the rest of her crew.

"Stay back or I'll run her through," Nathan warned. The curve of his cheeks—one bloodied from a cut—and the line of his jaw hardened with intent.

"You'd kill a woman?" Jackson demanded.

"Jack . . ." She started to tell him to stay back, but speaking pushed the blade deeper into her throat. She felt a sting, then a warm trickle slide a path down her neck to her chest.

"I'll kill one to save one."

She didn't know what Nathan meant by that, and found it hard to believe that a man born of blue blood would slit her throat outright. From her experience, the wealthy hired others to do their dirty work.

But from the bright metal flare in his eyes, the churning anger he revealed, she didn't want to take the chance that this time he might do his own killing. He didn't recognize her, but she hadn't expected him to, since she was wearing a mask, although a different kind from the one she'd worn at the ball.

Raising her hands out to her sides, she took a cautious step back, but he moved with her, keeping the steel tip pressed against her skin.

"I'm sure we can come to some agreement," she said carefully. She had to find a way to distract him, gain the upper hand. She'd been careless in not disarming the Englishman. A foolish mistake.

"Aye," he agreed. "Your crew will board the *Lady's Luck* and we'll take your vessel on to France."

"That's not exactly what I had in mind," she said as a desperate idea took shape.

"It's your only option." His eyes narrowed. "Besides dying, that is."

"I was thinking a contest would settle this. A duel." Yes, a duel, she thought. What better way to fight her enemy than hand to hand? No ships, no cannons, no distance and anonymity. Just the two of them using strength and skill.

"Against you?" His smirk told her he thought the idea of fighting a woman preposterous, which was fine with Jo. Let him believe her incapable of besting him; it would give her the advantage.

She said, "The first to disarm her—or his—opponent wins."

"And takes the healthy ship?" His voice was a growl of disbelief that she was offering to duel with him, but from the brief flicker in his eyes, she could tell he was already planning his strategy of attack.

"And the gold," she added as a final lure, since he seemed so attached to his money. *The greedy cur.*

"I already have you at my mercy. Why should I agree?"

"Because I won't tell my men to stand down unless you do. You might kill me, but you'll not draw another breath. And for a certainty, you'll never see France."

He considered her a moment, his expression speculative, distrusting. "You stand no chance of winning against me."

"Then you have nothing to lose."

"Order your men to stay out of it."

Since she couldn't turn her head without slicing her own throat, she glanced at Jackson from the corner of her eye. "This is between Lord Darvill and me. No one is to interfere, no matter what happens."

"I don't—" Jackson began to argue.

"Your word, Jack," she insisted.

He gave a reluctant nod. "No one will interfere."

She met Alcott's darkening gaze. "Satisfied?"

"I will be, once I'm on my way to France," he said with a twist of his lips that had nothing to do with a smile.

"Make this a fair fight, Captain," Jackson urged. "Let me duel in your place."

She should have known her best friend would offer to fight in her stead. Actually, she was surprised he hadn't tried to jerk her back to their ship and lock her away. She could already hear the lecture he would give her later. He hadn't wanted to attack the *Lady's Luck,* but sneak in as they'd done in the past.

But this was exactly what Jo wanted—had wanted since their first days aboard the *Sea Queen.* Morgan hadn't allowed them to engage in battle. Morgan had compassion for her fellow Englishmen, where Jo had none. For too long, she'd seen the wealthy take and gloat and then take some more, leaving the poor struggling simply to exist.

"He outweighs you and has a longer reach," Jackson added.

"I don't give a damn which one of you I best. But let's get on with it. My trip to France has been delayed long enough." He glanced aside to the smoldering forward deck. "Who knows how long before she sinks."

Jo ignored the alarm tightening her gut. She'd damaged Daniel's ship more than she'd intended, but surely it could make it back to port for repairs.

"You can't mean for me to pass on the opportunity to spar with a true aristocrat?" she said, though she knew fighting Nathan would be like dancing through fire. He was handsome, to be sure, but he was filled with deadly anger, and all that anger wanted to unleash itself on her.

She knew about anger, and she was more than ready to face his.

"He's a man with blue blood in his veins." She taunted him with a smile, but her lips felt cold and stiff. "A silk stocking who lives his life treading over the poor and helpless. I think it's time he met his match."

Nathan stepped back, withdrawing his sword, allowing her to lower her head. "Then let's get this done."

Jo ran her hand over her neck; her fingers came away wet and red with blood. She sliced her eyes up at her opponent. "You've drawn first blood, my lord. Seems I have some catching up to do."

"Shall we fight to the death?" A muscle pulsed in his jaw as if he were opposed to the idea.

"Nothing so drastic. Whoever is disarmed first loses."

She drew her sword, kissed it against his and took her fighting stance. Her free arm raised, her weight balanced on the balls of her feet, she looked Nathan in the eye and smiled. "I'm ready if you think you are."

He didn't respond but thrust his blade. Jo easily parried, stepping back, circling as he slashed and thrust, blocking her when she would sweep in for blood. She retreated and he followed, slicing his sword wide to the right. She checked the move. Steel shrieked and clattered. Their swords locked. She felt the weight in her arm and shoulder, the muscles straining down her back. She dodged left, but he moved closer, drawing their circle too tight for her to maneuver.

"A master taught you well," he said.

"I had no master," she replied, annoyed that she was breathing hard when he barely looked taxed.

"Self-taught?" He raised an arrogant brow as he moved her closer to the rail. Another few steps and she'd be trapped. "I'm impressed."

"Not yet, but you will be." She put her other hand against his chest and shoved. Breaking free, she skirted around him, then bore down, striking with her sword, the tip whistling again and again, pushing him back.

He parried each blow with ease, his blade a flash of silver in the burning sun. Sweat trickled beneath her mask, dripped down her jaw and into her cut, making it sting. Her muscles began to ache and her fingers cramped. But she wouldn't quit, not until she proved she could take him.

She had to hurry. She was growing tired, while he toyed with her, holding her off, controlling his own moves as if he were afraid of harming her—a woman. *That is his mistake.* She grinned, pouring more strength into her swings.

She lunged, and withdrew as he swung. He missed her blade. Jo slashed upward, catching his arm and leaving a five-inch slice. Blood poured like red tears from the gash.

"Ah, we're even," she said again, feeling her own blood beating frantically through her veins. "Now it's time to end this."

He glanced at his wound, then at her. Everything about him stilled, becoming tense and focused. "So it is."

Advancing, he swung his blade high. Jo caught his sword against hers. The impact vibrated her arm and rattled her teeth. He *had* been toying with her before, and now he meant to prove it. Jo felt a flash of panic, but shoved it aside. They broke apart. Nathan swung, catching her blade. Jo used a two-handed grip, blocking, stepping back in defense when she wanted to push forward and attack.

He wasn't going to quit or ease up or leave her an opening. She'd met an opponent worth fighting. A part of her was thrilled for the challenge; the realistic side of her felt a growing panic, knowing she could lose. *No, no, I refuse to yield to him. I'll not hand over my ship! And I won't forsake the children!*

Nathan locked her sword hilt to hilt. He twisted his wrist. The twin blades glittered; then one went flying. Jo gasped and held her empty hands out to her sides as her weapon landed with a clamor and slid across the deck and out of reach. Before she could curse or even move, he gripped her shirt in his fist and jerked her to him. He wrapped his sword arm around her waist, held her flush against his chest. Heat burned through her shirt. Her head filled with his scent—hot skin and sweat, something dark and forbidden like sin.

"Admit defeat," he demanded, his breathing as rushed and furious as her own.

Admit defeat? She swore the words would boil in her lungs before they'd pass her lips. "This isn't over."

"It is for you. But before I take my gold and leave you and the *Lady's Luck* behind, I want to know who it is I've been fighting." He ripped off her mask and tossed it down.

Jo shook her head and struggled to break free. His arm tightened, cutting off her air.

He caught her face in his hand and forced her to look at him. Stunned, he whispered, "My God."

She ceased her struggles. Panting, furious at herself and at him, she glared up at him. His eyes were narrowed, his expression one of surprise instead of anger. He searched her face, his gaze touching her eyes, her nose and mouth. Gripping a handful of her braided hair, he held it in his fist. She felt a shudder run through his body. Her own tensed, confused at what he might be thinking or feeling or what he might do next.

"Let her go," Jackson warned from behind her.

"You have no business playing pirate," Nathan told her, his teeth clenching as if he were becoming angry all over again. "You're a woman, for God's sake. You have no business risking your life."

"I might be a woman," she ground out. *Who's failed again and again!* "But I'm not playing, as you'll soon learn."

Her vision hazed as anger erupted. She'd lost the gold; she'd lost her chance to save countless babies from dying in the streets. She'd lost! God help her, she'd lost!

Fury burst from her with a growl. She shoved against Nathan's chest, giving her a breath of room, and reached for her knife at her side. The ruby-and-emerald hilt dug into her fingers. She jerked the blade free of the sheath and shoved. Something ripped, gave way. Nathan went stiff. Gasps sounded around her. He looked at her, his eyes wide and fierce. The gray irises faded, turning misty with dismay.

He staggered back a step. Jo glanced down. She couldn't see the metal blade, only her fingers curled tightly around the jeweled and gold-inlaid hilt.

The polished steel was buried in his side.

Blood pumped from the wound, warm and sticky, coating her fingers. It was red and thick and red . . . so much red! She looked at him, her heart beating in her throat. "Nathan . . ."

He swayed. The knife pulled free with a sucking sound that made her shiver and her stomach heave.

"Oh, God." She reached out, but couldn't bring herself to touch him.

Sweat beaded his forehead. His eyes glazed as he dropped to his knees. He watched her, searching her face. He opened his mouth, tried to speak, but no sound escaped.

"Where's the surgeon?" someone shouted. "Someone find the bloody surgeon!"

"Lauren," Nathan whispered.

Jo knelt before him. He gripped her face, smearing blood across her jaw. "I have to find her."

"Find who?" Jo held his shoulders when he lurched to the side.

"Lauren . . ."

His eyes closed and he went limp. Jo caught him but they both fell to the deck. Men began to shout and run. Orders were bellowed. She couldn't tell what was said or who said it. Nathan lay still, unmoving, his blood pooling beneath him onto the deck, soaking into wood, staining her clothes.

"I've killed him." A tremor sped across her scalp and down her spine. She pushed to her knees. "I've killed him. Oh, God."

She lost her balance, feeling the rocking of the ship for the first time since they'd begun their battle. Someone caught her arm and pulled her to her feet.

"Come with me, Jo." Jackson dragged her toward the planks connecting the ships.

"I can't leave." Her mind swam in a daze, a sickening red daze. *I've killed a man. An aristocrat.* It was what she'd wanted, what she'd dreamed of for half her life. She let her gaze scan the deck, seeing for the first time the wreckage she'd caused, the men wounded and bleeding, cradling their heads and arms, some whimpering from burns to their backs and legs. A violent shudder racked her body. She hadn't meant for this to happen. She hadn't. . . .

She had to leave, get off this ship. She turned and braced her hands to leverage herself onto the railing. What she saw stopped her. Blood coated her once-shiny blade. Red glimmered in the sun, warm and wet and alive. Nathan's blood.

Handsome, brooding Nathan, who'd called for a woman named Lauren with his dying breath. His wife? His lover? Was she waiting for him in France?

"What have I done?" She tried to open her fingers

and drop the knife. It belonged at the bottom of the ocean, where it was dark and desolate, where her deed could be forgotten. She willed her fingers to move, but they refused. Her hand shook, but it wouldn't let go. Denial tore through her body, threatening to erupt in a sob. She clenched her jaw, locking the cry inside. This was what she'd wanted; it was the way it had to be. It was her against the peerage. Things were turning out exactly as she'd planned. How long had she dreamed of ridding England of its nobility?

And now there was one less to worry about. She'd been victorious. She should be proud.

Only her victory tasted of blood, and pride had the scent of death.

Five

There is no mistake; there has been no mistake; and there shall be no mistake.

Jo didn't recall who said those words, or if she'd read them while in one of Madame Fournier's lessons, but she knew whoever had possessed such an arrogant thought had never buried a knife into another living soul.

There *were* mistakes, and she'd made one of the worst kind.

"Wesley, raise anchor!" Jackson shouted as the *Sea Witch* crew rushed to return to their own ship. "Hands, lay aloft to set tops'ls!"

"Jackson . . ." The words she'd intended to say stopped when her throat squeezed shut.

"Hurry, Jo!" He hauled her onto the plank, avoiding the knife she still gripped. "We've got the gold; now let's go!"

He shoved her ahead of him, but kept his hands firm on her waist. She moved in a daze, not seeing, not feeling. She knew the plank heaved dangerously beneath her feet, knew she could fall between the ships, be crushed against their massive hulls, but somehow it didn't matter.

I had to kill Nathan, she silently argued. *Mistake or no, I had to. He was going to take my ship, the gold. I couldn't let him.* She repeated the words in a mad rush, hoping they would relieve the pressure in her chest, the fear and horror screaming through her mind.

"Damn it, Jo, hurry!" Jackson said in a growl.

She reached the *Sea Witch*'s railing and was ready to drop onto the deck when she heard the shout behind her.

" 'E ain't dead. Turn 'im over. . . ."

Jo didn't hear the rest of the words. Her mind could focus only on three: *'E ain't dead.*

She faced the crew, no more than thirty feet away, huddled around Nathan, who was lying still, his bare chest painted with his own blood. An older man with a wiry beard bent over him and pressed a dirty cloth to Nathan's side. He called orders to a boy in ragged pants and shirt, who then darted off to do some task.

"Did you hear what they said?" She gripped Jackson's arm. "He's alive."

"Not for long. He's too badly wounded from your—" His voice cut off and he glanced away, as if he couldn't look at her. "We've got to go. They could still try to overrun our ship."

She shook her head. Her fingers flexed on the hilt of her knife. "No!"

"If I have to pick you up and carry you, I will," he threatened, his face stern with tension. "Now move."

"No." She tried to pass him. She had to return to the *Lady's Luck,* to see for herself if Nathan stood a chance of surviving.

Jack caught her around her waist and stopped her. "You can't help him."

"Maybe not, but I have to try." She had to right her wrong.

"If you go back you'll be captured. You'll be risking your men's lives, because we'll have to come after you."

"Then bring him to the *Sea Witch,*" Jo ordered, hearing the panic in her voice. "Please! He's still alive, Jackson."

"There's no use."

"Don't you see?" Her voice trembled with desperation. "If he dies, I'll no longer be a pirate breaking a few laws. I'll be a murderer!"

"Bloody hell." Jackson swiped a hand over his head, tearing off his mask, setting his wheat-colored hair loose about his face. "Wesley, Bishop." His jaw pulsed with anger. "Come with me." He glared at Jo. "You wait here."

She nodded and dropped onto her deck to make room for the other men to cross. She paced the railing, never taking her eyes off the *Lady's Luck*. The captain waved his fists, his fleshy cheeks turning as pink as his beard, as Jackson lifted Nathan's limp body and slung it over his shoulder. Her crewmen kept the other men at bay with drawn pistols and cutlasses, though the sailors didn't move to fight, seeming to want Nathan off their ship as much as she wanted him on hers.

The instant Jackson landed on her deck, she reached out to touch Nathan, but drew her hand back, her panic growing at the sight of his pale face. "Bring him to my cabin."

She turned to lead the way, but had to stop several times to wait as Jackson slowly navigated the narrow hatchway and corridor, taking care with his burden. Once they were in her room, she stood aside while Jack laid Nathan on top of her rumpled sheets. Jackson's shirt, from his shoulder down to his arm, was soaked with Nathan's blood. Jo looked away, though what she saw now made her want to run from the room.

Nathan's broad shoulders dwarfed her thin mattress. Blood streaked his chest, so much blood, becoming thick and dark at his side where his wound slowly seeped in a bright red pool onto the covers. A dozen tiny cuts crisscrossed his skin—wounds he'd suffered during the battle, she guessed. The black hairs on his right arm appeared to have been singed. His pants were dusty with smoke and ash, his legs so long his boots hung over the end of the bed.

"Bring me water and clean rags," she said to Jack. "And the surgeon's box."

"I'll fetch Cook to sew him up."

"No." She looked at the *Sea Queen* knife she still gripped. The blood had dried. Sunlight from the bank of windows glazed off the red steel blade, making her wonder if it had been forged in the fires of hell. No longer did it look like the symbol of strength and freedom, but a weapon crafted for killing.

"I'll take care of him," she said.

"You? What do you know about sewing up a hole in a man?"

"I put it there!" she snapped. "It's up to me to make it right."

Jackson drew a deep breath and searched her face. The tension in his shoulders eased, and understanding softened the creases bordering his eyes.

"I'll only be a moment." He left to fulfill her orders. In the companionway, he paused to rip off his ruined shirt, tossing it to the floor in a forgotten pile, never once looking back.

Jo dropped her knife on the desk, glad to have the dagger out of her hand. Yet her fingers ached. She could still feel the warm metal and polished gold that had once given her purpose, the hard gemstones that had always burrowed into her skin like protective charms. She wondered if she'd ever be able to pick the knife up again.

Nathan moaned and shifted on the bed. Jo hurried to his side, pressing her hands to his shoulders to keep him still. His skin was dry and hot, as if the fires he'd fought earlier were burning inside him now. He murmured something she didn't understand, which was just as well, she decided. She'd already heard the name of a woman he loved—a woman he might never see again.

"Do something," she told herself. She had to save

him. It was her responsibility—but how? Grace had been the one who had cared for the sick and injured aboard the *Sea Queen*. She'd had a natural talent, knowing what to say, what ointment to apply, what medicines to give for a cough or a fever. What she hadn't known through instinct, she'd learned through reading. Jo had been concerned only with visiting ports, meeting the locals and planning their next raid. Right now Jo would gladly trade all her knowledge of shipping lanes, star charts and tides for the chance to have Grace by her side.

But Grace wasn't on board the *Sea Witch;* she was safe in London, learning to be a perfect lady. Which meant Jo had only herself to rely on. Besides Cook, that was. She shook her head and grabbed one of Nathan's boots, pulling it off. She might be nearly clueless about how to stitch a wound, but she knew Nathan stood a better chance of surviving if she took a needle to his side instead of their cook—whose main experience was with slaughtering pigs.

Tugging off the second boot, she tossed it to the floor just as Jackson returned with the supplies. She took a clean cloth and pressed it to Nathan's wound to stanch the bleeding. Next she soaked another rag in water and began to wipe down his chest, grimacing at the dozen painful cuts he'd suffered. He's going to be scarred, she thought, aware of Jackson moving around behind her, and wishing he would leave.

She wanted to be alone with Nathan, give her nerves time to settle before she took a needle to his flesh. Minutes passed, and as they did, her conscience pushed to the surface. She'd wanted the gold so she could save the children. If she didn't help them, no one would. But was Nathan's life a fair trade? Before today she would have said yes, absolutely. He was an aristocrat. He didn't deserve her compassion. But to cause him harm . . . She pressed the back of her wrist to her forehead and pushed the question aside for later.

She rinsed the cloth and continued cleaning him. His skin was taut over his chest and ribs, and his muscles were corded like layered rope. His arms were well shaped, powerful, regardless that he was unconscious. And his hands . . . Jo picked one up and cleaned it with a fresh cloth. His fingers were long, lean, the same as his body, yet possessing a strength that made something inside her tremble. He wore a ring on the little finger of his right hand, a gold band with a falcon in flight, its sharp talons extended to snare its victim. She frowned, noting that he wore an identical one, only larger, on the ring finger of his left hand.

"If you're going to sew him up, you've got to use a needle and thread." Jackson shoved a three-inch-long piece of curved metal in front of her face. "You can't do it with your eyes."

She shot him a glare that lost its effect because she blushed.

"Are you sure you don't want me to call Cook?"

"I'm sure." She took the needle. "I can do this."

She lifted the rag she'd pressed to his side. The once-white cloth was dark red, heavy and warm. Her stomach heaved. The rag had absorbed so much blood. Still more drained from his wound.

Jackson held out a bottle.

Taking it, Jo looked at him uncertainly, then sniffed. "It's whiskey."

"Exactly."

"This isn't the time for a drink." Though she thought it might help calm her shaking hands.

"Pour it on the wound. I saw Grace do it when your uncle Simon stuck a fishing hook through his palm. He cursed a blue streak, for which Grace gave him a lecture."

She studied the amber liquid doubtfully. "Well, if Grace did it . . ." She upended the bottle, pouring the liquor onto the wound.

Nathan released a raw growl, his upper body jerking

off the bed. His legs thrashed; his hands clawed at the sheets.

"Hold him down." Jackson pinned his legs to the mattress, while Jo threw her weight across his shoulders.

Nathan drew deep, ragged breaths, turning his head from side to side. He clenched his jaw; then his body grew still. Jo started to rise, but stopped.

His eyes were open and glazed with pain. He stared at her, though she was almost certain he didn't recognize her. He probably didn't even know where he was or that he had a knife wound in his side.

"Pour some whiskey down his throat," Jackson suggested. "If you're going to sew him up, he's got to stay still, and he doesn't seem to be of a mind to listen to reason."

Jo carefully lifted Nathan's head and held the bottle to his lips. He surprised her by taking one deep gulp after another. He pulled back, coughing and grimacing before slipping back into a dazed state. She set the whiskey aside and found the needle where she'd dropped it among the ruined sheets.

Drawing two deep breaths, she clamped her teeth together. She had to do this; he wasn't going to die because of her mistake—she wasn't going to let him.

"I'm ready if you think you are," she said, repeating her taunt before their duel. His gaze was on her, but she had no idea if he understood.

She pierced Nathan's skin with the needle and felt her stomach turn over. He didn't move or call out or even twitch his hand. But she knew she was hurting him. She could feel his pain in her own side, feel the hooked needle slice through one side of the wound and then the other, pulling the torn edges together. She glanced up once, grateful to see his eyes were closed. Over and over she made her stitches, vowing she would reach the end before she retched.

"You look green, Jo," Jackson said close to her ear. "Are you all right?"

"Shut up." She swallowed and made herself continue.

"I never thought you were the squeamish type."

Neither did I, but then I'd never felt what it was like to stab a man. She didn't deserve the luxury of becoming ill. She had to look at him and touch him and make sure he survived.

"You did it, Jo," Jackson said quietly as she made her last stitch.

She nodded, afraid to speak. She tied off the thread and put the needle away. Taking out a jar, she spread salve over the wound. Nathan didn't stir or open those disturbing gray eyes, eyes that would condemn her for what she'd done. With Jackson's help, she wrapped strips of clean linen around his waist.

"Help me remove his pants." She reached for the top button of Nathan's trousers, but Jackson caught her wrist.

"What do you think you're doing?" He frowned at her as if she'd lost her mind.

"He's covered with dried blood. He needs to be cleaned."

"Not by you."

She would have smiled if she weren't feeling so ill. After spending years at sea, she'd seen her share of naked men. "You sound like a scolding father."

"And you're going to listen to me as if I were your father. You're not stripping him naked."

"I'm not Grace. I won't faint at the sight of a man's privates."

"You're still a woman, Jo, and there are some things even you don't need to see."

"Fine." She straightened, holding her hands up. "You do it then. Cover him with a blanket and I'll wash the rest."

"Turn your back," Jackson ordered.

"The sheets need to be changed as well. But that can wait until later." Lord knew she didn't want his stitches ripping open. She didn't think she could sew him up again.

Provided he lives through the night. Jo briefly closed her eyes. *He will live. He must!* Otherwise she wouldn't be able to look at the gold she'd taken from him without seeing it coated with his blood. She placed her supplies back into the surgeon's box.

"All right, you can turn around now."

She did, to find Jackson holding out the whiskey bottle.

"Take a drink," he commanded.

"I don't need—"

"Drink," he repeated, softer this time. "It will help your stomach."

She grudgingly took the bottle and upended it. Bitter liquid filled her mouth, then burned a path down her throat before catching fire in her stomach. She gasped a thready breath and shoved the bottle back into his hands. Her eyes blurred with tears.

"I said a drink, Jo." A somber smile lifted the corner of Jackson's mouth. "Not swig half the bottle."

"Well," she said, forcing air into her lungs, "my stomach is really not well."

He chuckled, then gathered the supplies and dirty linens. "Go to my cabin and rest. I'll watch over him."

She shook her head. "I'm staying here. You take the deck."

Jackson sighed with disapproval, but he merely said, "Where do you want to sail to?"

"Anywhere. Away from England, that is."

"Caribbean?"

She shrugged. "That's fine for now."

Jackson left her alone, closing the door behind him, sealing in the smells of blood and fear. Jo opened a paned window, one of many that lined the rear wall of her cabin. Cool air tasting of salt and sunshine flowed in, stirring her damp hair and raising goose bumps on her sweaty skin. She rubbed her arms and returned to the bed.

She sat in the small space by Nathan's side and watched him. Countless moments passed with neither of them moving. She listened to the comforting sound of the ocean rolling past the ship. The hull creaked with familiar whispers. She heard the muted voices of her men topside, but couldn't tell what they were saying. If she tried hard, she imagined she'd be able to hear seagulls swooping overhead, looking for a meal, though they were too far out to sea for birds to be flying.

Then there was the deep, slow rhythm of Nathan's breathing, one breath after another. She watched his chest rise and fall, counted the number of times his pulse beat at the base of his throat, a part of her terrified there wouldn't be another one to count.

She reached out and brushed black hair from his brow. *Soft.* The wavy length slipped through her fingers. She arched a brow. Who would have thought it? Even unconscious his features were taut, the carved cheekbones and solid jaw hard with pain—and anger. A frown creased his brow, and his lips remained pressed in a tight line.

Her hand hovered over his mouth. She was tempted to touch him, see if his lips were as firm as they seemed, as willful, as stubborn and arrogant. *He'd probably wake enough to bite me.* Which would be no more than she deserved.

Although Jo had wished Grace had been on board to help Nathan, she was glad Morgan hadn't been there to witness what she'd done. She didn't need her sister's reproachful looks to feel guilt; she was feeling enough as it was.

"You're going to live," she whispered, drawing her hand away before she gave in to the lure of touching him.

He had to survive, she thought, because her conscience couldn't endure anything else.

Something sharp and cold clawed through the dark side of Nathan's brain, bringing him out of oblivion. Pain that cut with a lethal edge sliced downward in a trail that gathered heat in his chest and flamed in his belly. He tried to touch his side where the sting of a thousand ant bites burned and festered. He couldn't move. His arms were heavy and sore. His head pounded so hard, he thought he would be left blind from the force.

Christ above, what had happened to him?

He focused on breathing, on controlling the aches that tightened his body. He clenched his hand, felt rough homespun sheets. He smelled damp air, heavy with salt and dew. Though his mind was sluggish, he knew he wasn't at his town house in London or in his bed at Winstone Castle. So where was he? He should know. There was something he had to do, something important. He felt the urgency in the sudden racing of his heart, the prickle at the base of his neck, but he couldn't remember . . . couldn't . . .

He managed to open his eyes a slit. Dark wood, weathered by age, rose above him to a flat roof of solid beams. A lantern, doused of light, swung from a hook like a pendulum, ticking off seconds, minutes. *Days?* How long had he been here, wherever "here" was?

It must be near dawn, he thought. Shadows blended with soft morning light, hazing the room with floating dust motes and traces of mist.

He turned his head slightly and grimaced at the resulting streak of pain. A part of him said to stop fighting, to sleep until the pressure eased. But somehow he knew he'd already slept too long. Gritting his teeth, he waited, and gradually the pain began to fade.

He saw a desk littered with papers and what looked

like scrolled charts or maps, as well as a silver ink bottle and a quill pen. He was on a ship, he thought dully. *A ship? Why?* Through a wall of square-paned windows, the blanket of gray sky was tinged pink from the rising sun.

Which way was he sailing? And where was he going? *I should know this. It's important that I know!* Yet the reason eluded him.

A sound drew his attention: a soft sigh, a murmur. He turned his head as far as he dared, yet saw no one, only a pile of clothes stacked on a chest, a cluster of books crowding wire-lined shelves, discarded plates of uneaten food. Maybe he'd imagined the noise. It might have been the wind stirring through the open window or the sound of his own breathing.

Then something brushed against his hand. Nathan looked down and felt surprise work through the drugged weight of his mind.

A woman sat on the floor beside his bunk, her head resting on her folded arms while she slept. Waves of deep auburn hair curled about her shoulders, partially covering her face. It had been braided at one time, though it looked as if she'd run her hands through it more than once. Wispy strands fluttered in the breeze. Hazy sunlight tangled in her hair, shooting threads of gold and cinnamon through its length.

Had she tended him while he'd been ill? His own angel of mercy?

He caught a fallen lock in his fingers. It was cool, smooth, like drawing satin across his flesh. Something clicked in his memory. He saw an image of himself holding a fistful of her hair, green eyes turning dark, smoldering with anger. Everything came back to him in a rush, making his head spin.

Lauren and Philip. The *Lady's Luck.* Pirates! A battle between the crews and a duel that he'd won—or so he'd thought.

This woman was no angel! He dropped her hair as if burned. She was a flame-haired witch!

She'd raided his ship, taken his gold. Then she'd stabbed him, trying to take his life as well. Fury burned hot in his side, spreading out, making his limbs shake. He wanted to wrap his hands around her throat and squeeze, to pay her back for what she'd done.

Was Lauren still alive? Or had he lost his ten remaining days? He pushed up onto his elbow. The wound in his side screamed in protest. He gritted his teeth and fell back onto the mattress, panting. He had to get off this ship, reach France, find his sister. Sweat coated his skin.

His mind spun, and a buzz filled his ears, as if a thousand bees had been set loose inside his head. His thoughts slipped away. He fought to hold on, struggled to stay above the creeping darkness. He couldn't stay here, at this woman's mercy.

His vision blurred, turning red—the color of blood, the color of auburn hair, the color that belonged to a witch.

Six

The banging of a door jolted Jo awake. She blinked and muttered a curse as sunlight stabbed her eyes. Rubbing the sleep away, she shot Jackson a glare. "I don't suppose you could be any louder?"

He set the tray of food he carried on the desk beside the other food she'd ignored. Facing her, he crossed his arms over his chest and gave her his best warning scowl. "Last night you promised you would eat."

"I wasn't hungry." She pushed herself off the floor onto her feet, stifling a groan. For three nights she'd slept in snatches, always waking in some odd position, her neck aching or her limbs numb. Her joints popped and moaned as she straightened to an upright position.

She picked up a slice of barley bread and bit into it, choosing to pass on the hard cheese and salted herring.

"How is the crew faring?" she asked. She hadn't stepped foot outside her cabin since the moment they'd brought Nathan on board. She knew that her men, some of them no more than boys on the verge of becoming men, had to be as concerned about their future as she was about hers.

"They're wondering if we're ever going to head someplace specific, or just sail around the Atlantic in one big circle."

"A circle, I imagine." She took a drink of water to

wash down the bread. They'd originally started for the Caribbean, but she'd changed the order, not wanting to sail so far from England. Now that she had the gold, she needed to return home as soon as possible, before the shacks the children were living in were destroyed. 'We can't start for home until I'm sure he's going to live."

Jackson furrowed his brow in thought, studying their . . . hostage? Captive? Unwanted passenger? Certainly not a guest. Jo didn't know how to categorize Nathan Alcott. When she tried, her chest began to ache, so she put it off and focused on healing him instead.

"He has more color today." Jackson laid a hand on Nathan's brow. "His fever seems to have broken. Have you changed his dressing?"

"Last night."

"And?"

"The swelling has gone down some. The lesion is still red, but I don't think it's infected," she said with more confidence than she felt. Each time she'd inspected his wound, she'd feared she'd find that red, telling streaks had crept across his body while she wasn't looking, leaving a diseased path and the stink of certain death.

Touching her chin with his finger, Jackson tilted her head back and studied her face. "You look like hell."

"And you're as charming as usual." She stepped around him and touched Nathan's forehead. His skin was cool, firm and smooth. She closed her eyes and sighed, feeling exhaustion lace through her mind.

"You think he'll live, then?" Jackson picked up a tray of stale food.

"I think he's too stubborn to die," she said thoughtfully, watching Nathan sleep. His eyes were closed, his face still, though she wouldn't say it was relaxed. Tension furrowed his brow into a slight frown; his lean cheeks and carved jaw seemed as hard and unyielding now as they'd been in the midst of her duel with him.

For hours and days she'd watched him fight off fever and battle his demons as he drifted in and out of consciousness. He had a strong heart, and a will to survive, for which she was grateful. She didn't want his death on her shoulders. She already carried the blame for Robby's fate, and in a way, Sammy's, too; she didn't wish to add another one.

But if Nathan recovered, it both solved a problem and created one. If he lived, she would escape being hunted down as a murderer. But she doubted he would forget about her and go on his way. He'd want her captured, punished. She'd stolen his gold, stabbed him and kept him from a woman named Lauren. No, Nathan Alcott, Marquess of Darvill, wouldn't forget—or forgive.

She'd never be able to return to London and visit her sisters for fear that he would spot her, recognize her and call her out for the pirate she was. A shudder raced up her spine. If King George ever learned what she'd done, she would be hanged, as would Morgan and possibly Daniel and Grace as well.

She squeezed her eyes closed. Bloody hell, what had she been thinking? How could she have been so careless? So foolish?

Because of the children, a voice answered from a stubborn part of her mind. *I have to protect the children.* Nathan had more money than half of England. Why had he fought her for a chest of gold? If only he'd let her leave, none of this would have happened.

"Jo," Jackson said, interrupting her thoughts.

She glanced at him. He filled the threshold of her doorway, his blond hair streaked by the sun, his tanned face all angles and strength. The gold hoop in his ear flashed, matching the sudden spark in his eyes. He'd been her friend for the best part of her life. He'd understood her fears, challenged her when he thought her wrong and made her laugh when she took herself too seriously. She might never have tried to sail the *Sea*

Witch if not for his support. Yet she'd endangered him, too.

"We have to move him off the ship before he learns who we are."

She nodded, knowing he was right. But the thought of abandoning Nathan made her stomach tighten. Unease inched over her skin, leaving her chilled. It was her responsibility to watch over him, to tend his wound. *I'll leave him only if I'm certain he will survive.* "What port are we close to?"

"We're two days out from the Canaries."

"Fine."

"It's not your fault, Jo," Jackson said solemnly, though the words were hollow, as if he didn't truly believe them.

She regarded him, but she couldn't answer—her throat had squeezed shut. It *was* her fault, all of this, but she was going to make it right. If the price she had to pay was never to step foot in London again, then she'd gladly pay it. The orphaned children would receive the money they needed and Nathan would live.

What more could she ask for?

Jo pressed the last spoonful of weak beef broth to Nathan's mouth. He swallowed by reflex, a small amount dribbling down his beard-stubbled chin. She dabbed it with a strip of cloth. His eyes remained closed, his face unmoving. His third day of unconsciousness was drawing to an end. Would he never wake? The gnawing worry circled her mind like a carrion crow waiting to land. At least he'd taken more broth today than he had before. But still, she wanted to see his eyes, hear his voice, know without a doubt that he'd live—even if it was to hate her for nearly killing him and stealing his gold.

She set the empty bowl on the floor, then soaked a cloth in a bucket of cool water. She ran it over his

warm chest, the healing cuts and bruises, taking care
not to disturb the bandage around his waist. She knew
his body now, every curved muscle in his shoulders,
the slope of his arms, the broad shape of his hands.
Black hair curled over his chest, swirling around dark
nipples, narrowing down to the flat of his stomach, an
area that repeatedly drew her eyes—and her curiosity.
She'd not removed the sheet that Jackson had draped
across his middle, though she'd been tempted to.

She ran the cloth over the lower half of his waist,
felt the muscles beneath his skin clench in response.
He stirred slightly, tensing, causing her stomach to
tighten as well. In a wave of anticipation that he might
wake, tingles sped through her body. Or was what she
felt something else altogether? The prickling sensation
was cool and disturbing, like imaginary fingers tickling
the tender underside of her skin.

Without thinking, she abandoned the wet cloth and
ran her bare hand down Nathan's thigh to his calf, then
up again, feeling the coarse hairs graze her palm. She
stopped below the hem of the sheet, debating whether
to continue. She'd done a dozen bold things in the past,
but what she considered doing now, lifting the sheet,
looking her fill, satisfying her curiosity, had to be the
most outrageous of them all.

She'd seen men naked before when they'd bathed
while anchored in some nameless cove. She hadn't been
amazed by any of them. Not even Jackson, who was
an awesome man in his own right, with his sandy blond
hair and rolling muscles. So why was Nathan different?
*Because Nathan is a breed of his own, as different from
my crew as the sun is from the moon.*

Something burned inside him, something she could
barely understand, an internal strength, a purpose that
lit his eyes with fired smoke. She recalled the night of
the mask. He'd been controlled and dangerous, as intriguing as shadows that shifted with the wind. His
pantherlike grace had captured her attention, drawing

her in, urging her to learn what emotion he kept hidden, what secrets. He was a challenge she wanted to face and test and conquer—however foolish that would be.

They would put him ashore in another day; she'd never see him again, never touch him or smell him—his rich scent that reminded her of darkness and mysteries, and things that were wild.

Jo straightened her shoulders. She wasn't one for wavering; why was she now? If she wanted to look at him, who was to stop her? She glanced at the door, making certain it was closed, then at Nathan's eyes; they were shut as well. She stood and lifted the sheet, tossing it aside before she could change her mind. Her breath lodged in her chest; blood pulsed beneath her skin, echoing in her ears, beating at the base of her throat.

She'd known what to expect, knew how men were built, so she hadn't thought she'd be surprised. But she was. Lying still with his arms resting by his sides, his legs so long they didn't fit on the bed, his manhood soft against his thigh, he seemed strong and vulnerable and . . . beautiful, she decided, while her body suddenly seemed quivery and weak.

Her gaze moved up to his face. His beard shadowed his stubborn jaw; even blacker lashes swept cheekbones that appeared carved from iron. And his mouth . . .

His lips were firm, the corners pulled into a frown, as if peace eluded him even in sleep.

"What would it take to make you smile, Nathan?" she whispered, then cursed her foolishness.

She shouldn't care a whit if he smiled or how he looked completely naked; her main concern was that he didn't die while under her care.

Yet she traced his lips with the tip of her finger. What would he taste like? she wondered. She knew his scent, the way his skin warmed against her hands; it seemed only right that she should know the flavor of his mouth. Would he be musky, like aged wood and smoke, or sweet, like sugared plums?

She smiled slyly, imagining Morgan's outrage if she ever learned what Jo was thinking—or what she wanted to do.

She'd been kissed before, by a sailor from another ship who'd taken the liberty without asking and had paid the price with a broken nose. A dockworker had tried as well, but he hadn't fared much better. And there had been Marcus, the tavern owner in Jamaica who'd caught her interest, but not for long. No man ever held her attention for long.

When she'd sailed from Jamaica, Marcus had accused her of running away from him and the relationship they could have had. Perhaps he'd been right, Jo thought grudgingly. She had run away, afraid he'd realize she wasn't as strong as she pretended to be. So she'd left, and in all her travels since she'd never met a man worth staying for. Staying meant risking her freedom, her independence. Her heart.

She'd never dared to risk her heart; nor had she dared to kiss an aristocrat, which was hardly surprising since her driving goal hadn't been to kiss one, but to kill one.

But that had been before she'd known what killing truly meant. She rubbed her palms against her pants, breaking away from the memory of her knife burrowing into Nathan's side. It was something she wanted to forget, but knew she never would.

She brought her thoughts back to the present. If she wanted to kiss him, now was her chance. There was nothing to stop her, except her own conscience, and she was too curious to listen to its warning.

"I'm going to kiss you, Nathan," she said in barely a whisper, sitting beside him and bending close.

She kept her eyes focused on his, watching for signs that he might wake. Her heart began to race, beating wildly, as if she were facing a storm. She held her breath and touched her mouth to his. His lips were firm, unyielding—a word she repeatedly found herself using in connection with him. His beard rasped against her skin. He was warm against her, but he didn't open his mouth, or respond the way she imagined he would—hungry, hard, demanding. His breathing didn't change. She didn't know what she'd hoped for—he was unconscious, after all. But she'd wanted more, his heat and temper, she wanted the challenge that had unfurled from him like a building gale when she'd met him at the ball, and again when she'd faced him on the deck of his ship.

She wanted the fire that had burned in his eyes.

But there was nothing.

She drew back slightly and sighed, disappointed and annoyed. She should have known better. Nothing ever worked out the way she planned. She had only to look at her past for a reminder of her sometimes dangerous, sometimes deadly mistakes. She could now add kissing Nathan to her list of errors, right after stabbing him.

Frowning, she looked down—and met a pair of cold gray eyes.

A gasp lodged in her throat. Nathan's icy gaze was clear and sharp and focused on her.

She pushed away. He gripped her neck with a strong hand and flipped her onto her back, pinning her to the mattress with his body.

"If you want me to kiss you," he said in a growl, his jaw hardening to match the fury blazing in his eyes, "all you had to do was ask."

Seven

Streaks of fiery pain shot up Nathan's side and exploded in his head, blinding him with piercing light. He gritted his teeth and sucked in a breath. The woman shoved against his shoulder; he caught her wrist, forced her hand above her head and pinned it there. Her other arm was trapped between them. He gulped in air, waited for the pain to ease.

Then he looked at her. Her disheveled red hair fell over the sheets and down her shoulders. Her eyes were as wide and defiant as the foaming sea, swirling with temper and fear. She should fear him, because right now he wanted to kill her.

"Who are you?" he demanded.

"Get off of me." She bucked her hips with surprising strength. Nathan pressed his knee between her thighs and held her down. She gasped, then clenched her jaw. Her eyes darkened with the promise of a fight.

"Answer my question."

"Who I am doesn't matter."

"I disagree. You tried to murder me"—a tremor tore through him—"after a fair duel, a duel I won."

Her chin tilted in a challenge, while her lashes lowered in a show of remorse—an emotion he didn't believe for a moment.

"Your name." He caught her other hand and jerked

it above her head, grimacing when his wound twinged in protest.

"Jo," she answered reluctantly. "My name is Jo."

"Well, Jo," he said, feeling her shiver, a reaction he sensed was due to her anger instead of fright. "How did you know I carried gold aboard the *Lady's Luck?*"

"Let me up and I'll tell you."

"Tell me now!" He shifted his bare leg higher up her thigh, burrowing tight against her center. She gasped and struggled, which only pushed her breasts against his chest. "You won't surprise me with your dagger again."

"I didn't mean to stab you." The way she spat the words, Nathan doubted she meant them. Not that it mattered.

"I suppose your burying that blade between my ribs was an accident?"

"I saved your life."

"You can explain your logic to me later. Right now there are two things I want to know. Where am I and where is my gold?"

"You're aboard my ship and the gold is safe with me, where it's going to stay." Her eyes glittered with insolence, like a cat's after capturing a mouse. And this cat thought she was going to hoard her prize for herself.

Nathan's muscles tightened. A tremor started in his chest and spanned out, fueling his strength and fury. He wrapped one hand around her throat, felt her wild pulse beat against his fingers. "I should kill you for what you've done."

Her expression stilled, but she didn't cry out or beg for mercy. Instead she fed the fire raging in his soul by saying, "You have more gold than any one man should have, Lord Darvill. What I've taken from you will hurt you not at all."

"You have no idea the damage you've caused!" Sweat coated his skin, chilling it where the wind blew in through the window in a rasping sweep. He felt himself stir, but it was a hot, angry sensation that filled his loins, hardening him against her thigh.

He knew she felt it as well, because her eyes widened with outrage. "Get off me, you lousy, bloody—"

"I'm not through with you yet."

"Rape me and I'll kill you for true next time."

"I wouldn't think a pirate such as you would object to rape; it's just another form of stealing, after all." He drew his hand down her chest, cupping his fingers around the underside of her breast. She lacked a corset or even a thin shift. Only her worn linen shirt separated her from his hand. He squeezed. She was soft and firm, full in his palm. Lust shot like wildfire through his veins. He gritted his teeth. "You kissed me while you thought I was unconscious. Is that not a form of rape?"

"Take your filthy hand off me," she demanded, her breath a hot tremor against his face.

He released her breast and skimmed his hand over her ribs to her stomach, where he stopped, his fingers flexing against her trim waist. From the glare in her eyes, she didn't seem to like this position any more than the last.

"You lousy son of a cur," she said with clenched jaw. The green of her gaze sliced like jagged glass—a brazen look, considering she was at his mercy. Perhaps he'd lost more blood than he'd realized, because he couldn't help noticing that Jo the pirate was as bold as she was beautiful. She was also a threat to Lauren's freedom.

"If you were awake," she admonished, "you should have said something."

"You expect me to play fair with a thief?"

Light from the overhead lantern flickered in the growing dusk, darkening her eyes to sage. Amusement suddenly glimmered in their depths, a spark that made his blood burn all the hotter. God above, who was this woman? And why did he lie here arguing with her when he should gag and bind her, then learn the full damage her delay had caused?

She shifted, rubbing her body against his groin, making him all the more aware of their positions. She lay nearly beneath him, her body flush against his, her thin shirt stretched taut over breasts ripe and firm, their nipples pebbled to tight points, his rigid sex pressed deep into her thigh. She wouldn't fight him for long. No, the wench would undoubtedly welcome the open battle, the clash of wills and body and sweat.

Her mouth curved with a brash dare. "All's fair on the open seas."

Would kissing her until her mouth was bruised and swollen be fair? He ground his lust under control. Now wasn't the time for sexual sport. "Not according to King George. Piracy is against the law, punishable by hanging. Or hadn't you heard?"

Her smile vanished and she arched her body into his, trying to throw him off. She was strong, Nathan realized, feeling the wound in his side twist and open, but not strong enough to escape him.

"I should have let you bleed to death," she snapped.

"I'm rather glad you didn't." He felt blood flow from his side in a warm stream, soaking into the bandage. "You've cost me enough as it is. Now you'll answer my questions."

"I've said all I'm going to say. You're on *my* ship, Lord Darvill. Your options are few."

"You're the captain?" He felt as if the vessel had suddenly taken a crazy dip over the edge of the earth.

"Aye, and the *Sea Witch* is my home." Her chin thrust outward with stubborn pride. "It will be yours, too, until I discard you at the first port we reach in the Canaries."

"I'm going to France," he said, seething, feeling anxiety and fury sear the nerves beneath his skin.

"But *I'm* not. And neither is my ship."

"You'll do as I say, Jo, or suffer the consequences."

Tremors bled through him, turning his lust to anger and anger to hot, furious lust; whether it was for sex or revenge, he didn't know and didn't care. She wouldn't keep him from reaching Lauren; nothing would stop him from saving his sister. Certainly not a willful thief with wanton eyes and a mocking smile!

"You're naked and wounded, Darvill, and my prisoner as well," she said as if she cared little that her hands were trapped in his, that her body was overpowered and vulnerable to his touch.

He expected her to scream for help. *Let her try.* He might be wounded, but he still possessed enough stamina to hold her captive, which would keep her men at bay. *But for how long?* How would holding her help him? There had to be a way to convince her to sail for Saint-Nazaire.

"You may think you have the advantage, but you can't defeat my men, Nathan." She whispered his name as if she were his lover. "Admit it, you're helpless and at my mercy."

"And you're at mine!"

With a growl of pure rage, his mouth closed over hers, hard and forceful, grinding until he heard her moan in pain. He forced her lips apart, plunged his tongue inside. Anger became a taste in his mouth, dark and wet and spicy with heat. He realized it was her he tasted, Jo the pirate, Jo the woman who was really a witch. He wanted to take her, see fear in her eyes, punish her for what she'd done.

This is madness!

The thought shouted through his mind, then again and again. He had to stop this, tie her up, find his clothes. With her as his hostage, he could force her men to sail to France. He'd retrieve his gold and exchange it for his sister's life.

But he pushed the kiss deeper, raked his tongue over the pirate's teeth, felt her shiver. He inhaled their mingled scents, his sweat and blood, her alarm, a hungry, primal scent that fanned through his lungs, seeped into his veins.

His fingers tightened over her waist, skimmed down to her thigh, lifting her leg so she cupped him more fully. She sucked in a breath, but didn't resist, which somehow fueled the anger tightening his skin.

"Damn you," he said under his breath, pulling away.

She stared at him, her lips parted and damp, swollen and red from the assault of his kiss. Her hands were fisted above her head. Each breath pushed through her lips as if the simple act were a struggle. Her eyes were glazed—with what emotion he couldn't guess. Dismay, fury, hatred—desire? It could have been one of them or none, or a combination of them all.

He pushed back onto his knees, keeping one of her hands in his. He glanced around the room for a pistol, a knife, any sort of weapon.

"You're bleeding." She touched the fingers of her free hand to her shirt. His blood stained a good portion of her blouse, spreading down to the bedsheets as well.

"So I am." He gave her a dubious glance, and fought the pain that burned like fire in his belly. "I hate to disappoint you, but it's not severe enough for me to bleed to death."

"If I'd wanted you dead I wouldn't have bothered to stitch you closed." The rigid set of her jaw convinced him that she regretted doing just that.

Gripping his wound, he rose from the bed. He swayed, and her wrist slipped from his hold. Sweat beaded his brow, dripping a cold path down the side of his face. His vision faded. Darkness swam into his mind, followed by shooting pinpoints of light. The dizziness came fast and furious. He was far weaker than he'd thought; even breathing was an effort. He spotted a gold dagger studded with jewels on the desk. *Was that the knife she stabbed me with?* He started for it, but his legs faltered as the ship rolled beneath his feet.

He made it as far as the chair and had to grip its back to keep from crashing to his knees.

He drew a deep breath, closed his eyes, and heard her walk past him. He watched her through lowered lashes as she retrieved the dagger and slipped it into a leather sheath at her hip. Her motions were sure, smooth, as if being armed were as natural as breaking one's fast.

"There's no use fighting me, Lord Darvill." The anger had fled from her eyes, leaving them cool and clear, and as green as polished jade. "You'll come to no harm while you're here. We should reach the Canaries within two days—"

"No!" They couldn't have sailed so far, and in the wrong direction. Dread sliced through him, penetrating just as her knife had.

"If you still want to travel to France, you shouldn't have trouble finding another ship to take you there."

"How long?"

She shrugged. "You may be in luck and find a vessel in port. Or it could be a week, a month. Who knows?"

"No, damn it!" He skirted the chair, catching the desk's edge to keep himself from falling. "How long has it been since you raided the *Lady's Luck?* Since you stabbed me?"

"Five days."

"Five . . ." Denial touched the back of Nathan's neck, a cold, shivery sensation, much like the scrape of stiff, dead fingers.

"Dear God," he whispered, staring sightlessly through a wall of windows that led to the blackened sea. He ran his hand through his hair. *Dear God, Lauren.* It had taken him three days after receiving Philip's letter to set sail. Now he'd lost another five. That left him only six to reclaim the ransom and reach Saint-Nazaire.

"You are going to take me to France," he told her, glaring at her, daring her to object.

She quirked a russet brow, her gaze flickering over his naked frame. "Am I now?"

"And you're going to return my gold to me." He came around the desk, his steps slow and careful, not caring that blood drained down his side, or that he was as naked as a stone. She was going to do as he ordered, or he'd make her suffer.

"I'm afraid I can't do that. I've already made plans for your fifty thousand pounds."

"I'll pay you that and more once my business in France is done."

"It's strange how men confuse being female with being stupid." She retreated a step, then stopped as if deciding to stand her ground. "I'm taking you to the Canaries, and nowhere else."

"That's unacceptable." He took another step, moving within reach of her.

"Life usually is." Her features hardened as if her words possessed a great deal more meaning. "Why are you so determined to reach France?"

Did he dare tell her? Philip had warned Nathan in his letter to keep the truth of Lauren's abduction between them. He'd informed Daniel and Mr. Fitzhugh because absolute secrecy had been impossible when he'd been given so little time to reach Saint-Nazaire. Besides, he trusted the two men—or he had until the *Sea Witch* had set upon him with full knowledge of the cache he'd carried. But that was a mystery he'd have to solve later. Right now he had to convince a pirate to do his bidding.

"My reasons don't concern you," he said, taking another step. "Just do as I say and I'll reward you."

She watched him move closer, her gaze scanning the length of his body, his chest, the wound in his side, and lower to his hips and privates and finally his legs. Evidently not finding him a threat, she said, "Thank you, but I already have my reward locked in the bays below."

Nathan reached out, surprising them both. He gripped her knife and jerked it from the sheath, raising it, poising the steel tip at Jo's throat before she could react. There was no way for her to move around him, and unless she dove through the window and into the sea, she was as good as trapped. Her chin came up a notch and her eyes narrowed in warning.

"You'll give the order to sail to Saint-Nazaire; then you will return my gold."

"Tell me why I should and I'll consider it." Her defiance took him by surprise. Either the woman had the courage of ten soldiers or she was a fool.

"If you don't do as I say," he warned with slow certainty, "my sister will die. And then you, sweet Jo, will do the same."

Eight

"Give up the gold or die. I can't say I care for either choice," Jo said, staring into Nathan's ash gray eyes, searching for any sign of wavering, a hint of deceit. His gaze didn't flicker from hers, didn't reveal a ruse or lie or the whisper of a trick. Could he be telling the truth? Was his sister's life truly at stake? If so, how could a chest full of coins save her?

The woman might be ill, but if so, Jo suspected the affliction troubling her had to be something far more foul than a sour stomach. Aristocrats played games with other people's lives the way the poor played with dice in filthy alleyways.

At the moment she was at a loss as to what to do: strike out or play coy? A decision eluded her, since all she could see were Nathan's angry eyes, his wide, sweat-slicked shoulders and the steel of her blade.

"I can be reasonable. You don't need the knife," she said, hoping to defuse the moment and give herself time to form a plan. She couldn't think clearly while he stood before her naked and crazed; she could only feel, and what she felt made her breath rush hot through her lungs. "And for God's sake, put something on."

The knife didn't move from her throat. "Do I have your word that you'll sail to France?"

"You want the word of a pirate?" she taunted. She had no intention of handing over the money, but she might consider taking him to Saint-Nazaire if he gave her a good enough reason. She'd nearly killed him, after all. Giving him transport would be the least she could do to atone for her mistake.

"I do."

"Why would you trust my word?"

"Because you could have left me to die, but you didn't. Somewhere behind those hard green eyes lies a conscience, however small and tainted it might be. I don't think you want my death—or my sister's—weighing on you."

"That *would* annoy me," she said with a half smile. No, she didn't need any more ghosts haunting her soul.

"Let's move aloft so you can give the order to change our heading." He didn't pull back to let her pass, and she wasn't about to maneuver around him. If she tried, she'd have to brush the length of her body against his. And she'd seen—and felt—enough of him for one day.

She forced her eyes to stay on his face. She wouldn't look at the sweep of black hair swirling over his chest, the layers of muscle that corded his stomach, the red-soaked bandage that trickled blood down his leg, or his sex, the impression of which still marked her thigh.

"Why don't we talk first," she said, placing her hand against his to urge the knife aside.

He refused to move. "You'll not distract me."

"I don't intend to." Though she wasn't sure that wasn't a lie in itself. "You need to dress, and I want to know the reason you're so determined to reach France."

He withdrew half a breath, but she could still feel the imprint of the knife's tip at her throat. A muscle pulsed in his jaw, as if he were gritting his teeth. Because he's angry, she wondered, or in pain? The guilt she'd battled for the injuries she'd caused him, as well as the destruction of Daniel's ship, swept up in a rising tide, hovering over her like a darkening cloud. She fought the shadows back, refusing to let them close.

There was nothing she could do about the *Lady's Luck*; its loss wouldn't affect Daniel's business too terribly, since he'd acquired the pirate ship when he'd raided Halo Jones's island.

Nathan was another matter entirely. She regretted stabbing him, but she'd righted that wrong. And perhaps she'd inconvenienced him, but he was an aristocrat—maybe it was time he learned how inconvenient life could really be.

But his sister, a voice worried in the back of her mind. The woman probably needs the gold to buy new gowns, Jo mentally argued.

"What are you scowling at?" he asked.

"What does your sister need the money for?" she demanded sarcastically. "A new gilded carriage pulled by matching thoroughbreds with plumes in their manes and bows in their tails?"

He didn't move, but the air around him seemed to harden.

"If she's truly in danger," Jo scoffed, "I'll discard my woolen pants and cutlass and dress like a lady."

"Perhaps, then, you'd care to change into a gown before giving the order to sail for France."

Jo frowned, regarding him.

"Don't try anything," Nathan admonished, stepping away and staggering.

Jo moved to help him, but stopped when he gave her a warning glare. She stood her ground and watched him return to the bed, her knife still clenched in his fist.

He sat and gathered a sheet across his lap. She sighed as her nerves slowly unwound. He might be covered, but she doubted she'd ever forget what he looked like: tall and strong, masculine and tempting, the way a man should be. Only now he was weak and sore with pain.

Taking the surgeon's box from the desk, she knelt in front of him. She reached for the bloodied bandage, but Nathan caught her wrist.

She met his stern gaze. "I'll not have you bleed all over my bed again."

"I'm fine."

She glanced at her ruined shirt, then studied his wan complexion and blood-streaked leg. "You look like you've fought a war—and lost."

Pushing his hand aside, she untied the wrappings and removed them, clenching her teeth when cloth stuck to skin. With a wet rag she cleaned the worst of the mess from his waist and lower leg, avoiding the parts in between, deciding Nathan could tend that area himself later. "Your stitches held, thank God."

"I told you I'm fine. Now order your ship to turn for France."

She spared him a glance. "As soon as we're through here. A few more minutes' delay won't matter." She soaked the rag in the bowl again, watching the water darken with swirls of red.

"Minutes could mean the difference between slavery and death, or life and freedom."

"Would you care to explain?" After applying more salve to aid the healing, Jo took a fresh strip of linen and wound it around Nathan's waist, taking care not to breathe when she came too close. Touching his heated skin was difficult enough; he felt like fiery satin, smooth, yet dangerous to touch. But there was something disturbing about his scent as well, something raw and powerful, a mixture that made her nerves feel wild and reckless.

"My sister . . ." Nathan looked over Jo's head, his eyes glazing as if he were seeing something besides the wire-rimmed shelves, jammed with books, maps and charts, along the side wall. It was the same look she'd seen on his face when he'd been in Daniel's study—

angry, determined, haunting. "Lauren is twelve years younger than I. I'm her guardian, and all she has."

And she's all you have? Jo wondered.

"She's not like you. She's softhearted." He glanced at Jo as if waiting for her to take offense. She merely quirked a brow and waited for him to continue. "She's gentle, too naive for her own good. She needs to be cared for, protected."

For a moment Jo could have sworn he was describing *her* sister, Grace.

"She's being held against her will." His body shook with suppressed rage beneath her hands.

"By who?" she asked.

"Philip de Maurier, a man I'm ashamed to say used to be Lauren's fiancé. If she is to survive, I must reach Saint-Nazaire within six days."

"With a chest containing fifty thousand pounds."

His gray eyes met hers. "Yes."

"What happens if you're late?" She tied off the clean linen and sat back on her heels.

"I won't be."

"But what if you are?" she pressed, crossing her arms beneath her breasts, a feeble attempt to keep his story from affecting her.

"The reason I ended their engagement is because I learned de Maurier was a slave trader. If I don't arrive on schedule he'll put her on a slave ship and send her to the colonies."

"Leaving England with one less aristocrat," she stated with derision. "How unfortunate."

Nathan caught her by the shirtfront and hauled her against him. "It's unfortunate, indeed. For Philip de Maurier for kidnapping Lauren, and for you for interfering with her rescue."

Her temper flared, rising in short, bright bursts. She was sorry she'd stabbed him, and she even sympathized with his need to find his sister, but she'd be damned before she'd tolerate his threats. "People are condemned to slave ships every day. More die in London streets from starvation! Where is your fear for them, your compassion, your resolve to rescue them? Men like you step over the poor the same way you step over trash in a ditch. What makes losing your sister so different?"

"You understand nothing. He has *my* sister." His face darkened and his eyes brightened with a blaze of emotion. Fear, Jo realized, flames of blinding fear. "It's my fault she's been taken!"

His expression changed; he seemed to close down, withdraw into himself. Had the admission of his blame surprised him, or had it made the guilt burrow that much deeper?

Jo drew in a steadying breath. Placing her hand over his wrist, she urged him to release her. His self-recrimination tugged at the guilt that was always nearby, threatening to swallow her whole. The depth of his resolve to free his sister was no less powerful than Jo's determination to see his kind pay for starting the war that took her brother's life.

They started the war, but I'm the one who let Robby die. She shoved the wounding thought away, but it had already struck a painful blow.

What would she do if Grace were in trouble? Would she cross an ocean, battle an enemy, threaten to kill? *That and more, without hesitation.* She had only to look at what she'd done for the children she'd promised to protect. She'd endangered her life and those of her crew. She'd broken laws. Risked attracting a king's wrath.

Nathan was willing to pay any price, make any sacrifice, to have his sister safe again. Did his actions make him so different from her?

Jo studied his taut features, the lines of stress bracketing his eyes, the hollowness in his cheeks. A five-day growth of beard shaded his jaw and chin, somehow making him more handsome than before.

Nathan was a man in pain, not from a stab wound

and stitches, she realized, but from a lesion to his heart and soul. *There's no worse enemy than a guilty conscience.* Since Robby's death, she'd lived with that enemy every day of her life; she knew the toll it took.

"When you reach Saint-Nazaire, what is your plan?" she asked.

He ran his hand through his black hair, causing the length to fall over his shoulder. It needs to be washed, she thought distantly, and trimmed.

"I'm to take the money to an abandoned monastery, where an exchange will be made."

"Do you trust this Philip de Maurier to honor his part of the demand?"

"I don't trust him at all."

"Yet you intend to walk into a deserted monastery, alone, with a cache of gold in the *hope* that he'll return your sister to you alive and healthy?"

"Sailing to Saint-Nazaire is the only thing you need to concern yourself with, Jo. My plans afterward don't affect you." His eyes hardened with distaste. "I promised to reward you for taking me there, and I shall."

"It's hard to claim a reward from a dead man."

"I don't intend to die, but I'm touched by your concern."

If only he knew how concerned she'd been over the last few days. She suppressed an angry scowl. He might not realize it, or want to admit it, but he was walking into a trap. And all because he loved his sister. She found such devotion in an aristocrat hard to believe.

Yet, for some reason, the thought of him dying with a knife in his back, after she'd repaired his side, didn't sit well with her. "You must have done something terrible to make this man kidnap your sister."

"Nothing he didn't deserve." Sweat beaded his brow, and his breathing seemed more labored than it had a moment ago. She saw a slight tremor in his arms, and knew he was on the verge of collapsing.

She rose and pressed her hand to his shoulder. "You need to rest."

"Not until we change course."

"Don't be stubborn, Nathan."

He gripped her wrist. "I'm the only hope she has. You must take me there."

"We'll discuss it after you've rested."

"Now!" He glared up at her, his eyes bright with fever. "Promise me."

She felt her resolve slipping. How could she keep her heart cold and uncaring when he seemed so desperate? Could she really let his sister suffer? Jo would have the gold she needed to help her wayward kids, but at what price? She stared deep into Nathan's gray eyes and clenched her jaw tight, realizing she wanted to ease the anger and desperation she saw there. Annoyed with him, and herself, she said, "I'll make the course change as soon as I leave here."

"Can I trust the word of a pirate?" he asked, his voice gruff, yet fading with his weakness.

She pushed his shoulder and he dropped back onto the tick mattress as if the strength had suddenly drained from his limbs.

"I may be a pirate, but I don't kidnap the innocent." She stopped herself, remembering four years ago when she and her sisters had taken Daniel against his will. If she looked at this from Nathan's point of view, she'd kidnapped him, as well. She wondered if there was some bizarre trait Jo and her sisters carried, causing them to take male captives. She shook her head at the thought.

Daniel had tried to seize Morgan for piracy, intending to watch her hang for a murder he'd thought she'd committed. This situation was completely different. Jo and Nathan had crossed paths, but they would soon go their separate ways. Without a doubt, their encounter wouldn't end the way Daniel and Morgan's had—in marriage. Which was fine with Jo, because she didn't intend ever to marry.

"I'll have you in Saint-Nazaire before your six days are up, Nathan," she said, though she doubted he could hear her. His eyes were closed, his breathing deep and constant. Shadows haunted the skin beneath his eyes. Belatedly, she thought she should have called for more broth. He needed to eat if he was to regain his strength and face the enemy awaiting him.

Lantern light glistened over his sweaty brow and the dark waves of hair that fell over it. She raised her hand to brush the strands away, but stopped herself. She'd touched him enough. It was better to keep her hands to herself, because the next time he awoke the battle between them would begin anew.

She had to keep her wits about her and prepare for the storm that was sure to come.

She would take him to Saint-Nazaire as she'd promised, but she wasn't giving up her gold.

Winter was in the air. The breeze whipped off the ocean's swells, stinging and biting into skin and bone. The sky rolled with temper and graying clouds, restless and moody, matching Nathan's state of mind. He welcomed the bracing cold, needed the numbing chill that sated the pain. There was a constant drumming beat beneath his skull and behind his eyes; the force of it had pulled him from a deep and dreamless sleep. He'd opened his eyes barely an hour ago to muted light, an empty cabin and a body racked with searing aches.

The *Sea Witch* rode the surf like a tireless whale, matching bow to sea, cutting a path swift and sure. Nathan clutched the balustrade to keep himself upright. The ship shuddered beneath his feet, vibrating up his legs, giving him a strange kind of strength. He felt the eyes of the crew on him. Vaguely he wondered what they were thinking, but he had no desire to make any effort to find out. They were sailing north by northwest, toward France. That was all that mattered to him now.

Yet their heading surprised him as well. Apparently he *could* trust the word of a pirate.

Jo was at the rear of the quarterdeck with a tall, muscular man with dusky blond hair. They were discussing a chart they'd spread over the binnacle box, their heads bent, completely absorbed in their conversation. Yet he knew Jo was aware of his presence on deck, just as he was aware of hers. Earlier, he'd felt her eyes on his back, sensed her thoughtful frown.

Something about the female pirate bothered him as much as it intrigued him. When he looked at her he saw a seductive woman with a coarse disposition—a strange and puzzling contradiction. She had hair as deep and rich as garnets. It should be upswept, pinned and curled so candlelight could catch its glow, not braided down her back with loose strands flying free, vulnerable to the attack of the wind. He recalled the feel of those thick, red waves sliding through his fingers, wrapping around his wrist.

She glanced up, spotting him, as if sensing his stare and hearing his thoughts. Even with the distance between them, he could tell her green eyes were almond-shaped, mesmerizing, and as secretive as a cat's on the prowl. There was nothing soft in her gaze, nothing meek or timid. It was challenging, bold and . . . *knowing,* as if she saw something in him he couldn't see for himself.

In a vague, distant way she reminded him of the woman he'd met the night of the ball—fiery eyes and cunning smiles and mysteries she refused to reveal. But there the similarities ended. Whoever the Emerald of London truly was, he couldn't imagine her wearing rough homespun pants, sturdy boots and a heavy wool coat like this pirate. *That* woman wouldn't have allowed anything but satin and lace against her creamy skin.

If only the Emerald were the one he was dealing

with now, he thought ruefully. He'd know how to control her, bait her with suggestive words and meaningful innuendos. Hell, he probably would have had her in his bed within an hour; she'd been brazen enough.

Jo the pirate was another matter altogether. If he were to risk bedding her, he wasn't so sure he'd escape with all his limbs intact.

Yet it was her mind he had to be wary of more than her temper or her sword arm. What was she planning now? How had she learned about his cache of gold? Those were things he had to focus on; not the color of her hair or the shape of her eyes. *Or the feel of her body.*

When he'd wrestled her onto her back in her cabin, he'd meant to terrorize her, gain her submission. But even half-crazed with pain, he'd registered the length of her body against his, the feel of her breast filling his palm. He closed his hand now, imagining he was touching her once again: soft, full, and entirely feminine. Another contradiction?

She straightened and started toward him, a half smile lifting her lips and bringing a light to her eyes. He watched her come, her gait sure, almost sensual, and found himself holding his breath, awaiting her arrival at his side.

The woman would dare anything, he realized: captain a pirate ship, lead a raid, stab a man—then kiss him when she thought him unaware. Their kiss. He'd meant it as a punishment, but whom had he punished? He could still imagine her spicy taste in his mouth, feel her heat, the willful fire that seemed to burn inside her. He shook himself and shifted the panels of his borrowed coat, letting crisp air rush in and cool his suddenly heated skin.

She stopped before him, planted her hands on her slender hips. Her gaze slid from his loose, blowing hair, then down to the soles of his boots. Her eyes met his with a flicker of amusement. "You almost look like one of the living."

"I almost feel like one."

"I see Jackson's clothes fit you well enough."

He arched a brow in question.

She nodded over her shoulder to the man she'd been discussing the charts with. "My first officer. The two of you are of the same build."

Nathan considered the younger man as he crossed the deck with a gait that said he'd been born to the sea. His attention seemed fixed on his captain. The black, woven wool pants, black linen shirt and coat did fit, and Nathan appreciated their warmth, but he didn't care for wearing another man's clothes. Especially one who watched Jo with a proprietary eye.

Her expression turned serious. "You should be resting. You're still not completely healed."

"I've been on my back long enough." He ran his fingers through his hair, a vain attempt to rub the pounding from his skull. "I feel like I've slept forever."

"Not forever. Only two days."

He nodded. And in three more he'd have Lauren back. "We're sailing north. I'm glad to know you've kept your word."

Her gaze flickered away. She faced the sea, her hands gripping the railing beside his, her fingers pressing the wood so hard the skin turned white. He felt a shift in her, a sudden tenseness that wasn't there a second ago. The fine hairs at the nape of his neck stirred in warning.

Gripping her arm, he forced her to face him. "We *are* sailing to France, aren't we?"

Her mouth pursed with annoyance. "Yes."

He heard a "but" behind her answer, and had the overwhelming urge to take her by the shoulders and shake her. But he couldn't risk alienating her or making her angry. Though he was loath to admit it, he needed her and her ship right now. But that didn't mean he would be weak and accepting. In a voice tight with control, he said, "You're lying."

"We're sailing to France." She tipped her head back to hold his gaze.

"And?"

She drew a deep breath as if stealing herself against a coming tide. "I've been thinking about your plan to meet Philip de Maurier."

Nathan released her arm, crossing his over his chest, feeling the dozen cuts and bruises he'd suffered. "Is that so?"

"You realize it's a trap."

"It's not your concern."

Her eyes narrowed and he felt a corresponding tingle scale down his spine. "I've made it my concern."

"We made a bargain, Jo. You take me to France and I'll pay you once we return to England."

She smiled, a shrewd, calculated pull of her comely lips. "Well, now, that's the problem I have with your plan. I already have your gold. I see no reason to return it to you, *hope* you survive your meeting and then take you to England, where likely as not, my reward will be your turning me over to the authorities."

"Unlike some people, my word is my honor."

"I'm sure it is." She brushed at a strand of hair the wind had whipped into her face. "But it's de Maurier's word that has me concerned at present. I've known people like him. Giving him the ransom won't win Lauren back."

"What are you suggesting?"

"I'll take you to Saint-Nazaire," she said with a confidence he didn't like. "I'll even help you rescue your sister."

"But?" he asked, every nerve in his body tightening as if she held an ax over his head, poised to fall.

"But you can't have the gold."

Nine

The deck rumbled beneath her feet like a monster stirring awake and none too pleased. For an instant Jo thought Nathan's rage, billowing out from his pores and limbs, and the heated furor in his eyes, had caused the vibration. Then she realized the sails had been adjusted for a change in heading.

Regardlesss, she took a cautious step back.

She hadn't expected him to welcome her decision to keep the gold. She'd known he'd be furious. But once he calmed down, he'd realize her plan made far more sense. At least she'd hoped he would. Nathan would live to see his sister; Jo would keep the money and share it with the poor. And Philip de Maurier, a slave trader who'd abducted a helpless woman, would get nothing.

Nathan took a threatening step forward. A muscle twitched in his cheek. "You aren't keeping the gold."

Jo forced herself to stand her ground. She'd faced sea captains and notorious pirates during her time on the *Sea Queen,* tough men who would have run her through with a cutlass if given the chance, but she'd never faced an adversary like Nathan. He possessed a quiet, feral energy, his presence intimidating while frustratingly compelling. Long ago she'd erected impenetrable walls to keep people at a distance—she'd had to, so no one would know how weak she really was—yet

he ignored those walls. But this was her ship, her crew
. . . and her gold! She'd be damned before she'd yield.

"You can consider it my fee for helping you," she
said.

"Helping me!" Before she realized his intent, he
gripped her throat, his fingers tightening, lifting her so
only the toes of her boots touched the deck.

She couldn't breathe, and felt her face turn hot from
lack of air.

"You little witch. I should kill you now!"

She clawed at his hand, but lacked the strength to
loosen his hold. Instinctively she reached for her knife
and ripped it from its sheath. Nathan caught her wrist
and jerked it aside, holding her arm over the railing.

"Drop it!" he ordered. "Into the sea. You tried to
kill me once with this knife; you'll not do it again."

"No!" She couldn't let go of the Sea Queen blade;
she'd lose everything if she did.

Nathan stiffened, his grip on her throat dropping
away. Jo doubled over, dragged in a breath, coughed,
and coughed again until she could breathe on her own.

"Do you want him overboard, Jo?" Jackson asked,
his tone remarkably calm.

She glanced up and saw her first officer stood behind
Nathan with a blade at the base of his neck. "Release
him," she said, her throat burning.

"Not without tying him up first," Jackson insisted.

"No." Jo straightened, meeting the hatred blazing
from Nathan's eyes. "I'm sure Lord Darvill won't try
to kill me again."

"Order your dog to release me and find out," he
said in a growl.

"You won't try anything." She resheathed her dagger,
then nodded to Jackson, who released Nathan with a
warning shove. "Harm me and you lose any chance of
seeing your sister again."

His face tightened, darkening with anger. He was
trapped and all but helpless; she knew it had to slash

his male pride to ribbons. It couldn't be helped, she thought. He had to be made to see reason.

"Listen to my plan, Nathan; then decide if mine makes better sense than facing de Maurier alone and unarmed."

"I'm not going against his instructions." His words were little more than a determined growl.

"Damn it, Nathan." Frustrated with his stubbornness, she paced in a tight circle. "It's a trap."

"It's a risk I have to take. De Maurier was explicit that I follow his instructions. Diverting from them means certain death for Lauren." He glared at Jackson and the rest of the crewmen who'd gathered to listen to them argue. A few men stepped out of his line of sight, as if not wanting his attention focused on them. Jo couldn't blame them.

"Besides," he said, "I won't be unarmed or unprepared."

"That's not good enough."

"I'm going to pay the ransom, Jo. Once Lauren is home and safe, I'll return to exact my revenge on Philip."

"And how will you pay the ransom? For that matter, how will you reach France if I decide not to take you?"

"You'd let my sister die?" Something cold and metallic hardened his stare. He hated her, she realized, feeling a jolt in her chest. She was bringing him to his knees, and he'd never forget—or forgive—her for it.

"It's you who'll be letting her die," she said.

"I want Lauren back." His eyes flashed like the tip of a blade poised in warning.

Jo wanted his sister safe as well, which surprised her. She didn't even know Lauren, and by all rights should hate the girl for her station alone. Rich and spoiled—what could possibly be worse or more useless? Jo decided she must be losing her mind—and her edge—to become entangled in Nathan's affairs. But call her a fool, she couldn't ignore the desperation in his eyes, the obvious love he bore his sister. She had to help.

A doubt forced its way into her mind: were her motives solely to save his sister? Or did erasing the hatred in Nathan's eyes have some part in it? It shouldn't bother her, but she didn't like the idea of his loathing her for all time.

She didn't know which reason was the true one, and it didn't matter. He was going to listen to her plan and agree, even if it killed him.

Nathan swayed out of rhythm with the ship's roil. Sweat beaded his brow, dripping down his temples despite the chilly gusts of wind. He was on the verge of collapse, she realized, but he refused to show any sign of weakness. She silently cursed him for pushing himself so hard, then admitted she shouldn't have expected anything less. She'd backed him into a corner. If he conceded while standing before her men, his pride would be injured beyond repair, giving him another reason to loathe her.

She nodded to Freddie, a boy of twelve who assisted the cook. "Bring food for Lord Darvill to my cabin." She swept her hand toward the hatchway, indicating that Nathan should join her. "We can finish this in private."

He walked past her, his back rigid despite the pain she knew he had to be suffering, his face harsh and cold. No one else seemed to notice his weakness; only she did, and only because she felt in tune with him. She could almost hear his thoughts, the rage beating through his veins, the oaths he wanted to shout at her. And the pain. She could feel the agony that tore at his heart and body alike.

She followed him, resisting the urge to lend him an arm. She shook her head at her own foolishness. He wouldn't welcome her help any more than he'd welcomed her aboard the *Lady's Luck*.

Once they were inside her cabin, away from prying eyes, Nathan's shoulders lost their stiffness. He gripped the top rail of a chair and wiped his brow with the back of his hand.

"Take a seat, Nathan."

He dropped into the scarred mahogany chair, closing his eyes and tilting his head back.

Sweat glistened on his face, dampening his hair, turning it to a length of wet sable. His face, while freshly shaven, was pale and drawn, the fine lines around his eyes bleached white. Jo frowned, hating to see him this way. She much preferred his hard cheeks tight with anger, his eyes inflamed with rage.

"Take off your coat." She retrieved the surgeon's box from a shelf.

"Tell me of your plan," he said, his voice flat and empty. He didn't move.

"Let me see to your wound first." She took hold of his shirt to pull it from his pants.

He caught her wrist, his fingers squeezing flesh to bone. "Don't touch me."

She swallowed. She'd never heard such contempt in a man's voice—in anyone's voice—before. Regret in a form she'd never known moved up her chest in a hot tide.

Raising her own wall of defense, she asked in a cutting tone, "I suppose you'd prefer to collapse at de Maurier's feet when you meet him."

"I'm to meet him, then?" he asked, the words twisting with sarcasm. "I'd thought you'd changed my plans."

She tugged free of his hold. Matching him glare for glare, she pulled his shirt loose. This time he didn't object, so she knelt before him and worked the buttons free. "I've made your plan better, is all."

"That remains to be seen."

"If it weren't for your sister I'd leave you at the nearest port." She pushed the fabric aside, prepared to see the bandage soaked with blood. She sighed in relief to find it clean and white against the hard, tanned ridges of his stomach. She leaned close to untie the bandage, her fingers brushing against his skin, fumbling. He was cool and firm, smooth except where the crisp black hair touched her fingers. Her chest clamped tight, making a full breath nearly impossible.

"Am I to thank you, then?"

She slanted him a look and offered up a mocking grin. "You should. I'm helping you out of the kindness of my heart."

"You, my dear Jo," he said, his voice as gruff as the look in his eyes, "are a thief and a cutthroat. You have no heart."

Her pretense of a smile faded as she forced her attention to the bandage. She had a heart. She knew she did because it hurt every time she thought about her brother and Sammy, every time she patrolled the streets of London in search of new faces that were too young and too thin and too filled with desperation. She had a heart, all right, and she was wasting it by worrying about a self-serving, arrogant knave like Nathan Alcott who thought about no one but himself and his spoiled, worthless sister.

She slapped the wrapping against his chest and pushed to her feet. "Tend your own wound, Nathan. I've had enough of your taunts."

He caught both her wrists and jerked her down between his spread legs. "You put it there; it's your responsibility to see that it heals."

"Go to hell," she spat through gritted teeth.

"I did the day I met you."

She pushed against his bare chest, but she couldn't work herself free. The skin that had been cool only moments ago now burned with a fierceness that matched his eyes.

"Release me," she ordered.

A scowl lifted the corner of his mouth. "So you can reach for the knife you're so fond of? I think not."

Jo struggled, but even in his weakened state, he was

too strong. Damn it, she wanted to scream in frustration. He wrestled her arms behind her back and locked both her wrists in one of his hands. He pressed her tightly against his chest, their faces mere inches apart. His breath rushed hot and moist over her cheeks and jaw, into her mouth.

"You cannot beat me, Jo."

"I have a ship and a crew behind me. You have nothing but what I give you."

"Is that so?" A flare brightened his eyes, a challenge she recognized, but not soon enough to try to avoid it.

His mouth crushed over hers, hard and biting, ravaging with a savage need. He forced her mouth open, drove his tongue inside. His free hand burrowed into her hair, holding her to him, tilting her so she had to take him deeper. He tasted of musk and male strength, of rage and madness.

I've done this to him. The thought came unbidden and unwanted. *I didn't start the wars; I didn't create the victims,* she tried to argue. *People get hurt; Nathan is now one of them.* But it did no good. She felt his pain, the fear clenching his muscles, the desperation in his kiss, as rough as it was.

She had to stop him—and herself—before they took the kiss too far. There was too much anger, too many emotions singeing the air around them. She forced her body to relax. She softened her mouth and kissed him back, trying to tell him with actions what he refused to hear. She intended to help him, wanted to help him. She had to.

"Nathan," she whispered as she gulped a breath.

He released her and reached for the hilt of her knife at her waist. Jo sucked in a breath, tensing, but he tossed it across the room, where it landed with a clatter and skidded out of sight.

"No more tricks, damn you," he said, his words and breath hot against her face.

He loosened his hold on her wrist. She pressed her palm to his face, cupping the unyielding line of his jaw.

"No tricks." Her fingers slid into the damp hair at his temples. Her nerves tightened in her belly, twisting like a rope, tighter and tighter and tighter, working its way into her core. What was this man doing to her? Why did he affect her in ways she could barely understand?

Nathan caught her backside and hauled her flush against him. She gasped and closed her eyes, dropping her forehead against his chin.

He wanted her. And something inside her strained for him in return. If only it were that simple. If only she could kiss him, guide him to the bed and let him show her the things she'd only imagined. . . . If only . . . but she couldn't. His blood might be on fire, but he wanted to take her body, drain her soul and claim his revenge. Nothing more. And that was a war she didn't know how to fight.

She heard a faint knock, then the turn of a latch. She pulled back, surprised Nathan let her, just as the door swung open and Freddie entered the room carrying a tray laden with food. She stayed where she was, afraid to move, certain her legs wouldn't support her if she tried to stand.

"On the desk will be fine, Freddie," she said, her voice hoarse and unrecognizable. She was thankful the boy failed to notice.

On his way out, he stopped to say, "Mr. Jackson says 'e needs ye topside."

Jo nodded and motioned for him to shut the door behind him. Once they were alone, she glanced at Nathan. He studied her, his expression closed, remote. Had their kiss not affected him at all? Eased his anger? She saw no sign in his eyes, no loosening of his jaw, no softening of his lips. Perhaps it hadn't overwhelmed him as it had her, she thought, wanting to feel angry when all she felt was regret and humiliation.

She could be just as cold and distant, she decided, tilting her chin. She'd practiced keeping her emotions at bay longer than she'd practiced with a sword, far longer than she'd practiced with manners or curtsies or country dances.

She pushed to her feet and stepped back, keeping her gaze locked on his, though it took every bit of will she possessed to hold his solemn stare. "You will meet de Maurier as planned," she said, deciding it safer to ignore the kiss and focus on what lay ahead. "But you won't be alone."

"I suppose you'll be with me."

"As well as a handful of my men. We're going to protect your back—"

"While you protect your gold." His tone had a wooden quality she was beginning to hate.

"This kidnapper of yours won't have a chance to get close to the gold."

"And why is that?"

She allowed a confident smile that felt gritty and strained. "Because I intend to stop him."

Ten

Night wrapped the *Sea Witch* in a cold, dark blanket, an impenetrable void that raised the fine hairs on the nape of Nathan's neck. Throughout the day, gray, turbulent clouds had chased the ship, threatening rain but never delivering. At dusk, a barrier of fog had pressed down from the sky like a gigantic wall being lowered to block their way. Stars, the moon, all traces of light had vanished, leaving only the eerie sound of a moaning ship, the whispering voices of wood and nail that drifted through the air and mind.

The vessel had pushed deeper and deeper into the black space, steadily cresting unseen waves. Wind whistled across the shadowy deck, slipping around towering masts full of sail, the wheel, the unfortunate few still stationed aloft to carry on their watch.

Nathan repeatedly had to quell the urge to order the pirates to drop anchor and wait for the suppressing dark to lift. They risked running aground or ramming another ship. The demand to slow down worked its way up his throat, but he bit it back. Pushing on like a blind man was madness, but he couldn't risk a delay, not when they were so close to reaching France. Besides, the crew didn't seem to be disturbed by the nerve-racking hellhole that had befallen them. Perhaps this unholy vacuum was commonplace, though Nathan didn't think so.

He'd traveled by sea often during his thirty years—to Europe, to the colonies, the Caribbean—but never had he experienced a night such as this. The air was so cold it seemed to pour frigid water into his limbs, the world so dark and silent he wondered if he and the crew were the only ones left alive.

He paced the deck like a moth searching for the warmth of a flame, moving from one dim lantern to the next, studying the men who seemed little more than boys as they huddled inside their coats and gloves. He received a few nods of acknowledgment as he passed them, but he didn't stop to talk, though he knew he should. Some would accompany him to the monastery; he ought to know their temperaments, their abilities. God help them if they acted foolishly and jeopardized Lauren's life. Yet he continued to walk, his hands buried deep in the pockets of his borrowed coat, his face lifted to the slap of wind—just as he'd done since his last argument with Jo.

The thought of her made his jaw clench. Sweet Jesus, the woman exasperated him every time he laid eyes on her. Who the hell was she? Where had she come from? Why had she turned to pirating? And why the blazes couldn't he keep his hands to himself when she was near? Especially when his every thought should be centered on Lauren?

He raked his fingers through his damp hair to dispel some of his tension, but it didn't help. Jo was reckless, stubborn and as beautiful as she was willful. What would make her risk her life on the whims of the sea, raiding ships, challenging men to duels? She should be at home—somewhere, anywhere—with a husband to keep her in hand. He imagined her with half a dozen children, all with red hair and green eyes, clinging to her skirts, making demands. *That* would keep her out of trouble, he thought, releasing a sigh that frosted the cold air.

She would no longer be Jo the pirate. He didn't see her as a lady, either. Just a woman.

Just a woman, a voice in his mind repeated. Nathan stopped at the bow of the ship and closed his eyes, wishing the wind would sweep the musky, heated scent of her from his skin, erase the feel of her lips from his. She was as wild and untamed as the ocean she called home, and as unpredictable. Why the hell had he kissed her? Because she'd refused to return the ransom money to him? For her trickery? She deserved far worse punishment than a kiss.

Yet he could still feel the raging emotions that had ripped through him as vividly as he could feel the curve of her lips, the heat of her mouth, the tremor in her hands as she'd tried to push free.

He'd never felt anything so powerful, so overwhelming. He'd been blinded by the need to punish and take and control. That he'd done, and had sensed some small victory—until she'd kissed him back with an urgency of her own.

Despite the bite in the wind, as well as the worry for his sister's safety and his impending meeting with Philip, Nathan felt himself stir in response, harden against his pants, just as he had when he'd held her trapped in his arms. He must be out of his mind to want a woman such as her. She'd brought him nothing but trouble, and he suspected there was more to come. With a perverse twitch of his lips, he decided that whoever had given the *Sea Witch* her name hadn't been thinking about the ship, but her captain.

He shook his head. Some base part of him might want her, but he'd never forgive her for forcing him to agree to her plan to accompany him to the monastery. If things went awry, if Lauren's safety was further jeopardized . . .

He clenched his hands inside his pockets as his anger returned, as the heat beneath his skin gathered and built. He wanted to grab onto the emotion, twist it into a burning force. He drew a deep breath, fought the anger down and forced his mind to clear. He was used to dealing with problems logically, methodically. Emotions would get him nowhere, especially now. It was best he put them away and play the cards he'd been dealt, lousy though they were.

Besides, as furious as he was with Jo, he knew he should be grateful, as well. Any other pirate would have left him aboard the *Lady's Luck*, where he might have met his death, ensuring Lauren's fate. Yet Jo had brought him aboard her ship, caring for him as if he were a fallen mate. It was her guilty conscience that had motivated her to save him; that he knew without question. Which left him with another puzzle to ferret out: what kind of pirate was motivated by guilt? What were the odds of such a pirate living a long, if nefarious, life?

It was the "long" part that troubled him. If she continued down her chosen path, she wouldn't survive another year. Merchant vessels weren't as easily targeted as they'd once been, and the Royal Navy still patrolled the seas, protecting what belonged to the Crown. Which meant pirates rarely received mercy. He felt an uneasy shift inside his chest, but ignored it and focused instead on Jo's weakness: her guilty conscience. He frowned into the dark. She was gruff and brazen, yet somewhere inside her hid a tender nature. He imagined she'd go to her grave before admitting she possessed such a trait. Was it a weakness he could use against her?

Something pulled at Nathan's sleeve, startling him. He glanced down to see the shadowed face of a young boy, the same one who'd brought food to Jo's cabin earlier.

"Cap'n wants ye below."

Nathan was tempted to send a message back telling the captain she could go to hell. But that would be his anger speaking and not his common sense. Jo had forced him onto a proverbial gangplank. Though it infuriated him to admit it, she held the power to either send him plunging into the sea or to pull him back to the safety of the deck.

He had no choice but to cooperate with her. After he had Lauren safe at home, he vowed, clamping his jaw tight, he'd find a way to deal with Jo.

He followed the boy belowdecks, shivering like a dog shaking off rain as he stepped out of the wind. He expected to be led to her quarters, but the boy took him down a narrow companionway to the bow of the ship, where light glowed like a beacon through a low portal. Nathan ducked through the archway and came to a stop. The long, narrow room had dozens of hammocks hanging from hooks in the ceiling: the crew's quarters. Most beds were full, though no one seemed to be sleeping. They were facing the far corner, where Jo and her guard dog, Jackson, were holding court.

Nathan moved between the rows of floating beds, straining to hear what was being discussed.

"Macklin Renshaw," she addressed a lean young man with a pointed black beard and thin mustache, his eyes as dark and shrewd as a raven's. "You, Eric and Kevin will come with me. Dillon"—she nodded to another boy nearing manhood, built as thick and solid as an oak mast—"you, Bishop, Theo and Nyle will follow Jackson's lead."

There were nods of agreement, and those chosen exchanged cocky grins. Nathan wanted to protest. They were little more than boys. *Boys who succeeded in bringing the* Lady's Luck *to her knees.*

"I want all of you armed with bows, with plenty of arrows. And knives." Nathan glanced at the dagger Jo wore as if it were a part of her body. Did she ever go without it? he wondered, touching his injured side.

"What about pistols?" one of the boys, Macklin, asked.

Jo hesitated. "I don't think they'll be necessary for what I have in mind."

"Which is what?" Nathan's voice boomed in the quiet room. Fifty startled gazes turned toward him.

Jo crossed her arms beneath her breasts, drawing her shirt tight over full mounds. Nathan cursed himself for noticing. He also noticed the shadows beneath her eyes, the drawn tightness along her cheeks.

In a commanding tone lacking any semblance of femininity, she asked, "What do you know about the monastery where you're to meet de Maurier?"

Had she really returned his kiss? he wondered. The woman before him now resembled the pirate who'd tried to kill him, not the one who'd slept at his bedside while he lay feverish. This wasn't the woman who'd tended his wounds with callused hands and a tender touch, but a pirate planning a raid.

He shrugged. "The monastery is abandoned and on the outskirts of Saint-Nazaire. That's all I know."

"We can assume it's in a ruined state," she stated sharply.

"Does that matter?"

She smiled, a surprising lift of her full mouth. The small act fired her cheeks with color and lit her eyes with a cunning green light. The softhearted woman vanished, as did the harsh, rigid captain. Standing before him was a woman eager for adventure. But why? Was it because she wanted to keep the gold? She already had it, and nothing he could do would change that. So why was she risking herself, her crew, the very gold she craved, to save Lauren? Did she really mean to right the wrong she'd caused? Or did she have something else in mind? That was what he had to know.

"The setting can mean the difference between success and failure, Lord Darvill," she explained.

It occurred to Nathan that she called him by his title whenever they were with others, yet used his given name when they were alone. Was that another clue— another weakness—in her character? Was the fearless pirate captain only a ruse for her men's benefit? Sweet Jesus, he wished he knew.

"There will be ten of us going ashore," she continued.

"Only ten? I would think you'd take the entire crew. You could render the building to rubble, as you did the *Lady's Luck.*"

She regarded him with a slanted gaze; the pulse in her jaw beat in rhythm with the seconds ticking by. "Our intention isn't to bring down the building. Just one man will do. You'll wait for de Maurier in the nave while we circle the structure."

"What if he brings other men?" He clenched his hands. Everything in him rejected taking orders from a woman. "I won't have you starting a battle while he still has my sister."

Her self-assured grin returned. "Don't worry, Lord Darvill. De Maurier won't even know we're there."

But I'll know you're there, he thought. *And I don't trust you any more than I trust the slave trader.*

"We'll infiltrate the monastery while you make the exchange. Once your sister is safe in your hands, we'll capture de Maurier and reclaim the gold."

"I don't want him killed," Nathan said.

She shrugged. "If that's the way you want it."

"If this scheme of yours works, and it had better work," he added with a scowl, "I want him brought back to London."

"Consider it done. Now tell me the exact terms of your meeting with de Maurier."

"I'm to meet him at midnight on the fourteenth day from when the letter was postmarked." He no longer had possession of the note—it was either burned or lost on the *Lady's Luck* deck with his coat and Lauren's lock of hair, but he knew the message by heart.

She nodded to her men, her jaw tightening as if to hide her fatigue. "The wind's been with us. If our sheets stay full, we'll reach Saint-Nazaire sometime tomorrow, giving us two days' leeway of Lord Darvill's schedule. Now get some rest."

Moving past the men, she brushed by Nathan without a word. He turned, following her into the companionway. Catching her arm, he pulled her to a stop. "I have some questions for you."

"Later," she said, tugging her arm.

"Now." He tightened his fingers around her flesh and pulled her closer.

"I'm busy, Nathan."

"Why are you doing this?" he demanded, though he kept his voice low, not wanting to attract her crew's attention.

"What are you talking about?"

"Offering to help rescue Lauren. I find it hard to believe that you simply want to do a good deed."

"You know nothing about me," she said, her voice shaking, making him think there was more to her answer.

"Then tell me, damn it."

She opened her mouth as if to answer, then snapped it shut. Straightening, she glanced into the hallway beyond his shoulder.

"Is there a problem, Captain?"

Nathan muttered a curse. Hardening his features, he turned and glared at Jackson, who stood at his back. "She's fine."

"Take your hand off her."

Nathan had her, and by God, he wasn't letting her go until he got some answers. "Stay out of this."

"I said release her." Even in the gloomy hallway, Nathan sensed that Jackson was poised to fight. The air changed, growing warm, humming with tension. They were of the same build, but Jackson was younger, plus he wasn't wounded. Nathan didn't care.

He released Jo. If her first officer wanted a fight, he'd be only too happy to oblige. He was through being forced down a path not of his choosing. He faced his opponent. It might not win him Lauren's freedom, but hitting something solid with his fists would make him feel a hell of a lot better.

Before he could lift his hands or utter another word, Jo was between them, one palm planted on each of their chests.

"Normally I don't have anything against a good brawl," she said, "but this isn't the time."

She released her first officer. "Jackson, you're on watch. I'll take the next."

The other man hesitated, and Nathan expected him to argue, but he merely said, "Call if you need me." Then he was gone.

"How do you do it?" Nathan heard himself ask.

She rounded on him, her hands planted on her hips. "How do I keep from gagging you and locking you in the hold? I'm not quite sure. My willpower amazes even me."

He ignored her quip. "How do you convince your men to follow you on such a reckless mission?"

"There are two things you need to understand about my crew, Nathan." Her voice was teeming with anger as she jabbed her finger into his chest. "One, they don't question my decisions, and two, they believe in my cause."

"And what *is* your cause?"

"Nothing that concerns you, though it should." She jerked her hand back.

"Obviously it has something to do with my gold. I don't care for the thought of it being squandered in some port, used for drinking and whoring. Or in your case, I should say just drinking."

"You don't know anything about me, so don't—"

"Which is the problem. Why don't you tell me?"

She took a step back. "You know all you need to."

He pinned her against the wall, grabbing her wrists and holding them out beside her, well away from her knife. "Why are you helping me?"

"I've already told you. I don't want to be responsible for your sister's death."

"I find that hard to believe. You're a pirate, and anyone claiming to be a *real* pirate would take the gold, dump me overboard and sail away. Unless you have another plan? Such as holding Lauren for ransom instead."

In the faint light, he saw Jo's eyes widen before they narrowed in a silent threat. "Believe what you will, Nathan; it makes no matter to me."

"I would ask for your word, but this time I think it would be worthless."

She ripped her hands free and shoved against his chest. He staggered back a step and clamped his jaw tight as pain from his wound erupted beneath his skin.

He leaned against the wall, feeling sweat bead his brow and drip down his temple. "If you are speaking the truth, Jo, and really want to help save Lauren, then stay out of this. Your coming to the monastery, defying Philip's instructions, is too great a risk. I meant it when I said I'd pay you for bringing me to France."

"I don't doubt you did, but I prefer my way. The odds are better."

"Then let Jackson and his men accompany me while you stay on board the *Sea Witch.*"

"Why?"

"I've fought you twice and both times I've bested you." Philip wouldn't hand Lauren over without some sort of test or battle, be it mental or physical. He didn't want Jo caught in the middle if things turned dangerous. The woman wasn't as tough as she liked to pretend. He shouldn't care if she were hurt—she'd stabbed him without a thought—but the idea of her being harmed disturbed him, and it was a distraction he didn't need.

"So therefore I'm inept?" She quirked a brow.

"You could get hurt." It was closer to the truth, but he didn't dare provoke her further.

"Your concern is touching, Nathan, but I can take care of myself. I've been doing it for a long time now."

"Then understand this. Once we reach Saint-Nazaire, the only thing that will matter to me is Lauren. I won't be responsible for you."

"I'd never assumed you would be," she whispered, her voice sounding detached and . . . lonely.

The notion caught him off guard. Was this another glimpse of the woman behind the pirate's mask? She stared at him, not speaking, as if she, too, was aware of what she'd revealed. She had more nerve and more courage than any person he'd ever known. She commanded a band of wayward men, led attacks, and bore the responsibility of everyone's welfare, yet something told him her strength was a disguise, a mask she wore to keep the world at bay.

His instinct also told him that she was the one in need of protection.

A stream of rare English sunshine beamed through the open window, bathing Robby's face, flushing his cheeks, lighting his eyes like bits of polished stone. He laughed his contagious laugh, a small, chirping sound that shook his small body and stole his breath.

"He looks funny, Joanna." Robby held up the toy soldier in his short, stubby fingers so she could see better.

"You insult me, Robby," Jo said, pretending to frown. "If he's to protect our country, he must look severe."

"But his nose is on the side of his face and his mouth is crooked."

Jo pressed her lips together to keep her own laughter from bubbling out. She'd made a mess of the tiny soldier's face, but it had been her first attempt at painting. She held out her hand and sighed. "Give him over, then, and I'll try to fix him."

Robby clutched the toy to his narrow chest, which rumbled with each breath he drew. "No, he's my favorite."

"*You can't have a soldier with a lopsided mouth and nose. How will he ever scare the enemy?*"

"*He reminds me of you.*"

"*So you think I'm funny-looking, too? I'll have you know my nose is right where it's supposed to be.*" *She tickled him, trying to wrestle the toy from his grip.* "*Give him to me, Robby. I must fix him.*"

"*No!*" *he squealed, giggling so hard his face turned pink.*

Jo caught the toy and took it from his hand. "*Aha! I've got it.*"

Robby's laughter abruptly stopped. His wiggling body vanished from her arms, leaving them weightless and empty. Jo frowned, confused. "*Robby?*"

She glanced around their simple cottage, the wooden rocker by the hearth, the battered table and well-worn benches, the shelves crowded with metal pots, plates and tin cups. Her little brother was nowhere in sight. He had to be here somewhere, she thought, trying a smile that wouldn't come. "*Robby?*"

The rough walls blurred, faded, then dissolved like snow drizzled by warm rain.

"*Robby?*" *Her voice echoed, sounding strange and hollow.* "*Where are you?*"

There was no answer, no laughter nor childlike voice. She stared at the toy in her hand with its misplaced nose and crooked smile. "*Robby? Come back. Robby! I'll leave it the way you like. Only come back!*"

Nothing. No sound, no light, nothing. She was alone. Panic rushed hot beneath her skin, and tears built in a river behind her eyes.

"*Robby. Come back. Robby! Robby!*"

A touch on her shoulder jolted Jo awake. She lurched upright and dragged in a deep breath, then another. She had to find her brother. She had—

She stopped and squeezed her eyes closed. *A dream,*

it was just a dream. Robby wasn't here. He was gone, dead, buried behind the church in Dunmore for the past twelve years. But she could smell him, the childish, clean scent of his skin, like butter and jam. She could still hear his voice, laughing and young. Forever young.

She pulled the rope necklace from her shirt and gripped the toy soldier in her fist, focusing on breathing. She pressed her other hand to her face, felt the cold sweat layering her skin. The tears of her dream became real, pushing against the backs of her eyes in a burning tide. She clenched her jaw. She couldn't let them fall. Not once since his death had she cried, and she couldn't do so now. That would be giving up her pain, letting it out when she was determined to hold it in.

"Jo."

Nathan's coaxing voice broke through her grief. She sucked in a breath. She couldn't look up, didn't want him to see her like this. He had no right to see her like this.

"You were dreaming." He stood beside the bunk, all but cloaked in shadows. She didn't need to see his eyes to know he was watching her intently, his brows pulled into a frown.

She glanced around the narrow room, remembering that she'd borrowed Jackson's cabin to catch a few hours' sleep, not wanting to return to her chamber and face Nathan. Straightening her back, she ran her hand through her tangled hair, trying to dispel the remnants of her past and gain some composure. "It was nothing."

"Who's Robby?"

The question bruised her as if he'd struck her with his fist. She almost snapped that it wasn't any of his concern, but she looked at him and the words lodged in her throat. Dim light filtered through the window slit in Jackson's cabin, softening Nathan's dark eyes, turning them moody and thoughtful.

Why was he here? She tried to think of something to get rid of him, but couldn't manage to form a coherent thought. Her emotions where he was concerned were too unstable, too confusing. Having him see her like this, trembling and unsure, didn't help. She pushed to her feet, but the tight confines of the room made it impossible to move past him.

"How far are we from Saint-Nazaire?" she asked, furious that she couldn't control the quaver in her voice.

"We've arrived." She could feel his curious frown, hear the questions he wanted to ask, but didn't.

She was grateful for that. Maybe they could both pretend she hadn't been having a nightmare, hadn't called out for the brother she'd sent to the grave.

Then his words sank in. "We've *reached* Saint-Nazaire?"

"About an hour ago."

She pressed a hand to her head to stop the dull throbbing that always followed whenever she dreamed of her brother. "Why didn't someone wake me?"

"You're asking the wrong person, but I think your first officer decided you needed to sleep."

"Damn Jackson," she muttered, trying to push past Nathan.

He placed his hands on her hips as if he had every right to. "This once, I agreed with him."

There was something in his voice, a subtle compassion that kept her from whipping out a retort. "Let me pass, Nathan. I must see to my ship."

"There's something I want to ask you first."

"What is it?" she asked, her skin tightening with anxiety. It was his gentle tone that rattled her nerves, she decided. It wasn't something she would have expected from him. She much preferred the battle of wits and swords to the deviousness of shadowed rooms and caring words.

"What's your name?"

"What nonsense is this? You already know it."

"Your full name."

She stared at him, unable to speak because of the unsettling warmth flooding her mind and tingling down her limbs. Perhaps it was the dream, the vivid memories of her brother that had her so panicky, feeling so out of sorts. It wasn't Nathan's deep, rumbling voice or his masculine scent of wood and smoke or the heat of his hands firm on her hips. "Let me pass."

"Your name."

"You are infuriating, do you know that? I should have left you aboard the *Lady's Luck.*"

He stepped closer, bringing his heat and musky smell so close they filled her lungs. "Tell me."

"Jo . . . Joanna," she admitted, only so he'd let her go.

"And your surname?"

"Fi—" She stopped herself. She couldn't tell him her surname was Fisk. He might connect her to Morgan; then her secret would be out. Everyone—the king included—would know she'd returned to pirating. The consequences would be severe and fatal. But she had to tell him something or he'd never let her leave the cabin. "Finn."

"Joanna Finn."

"Yes, now get out of my way."

He released her, but lifted the wooden soldier tied with a leather cord. The toy looked ridiculously small and fragile in his large palm. She started to rip the trinket from him, not wanting to hear his jests about her choice of accessories, but his expression turned contemplative rather than critical.

"What is this?"

She could imagine the thoughts buzzing through his head. Why would a woman wear a child's toy around her neck? *I wear it as a reminder that I caused Robby's death.* But she couldn't tell him that, so she settled for a partial truth. "It belonged to my brother."

"A keepsake," he whispered as if he understood. He

looked at the small ring he wore on the little finger of his right hand.

She nodded.

"Have I seen him? Is he a member of your crew?"

"He's dead." The flatness of her voice surprised her. Evidently it surprised Nathan, too, because his gaze narrowed on her. "Was he your only sibling?"

Don't tell him anything more. He doesn't care about you or Robby. He's setting a trap. Yet she heard herself say, "I have two sisters."

"Tell me about them."

Clenching her jaw, she snatched the soldier back and stuffed it down her shirt, welcoming the comfort of hard wood against her skin. "You've done enough prying for one day."

She tried to push past him, but he kept her from leaving by holding his hand at her waist. Heat unfurled from the touch, spiraling out like fingers of wicked lightning. "It's a simple question. What are their names?"

"What does it matter?" She slapped his hand away, but it was too late; she could still feel the shape of his fingers imbedded in her skin, feel the strange, coiling tension tighten in her stomach, winding her into knots.

"I'm curious about you."

"It's your sister you should be thinking about, not me."

"I just want to . . . Hell . . ." He swiped a hand through his hair and sighed, the sound raw with exasperation. Moonlight illuminated his jaw in cool gray light, revealing the muscles tightening and flexing over and over, like a heartbeat fueled by frustration instead of blood. "I don't know what I want where you're concerned, Jo."

You want to kiss me again. The thought flashed through her mind out of nowhere. She almost slapped her hand over her mouth, afraid the words might slip out. What was wrong with her? She couldn't think about his hands or the sound of his voice or his blasted kiss. She had to focus on rescuing his sister; then she'd abandon them both in Saint-Nazaire.

Something inside her chest clenched in protest. She shoved her hesitancy aside. Nathan had means; he could find his own way home. She'd be rid of him and the chaotic feelings he stirred inside her. Then she'd be free to focus on the children who still needed her. They were what mattered most; not Nathan or Lauren or the shipload of guilt Jo carried on her back.

She pushed him away and this time he allowed her to pass. But she paused in the doorway. Without turning to look at him, she said, "This time tomorrow you'll have your sister back, and my debt to you will be repaid."

"As will mine, *if* Lauren is returned unharmed."

Nodding, she felt her lungs, her heart, her very breath quiver. "The time we've had to suffer in each other's company is almost at an end."

"Is that what you believe?"

She tensed at the quiet warning, feeling the anger behind his words. The air in the room shifted, growing warm, as if a wall of hot, pulsing air were pushing against her back. She glanced over her shoulder. His eyes were molded shavings of dark metal, harsh and unreadable. A shiver ripped up her spine. She turned and hurried away, leaving him alone.

They would be finished with each other, she vowed. They would be. Soon.

Eleven

The night was full of moon, a hammered disk of silver hanging in the bright black sky. Beams of polished gray light speared through wisps of drifting clouds. Icy wind caught their vaporous tails, twisting them into threads of slippery mist.

It was an ill omen if Jo had ever seen one. A coal black night would have served them better. Now they would have to use extra care not to be seen as they approached the monastery.

Dressed in pitch-colored pants and shirt, she knelt behind a stone wall that at one time would have reached her waist, but storms, wind and countless years had broken its strength, chiseling holes through some parts, while completely destroying others. Her men fanned out on either side of her, Jackson to her right, all gripping their weapons, all quiet and wary, waiting for her signal to move.

She considered the towering mass of sooty stone walls on the knoll before her, rising into the night like a ragged beast. There was no roof, only the remains of crumbling turrets, empty wall walks and black windows looking out with watchful eyes. If this had once been a place of holy worship, any divine protection the monks had offered had long since fled.

A foreboding wind snaked through the dark, sending a shiver down Jo's back. She craned her neck to better see the entrance, but skeletal trees with thorny white limbs and dying brush blocked her view. Nathan had to be inside the abandoned nave by now, with the cache of gold at his side, waiting for Philip de Maurier to appear, hopefully with Lauren in tow. If he didn't have her . . . Jo didn't want to think about what they would be forced to do then. But one thing was for certain: if de Maurier tried to double-cross Nathan, he wouldn't get away with it.

Jo forced herself to release a breath to steady her nerves. She'd always loved the adventure, the unknown possibilities a raid brought, but this was a far different raid from any in her past. Someone's life depended on her success. She just wanted this over with so she could return to London, to Mira Fenner and the children, where she might do some good.

"The moon's listing, Cap'n," Macklin whispered.

"So it is. Everyone knows their positions. Take care not to be seen. We don't want de Maurier to know we're here."

She looked at each of the young men who followed her, their faces deceptively pale and cold in the ghostly light. Lifting her crossbow from her back, she murmured, "With sword we meet."

Her crew added their hushed voices to her own. "Our revenge is sweet."

Dead leaves swept through the barren nave, swirling in corners and along lichen-covered walls. The sound was haunting, disturbing, like the rattle of old bones—a fitting sound for a monastery built of eroding stone and chipped mortar and long-forgotten prayers.

From the shadowed entryway, Nathan scanned the deserted arcade, the blackened pillars that stood like mammoth spears imbedded deep into the ground. Misshapen rocks, beams from the rotted roof and scraps of rusted steel littered the floor. Weeds that would brush a horse's belly grew where hard wooden pews might have sat in orderly rows. Surrounding it all were walls that were tall, imposing, yet intangible, as if they were made of black smoke and would blow away with the wind.

For a brief instant he thought about the people who had come here to pray on bent knee, their hearts full of hope or in need of guidance. If he tried praying now, would he be heard? Would Lauren be returned to him unharmed? He didn't dare relax his guard and bow his head in prayer to find out.

Everywhere he looked, shadows moved over towering walls and cluttered floors, across tumbled partitions and obscure halls. There were a thousand places to hide. Philip could be anywhere, before him at the dais, or above him, on the second-floor balcony. Or behind him, lurking in the darkness like the criminal he was.

Wind blew cold beneath his jacket, chilling the sweat coating his neck, chest and back. He'd waited two weeks to confront Philip with his treachery, and now the moment was at hand. He clenched his fists to keep from touching the pistol he had tucked into his waistband. He was grateful to have the weapon, though it still surprised him that Jackson had been the one to give it to him.

No man should face his enemy unarmed, the first officer had said. Nathan had stared at the pirate, cautious, wary, wondering if this was some kind of trick. He could have easily shot Jackson, but the man had regarded him with a cocky grin that said he knew Nathan wouldn't.

He'd tucked the weapon away, annoyed that Jackson was right. It irked him to admit it, but he welcomed having the pirates to guard his back. Like the temptation to pray, he set thoughts about Jackson aside.

Where the hell was Philip? And more important, where was Lauren? The hour of midnight had passed, and still Nathan waited, his nerves twisting tighter with every second he stood alone, listening to nothing but the hoot of a distant owl and the moan of lifeless wind. He glanced around him, then above at the balcony. Parts of the flooring were missing altogether. The rotted boards that remained were too decayed to support the weight of a dozen rats. He saw no sign of Jo or her men. Perhaps they'd fled, leaving him on his own? He discarded the thought. He had the gold safely by his side. Jo wouldn't leave without her reward. No, she was slinking through the dark, waiting just as he was for Philip and Lauren to appear.

He lifted the chest, clamping his jaw tight as his side stretched in protest and his body strained with an infuriating weakness. He didn't worry about the wound opening; Jo had tended him well and he was healing quickly. He'd have a scar to remember her by, though he doubted he'd ever forget her.

Moving to the center of the building, out into the open where Philip would be sure to see him, he scanned the gallery, wondering where his pirate was hiding.

His pirate. The phrase meant nothing, he assured himself.

Yet a part of him hoped she stayed out of sight. Aye, she was skilled with a sword, but she wasn't as accomplished as she believed. The woman was a fool for wielding a sword in the first place, he thought, scowling. She had no business living the dangerous life of a pirate. Jo—Joanna—was too spirited, too beautiful to risk her life by thieving, no matter what her reason.

He'd bet his chest of gold, however, that her motivation for raiding ships involved her brother, Robby. He shook his head. Jo's behavior was a puzzle that would have to wait until later to be solved. As was the mystery of her name. Finn. He no more believed that to be her surname than he believed Philip would apologize for kidnapping Lauren. Jo had hesitated when she'd answered, and when she'd finally volunteered a name her voice had lacked conviction. Obviously she was trying to hide something, but what?

A noise beyond the dais caught his attention: the crunch of leaves beneath boots. He set the chest at his feet and peered into the darkness, holding his breath, flexing his hand, preparing to draw the pistol if need be. *Wait,* he cautioned himself. *Wait.*

Shadows stirred at the base of the far wall, growing darker, separating, taking shape. The skin prickled at the nape of his neck. *Come out of hiding, you bastard,* he wanted to shout. But he didn't. He remained still, his hands coated with sweat, his breath icing in his lungs.

"I knew I could count on you to be on time," a familiar voice taunted.

Nathan willed his jaw to unclench. "Did you think I wouldn't come?"

"And risk losing your precious sister?" Philip laughed, a brittle sound that sliced through the night like grated glass.

"I've brought the gold. Return Lauren to me and it's yours."

"That sounds suspiciously like a command, but I must be mistaken." Philip stepped into a beam of ashen light. "We both know you're in no position to command—or *demand*—anything."

"I've followed the terms of your letter." Nathan's heart beat a frantic rhythm as he searched for Lauren in the shadows where Philip had emerged. He didn't see any sign of her, and had to fight down a surge of adrenaline. He was so close. In a few more minutes this might all be over, but only if he handled Philip with the care he would use handling a poisonous snake. "I want to see my sister."

"Oh, I'm sure you do." Philip took another slow step, then another, creeping forward, closer to Nathan. He stopped when he was twenty feet away, his arms straight at his sides, his legs planted slightly apart. A slice of moonshine dulled his tailored suit to funereal gray, hollowed his eyes and drained his cheeks to a pasty mask. His pencil mustache became a black slash across his upper lip.

The mark of the devil, Nathan thought.

"Where's my sister?" he demanded, tempted to rush Philip, catch him by the throat and squeeze until he ceased to breathe. Every nerve and muscle burned for revenge, demanding he move, act, put the slave trader out of his misery for good.

But he stood still, forcing his breathing to calm. He couldn't lose control. That was what Philip wanted. He'd known the blackguard would draw their meeting out, make him squirm before relinquishing his sister. *This is a game, one I have to play if I want Lauren back.*

"Making demands again, Darvill?"

"We can make an even trade," Nathan offered. "Bring Lauren into the open. I'll take her away and leave the gold behind." He backed up a step to show his willingness to concede.

"I think not. You'll leave now."

"Not without my sister."

"Watch your tone, Darvill. I'm feeling generous at the moment, but that can change. As it happens, Lauren isn't here."

"What do you mean?" he asked in a controlled tone, yet the words hammered through his mind.

"Just what I said. She's not here." There was a scattering of pebbles on the balcony. Tiny rocks fell, landing on the floor behind Philip. He didn't look up or even flinch. Either he hadn't heard the noise, Nathan decided, or he wasn't bothered by the disturbance because he knew what had caused it.

Or was it Jo moving around up there? He prayed she didn't show herself. Not yet, not when he had no idea what Philip had done with his sister.

"If you've already put her on a slave ship then my

gold won't do you any good," Nathan warned. "Because you'll be dead before you can come close enough to touch it."

"First you issue commands; now you're making threats." Philip grinned, though something malicious flashed in his eyes. "Your sister is somewhere close, being well cared for, I assure you. But she's also so well hidden you'll never find her."

De Maurier's grin twisted into a thin, ugly line. "I've had a change of heart since I sent you my letter. I've decided you haven't suffered enough, the way I have since you ruined me."

"You caused your own downfall by lying about your business dealings."

"If I'd told you up front that I sold slaves, would you have given your sister to me with your blessing?" Philip scowled. "I think not."

"Slave trading? Kidnapping a woman you'd professed to love? Where does it end with you?"

"Oh, I did care about Lauren. But I cared about her fortune more." Philip chuckled. "Which brings us to your last question. Where does it end? Not here and now, I'm afraid. As I said, I've had a change of heart. Leave the chest where it is, turn around and leave, Darvill. You'll find a room waiting for you at the Grand Falaise Inn in Saint-Nazaire."

"I'm not going anywhere without Lauren."

"You'll do exactly what I tell you to do," Philip ordered. "I've decided fifty thousand pounds doesn't begin to make amends for the damage you've done me. I want another hundred thousand pounds delivered within the month. If you deliver it without fail, I'll send Lauren to you. That is, once I tire of her."

"You son of a—"

"The gold is *mine*, Darvill." Philip raised his arm, revealing a pistol as black as his soul. With a steady hand, he pulled the hammer back until a cold, metal click vibrated the air. "Or your sister's life will be damned."

Jo froze. Rocks burrowed into her knees where she knelt on the decaying gallery floor. Wind blew in through the roofless ceiling, grazing her neck, whispering chants in a shivery breath. She knew the placement of her men, all crouched in the shadows, well armed and waiting, just like her. She'd chosen the cover of a crumbled pile of railing. Here, on the balcony, she had a view of the nave, the entrance, the stone stairs to her left and the second-floor hallway leading to rooms that no longer existed.

Her senses were alert, fine-tuned; she could hear her heartbeat, frantic and wild against her temple, taste the metallic flavor of fear in her mouth, feel the outrage pulse through her mind.

Nathan.

She wanted to scream his name, but knew she couldn't move, couldn't breathe for fear of what might happen. She pushed to her feet, heard the termite-infested planks give with strain, and brought her crossbow to her shoulder. In a move that felt cold and detached, she took aim down the quarrel's shaft, leveling the steel tip at Philip de Maurier's heart. She kept her finger poised over the trigger, not firing, yet she could almost hear the arrow take flight, hissing through the air, finding its target with a quiet blow.

After stabbing Nathan, she'd sworn never to take another person's life. She'd thought nothing would possibly drive her to such a rash act again. But watching de Maurier hold a cocked pistol on Nathan, seeing the malicious twist of his mouth, hearing the vindictiveness of his words, she set her vow aside. The slave trader wasn't going to hurt Nathan. Not while she still had breath in her body.

She touched the crossbow's trigger, balanced to fire

with a slight caress. It would take no effort on her part to pull it back, release the weapon, stop Philip's threat here and now, yet she felt her arm and shoulders tense. Sweat dripped down her brow, into her eyes, stinging them.

As tempted as she was to fire, she couldn't; Lauren hadn't been rescued yet. Nathan would never forgive her if she acted too quickly, sealing his sister's fate.

She lowered her aim, targeting Philip's leg instead. Perhaps if he were wounded, writhing in pain, he might be inclined to reveal the girl's whereabouts.

"Killing me won't end this," Nathan warned, his voice floating up the sullen walls.

"Won't it?" Philip taunted. "As I instructed, you came alone. It will be weeks before anyone thinks to look for you; then it will be too late. I'll be gone from here. You'll be dead, and Lauren . . . Well, what can I say about your beautiful sister? If you don't cooperate and send for the rest of my money, I'll sell her as a slave in the colonies. She'll fetch quite a handsome price. She would undoubtedly bring more if she were a virgin, but since she isn't—"

Nathan released a furious growl and lunged forward.

Philip leveled his arm. "Another step and I'll fire."

Nathan stopped, his hands clenching again and again at his sides, his face a mask of rage.

"This is my payback, Darvill. You ruined me, cost me my ships and my fortune. Turned all of London against me. I lost everything because of you."

"It was no more than you deserved."

"That's funny. That's precisely how I feel about shooting you."

Nathan glanced up. His eyes widened with surprise, then flashed with rage. Jo followed his line of sight and saw a man she didn't recognize standing on the balcony across from her, holding a musket trained on Nathan. She didn't think. She acted. She brought the crossbow around, aimed without thought and pulled the trigger. The bow recoiled, and the wooden butt kicked back and jarred her shoulder. The quarrel split the air, then found its victim.

The man screamed as his body flew back, landing with a sickening thud of bone and rotted wood. The flooring creaked, then split, giving way in a tumbling roar of falling planks, stone and dust. She saw the musket fly out of his hands; then it became lost in the rubble.

Philip ducked to miss the falling debris. He bellowed a curse. Nathan reached for his pistol, but it was too late. Philip fired. Jo saw a flash of powder, a plume of smoke.

She lurched to her feet. "Nathan!"

He staggered back and fell, his arms spread to his sides, his gaze locked on the moon-bright sky. "Nathan!"

She heard her men scrambling from the dark, saw Philip turn and spot her crew. He looked at the chest of gold, his expression greedy and furious, but the ransom was too far for him to reach.

"I don't know who you are, but you've made a mistake by joining Darvill," Philip shouted, edging away. "Nathan, I hope you're still alive, because I want you to spend every day knowing you'll *never* see your sister again."

Jo pulled another arrow from her pack, then slipped it into the notch. *Calm. Smooth. Easy. Don't rush.* Philip dropped his useless gun and pulled out a knife as he turned and ran for a shattered hole in the wall.

"You're not going to get away," she said between clenched teeth. The quarrel clicked into place. She took aim—on nothing. Philip was gone.

She lowered the crossbow and stared at the spot where he'd been only a second ago. *No. No!*

Jo spun for the stairs, shouting to whoever could hear, "Macklin, Eric, someone, go after him!"

Her men could catch de Maurier. She had to reach Nathan. Her heart beat against her chest, threatening to burst. She should have shot de Maurier first. Why hadn't she fired? *Why, damn it, why?*

Reaching the ground floor, she ran blindly through a shadowed maze littered with debris. She tripped, banging her shoulder against something hard and cold. The crossbow dropped from her numb fingers. She pushed on without it, but drew her dagger in case there were more of Philip's men about. Stumbling into the nave, she paused only long enough to see Jackson kneeling by Nathan's side.

She ran through the weeds and collapsed beside him, her breath coming harsh and fast. "Is he dead?"

"Not yet," Nathan answered, the words sharp with fury. He struggled to sit up and winced. "Bloody hell."

Her hands trembling, Jo resheathed her knife as Jackson helped Nathan sit upright. Sweat glistened on his face, intensifying the dark anger in his eyes.

"I thought he'd shot you," she said, feeling her eyes burn and her throat close. A crazy, wild panic raced through her veins. He wasn't dead, but alive. *Alive.* She repeated the word over and over, but it was slow to sink in. "You fell—"

"He grazed my arm."

Jo reached for the spot he'd indicated, but Nathan pushed her hands away. "I have to stop him."

"We will," Jackson vowed.

Macklin came hobbling up to them, supporting Theo by the waist. "Sorry, Cap'n," Mac said. " 'E got away."

"Theo, are you hurt?" What had her delay cost? She should have shot de Maurier. She should have!

"Just a knot on me head, Cap'n." The young man pressed his palm to the side of his scalp. His coat was disheveled and ripped at the sleeve. " 'E surprised me, shooting out of the dark, an' all. Clubbed me with the butt of his knife. Then he jumped on his horse."

Nathan struggled to stand. Jo clenched her hands at her sides to keep from helping him. He wouldn't welcome her aid, not after she'd ruined his chance of finding Lauren.

"My God." Nathan paced in a circle, ran his hand through his hair. "What will he do to her now?"

"He wouldn't dare harm her," she told him, though the words felt like a lie even as she said them. De Maurier was wicked and cunning. The possibility that Lauren was already on a slave ship—or dead—was all too real. "Are there any more of de Maurier's men about?"

"None that we've caught sight of, Cap'n," Eric said.

"We might have lost that accursed slave trader." Dillon smiled and pointed over his shoulder with his thumb. "But we got ourselves something else."

"Explain," Nathan demanded.

"De Maurier's man still lives."

Jo met Nathan's murderous gaze, and saw a muscle pulse in his jaw. *He blames me for Philip's escape.* An ache far too real to be her imagination twisted inside her. She tried to dismiss it, to harden herself to what the tightness in her chest might mean. She reminded herself that she'd brought him to France as she'd promised. Philip's escape wasn't entirely her fault. Staying longer to find his sister didn't have to concern her.

But it did. For some reason she couldn't explain, it did!

Because she cared for Nathan. *No.* She pushed the possibility away. She couldn't care about him. She wouldn't let herself!

Walk away, she told herself. *Take the gold and give it to the children you've sworn to help. They need you more than Nathan does. Walk away.* Something inside her, something buried so deep she didn't recognize it as a part of herself, resisted, whispering that she couldn't turn her back on Nathan. Not now.

Maybe not ever

Twelve

The wound was deep, but whether it proved to be fatal depended on the assassin's answers. Cold, savage anger hardened Nathan's arms, his spine, the very breath that tore through his lungs. Jo's men had lifted fallen beams and boards from the man's body. He lay on his back, the moon's glow full on his sweat-slick face. His hands spasmed against his stomach, reaching for the arrow, only to fall away. He muttered a prayer in English, half recognizable, then gritted his teeth on a string of curses.

Nathan knelt beside him, studying the quarrel where it impaled the man's chest, missing both heart and lung while destroying flesh and bone. If that were his only injury, he might survive, but there was no telling what damage the fall had done that couldn't be seen.

Broken limbs and injured organs didn't matter, Nathan decided. The blood pumping in shiny black rivulets would take the man's life unless something was done, and quickly, though a dark, unrecognizable part of Nathan wanted the man to suffer for the role he had played in Philip's conspiracy. Jo dropped to her knees opposite Nathan. He glanced at her, but she remained quiet, her hands fisted on her thighs, evidently waiting for him to lead the questioning.

"Where's my sister?" he demanded.

"Please 'elp me," he begged in a thick Cockney accent.

"Tell me why I should. You tried to kill me."

"I was . . . I was only follow'n orders. I weren't gonna shoot. On me life . . ." He spotted Jo and gulped a breath. Reaching out, he groped the air with a bloody hand. "Please . . . lady, the pain . . ."

She glanced at Nathan. He couldn't read the emotion stirring behind her green eyes, but her jaw was taut, her shoulders stiff.

"You'd better hurry," she said, her tone controlled, detached.

Because the man might die, Nathan wondered, taking any information with him? Or because she wanted to save the man's life the way she'd saved his? If that was the case, it made her the most peculiar pirate he'd ever heard of—one who inflicted wounds only so she could heal them.

"You'll answer my question." Nathan made himself ignore the man's suffering. His injuries were no more than he deserved. "I'll leave you here where you're certain to die, and not necessarily from your wounds. Wolves roam this part of the country," he said, not knowing if that were true. "They've undoubtedly caught the scent of your blood by now."

Sobbing, the man gripped Nathan's arm, leaving a streak of black blood on his white sleeve. "I'll tell ye, just please, please, don't leave me 'ere."

"Where is de Maurier hiding my sister?"

"I don't know. 'E never told me—"

"Let's go." Nathan started to rise, but the man's grip tightened, his dirty nails cutting through fabric and digging into Nathan's skin.

"I swear, I don't know where he's keep'n the girl."

"But you know something else." Jo's brow dipped in a frown.

"Aye, aye, that I do." Their captive gritted his teeth and groaned. "De Maurier . . ." He sucked in a breath, then another, frosting the air with his moan. " 'E's staying near here, with a bloke named Marquess Fulepet. Could be she's there."

"Fulepet?" Nathan sat back on his heels and scowled into the gloomy night. If Fulepet and de Maurier had joined forces . . . A chill sped down Nathan's spine as the dire implications sank in.

"Do you know him?" Jo asked.

Nathan nodded. "Unfortunately, and well enough to know that the marquess's character is only slightly better than de Maurier's."

"At least we have a place to start." Jo pushed to her feet and stared down at their captive. "What's your name?"

"Rubin." He coughed, then shivered as if he'd taken a chill. "Rubin Sweeney."

"Macklin, Dillon, Eric. Take Mr. Sweeney to the *Sea Witch.*" She turned and started walking away, but added over her shoulder, "Jack, make sure he doesn't die."

Jackson stared after her, his eyes wide as if he were in awe. Then he murmured, "It seems our bloodthirsty Jo has turned over a new leaf. If only Morgan could see this."

The comment hadn't been meant for anyone else's ears, but Nathan heard and frowned, not understanding what the pirate meant. Briefly, he wondered who Morgan was, and why he would be interested in a change in Jo. Was he a lover? A husband? Remembering the way she'd kissed him, Nathan discounted the possibility that she was married. He narrowed his gaze on her back, then swiped a hand through his hair, agitated that he'd allowed thoughts of Jo to intrude.

"Why would you be wanting Sweeney to live?" the first officer called after her.

As Nathan pushed to his feet, Jackson smiled and winked at him as if they shared a private joke, as if Lauren's life weren't in even more danger than before.

Nathan's insides twisted with impatience. He had to

reach town, hire a horse, maybe question the local villagers before riding to Fulepet's estate.

"Sweeney's not an aristocrat," Jo answered absently, her hands propped on her hips as she studied the leaf-scattered ground.

"No, he isn't," Jackson stated. "But Lord Darvill is, yet you saved him."

"Jackson," Jo snapped, not bothering to turn around. "For the love of Mary, just see to the man!"

Nathan turned away, furious that the pirate could take the situation so lightly.

"Captain!" Jackson called out again.

"Jack, I'm going to shoot *you* next if you don't stop pestering me."

Nathan thought he might give her his gun so she could carry out her threat.

"Where are you going to be while I'm playing nursemaid?" Jackson asked, though half his attention was on his men rigging a litter for Sweeney.

"With Lord Darvill, paying a visit to Marquess Fulepet." She turned and arched a brow, daring anyone to object.

"No, you're not." Nathan glared at her. Her expression turned even more determined in the shadowy dark.

"Yes, I am." She headed for a dismal corner within the monastery and disappeared behind a crumbling wall.

He followed her, not stopping even when darkness swallowed him into its blinding void. He used the wall to his right to guide him, scraping his hand against the teeth of jagged stone. "Damn it, Jo, where are you?"

Muffled footsteps and the rustle of grass and leaves came directly ahead of him. He quickened his pace, his eyes wide yet seeing nothing but distorted shapes of black on black. Icy wind stirred the scents of moldy earth and withering stones as it whistled through a hundred cracks within the walls.

Never had he met a more infuriating woman. He'd

spent his adult life running his estate, leading his people, finding solutions to their problems. Yet in one fell swoop, a blasted redheaded, green-eyed woman had taken all of that from him.

That was going to change. He'd listened to her plan, allowed her to bring her men to his rendezvous with de Maurier, but what good had it done him? He'd been shot, Philip had escaped and Lauren was still in danger.

"Bloody hell," he swore under his breath, deciding to wring Jo's neck—as soon as he found her!

He barreled into a body soft and curved and smelling of soap and wind, a combination that was uniquely Jo. He heard her gasp as she started to fall. Nathan caught her around her waist and steadied them both.

"What are you doing?" she demanded, pushing one hand against his chest.

"I might ask the same of you." He couldn't see her, but he felt the tremor that passed through her hips and into his palms. "Where do you think you're going?"

"I dropped my crossbow when I was trying to reach you. Fool that I am," she added sourly.

"You must have the senses of a bat," was all he could say. Had she been concerned for him? Now that he thought about it, she'd seemed shaken, her voice thready when she'd reached him, but he'd attributed it to anger—not worry—and certainly not worry for him. God, what was he thinking? Jo's state of mind didn't matter. He had to leave, *now,* find Philip, and confront Fulepet.

"Excellent night vision is a must for any pirate. It's just one of my many talents."

"You aren't going with me to Fulepet's," he said, returning to the reason he'd followed her.

"Don't be stubborn, Nathan," she said as if speaking to a disgruntled child. "You need me."

"Like hell I do. You've been nothing but a thorn—or should I say a knife—in my side since the moment I laid eyes on you. I've had enough of your interference."

"De Maurier set you up. He never intended to release Lauren."

"It was a chance I had to take."

"It was a chance that almost got you killed," she ground out, her voice tight with impatience.

The sting where the bullet had grazed his arm flared at the reminder. "Now that I know what I'm up against, it will be different when I find Philip."

"Will it? How?" she demanded. "You said yourself that Fulepet is of questionable character. What if he's involved with Philip's scheme?"

"Which is why you're not going. It's too dangerous."

He turned and made his way out of the dark, aware of Jo following close behind. In the nave, her men were fashioning a pallet of fallen limbs with which to carry their prisoner. He continued past them. He'd suffered Jo's interference because he'd had no choice. But he'd reached Saint-Nazaire. He didn't need her any longer, and he'd be damned if he'd let her hinder him, or further jeopardize his chance of rescuing Lauren.

"Nathan," Jo called from behind him.

He ignored her and passed through the eroded walls and cracked stone that had once been the monastery's entrance.

"Nathan!" she repeated, her temper making his name as vile as a curse.

"You brought me to Saint-Nazaire, Jo; your debt for stabbing me is paid." Knowing he'd wasted too much time already, he abruptly stopped and faced her, watching her come to a sliding halt on the graveled path. Philip would undoubtedly be furious for having been thwarted. If he turned that anger on Lauren . . .

"I have no more need of your . . . assistance," he said with a clenched jaw.

Gripping the crossbow in one hand, she tossed her braid onto her back and tilted her chin. "If my men and I hadn't *assisted* you tonight, events would have turned out quite differently. To begin with, you'd be dead. Philip would have your money. Your sister, *if* she's still alive, would be doomed to become a slave."

"Which could still happen if I don't stop wasting time with you and find her."

"You can't do it alone."

"Your helping me ends tonight." He would do anything to save Lauren, but Jo's interference would only complicate matters. He couldn't control her, and if Philip changed the rules again, he couldn't be certain that Jo wouldn't do something that would risk herself *and* his sister.

Having Jo and her men hiding in the monastery had been a double-edged sword. She had prevented Philip from murdering him in cold blood, but now his sister's future, her very life, hung over a precipice.

Jo drew a deep breath, her gaze breaking from his to scan the dark hills that stirred with shadows and ghosts from a forgotten time. "I told you I'd help get your sister back."

"This isn't your concern."

"It is!" she shouted, then froze and stared at the ground. "I had him. I could have stopped him."

A chill grazed Nathan's neck. "What did you say?"

"I had a clear shot at Philip." She threw the crossbow at his feet. "With one squeeze of the trigger, I could have ended his sorry life, or at least wounded him, kept him from escaping."

"Why didn't you?"

Her gaze flickered to him, then moved away. "I kept thinking about Lauren. Where was she? Was she alive or hurt? When she didn't appear, I decided to wait and see what would happen."

"You made the right decision, Jo." Nathan sighed, feeling his anger mollify into something he could control. "Who knows, killing Philip might have put Lauren in greater danger."

She remained quiet, and for a moment Nathan thought she was going to relent. Perhaps it was her troubled conscience that made her so stubborn, but he knew parting now would be best for them both. He already had a plan in mind that would gain him access to Fulepet's estate, and his plan didn't include Jo.

Her gaze came back to his, and what he saw made his heart lurch in warning. The green of her eyes was dark, nearly black in the night, and her face was filled with an emotion too raw to define.

"I have hated aristocrats for most of my life," she said, the words so sharp they almost quivered.

"I don't have time for this, Jo."

She ignored him and touched her shirt. Instinctively he knew she was seeking reassurance from the toy soldier she wore. "Every day I vowed to make your kind pay for the things you'd stolen from me."

He didn't know why she was telling him this, and why now. Every instinct told him to turn and leave her behind. He didn't want to hear about her demons. Yet despite the urgency icing his skin, his boots remained rooted to the ground.

"What did we steal?" he heard himself ask.

A sad smile lifted one corner of her mouth. "My parents, my brother." She shook her head as if banishing a painful vision. "The point, Nathan, is that I believed every accursed nobleman in England to be vain and greedy and filled with selfish disdain. People of your class let others suffer—without a care. . . ."

She paused to square her shoulders. "Yet you are willing to risk your life to save your sister."

"Would you not do the same to save yours?" he asked.

"Without question."

"Then you understand I have to do what I think is right."

"I'm going to Fulepet's estate with you." She held

up a hand when he started to object. "I'm not going to let you go alone."

"Jo," Nathan said, struggling to be patient when he really wanted to shake some sense into her stubborn head. "I don't pretend to understand what happened to you or your family, but I can understand your grievances against the rich. But what does that have to do with you helping me find Lauren?"

"You're different."

The statement, so simplistic, so direct, and so misguided took him back. Damn her, he thought. How could two simple words manage to unsettle him so quickly and so deeply? *Because she believes them to be true?* Or was it because he knew them for the lie they were? He was no different from the noblemen she hated; he realized that now.

He'd sat in judgment of Philip. Perhaps he'd gone too far by ruining de Maurier, but when he'd discovered Philip's secret dealings in slavery, he'd been furious and had made his opinions known. *If I had just called off the engagement, perhaps Philip wouldn't have become desperate, and wouldn't have been driven to kidnap Lauren to gain his revenge.*

Leaving Philip free to dupe another innocent young heiress, Nathan thought with a scowl. He couldn't excuse Philip for the atrocities he'd committed, but as difficult as it was to admit, Nathan knew he was partly to blame for this nightmare.

"I'm not so different from the rest of my peers," he said.

"I disagree." She gave a negligent shrug of her shoulders. "Though I could be wrong. But in the event I am right, I think you might be worth helping."

He stared at her, not knowing what to say.

"Don't let it go to your head, Nathan." She narrowed her eyes in annoyance. "I'm still ready to be done with you."

"Then be done now." He said the words, but they

lacked conviction. He knew it would be insane to allow Jo to accompany him, but the idea of having her by his side lent a strange kind of comfort. Still, he couldn't allow it. But how to convince her? Knowing her stubborn mind, she'd go to Fulepet's on her own if he didn't find a valid reason for her to stay behind.

"You need me to guard your back."

"Jo." Taking her cold hand into his warmer one, he ran his fingers over her palm, felt her calluses, and realized he preferred her strong, firm skin to the plump softness of other women he'd known. God help him, she was so unique, so strong.

If only times were different and he weren't a marquess, and she weren't a pirate. . . . He stopped his line of thought, knowing it wouldn't do either of them any good.

"I'm grateful you want to help me, but I'll be playing a dangerous game. Every move I make from this moment forward could mean the difference between life and death."

"And what do you know of dangerous games?" she taunted.

"I know that if I have a pirate tagging along, the marquess will become suspicious. What will he think if I show up with a woman who wears rough-spun pants and shirt, and carries a dagger? What information would he tell me?"

What if he learns who you are, what you are, and reports you to the authorities? She'd be arrested, deported to England, tried and hanged. A shiver that had nothing to do with the cold ran down his back. He'd once vowed to see her arrested for piracy, but that had been before he'd come to know her. She might be a thief, but the thought of her meeting such a grisly end sickened him.

She glanced down at her pants, her scuffed boots, then regarded him with a tolerant look. "I can change my clothes."

"Clothes alone do not make a lady," he scoffed.

"Of course not." In a tone that was decidedly more derisive than self-conscious, she added, "After all, what is a lady without her manners and petty wiles, her simpering and thirst for gossip?"

The image of the temptress he'd met the night of Daniel's ball appeared in his mind unbidden. Lush red hair, the color of fire and gold, piled in a thick silk rope on her head, rose-tinted lips made for teasing and smiling and deep, soul-aching kisses. And almond-shaped eyes, their emerald depths glittering with mischief and temptation. If his mystery lady were here, he imagined she would entice Marquess Fulepet into confessing all he knew with a few velvety words and suggestive glances.

Whereas Jo would likely use the steel tip of her dagger.

"If I can pass for a lady," Jo said, lifting her chin in a challenging tilt, "will you agree to let me come with you?"

Knowing the sea would turn to freshwater before Jo could pass for a lady, Nathan decided he had nothing to lose by relenting. "If you pass, and by that I mean in every aspect of a lady, then I'll concede and you can join me."

But she wouldn't be able to impersonate a refined lady. Jo might affect him as no other woman ever had—including the masked lady from the ball—but Jo was a pirate, a crass, opinionated thief.

There was no chance she could be anything else.

Thirteen

"Have you lost your mind?" Jackson demanded, plowing the fingers of one hand through his wheat-colored hair, stirring it so it stood up on end. His eyes took on a crazed, murderous gleam.

"Possibly." Jo wrapped the corset around her body, adjusting it so the white ruffle of her silk shift showed above the stiff edge. "If I had time to think about what I'm doing, I'd probably call myself a fool."

"I have no business being in here. Not with you looking like . . . like this!" His glare veered away from her and focused on the plain chest he'd retrieved from the hold. Inside were items she kept for an emergency such as this. Petticoats, stockings and an effusion of satin gowns spilled over the edge and onto the floor.

"Someone has to help me dress." The stiff whale-bone stay dug into her hips. Jo scowled at the contraption. It wasn't even laced and already it was making her miserable. "Don't just stand there. Give me a hand."

"I tended to Rubin Sweeney like you wanted, but asking me to tie you into that gadget is going too far. Even for you."

"How is he faring?" She'd regretted leaving Jackson with the burden of caring for their prisoner. But she'd had a dozen things to see to before she left with

Nathan. Only now did she notice the dark circles beneath Jackson's eyes, the grim lines about his mouth.

"Sweeney survived the night, and might see another." He stared out the window, his face bathed in the soft orange glow of evening light. She followed his gaze just as the sun shimmered and dipped, touching the border of France, spreading a quivering wave into the cold blue sky.

"He's lucky he didn't break any bones," Jackson commented, drawing her attention back to him. "If he fights the fever, he might live. What do you plan to do with him?"

"It's up to Nathan. I, for one, don't want to involve the authorities. Once Sweeney's strong enough to stand on his own, I'd prefer to drop him off at the nearest port."

"As I recall," Jack mused with a sideways glance, "that was your plan for Darvill, yet *he's* still with us."

"And he'll leave without me if I don't hurry." She held up one of the corset strings. "Do you mind?"

"Darvill returned with a carriage only a short while ago. He's in my cabin changing into clothes I had stored below."

"I'm grateful you offered him your suit," she said, willing her teeth not to clench. "Now will you please help me?"

He crossed his arms over his solid chest and turned his back to her. "I'm your first officer, not your lady's maid."

She wanted to curse with exasperation. She and Jackson had practically grown up together, surviving storms, raids, the perils of London society. She was closer to him than she was to her own sisters. Who would have thought he'd suddenly turn squeamish about seeing her in her undergarments?

"You can be an officer later, Jack. Right now I'm in need of a maid."

He glared at her over his shoulder, his tiger eyes

dark with disapproval. "I don't want you going with him."

She heard the concern in his voice, but chose to ignore it. "I won't be going anywhere unless I get into this blasted gown."

"If by some miracle you pass for a lady and Darvill agrees to take you, I'm coming along."

"No. It's better if only the two of us go." Holding the corset in place with one hand, she lifted her quilted petticoat with the other and walked barefoot around Jackson, presenting her back to him. "I don't want it to look like we're invading Fulepet's domain. If he knows about de Maurier's blackmail plot, the marquess will be suspicious enough as it is when we arrive on his doorstep."

"Which is why it's too dangerous, Jo. Did you learn nothing from your duel with Darvill? You can be cornered, trapped, or worse."

"I intend to be careful. If the marquess *believes* he has the upper hand, it will give Nathan and me the advantage. Now tie, Jack."

"Darvill is right in wanting to leave you behind," he said, keeping his arms locked across his chest. "Besides, his sister is none of our business. We brought him to Saint-Nazaire. We should take the gold and sail for Mira Fenner. Or have you forgotten the reason we went after Darvill in the first place?"

"Of course I haven't forgotten." She counted to ten—quickly—resolved not to lose her temper. "We'll return to London as soon as we find Lauren Alcott."

"The girl isn't the reason you're so determined to help him."

The quiet certainty in Jack's voice unnerved her. Could he possibly know how Nathan affected her? She thought she'd kept her emotions hidden. She didn't want anyone to know—didn't even want to admit it to herself—but sometime during the last two weeks, she'd stopped think-

ing about Nathan as an aristocrat to hate, and now
thought of him as a man to admire, even care for.

She gritted her teeth against the thought. Bloody hell,
what a milksop she was turning out to be. "Are you
going to lace me up or do I have to call Nathan in
here to help me?"

"Tell me something, Jo." Jackson sighed and took
the corset strings in hand, yanking them so hard she
stumbled back, nearly falling onto her backside. He
pushed her forward and tugged again, more gently this
time. "When did he stop being Lord Darvill and become *Nathan?*"

"What kind of inane question is that?"

"One you should think about." After lacing her so
tightly she could scarcely breathe, he tied the strings
off and stepped away. "There, I'm done."

"Now the dress."

"Joanna," he warned in a growl he used only when
his patience was at an end.

"Be reasonable, Jack. The buttons are down the back.
I can't reach them." She lifted the yards of sapphire
blue silk off the bed and worked the dress over her
head.

Of all the gowns she'd stored, she'd chosen the deep
blue because she knew without a doubt that blue
wouldn't clash with her hair. Style and color schemes
had been Grace's domain. Jo hadn't cared a whit about
fashion—much to Madame Fournier's distress. With her
arms through the three-quarter-length sleeves, she
smoothed the pleated skirt over her petticoat before
glancing up.

Jack's mouth thinned with irritation. "I made a mistake; I see that now. When I brought your trunk up
from the hold, I should have thrown it overboard."

"Jack, my dear, you're beginning to sound like a
nagging husband. You should be complimenting me on
being prepared."

"The buttons," he said with scowl. "And that's all.

I'll give you fair warning: don't ask me to fix your hair or I'll take the scissors to it."

"Oh, Lord!" She grabbed a handful of her braid.

While Nathan had been off hiring a coach and horses, she'd taken the time to bathe and scrub her hair clean, wrapping it in a plait afterward, as was her habit. Dozens of thin red strands had escaped as they'd dried, twisting into tight, rebellious curls. Removing the string she'd tied to the end, she began unwinding her hair, running her fingers through the length until it bunched and crimped around her shoulders and down her back.

"A rat's nest," she said with disgust. "What am I going to do with it?"

"You could call this whole thing off and leave it as it is," he suggested, working his way up the line of dainty blue pearl buttons on her dress.

"Whose side are you on?"

Jackson rested his hands on her shoulders, a firm weight that lent strength and friendship, until they squeezed a little too hard. She thought he might be considering wringing her neck. "Yours, Jo. I'll always be on your side."

"Then stop fighting me. I'm going to help Nathan."

"Because you stabbed him?"

"Because he's not like the others. He's—"

"There can't be anything between the two of you," he said, catching her completely off guard. She tried to whip around and face him, but he held her still. "You know that, don't you?"

She glared over her shoulder at him. "I don't *want* anything to happen between him and me."

"No? I've seen the way you look at him." Jack's gaze narrowed with a shrewdness that made her want to squirm. "And I've noticed the way he looks at you."

"We don't look at each other"—she stumbled, at a loss for words—"like *that.*"

"Don't you?

"Of course not. And you should be seeing to the ship instead of spying on Nath—Lord Darvill and me."

"I just don't want to see your heart broken." Turning her so she fully faced him, he tapped her beneath her chin with his forefinger. "The man may not be the arrogant nobleman you'd first thought him to be, but he's still a nobleman."

Jackson opened the door to leave, but paused on the threshold. "A man like him will surely break your heart."

"Morgan married an aristocrat," Jo challenged.

"That she did, and your sister and Daniel are happy, but only because Daniel's a better man than most. What are the odds of a match like theirs happening again? One in a million? It's not worth the risk, Jo."

The door closed behind Jackson, shutting her inside the small cabin—a dangerous place to be when her thoughts were suddenly crashing through her mind, surging like frantic waves. She'd never expected to find a husband like Morgan's. That would take a miracle, and frankly, Jo knew there were no miracles in her future.

That was why she had learned to guard her heart so well, she thought defiantly. To stop anyone from reaching in, touching her, leaving a mark that would only turn to pain. Jackson didn't know what he was talking about. She wouldn't let anyone, least of all Nathan, get close enough to hurt her. Pacing the tight space, she picked up the toy soldier from the desk, but slammed it down again and turned away.

The girl isn't the reason you're so determined to help him.

She could hear Jackson's voice, so calm, so sure. Jo closed her eyes. *So right.* She'd promised to help find Lauren, but she had to face the truth: that wasn't her real reason for staying in Saint-Nazaire.

She didn't want to leave Nathan. Not yet.

For some strange, infuriating reason, she didn't want

to leave him. It was because of his kiss, the way he
made her feel, as if she didn't know herself. As hard
as she'd tried, she couldn't forget the force of his touch,
the desperate, searching feel of his mouth against hers,
the heat of his hands, as if he'd wanted to pull her
inside him so she could calm that heat, or maybe fuel
it—she didn't know.

Her response had been just as powerful, just as
needy. There was a fire between them, but it had only
begun to burn. If given a chance, the bond would grow
and spread; it would demand more of her, taking more
than she wanted to give, taking and taking until it consumed them both. It could happen so easily. Just one
kiss . . .

She had to stop it. She saw that now, saw just how
dangerous they were together.

"I've been a fool," she whispered, swallowing hard.
Why hadn't she seen that before now? Jackson was
right. She and Nathan had shared intense, driving
kisses, but nothing more could come of them—nothing
besides confusion and heartache.

She'd already allowed Nathan to turn her thinking
upside down. The weather had turned cold during her
trip to France. The children in Mira's care had to be
in desperate need of blankets, hot food and coal for the
stoves. *They* were her priority, not her unruly attraction
for a man so far removed from her station that any
feelings they might share would be deemed laughable.

Worse, she'd risked not only the children's well-being;
she'd also endangered her crew's lives by lingering in
France.

By dressing as a lady she put them at even greater
risk. If Nathan realized she was the woman he'd danced
with at the masked ball, all would be lost. She hadn't
worried about discovery before now because she'd worn
a half-mask that night. Since then he'd seen her only
in pants and poorly woven shirts, scuffed-up boots. And
her hair . . . She lifted a handful of red tangles, crushed

them in her fist. He'd only seen it braided, not brushed until it gleamed, wrapped in elegant curls, twisted about her head and strung with glittering jade beads. If she added that final touch before presenting herself for his test, would he recognize her as the Emerald of London? Did she dare take that chance? Just so she could be near him for another few days?

The answer came to her fast and hard: she couldn't. Not when her crew's lives were at stake. Not when her sisters could be exposed because of her carelessness. Not when the children were depending on her for their survival!

Nathan would have to find Lauren on his own. He wouldn't argue about going without her; that was the way he wanted it anyway. But just to abandon him . . . She pressed her hands to her stomach, but the quivering didn't ease.

"I'll leave him enough gold to cover his expenses, and passage for two to England. That will settle any debt I owe him, once and for all."

She reached behind her for the gown's top button, and realized she'd have to rip the buttons off if she wanted out of the dress. As soon as she changed into her pants and work shirt, she'd tell Nathan of her decision.

"Well, I'll be damned."

Jo gritted her teeth. *God, no. Not now. He can't see me now.* But Nathan was behind her; she could feel his eyes watching her, studying her from the top of her snarled hair to her bare toes. Fighting a flush of heat that raced beneath her skin, she faced the door.

Wearing a pair of saddle brown pants tucked into knee-high black boots, he filled the portal, his stance negligent, yet she sensed a tenseness about him. His frock coat of soft black wool, with simple gold frogs lining the lapels, covered a matching waistcoat. A white linen cravat was tied loosely about his neck. Over it all, a plain cape of heavy wool draped his shoulders.

It occurred to her that Jackson had never looked so wonderful.

Standing in her cramped cabin, Nathan seemed every bit the lord, a man of privilege and power. The air almost trembled with his presence, a confident aura she'd always associated with the wealthy. Nathan possessed self-assurance in spades. He seemed larger somehow, taller, and even further beyond her reach. She couldn't imagine calling *this* Nathan by his given name.

He was Lord Darvill, through and through.

Something inside her twisted, and it took a moment for her to recognize the ache. Loss, she thought, astonished. She felt the pain of losing all over again, that wrenching disappointment, the helpless sensation when something valuable began to slip through her fingers and she couldn't stop it, no matter how hard she tried, or how tightly she squeezed her hands closed.

Fool, she called herself.

He wasn't hers to lose; he never had been. The pain she felt had to be the corset cutting into her ribs.

Jo clenched her jaw. This time she called herself a liar.

Nathan stared in silence, stunned, his hand on the metal door latch, his boots feeling heavy, as if they'd suddenly rooted themselves to the floor. He was aware of a warm stir of air against his face, while a cold draft brushed at his back, lifting the hair he'd recently washed and tied in a queue. He sensed, rather than saw, a brazier burning nearby, heard men moving about above deck, knew that time was ticking by at a faster and faster pace. But he was aware of those things as if from a distance. Every part of him seemed fine-tuned and focused on the impossible vision before him.

"What are you staring at?" Jo demanded, her hands coming to her hips.

"The question isn't what, but *who?*"

Her expressive green eyes flashed with . . . With what? Nathan wondered. Outrage, panic? He wasn't sure which, but he knew whatever emotion she felt, it was volatile.

She furrowed her brow, glaring at him with suspicion. "What do you mean by that? You know who I am."

Nathan stepped fully into the room, shutting the door behind him, unable to tear his gaze from her auburn hair, pulled across her left shoulder, draping her chest in a thick, shining wave, the burnished-gold ends curling at her narrow waist. The temptation to burrow his hand into its length and wrap it around his fist was almost too powerful to ignore. But he stayed the urge and forced his thoughts toward the pragmatic instead of the enticing.

He'd known she was slender, but her grubby pants and shirt had disguised her build. The tightly cinched gown, however, did not. The blue dress was simple in design, formfitting, scooping low across the full swells of her breasts, hugging the shape of her body until it reached her hips, where the skirt flared slightly with the aid of petticoats, he noted, instead of a stiff cane farthingale.

Yet the gown's simplicity was what took his breath away, made the attraction he felt for her slip from his control, causing his body to respond and harden.

He realized the name Jo didn't suit the woman before him. She was Joanna, a woman capable of any number of things—including seduction, if he gave the slightest encouragement.

He gave himself a mental shake. What in bloody hell was he thinking? He'd grown impatient waiting for her above deck, so he'd come to her cabin to tell her that nothing she did could possibly convince him that she could pass for a lady.

Her skills with manners and proper decorum were still in question, but to look at her . . . Nathan muttered a curse. Clasping his hands behind his back, he walked around her, trying to find something he could object to. But God help him, she was beautiful. She'd been incredibly alluring in her worn sailor's garb, but in a sapphire blue gown that added fire to her hair and a soft glow to her creamy skin, she was irresistible.

He paused at her back, catching her scent of soap and water and warm skin. Fresh smells, innocent, yet they invoked a tightening in his loins, a feral need to wrap his arm around her waist and draw her back against him, touch his lips to the base of her neck. Taste her.

Drawing a shallow breath, he stared at the curve of her throat, the exposed length of her shoulder. She looked so soft, her skin slightly tanned and sprinkled with pale freckles.

A memory nudged the back of his mind. Powderless skin, pale freckles. Frowning, he tried to pull the meaning forward but it stayed in the shadows, just out of reach.

"If you're through gawking, I have something to tell you."

"You usually do," he said, then ran his finger over the ridge of her shoulder, drawing a surprised gasp from her, which was followed by a shudder.

"You have freckles," he said, not sure why that should have caught his attention. But it had, and it was a fact that made him frown.

She jerked away, spinning to face him, giving him a full view of the color in her cheeks, a heated glow that bled down to her curving breasts, tinting them pink—breasts he still remembered the shape and feel of, a sensation he wished beyond all reason that he could feel again.

"Yes, my skin is flawed," she said with her jaw clenched. "Which means I could never pass for a true lady. I guess you'll have to visit the marquess without me."

Nathan quirked a brow, taken back by her sudden reversal. What was she up to? Had something happened to change her mind? He knew her well enough to be suspicious of anything she did, and her abrupt concession piqued his suspicions to a new level. "Ladies have been known to have freckles."

"No self-respecting ladies." She moved around him so the desk stood as a solid oak barrier.

Did she feel in need of protection? From him? His instincts went on alert.

"In any case," she added, "it doesn't matter. I've decided against accompanying you."

"Is that so? May I ask why?"

"I have business to attend to in England. Tending your wounds, then bringing you here, has delayed my plans for too long."

"It's too late to sail out tonight." Her knife with the imbedded gemstones lay on the desk. He picked it up, twirling the blade over and over so light from the overhead lantern glittered off the polished steel edge. "You should wait until morning."

"I've wasted enough time on you, Darvill." She glanced at the dagger as if she wanted to snatch it from his hands. "To be fair, though, I've decided to leave you with enough gold to see you and your sister home." She reached into a drawer, then tossed him a leather pouch.

He caught it, felt the weight of at least a dozen coins inside, enough to buy every cabin on ten ships, if his estimate was correct. Why did she want to be through with him so suddenly, when only a few hours before she'd been as stubborn as a mule about guarding his back and helping to secure Lauren's freedom?

There was a reason Jo wanted to be away from him, and he doubted it had anything to do with her "business" in England.

She ran her hand through her hair, twisting long strands so the soft sheen of lantern light glistened off curls as rich and dark as garnets. The blue gown complemented her fiery coloring, but he wondered what she'd look like in green, a deep, seductive emerald that would match her eyes.

The memory he'd been reaching for earlier stirred again, coming closer. Jade beads. She needed jade beads threaded throughout her hair, and a half-mask of gold to cover her face, finished with jewel green ostrich feathers.

A mask just like the mystery woman had worn at Daniel's ball. *The Emerald of London.*

The phrase buzzed through Nathan's mind. He frowned, took a step back and looked at her hair, trying to imagine it upswept, curled and pinned. And powderless in a show of fashion rebellion. A rebel, just like Jo herself.

He pictured her with a mask covering her forehead, her cheeks, the bridge of her nose. His breath hissed through his clenched teeth. It couldn't be, but the image fit almost too perfectly.

"Why are you staring at me like that?" she said, sounding more agitated than offended. "Don't you know it's rude?"

"Who are you?" he asked, still doubting his own eyes and the questions spinning through his head.

"I've already told you who I am." She turned away, crossing her arms over her waist as she stared out the paned windows. "Our business is done, Lord Darvill. You're free to leave."

He didn't move except to study her tense shoulders, the rigid stiffness of her back. The Emerald of London and Jo couldn't be the same woman. Yet he couldn't dismiss the nagging possibility. How many times had he thought of the mystery lady when he'd been in Jo's presence? They looked so much alike—both bold and brazen, willful. And beautiful. All that red hair and creamy skin, the dusting of freckles. And her lips that were meant for kissing . . .

Good God. Nathan ran his hand over his mouth, remembering too well how she felt and tasted. Jo was the Emerald of London. A part of him continued to deny it, but he knew—something inside him, his instinct or his reasoning knew—that the two women were one and the same. Pieces of the puzzle moved and connected, creating a picture that began to make sense.

That would help explain why Jo had known about his shipment of gold. *She'd* been at the party. And he knew she was both cunning and daring. Could she have overheard his conversation with Daniel and Mr. Fitzhugh without his realizing it? He knew the answer to that question.

Damn her! What kind of game does she think she's playing? He wanted to ask the question out loud, demand an answer. But now wasn't the time. He'd had every intention of going to Marquess Fulepet's alone, but now he wasn't about to let Jo—Joanna—Finn, or whatever her real name was, out of his sight.

He wanted answers from her, and he was bloody well going to get them—after she helped him rescue Lauren.

Fourteen

"I'm sailing within the hour, Darvill." Jo kept her back to him, her arms tight around her waist. "Unless you intend to sail with me, I suggest you leave. Now."

Nothing. No answer, no movement.

Her nerves hummed with confusion. Why wasn't he leaving, dashing from the ship? She thought he'd be relieved to finally be free of her interference.

Lights flickered on one by one throughout the town of Saint-Nazaire, filling the windows of cottages and taverns, the two inns that lined the main street, shining through like a beacon against a darkening backdrop of buildings and sky. Jo watched the night sweep in with amazing speed, focusing on it instead of the man behind her. Anything except the man behind her.

He kept still, studying her, contemplating something, thinking about Lord knew what. *Who are you?* She didn't even want to consider what he'd meant by those words.

Hearing the rustle of clothes and the creak of wood, she closed her eyes and sighed. He'd be gone soon. She'd be able to order the anchors raised and sail for home. Maybe she wouldn't even wait for morning. She'd never see Nathan again, and could put to rest her fear of discovery.

A heavy weight settled on her shoulders. Jo gasped and spun around. Nathan stood behind her, catching the black velvet cloak he'd placed on her shoulders as it fell to the ground.

"There's no need to be nervous about meeting Fulepet," he said as calmly as if they were attending a tea. He held the cape up for her to slip on.

"I told you I'm not going."

A fire leaped into his eyes, a light brighter than any reflection a lantern could produce. Anger, exasperation, suspicion? She couldn't tell, and a part of her didn't want to know. *Does he suspect who I really am?* She buried the nagging fear. If he knew, he'd call her out, demand to know if she and the Emerald of London were one and the same.

"It's true," he said. "I didn't want you accompanying me." He stepped behind her to drape the cloak around her shoulders. It was a simple move, but the weight of the fabric, the pressure of his hands, trapped her as surely as iron chains.

"But I was wrong. I do need you." His words were a warm brush against her ear. Reaching in front of her, he tied the corded strings. "Fulepet will be much less suspicious if I arrive with a beautiful woman on my arm. And if by some miracle Philip has returned there, he might be less likely to shoot me with you as a witness."

"Or he might decide to shoot us both." She tried to move away, but Nathan gripped her shoulders, stopping her. He slid his palms down her arms. Tingles scurried like sparks across her skin, creating a heat as erotic as it was unwanted.

"Are you afraid?"

The question hadn't been taunting, yet her chin jutted upward in defense. "I'm not afraid of anything."

He pulled her against his chest. "I won't let anything happen to you, Jo."

The sincerity of his words warmed something deep inside her. No man had ever offered to take care of her, watch over her. Morgan had been like her parent after theirs had died, but this was different. She didn't need Nathan's protection, but that he offered . . .

"Traveling to the marquess's home and questioning him about Philip's whereabouts will take only a few hours. I promise to have you back in time to sail with the morning tide."

"Nathan—"

He raised his hand, interrupting her. "Please, for Lauren's sake."

She wanted to say no. The word was on the tip of her tongue, but she couldn't force it out. Even the ability to curse seemed beyond her. She took a calming breath and tried to think rationally. What harm could a few hours cause? If she left Nathan now, it would be like running, admitting defeat, admitting that she couldn't control her feelings for him.

They could visit Fulepet, and if Lauren and Philip weren't there, she could return to the *Sea Witch* and head for England. The delay would cost her nothing, and there was still a chance that Nathan could save the sister he dearly loved. Could she live with herself if she robbed him of that chance?

The alternative was to have Jackson and Dillon forcefully remove him from her ship. That image turned her stomach.

Facing Nathan, she crossed her arms over her chest. "I'll give you until morning. If we haven't found your sister by then, you're on your own."

"Thank you."

She gave him a curt nod. "Now I think—"

Nathan gripped her neck and pulled her to him, clamping his mouth over hers, cutting off breath and words alike. She broke free long enough to gasp in surprise. He tilted his head, taking the advantage. Fitting their lips tightly, he slipped his tongue into her mouth, flooding her with his taste. Jo gripped his coat in her fists, tried to breathe, but the floor spun beneath her feet.

"Nathan—" She couldn't manage anything more. He eased his hold, cradling her against him even while he deepened the kiss, stunning her nerves, turning them to liquid. She should fight, but this kiss . . . What was he doing to her? It wasn't anything like the others. The times before had been hard and angry, a battle over who would win. Or perhaps they'd been about something more primitive: a battle over who would survive.

But this . . . this was velvet and heat, a seduction that trailed liquid smoke through her veins. The taste of brandy mingled with the taste of Nathan; the combination filled her mouth, making her want to groan with pleasure. Somehow she held the sound back. His hands slid around her waist, fitting to the curve of her spine. Her skin tightened; her nerves started a slow swirl that promised to lift her off her feet.

God help her, he was making her want him even more than she had before. She couldn't let him. She couldn't! She might never sail away from him if she didn't stop him now.

Pushing against his chest, she broke free, surprised that he let her. She pressed the back of her hand to her mouth. Her lips were swollen, sensitive, tingling with the need for more.

"Don't ever do that again," she warned.

A rueful smile curved his lips, making her think that once again the kiss hadn't affected him nearly as much as it had her. But when he spoke, and she heard the strain in his voice, she knew he wasn't as calm as he appeared.

"I apologize, but you're incredibly beautiful tonight. Much too beautiful"—he fingered a strand of her hair—"to waste your life being a pirate."

She jerked her hair out of his reach. "Don't concern yourself over my welfare, Nathan. After tonight you'll never see me again."

A volatile emotion stirred in his eyes, but it vanished so quickly she wondered if it had been a trick of the light. He nodded and extended his hand, letting her lead the way.

Glaring a warning for him to keep his distance, she didn't leave the cabin, but lifted the hem of her skirt—realizing she had yet to put on her shoes—and exposed her bare leg.

"Jo," he croaked as if something were caught in his throat. "What are you doing?"

Taking the *Sea Queen* blade from the desk, she slid it with a quick, practiced move into the leather sheath strapped to her thigh. "You told me before that a dress doesn't make a lady. And you were right. I'm a pirate, and pirates are always prepared."

Chateau de Noir Bois shot from the ground with walls as steep and perilous as granite cliffs. The castle was tall and imposing. The square, fitted stones were dark with soot and age, as if the wars of centuries past had soaked into their flinty pores, coating them with memories that couldn't be washed clean.

In a tower window, high against the mist-shrouded night, a weak glow flickered like a fading star. Nathan wondered if even the candles were wary of burning too brightly. Along the outer walls, the battlements circling the massive structure, even the stone gatehouse leading into what he assumed to be a bailey, darkness crept around them like a living thing. From the watchtower to the round, crenellated turrets, no torches were lit to reveal whether anyone stirred within the forbidding castle. Only the wash of a waning moon beyond scuttling clouds gave what little light there was to be had, turning the walls gray and giving life to the fog that swirled two feet above the ground.

Perhaps Fulepet had left for the evening, or had already retired. Or perhaps this was a grim warning that visitors weren't welcome?

Nathan hated to disappoint Marquess Fulepet, but he

wasn't about to be intimidated. Flicking the reins, he drove the hired carriage beneath the gatehouse and into the bailey's oppressive darkness. The crunch of wheels against gravel and the swirl of biting wind were the only sounds. With a creak of wood and leather and a rattle from the harness, Nathan drew the team of horses to a halt before a set of stairs that led to fifteen-foot doors as ominous as the surrounding walls.

Was Philip ensconced behind those doors? Was his sister? Anxiety tightened like a cord around Nathan's chest. Would he meet another ambush? Belatedly, he realized his foolishness by bringing Jo. She shouldn't be here, but safe on her own ship, sailing as far away from him as she could get.

He glanced at her, wrapped in the shadow of her cape. Her skin was colorless, her lips a faint outline, but there was a gleam in her eyes that had little to do with the moon. He could feel her mood, as well: grim, apprehensive—a state of mind that matched his own. She'd refused to ride inside the carriage, which shouldn't have surprised him, but he'd have preferred some distance from her. Even as he focused on the upcoming meeting, his thoughts were continually interrupted with questions about Jo's identity. Where did she come from, what had caused her to lead a double life? They were questions that would have to wait until later to be answered.

Leaping down from the high seat, he turned and took her by the waist, helping her to the ground.

"I'm beginning to think all of France was built from gloom," she said, frowning at the closed doors.

"Not the warm welcome you'd expect," he agreed. But Nathan wasn't entirely surprised. After all, he'd met Marquess Fulepet.

Before leaving the ship, Jo had coiled her hair into a simple chignon at the nape of her neck. The change stunned him by turning her features regal, almost unapproachable. She was a woman as haute as any he'd ever seen—a vast departure from the spirited pirate he'd come to know. She touched the neat bun now, as any lady might after subjecting her coiffure to the winds. Then she propped her hands on her waist, her narrowed gaze scanning the grounds with open wariness, giving him a glimpse of the pirate beneath her disguise.

"A groom should have heard our arrival and come running," she said, her tone calculating. "Do you think I'll have to haul my trunk in myself?"

"Let's hope we don't have to carry this deception that far. If this is Fulepet's way of greeting guests, this could be a very brief visit."

"We only need one night."

She sounded so sure and confident, when doubts plagued Nathan like a festering sore. What if Lauren wasn't here? If Fulepet refused to cooperate and reveal what he knew about Philip, what in God's name would he do then? Or if Philip were hiding within the desolate walls, how would he stop himself from killing the man outright?

Nathan touched his coat pocket, felt the bulging shape of a pistol, and pushed his worries aside. *One thing at a time.* First he'd deal with Fulepet; then he'd face whatever came next.

"How do you intend to explain my traveling alone with you?" she asked as he took her by the arm and led her up the stone steps, which were worn thin by the passing years.

"There's only one solution to be had," he said, wondering how she would accept his decision. "You'll be my wife for the evening."

He felt her gaze pin him, even in the dark. Her face was in shadow, hiding her expression. Was she outraged? Shocked? Intrigued? He realized it was just as well he couldn't see her face. If she was intrigued and looked anywhere close to the green-eyed temptress she did earlier, he'd kiss her again.

"Your wife," she said as if the idea amused her. "If

we survive tonight, we might laugh about this one day."
She touched his arm.

"If de Maurier is staying here, then Fulepet will
know it's a lie."

"Yes, but I'm trusting that his curiosity will be
piqued and he'll let us play out our charade."

"Do you really believe he'll allow us to stay?"

"It doesn't matter. With or without his consent, I intend to search every inch of his estate."

After a gray-haired butler reluctantly allowed them
entrance, they were left in the main hall to wait like
lowly messengers. Nathan had never visited Chateau de
Noir Bois before. The towering walls groped upward,
disappearing into the dark void above, leaving him to
wonder if the ceiling was actually connected to the
night sky. There were no tapestries lining the immense
staircase, no paintings of ancestors, coats of arms or
displays of weapons. The castle was as barren as it was
cold.

He suppressed a shiver as he imagined the possibility
of Lauren's being held in such a dismal place. His sister
was far too fragile, both of body and spirit, to withstand
such harsh surroundings—unlike Jo, who would have
undoubtedly found a way to escape by now, taking her
captors prisoner in the process.

Briefly he thought of his own home, Winstone Castle, in the Lake District far to the north of London.
Snow might have fallen by now, dusting the centuries-
old oaks and pines. He pictured Jo as she looked now,
riding through his wheat fields, past forests wild and
untouched, greeting the villagers who lived nearby. His
imagination took the scene further, picturing her barefoot, with her hair free of pins and at the mercy of the
wind.

Muttering a curse for his disturbing and useless
thoughts, he glanced at her. Her brow was dipped in a
frown as she studied the imposing room. Her frown
deepened to a scowl, and he didn't have to ask to know

she didn't like what she saw. For once they agreed, because neither did he.

The echo of footsteps drew his attention to the grand staircase. Marquess Fulepet was descending the steps at a leisurely pace, his gaze as gritty and formidable as the stone walls that protected his home. His brows were drawn tight over a face shaped by hard lines and unforgiving angles. The blue-black whiskers covering his cheeks, his upper lip and his square-cut jaw seemed to make him all the harder, as if he'd never known a smile, and laughter was unheard-of.

Not until Nathan felt a shiver run through Jo's spine did he realize he'd placed his hand at her back. His fingers tightened instinctively on her waist. Was she nervous? Afraid? Did she wish she'd fought harder to remain on board the *Sea Witch?*

Or was it excitement she felt? He should have left her on her ship. She should be on her way to wherever it was she'd come from. Instead he'd foolishly disregarded her safety so he could learn her real identity. Jo might be cunning and more daring than any woman should be, but she was no match for Fulepet.

"Lord Darvill," the marquess droned in a thick French accent as he came to a halt before them. He bowed, a stiff bend at the waist, while he kept the fingers of one hand tucked inside the pocket of his scarlet waistcoat. "What an unexpected surprise."

From the stern set of Fulepet's mouth and the flat sheen of his eyes, Nathan doubted anything surprised the man. He returned the bow. "I apologize for arriving unannounced, but events occurred in such a way as to prevent my sending word ahead."

"Yes," he said slowly, giving a wealth of meaning to the single word. His attention shifted to Jo. "And who is this you've brought with you?"

"Allow me to present my new bride, Joanna." He held his breath, not knowing how Jo would behave. She merely gave the marquess a winsome smile that made her eyes glitter like green jewels.

"I had not heard you'd married, Lord Darvill." Fulepet took Jo's hand and kissed it, lingering seconds too long for Nathan's liking. "I'm pleased to make your acquaintance, Lady Darvill."

"As am I, Monsieur Fulepet." Jo performed a perfect curtsy, then tugged her hand free. "I hope we haven't caused you any inconvenience."

"Not at all." He clasped his hands behind his back, and in a flash his expression shifted, becoming sharp, uncompromising. "What brings you to France, Darvill?"

Nathan had hoped the marquess would invite them in, make a pretense of welcoming them into his home; evidently Fulepet didn't care for charades any more than Nathan did. "I'm hoping to catch up to my sister, Lauren. She's traveling with her companion, the dowager Easterly. Do you know the dowager?"

"No."

Despite the curt answer, Nathan forced himself to smile. "They're supposed to be in the area. You haven't seen them, or perhaps heard of their arrival in town?"

"I rarely pay attention to the local gossip."

"Of course not," Nathan said tightly, wanting to smash the disinterested look from Fulepet's face. "We're simply anxious to find Lauren. Joanna and I weren't sure when my sister planned to return to London, so we went ahead with a small wedding. I want to tell Lauren about our marriage in person, and introduce her to her new sister-in-law."

"So you traveled all the way to Saint-Nazaire?" Fulepet quirked a brow, clearly doubting every word Nathan said.

"As part of our honeymoon trip," Jo interrupted, placing her hand on Nathan's chest. "We made port in Concarneau, where they were supposed to be."

Nathan knew she was playing her role—and exceedingly well—but her touch only made his gut tighten into a harder knot.

"Once we learned Nathan's sister and the dowager traveled south, well, we hired a coach and set out after them. It's my fault we're here at all, monsieur. It's silly, really, and Nathan should be furious with me for making such a foolish request, especially given the late hour. But he indulged me this once."

Nathan stared down at his "wife," who smiled at him as if she *were* a glowing bride. He'd never heard Jo prattle before, or use such an innocent tone. Half of him dreaded what she'd say next; the other half couldn't wait to hear.

"The countryside is so . . . beautiful," she said, forcing the last word out as if it had stuck to the roof of her mouth. "I pleaded with Nathan to continue on. Before I knew it, the sun had begun to set. We had no choice but proceed in the dark until we reached your lovely town. That's when my husband mentioned you lived nearby, and I knew we had to visit. It would have been unforgivably rude if we'd gone into the village without first calling on you."

"Unforgivable indeed," Fulepet commented dryly, though he examined Jo as if she were a piece of cheese sitting in the middle of a mousetrap.

She stepped away from Nathan, and he had to stifle the impulse to draw her back to his side. Her gaze slid over the marble and stone foyer before settling back on their ungracious host. "I'd love to take a tour of your home, Monsieur Fulepet. Has it been in your family long?"

"Seven generations, madam. But I'm afraid a tour is out of the question."

Jo laughed, a low, smoky sound that warmed the halls. "I wouldn't dream of troubling you with something so tedious tonight, my lord. In the morning, perhaps?"

She tilted her head at a decidedly feminine angle,

exposing her long neck, the slope of her breasts; it was a breath-stopping pose Nathan remembered well from the night of the mask. If he had any lingering doubts that Jo was the Emerald of London, he didn't any longer. She was using the same smiles, the same throaty laughter on Fulepet that she'd used on him.

The witch.

Though for tonight, her unique ability of combining seduction and innocent charm might serve to find Lauren.

Fulepet's mouth twitched with annoyance. "The morning would be fine. When you return—"

"Wonderful!" Jo clasped her hands together, then sighed with relief. "I look forward to it. Now if you'd be so kind as to have your butler show me to our rooms, I'll retire for the night. This has been such a long day, and I'm sure you two men have a lot of catching up to do."

"Joanna," Nathan warned, wondering what she was up to, and not liking the possibilities that came to mind. "Perhaps you'd like a sherry first."

"No," she said with a maidenly shake of her head. "I'm fine, thank you."

Fulepet stared at her, his face turning red beneath his beard. "You might find my accommodations lacking, mademoiselle. The inn in town would undoubtedly better suit you and your husband's needs."

"Nonsense." She smiled with such innocence Nathan could almost believe she didn't realize Fulepet didn't want them to stay. Walking to the staircase, she ran her palm over the railing. Her hand seemed small, delicate, unbelievably frail against the dull stone. "I find your home charming. I promise we won't be in your way, and tomorrow we'll be gone, continuing our search for Lauren."

A muscle throbbed at the base of the marquess's neck, but he gave a reluctant nod. "Very well."

The gray-haired butler appeared, from which shadowed corner, Nathan couldn't have said.

"Show Lady Darvill to the east wing," Fulepet ordered. "The Crystal Suite."

"Oui, monsieur."

Turning to Jo, the marquess informed her, "I have no lady's maid to tend you."

"I have no need of one, my lord, but thank you for thinking of me." She crossed to Nathan, reached up and kissed his cheek, a warm brush of lips and breath. "Enjoy yourself, husband. I shall see you later."

She turned in a swish of satin, her back straight, her shoulders squared and prim as she hurried up the stairs after the butler—up into the darkened second floor, where he wouldn't be able to see her, know what she was up to, know if she was safe.

Nathan gripped his hands behind his back to keep from going after her. She wouldn't try anything foolish, he reassured himself. But he didn't believe it. Any other woman would have remained glued to his side for fear of what she'd find lurking on the darkened floors above. But not Jo. He didn't believe for a minute that she planned on retiring to the safe confines of their room. He wondered if Fulepet doubted her intentions as well.

Whatever she had planned, she had better be careful, he thought, tempted beyond belief to grab hold of her and shake some sense into her foolish head. If Fulepet suspected . . . If Jo were hurt . . . Nathan couldn't finish the thoughts. Instead he turned his attention to the opportunity at hand. It was time to ask the marquess a few overt questions about Lauren and Philip. At the moment, he had to trust that Jo would take care of herself.

"She is headstrong, that wife of yours," Fulepet said in a tone that matched the chill in his eyes. "I like that in a woman."

The apprehension in Nathan's stomach turned to ice. He didn't want a man like Fulepet liking anything about

Jo. He didn't even want the man to look at her. And what about Lauren? How did Fulepet feel about women who were as headstrong as a mouse? Once again he prayed his sister wasn't being held at Chateau de Noir Bois. If there were a god, he wouldn't subject his gentle, guileless sister to the mercy of such a cold, forbidding man.

"Since your wife has conveniently left us alone," Fulepet said, his mouth thinning into a sneer, "why don't you tell me why the hell you're really here."

Stone floors shouldn't echo when you crossed them, turning your own footsteps into the sounds of pursuit, Jo thought as she glanced behind her and saw nothing beyond the darkness closing in. Lanterns shouldn't sit cold and unused in endless hallways, either. But both were the case in the east wing of Chateau de Noir Bois.

The candle the nameless butler carried couldn't push the dark back far enough to suit her. The walls pressed in, becoming tighter the farther they walked. The floor seemed to rise beneath her feet, the ceiling to push lower until she thought she could reach up and touch it. The air smelled dank, old, like rotted wood and a hundred other things long since dead. But as bad as it smelled, she dragged in one lungful after another.

Deciding to search the castle on her own had to be the most half-witted idea she'd ever had. What she wouldn't give to be on the open sea, braced on the deck of her ship, welcoming whatever challenge the ocean tossed in her face. Instead she was walking half-blind down an accursed tunnel that ended Lord knew where.

She followed the stooped butler around another corner, turning right this time, and continued deeper into a well of blackness. That made two rights, a left and another right. She had to keep her bearings or she'd never find her way out of the castle's maze to conduct her own search. She kept an eye out for any landmarks—paintings, statues, furniture—but there was nothing, only bare walls the color of dried blood.

The castle was larger than she'd have believed. Jo had to face the truth: if Lauren were here, their chances of finding her were almost nonexistent.

"This way, mademoiselle." The butler opened a door papered in the same burgundy shade as the endless walls. Even the metal handle was inset to disguise its presence. Jo imagined what the hallway must look like in full light: one long, continuous corridor of bloodred with no windows or doors—no obvious way out.

Just what kind of man was Marquess Fulepet? He resented the arrival of guests, and seemed as austere and dismal as the castle he lived in, a castle devoid of light and warmth and filled with hallways designed to fool the eye into believing they had no end.

If he knew where Lauren was, what did that mean for the girl? What would he have done to her in the time she'd been taken captive? And how could she have survived if she was at the mercy of both Fulepet and Philip de Maurier?

Jo suppressed a shudder and stiffened her spine along with her resolve. She'd given Nathan until morning to find Lauren, and she couldn't leave until she knew the girl was alive and safe.

She trailed the butler into the bedchamber just as he lit a three-tiered candelabra on a bedside table. Welcome light pushed into the gloomy corners and reflected off the paneled ceiling. Jo started to sigh with relief, but it caught in her throat as the butler hurried from the room without a word, closing the door behind him with a loud click. A chill shivered up her back.

"What the bloody hell?" *Does Fulepet think he can lock me in?* Fisting her hands, she ran to the black walnut door, gripped the cold metal knob and yanked. The door opened with a whoosh. A gust of musty air washed her face. She stepped back, pressed one hand to her trembling stomach, and stared at the gaping darkness beyond the threshold. She wasn't locked in, but for some reason that didn't help settle her nerves, which had twisted into even tighter knots during the last few seconds.

With her other hand, she felt for the knife strapped to her thigh. The familiar shape bolstered her confidence, but not enough. Lifting her skirt, she slipped the dagger from the sheath, clenching her fingers around the cold hilt. The metal handle felt good, solid, hard against her palm. Drawing a deep breath, she felt her control return and strengthen. She'd let her imagination run away with her. And who wouldn't while standing alone in a castle that should appear only in one's nightmares?

Giving the room a cursory look, she noted a fourposter bed; the sagging mattress was covered with a black, gold-trimmed quilt and a fine layer of dust. The only other furnishings were a table that held the candelabra, two high-backed chairs before an empty hearth, and an oversize wardrobe with beveled mirrors. She considered opening the cabinet and peering inside, then decided that if something lurked within, she didn't want to know.

"Don't be such a coward," she grumbled in disgust. She'd never been one to frighten easily, and it annoyed her that she'd allowed herself to become frightened now. The castle might have the warmth of a medieval dungeon, but it was made of stone and mortar—nothing more. Certainly there was nothing within the damp walls to be frightened of—it was Philip de Maurier and Marquess Fulepet that posed the greatest threat.

Regardless, as she lifted one taper from the candelabra and headed out into the dark hallway, the hairs on the nape of her neck rose in warning.

"Mortar and stone," she whispered to herself, tightening her hold on her knife. "There's nothing here but mortar and stone."

Fifteen

"The Lord will abhor both the bloodthirsty and deceitful man," Fulepet murmured, staring at the empty space above the massive hearth, seeing what, Nathan couldn't begin to guess. A missing portrait, a tapestry of the family crest? Whatever it had been, only gray-mortared stone remained.

He narrowed his gaze on his host and felt his muscles tense with the need for action. They'd moved into Fulepet's drawing room, and for the past ten minutes the marquess had roamed the room, muttering cryptic verses ranging from Shakespeare to the Bible, as if he'd forgotten Nathan existed.

Seated in a hard, slatted chair so worn the stain on the carved arms had begun to fade, he took a sip of brandy Fulepet had grudgingly provided. The pungent taste sharpened on his tongue, then spread a numbing warmth down his throat and across his chest, but he hardly noticed.

Few candles had been lit, but even in the dim light, Nathan could tell the spacious room had once been grand, undoubtedly furnished with mahogany chairs polished until they'd gleamed. Gilded tables must have been set with valuable trinkets, and chandeliers of Irish cut glass might have hung from the gaping black holes in the ceiling.

Only a few unremarkable pieces were scattered about

now, all scarred and coated with dust, creating an emptiness, a degrading solemnness that seeped through skin and bone.

Even the struggling flames, burning in the ash-packed hearth beside him, looked cold and forlorn.

It was obvious to Nathan now why the castle had seemed inhospitable when he'd first arrived. What was the point of lighting torches along the stone battlements if Fulepet had no one in his service to stand watch? Hiring guards took money—something Fulepet was clearly without. From the looks of things, the man was in danger of losing what was left of his heritage. Nathan wondered how far Fulepet would go to keep that from happening. Kidnapping, extortion?

"State your reasons for coming here, Darvill," the marquess demanded abruptly. Standing by the far table, his face half cloaked in shadows, he tossed back his tumbler of brandy. Pouring another, he nursed it slowly.

"It's as I said earlier." Nathan set his drink aside on a battered table. If he hoped to glean any information from Fulepet, he had to keep his anger under control and his head clear. "I'm in search of my sister."

"And you just happened to come looking for her in my home?" Flames leaped in the hearth, growing brighter for an instant as they seared another log with a crackling, licking sound. The glow reflected off Fulepet's black hair, making it shine where it was slicked back against his head. Yet his eyes absorbed the light, consuming it the way the flames consumed the wood.

"It seems curious to me that you'd drag your wife about the countryside on your honeymoon—if she is indeed your wife."

"Why would you doubt me?" Nathan returned the man's probing stare.

"Why doubt you indeed?" The marquess smiled, but the effort merely hardened his eyes.

"If you must know the truth, I'm concerned for

Lauren's welfare. She was recently engaged to Philip de Maurier." Nathan rose from his chair. Straightening his sleeves as if he had no other cares in the world, as if his muscles weren't twisted into bitter knots, he asked, "Do you know him?"

"We're acquaintances."

Nathan forced his hands not to clench, forced himself not to grab Fulepet by the throat and wring more than a cryptic answer from him.

"Things went badly between them," he continued, amazed his voice sounded normal, calm, as if someone else were speaking altogether. "The engagement was called off, leaving my sister heartbroken, which is why she went abroad with her companion."

"I'm sure she's stronger than you give her credit for." His smile turned spiteful. "Women usually are."

Nathan held Fulepet's indifferent gaze, tried to probe deeper, discern what he'd meant. The fire's warmth leaked into the room, brushed against his neck, but it wasn't enough to stop his blood from chilling in his veins.

Deciding to end their verbal sparring and come to the point, he asked, "Have you seen Philip de Maurier lately?"

"Why do you ask?"

"I would hate for Lauren to chance meeting him. She needs to put him in her past, move on." Silence fell into the room, lying between them like a challenge tossed down. "Have you seen him?"

Time ticked by without the marquess answering, and with each passing second, Nathan felt his blood pulse harder and harder against the base of his throat. Fulepet knew something, knew where Lauren was, or at least what had happened to her.

Topping off his tumbler of brandy, Fulepet admitted, "De Maurier was here some time ago, but he soon left."

"Do you know to where?" Nathan asked, knowing

Philip hadn't left at all. The bastard was here; either he was hiding, biding his time until he could think of another way to blackmail Nathan, or he was planning a way to escape. If he had escape in mind, would he try sailing away, taking Lauren with him? He wouldn't get far if that was his plan. Before leaving for the chateau, Nathan had stationed Jo's men along the dock to keep a lookout for anyone who tried to board the other ships in the harbor.

Fulepet shrugged. "I believe he mentioned Paris. Unless your sister traveled to the city, I doubt she has encountered him."

"I hope not."

"But who can really say? Sometimes fate decides two people should remain together."

Fate had nothing to do with Lauren being kidnapped, Nathan inwardly seethed. His temper was reaching a dangerous level. He had to get away from Fulepet before he said something that might endanger Lauren even more. She was here, or at least close by; he felt it in every pore in his body.

Listening to his instincts, he forced himself to bow. "The hour grows late. If you don't mind, I believe I'll join my wife."

"Yes, you'll want to resume the search for your dear sister early. Who knows, luck may be with you. The villagers may know something of her whereabouts."

The butler who'd shown Jo upstairs appeared in the doorway as if he'd been standing there all along.

"Patrik will show you the way." Fulepet took his empty glass and turned, moving deeper into the gloomy corner, his measured footsteps resonating like the brooding echo of a drum.

Before Nathan could escape the room, the marquess's voice slipped through the dark: "A word of warning, Darvill. Don't roam the halls tonight. The castle is old, and there are many hazards. I would hate to see you

or your"—he paused as if to add weight to his words—
"*wife* come to harm."

Nathan followed the butler into the entryway and up
the stone steps, his skin crawling with the need to run
past the old man. He'd be damned if he'd heed Fulepet's
warning. He intended to tear the castle apart, one room
at a time.

Lauren was here. She was here! And he wasn't going
to leave until he found her.

Wind whistled through cracks in the walls, threatening to douse the candle's weak flame. Where the draft
came from, Jo couldn't begin to guess. If she could
trust her sense of direction, she should be deep in the
bowels of the castle by now, far from any windows or
doors, beyond the reach of any breeze.

At least half an hour had passed since she'd left her
room, gripping her knife in one hand and the dripping
candle in the other. She'd kept to the walls, looking for
a way off the second floor that didn't involve the main
staircase. It only made sense that if Lauren was in the
castle, Fulepet wouldn't put Jo and Nathan anywhere
near her.

When she'd found a spiral staircase that seemed
carved from solid stone, winding down deeper and
deeper into the heart of the castle, she'd considered it
a good omen—until she'd begun the descent. Streams
of cobwebs hung from the walls, clinging to her cape,
her face, tangling in her hair. More than once she'd had
to stifle a startled curse, and will her pounding heart
to move out of her throat. Muttering oaths that would
have turned Nathan's ears red, she refused to give in
to the panic that dried her mouth and coated her palms
with sweat.

This was part of the adventure, a raid like any other.
Only on this raid, the walls inched closer with each
step until she couldn't move without brushing against

the cold, rough surface. Even the air seemed thinner, smelling old, musty and dank. She heard sounds of dripping water, the curl of shifting air, her own ragged breathing. If there were voices or people moving about, she couldn't hear them. Everything had narrowed down to the confining walls, the oppressive dark, the claustrophobic fear that she was trapped in a box.

With nothing but her lone candle to guide her, her eyes burned from staring hard into the pressing black space, trying to make out some shape, a door, a passageway, something besides the circular walls that descended alongside her.

Perhaps she should go back and wait for Nathan, she thought, feeling dizzy as she continued winding down and down. She discarded the idea. He would keep Fulepet occupied, giving her the perfect opportunity to find Lauren.

"Or become lost," she muttered.

Jo cursed again and used her knife to bat away ropy spiderwebs that floated before her like dull gray yarn. The air shifted, sweeping beneath her cape, chilling her legs and arms. She continued her slow descent, feeling the stone steps and the scattering of pebbles beneath her slippers, wondering if her next step would be a trick and she'd go plunging off into a bottomless pit.

All at once the walls pulled away, opening to a cavern black and endless. Holding the candle aloft, she realized it wasn't an abyss, but the bottom of the stairs. She would have sighed with relief, but her breath froze in her lungs. Faint light revealed the outline of heavy wooden doors coated with layers of mildew and grime. She moved deeper into the room and saw that the doors were set close together, one after the other, creating a wall along either side of her. They continued on, disappearing into a tunnel of black. Some had iron bars where small windows had been cut out. Others were solid, but all had enormous locks with metal rings for handles. If the doors opened to cells, and Jo had a sick feeling that they did, the rooms would hardly be more than the width of a man's shoulders.

"Please don't let me find Lauren down here," Jo whispered, then clenched her jaw as her words echoed down the corridor, turning her one voice into many.

She held her breath, listened to the dark, and heard only the drip of water, the buzz of warning in her mind. Nothing else. No one stirred, or shouted for her to remain where she was. No guards, no Fulepet or Philip de Maurier to stop her search. Releasing a shaky breath, she moved deeper into the chamber.

"Lauren," she whispered, but the name came out rough, choked, unrecognizable. Jo cleared her throat and tried again, though she didn't raise her voice too high. "Lauren, are you here?"

Nothing. No cries or whimpers or calls for help. Nothing.

If the girl was here, she could be asleep, or too weak to answer. If that was the case, it meant Jo would have to open and check each cell. She turned in a circle, searching the shadows, not caring for that option at all. But she had no other choice; she couldn't leave if there was the slightest chance Nathan's sister was being held in this hellhole.

Going to the first door on her left, she rose up on her toes to peer through the barred window, but it was too high for her to see inside, and the candle did nothing to pierce the murky dark. She held the knife and candle in one hand, gripped the round iron handle with the other and pulled, but the door didn't budge. Leaning back, she pulled harder, straining until her muscles burned. Finally the door gave with a groan and a mist of falling dust as it swung open wide.

Jo stumbled back. The candle's flame danced and flickered, almost going out before settling into a constant burn once more. Her pulse raced, hammering against her chest, the base of her throat. She pushed the door wider, stepped up to the threshold, and raised the taper.

Old straw, the color of mud, lay in shreds across the dirt-packed floor. Jo took another step closer, leaning into the chamber to better see. The walls to either side were no more than three feet apart, and were black and slick in the candle's glow. The air inside smelled of rot and mildew, of despair and even death. How could anyone survive, even for one day, being locked in such a horrid place, closed off with no light, no wind, the hope of freedom all but lost?

She could imagine the sound of the door banging shut, trapping the poor prisoner inside, the grinding of the key as it turned in the lock. Just the thought made her grip the doorway and draw in a lungful of rancid air.

Thick, heavy chains with iron cuffs were attached to the far back wall. They lay on the floor, half-buried in debris, unlocked and empty, as was the rest of the cell.

"Thank God," she whispered as relief washed through her. She closed her eyes, but only briefly. She wasn't finished. There were at least a dozen more cells to check before she knew for certain that Lauren wasn't here.

She heard a muffled sound, then the tap of falling pebbles. A chill grazed her neck, followed by a rush of goose bumps. She glanced to the side without turning her head, but couldn't see into the main room. Someone was behind her, watching her. She held her breath, felt her body go cold. Still holding the knife and candle together, she took the dagger in her free hand, tightening her grip, ready to turn and fight whoever stalked her. If it was Fulepet, so be it. But if it was de Maurier, then so much the better.

An arm shot around her waist, lifting her off her feet before she could move. Jo sliced her knife down and back to catch the man in the side. He clamped his hand around her wrist, jerking it up above her head. She struggled and pulled to free her arm. Her attacker's fingers tightened on her wrist, squeezing the bone. She cried out, the sound ricocheting throughout the room. He released her waist, dropping her to the floor. His hand pressed over her mouth, stopping the sound in midair.

Jo struggled to breathe, stiffening as he held her head tightly against his chest. Confined in her dress and cloak, with one hand trapped, the other holding the candle, she knew her options were few. But giving up wasn't one of them. She flung the candle behind her, hoping to catch the man's hair on fire. But the flame was snuffed out. Blackness swallowed the room, the cell, the door.

The cell! God, please don't let him lock me in that cell!

Panic surged through her limbs. She dug in with her feet, pushing, twisting in the man's hold, felt the skin on her arm burn where he held her. She faced him, shoved one-handed against his chest.

"Let me go!"

She stomped her heel on his instep, heard him grunt, felt him bend slightly at the waist. She rammed her elbow into his stomach, tried to wrench her other wrist free. But he held her, his grip turning to iron. He caught her free hand, forced her back against the open door.

"Stop—" he began.

Jo lifted her foot to kick him, but he flattened his body to hers, trapping her against the wood, her arms pinned at the sides of her head. Her breath came in harsh, burning pants. She had to get free, find the stairs, run, find Nathan!

"What in bloody hell do you think you're doing?" he demanded.

Jo caught her breath, recognizing the voice, the grating, *angry* voice. She stared hard into the pitch-black space. She couldn't see anything, no outlines, no shapes. But she felt his hands on her wrists, felt the length of his body locked against hers. Forcing her mind to focus and listen to her senses, she realized her mistake.

"Nath . . . Nathan, is that you?"

"Fortunately for you, yes."

She tugged her hands, and this time he released her. "Why didn't you say something instead of grabbing me from behind?" she demanded, fighting to calm her breathing. Clenching her fingers around the hilt of her knife, remembering she'd tried to stab her attacker, she added in a voice that trembled with fury, "I could have killed you."

"Which is why I restrained you first." His hand was on her face, warm and solid, cupping her cheek. "Did I hurt you?"

"You scared a few years off my life," she complained as her beating heart returned to as close to normal as it was likely to get while she remained in the dungeon. Her wrist throbbed but she ignored the ache. "I thought you were going to lock me in the cell."

He grunted and released her. "Perhaps I should; that way I'll know precisely where you are. I have only myself to blame, though. I knew you wouldn't stay in your room."

"Then you should have also known I would be trying to find Lauren," Jo argued, hating that she couldn't see his face.

Just then she heard the familiar striking sound of flint, then saw a beautiful flare of light as the thin taper he held caught and began to burn. Though his mouth was pressed into a thin line and worry darkened his eyes to stormy gray, she was relieved to see him. So relieved, she found it hard not to wrap her arms around his neck and press her face into his chest. She'd slit her own throat before admitting it, but feeling his arms around her right now would do wonders for settling her nerves.

Glancing away from him and ignoring the vulnerable feeling, she asked, "How did you find me?"

"It wasn't hard. I just had to think like a pirate." He reached down and retrieved the candle she'd thrown at him. He lit it, pushing the shadows farther back.

"Either I'm becoming too predictable," she commented dryly, "or you're more cunning than I thought. Perhaps you should join my crew?"

"Predictable would never describe you, Jo," he said, keeping his voice low as he checked the next cell.

She glanced warily at the stairs behind her. "Are you certain no one followed you?"

"I'm not certain of anything, except that Fulepet knows more than he's telling and that my sister is close by. But to answer your question, no, no one followed me. While searching for you I spotted Fulepet retiring to his room."

"Did he say anything more after I left, give some sort of clue to Lauren's whereabouts?"

Nathan shook his head. "It's just a feeling I have."

"A feeling I share." That earned her a startled look. Jo glanced down the dark passageway. "I still need to search the rest of these chambers."

"We won't find her here." Nathan handed her one taper.

"How can you be so sure?"

"Besides our passing, I doubt the stairwell has been used in years."

Jo hadn't thought about that, but then she had little experience with musty old castles. "There could be another way down here."

"I doubt it." Taking hold of her elbow, he led her to the stairs. "There are a hundred other places Fulepet could be hiding her, so there's no time to waste. I don't suppose you'd wait in your room while I search for Lauren?"

"No, I don't suppose I would."

Nathan stopped on the first step, turning to look down at her. "Then stay by my side. Fulepet isn't a fool. He knows we're up to something. He suspects you aren't my wife."

Jo wasn't surprised. She doubted that Fulepet's soulless black eyes missed anything. "What else did he tell you?"

"He admitted knowing Philip, but claimed he hadn't seen him in some time. If it's as Rubin Sweeney said and de Maurier was staying here, then Fulepet knows I met Philip yesterday."

"He's covering for him."

"Exactly." Nathan tucked a loose strand of her hair behind her ear. His frown became even more severe. "Which is why I regret bringing you with me. Fulepet was never a congenial man, but if he's conspiring with Philip, he's not only desperate, he's dangerous."

"I can take care of myself." Yet her heart fluttered against her chest. The worry for his sister that never left his eyes was still there, but something else had joined it: concern for her. Jo tried telling herself it was nothing, a play of flickering light and shadow. Certainly nothing more.

But what if he did care for me?

Jo stopped herself from asking any more "what if" questions. She was here for Lauren's sake, and Nathan's. Not because she felt something for him, and not because she hoped that he might feel something for her in return.

"I don't want to see you hurt." His voice was barely a whisper, yet she heard every word. "Promise me you'll do whatever I say."

She arched a brow, a futile attempt to shrug off any hidden meaning. "You mean follow your orders?"

He cupped her face in his palm, running the pad of his thumb across her cheek. "Promise me."

Don't pretend to care about me, she wanted to tell

him. *And don't make me care about you!* It undercut her objective, her resolve to find Lauren—and then walk away from them both for good.

Sixteen

Nathan led Jo through one winding hallway after another, up stairwells meant for servants and into rooms that had been emptied of furniture before being sealed off and abandoned. The dark smelled of age and dust and ghosts from a time long past. Everywhere they searched, they found little sign of life and nothing of Lauren.

When they'd chanced upon a ballroom draped in cobwebs and grime, Nathan had wondered again what dilemma had befallen Fulepet. Whatever had happened—poor investments, gambling debts, war— it had been severe enough to cause the downfall of a prosperous family seven generations old.

He had no idea how much time had passed since they'd left the dungeon. One hour? Two? Six? They'd yet to cross paths with the butler, a maid or a guard. At any moment he expected to turn a corner and find Fulepet, or possibly Philip, with Lauren in his arms, a gun aimed at her head.

With each room they encountered and searched, a new battle of relief and anxiety began inside him. He knew his sister was close, yet the odds of finding her seemed to grow more impossible with each step he took.

"She's not here." Joining him in the hall after searching one of a dozen bedchambers, Jo held her waning candle aloft and looked farther down the passageway. Soft light warmed her cheeks to cream, shadowed the curve of her jaw, brightened the resolve shining in her eyes.

She seemed tireless, and almost as determined as he to search every nook and crevice—and just as frustrated that they'd found no sign of his sister.

"Perhaps she's not in the castle," Jo reflected as they moved to the next room. "If Fulepet owns cottages for his tenants, he could be hiding her in one of them."

"Possibly. If we fail to find her tonight, I'll learn the whereabouts of his cottages and search them tomorrow."

Jo stopped and stared at him, indecision darkening her eyes. She started to say something, but paused, then snapped her mouth shut. He wondered what she'd been about to say—that he couldn't search Fulepet's estate alone if he hoped to find Lauren, that she would stay and help him?

If that had been her intent, he didn't blame her for not making the offer. He wouldn't have accepted it if she had, in any case. He didn't trust Fulepet, and not knowing where Philip was hiding made the situation only that much more dangerous. The sooner she was safe aboard the *Sea Witch*, the better.

Safe, and away from me. Nathan pushed the uneasy thought away. He didn't have time to think about how Jo's leaving would bother him. She affected him on a level no other woman ever had, and as crazy as it sounded, he knew he would miss her once she was gone. But that was something he'd have to contemplate later.

"I'll take the next room on the right." Jo started off again. "You take the left."

Nathan heard a shuffling noise, faint, but growing louder in the passageway behind them. He caught her hand and pulled her toward the closest door. Urging her inside a bedroom, he shut the door behind them. They blew out their candles.

"What is it?" she asked in a faint whisper.

"Someone's coming." Nathan eased the door ajar so he could see into the dark hallway. Jo gripped his arm, watching him, but she didn't say anything more. Within seconds light flooded the corridor and the shuffling became footsteps, slow, evenly paced, unhurried.

A man dressed in black clothing and carrying a lantern came into view. Nathan shut the door, waited a moment, then eased it open again. Light moved along the papered walls, gradually fading. Easing out into the hall, Nathan watched the man walk toward the end of the corridor. Black hair, dark clothing, his gait slow and methodical—it could be none other than Marquess Fulepet. But where was he going? His bedchamber was in another part of the castle. Could Lauren be so close? There were only a few more rooms. . . .

Fulepet stopped at the farthest door, opened it and disappeared inside.

Apprehension, fear, anger—they all pulsed through Nathan's veins, demanding he pursue Fulepet, confront him now. But he knew he couldn't barge in blind, with no idea as to what or who was there or what he'd find. If Lauren was inside, there could be men of Rubin Sweeney's ilk guarding her. Acting rashly would only endanger his sister's life. And he'd caused her enough harm already. He stepped back into the room, and felt more than saw Jo's questioning gaze.

"That was Fulepet," he whispered, feeling as if an iron band were tightening around his chest.

"Do we go after him?" Her voice was calm, forceful, though edged with impatience.

"No." He surprised himself by wrapping his arm around her waist and drawing her to his side. She didn't resist, giving him her strength, for which he was grateful. He pressed his lips to her temple and stared over her head into the shrouded room, his thoughts remaining on the man, and hopefully the woman, down the hall. "Now we wait."

Time had slowed to the sound of their breathing, the creak of wood as the floors and overhead beams settled around them, the rustle of Jo's gown as she fidgeted at his side. Nathan kept watch through the crack in the door for any sign of movement, a glimmer of light, the tread of Fulepet's footsteps. The chilled air had long since seeped through Nathan's coat and vest, soaked through his skin, numbed muscles taut with the need for action.

But he forced himself to wait.

Jo had remained close by his side, huddled in her cloak. He could feel her glaring at the door, sense her eagerness to leave the empty bedroom and confront Fulepet. If she disagreed with his decision to wait for the marquess to reappear before they searched the far room, she didn't say so. But she'd refused to resheath her knife when Nathan had suggested it. Moonlight streaming through a window reflected off its steel blade, reminding him that while she might not have a man's strength, she knew how to defend herself.

He touched the pistol tucked into the waist of his pants and prayed it wouldn't come to that.

But he couldn't delay much longer. If Lauren was being held in the other room, why was Fulepet there? What was he doing to her? And where the hell was Philip?

Or was he wasting his time altogether? Could Philip have already followed through with his threat and put Lauren on a slave ship? Nathan couldn't bear to consider the possibility. But Jo's men were watching the docks; if Philip tried to leave, they would apprehend him.

When he found Lauren, and he swore he would, he wanted to take her from the castle without raising an alarm; she'd suffered enough, and he didn't want to openly challenge Fulepet or de Maurier now, and risk endangering her life even more. But he might not have any other choice; leaving his sister at their mercy another moment went against every instinct he possessed.

"I have an idea," Jo whispered, her face a study of concentration in the faint light.

Nathan gave her credit for waiting so long to offer a suggestion. "And that would be?"

"We return to the *Sea Witch* and gather my crew. Fulepet has no defenses in place. We can return here in force and take the castle. Stop all this sneaking around."

"I thought you were going to sail for England at sunup?"

Her chin tilted. "I still could if you do as I suggest."

"Thank you." He reached up and stroked her soft cheek, an act that comforted him as much as it stirred him. "But there's no need to risk your men. I believe this will soon be over."

"Nathan, what is he—"

"Shh." Light and shadows danced over the walls, becoming brighter. He closed the door, leaving only a slight crack. The glow from the lantern flared as Fulepet came abreast of them, shining off his slick black hair while washing his face of all color.

Then he was gone around the corner, hopefully returning to his room. *Unless he intends to check on us.* If that was the case, Nathan had to hurry.

He opened the door and entered the hall, heading for the far room with Jo close on his heels. Her skirts rustled as loud as a barroom shout in the quiet. For once, he wished she were wearing her breeches and boots.

Drawing his pistol, anticipating the door to be locked, he turned the knob and raised a brow in surprise. With a soft click, the door opened. He expected to see a dust-filled chamber, unfurnished like the rest, or Lauren asleep on a cot, her beautiful face bathed in cold moonlight.

Instead he saw a cavern as dark as the dungeon they'd left below.

"Light a candle," Jo said, holding hers out for him.

He retrieved the flint from his pocket, and within a minute a flame glowed like a beacon in the stifling dark.

"Look." She held the candle aloft, revealing not a room, but a set of stairs winding upward, where they disappeared. She started to go in.

Nathan caught her arm and held her back. "After me."

Ignoring her disgruntled look, he started up the steps. They were as narrow and steep as the stairs he'd taken to find Jo earlier, only these had been swept clean of spiderwebs and filth. He continued spiraling upward, one step after another, one floor after another, until he felt a burn in his thighs. He wondered how Jo was faring, but he didn't stop to ask. He heard her behind him, her breath slightly louder than his own.

Finally they reached a narrow landing. A hallway extended off to his left, where it curved, revealing a faint light. The passageway to his right was dark and quiet. Opting for the shadows, he turned right, stopping at a vacant alcove made of rough stone that, if he were to guess, had begun crumbling during the previous century.

Giving the candle to Jo, he motioned for her to stay back. With his pistol raised, he retraced his steps down the hallway slowly, careful not to make a sound, not knowing what or whom to expect. Reaching the turn in the wall, he peered around the corner. A lantern hung from a hook in the ceiling, illuminating a heavy oak door that undoubtedly led to a tower room. *And Lauren?* A man with the thick hairy arms of a blacksmith sat on a stool with a gun balanced on his lap.

He held a thin blade in his beefy hands, his attention focused on the piece of wood he was whittling.

Nathan's pulse hammered against his temples. He leaned back against the wall, then returned to the alcove. "There's a guard."

"Lauren must be there."

He held his pistol up to the candle and checked the chamber. "You wait here. If all goes well I'll return shortly, with my sister."

"Is he armed?"

"Just do as I say, Jo."

"We don't want to alert the rest of the household."

"I don't intend to."

"Hold this." She shoved the taper into his free hand, then lifted her skirt up to her thigh and resheathed her knife. Taking the candle back, she smiled and said, "Thank you."

Before Nathan could guess her intent, she hurried past him, calling out, "Hello, hello, is anyone there?"

"Damn it, Jo," Nathan said under his breath. He went after her, but stopped when he heard the scrape of wood, then a clatter as if the guard had overturned his footstool. He raised his pistol, but couldn't possibly fire it in the narrow corridor with Jo in the way.

"Who goes there?" the man barked in a grizzly voice.

"Oh, finally I've found someone," Jo said, her voice turning as shrill as a flustered female's. She paused and glanced over her shoulder at Nathan, her eyes narrowing with a silent message.

He understood her meaning all too well, and vowed to wring her neck later if they escaped alive. But he backed into the alcove, holding his gun, feeling useless and fuming with fury.

"Sir," she said, "oh, thank the Lord, I found you. I'm in need of aid."

"Who are ye?" the man asked, his voice as gruff and unforgiving as the stone walls.

"I'm Lady Darvill, and I'm as lost as a mouse in a labyrinth." She laughed, though she sounded breathless and shaken. "I feel like such a ninny, really. I left my room—"

"Ye shouldn't be wandering the castle."

Nathan imagined the man training his gun on Jo with one hand while fingering his thin blade with the other. Damn it, he couldn't stand there, yet if he moved and tried to shoot the guard, Jo might be hit in the crossfire.

"I know that now, believe me. But I was in need . . . well . . . in need of the privy, if you must know . . . and, well, I became lost. I couldn't find my way back to my room. The harder I tried, the more lost I became."

"Well, your room ain't up 'ere."

"I realize that," Jo said, sounding miffed. Then she paused, and Nathan could almost hear her scheming mind at work. "If you'd be so kind as to show me the way, I'd be forever in your debt."

"I can't leave my post."

"But it will take only a few moments."

"You'll 'ave to find the way on your own, lady."

"Then I'm sure to be lost until morning." After a weighty pause, she added, "If you can't leave right now I suppose I could wait until your duty here is finished."

"Ye can't stay 'ere with me."

"Well, I'm not going to wander through the castle alone again. Who knows where I'll end up? The moat could be next."

"We ain't got a moat."

Jo sighed, a small huff that seemed more annoyed than distressed to Nathan's ears. "I'm sure Marquess Fulepet will reward you for taking care of one of his guests."

"I already told ye—"

"Please," Jo said, softening the word to a velvety plea. Nathan wondered if she'd tilted her head and smiled her alluring smile. Hearing the guard's next words, he felt sure she had.

"Ah, bleed'n hell. I can't 'ave ye yacking away up 'ere with me. I'll take ye tae your room, but ye better not lag behind, 'cause if ye do, I'll not stop tae go look'n for ye."

"Oh, thank you, thank you. I'm in the Crystal Suite. In the east wing. Are you familiar with it?"

Nathan waited in the alcove, listening to the fading shuffle of footsteps and Jo's chatter. He still couldn't believe her audacity at luring the guard away. The next time he saw her, he'd definitely wring her neck; then he'd kiss her.

Leaving the alcove, he hurried down the hall. He had five minutes—ten at most—before the guard returned. Reaching the door, he tucked his pistol into his waistband. An iron bolt driven into the thick-beamed door frame secured the door instead of a lock. If he'd needed a key, he'd have had no choice but to break the lock by shooting it—which would have brought the guard running back for certain.

Sliding the bolt free, he eased the door open. Light sliced into a circular room, revealing stone-block walls, two arrow loops for windows, a wooden floor swept clean and a narrow cot, empty except for a rumpled blanket.

He stepped farther into the room, searching the shadows. She had to be here. She had to be. They were running out of places to search. "Lauren?"

The blow came hard across his shoulders, stunning him, knocking him forward, almost to his knees.

"I warned you I'd tolerate no more!"

Nathan caught his balance and spun around just as a wooden club shot from the dark. He raised his arm to ward off the blow, but shifted and caught the club instead, jerking it out of his assailant's hands.

Lauren stumbled forward into the light, her black hair a tangled rope around her face and shoulders, her eyes narrowed, half-wild. Then they widened with disbelief.

Her ruby-colored gown was ripped at the shoulder; the skirt was little more than shredded rags. "Nathan—"

He tossed the stick aside and gripped her shoulders. "Are you all right?"

"Nathan." She looked him over, frowning as if she couldn't believe what she saw. "You're here. You're—"

"I've come to take you home."

She looked up at him, her eyes suddenly shimmering with unshed tears. Then she leaped up, throwing her arms around his neck and burying her face in his chest. "You came. I knew you would. I knew it. I told them they wouldn't get away with holding me for ransom. I told them. I told . . ."

Nathan held her tight, listening to her babbling, the wonderful, teary sound of her voice. Relief flooded him in a staggering wave. The fear that had gripped his heart for two agonizing weeks finally loosened its hold. He still had to get her home, but nothing would stop him, not now that he'd found her.

Lauren released him and stepped away. Then she did the unbelievable. She struck his chest with her clenched fists and demanded, "What took you so long?"

"I . . . Lauren . . ." Color rode high in her cheeks, and her eyes glittered with anger. *Anger?* "I came as soon as I could."

"I've been here for weeks." She propped one hand on her hip; the other she pressed to her forehead. "I thought I was going to have to find a way to escape on my own."

He could hardly believe the words or the temper coming from his once amiable sister. What had Fulepet done to her? Guilt pinched the muscles between his shoulder blades. He took her by the hand and led her out the door. "I don't have time to explain. We must hurry."

She followed without another word, keeping close to his side. Taking the lantern from the hook, he led the way down the winding stairs, praying with each step that he didn't meet the guard on his way back up. He wouldn't hesitate to shoot the man, but that was something he didn't want Lauren to see.

Reaching the hallway without being intercepted, Nathan decided not to test his luck. He extinguished the lantern and left it in a corner.

"What are you doing?" Lauren whispered. "We need the light. I've seen this castle. It's enormous. We'll never find our way out."

"Just stay close to me." He kept hold of her hand, pulling her behind him, stopping every few feet to listen. The corridor was quiet, lined with empty rooms and cold air that chilled the sweat beading on his brow.

He retraced the way he'd come with Jo, turning down long passageways, staying close to the walls, alert for a place to hide in case they encountered the guard. By the time he reached the staircase that would take him down to the second-floor landing—and hopefully to Jo—the muscles in his back were corded knots. He paused in the shadows.

"How much farther?" Lauren asked.

The stubbornness in her tone surprised him; he'd never heard it before. He'd expected his sister to crumble into a fit of tears once he found her, cling to him, collapse into a faint. He didn't know what to make of the change, but he was grateful for it.

"Once we reach the second-floor gallery," he told her, "we'll go down to the east wing. Jo's there—"

"Who?"

"Someone who helped me find you," he whispered. "I have a carriage waiting and a ship that will take us to—"

Lauren clamped her hand over his mouth. In the dim light he saw her shake her head; then he heard footsteps coming hard and fast, followed by the erratic glow of a lantern. He pulled Lauren deeper into a shadowed nook, pressing her back against the wall.

The guard vaulted up the stairs and ran past them

without a sideways glance. Once the man vanished from sight, Nathan ground out a curse. As fast as the man was running, they had only a minute, maybe two, before he discovered Lauren was missing.

"Hurry." He raced down the stairs, catching Lauren when she tripped and fell. As he reached the gallery leading to the east wing a bell erupted, echoing a shrill alarm throughout the deserted halls.

He looked down the darkened passageway. Jo would surely be there in their room, waiting for him.

"Nathan, we have to go! They're coming!" Lauren tugged on his sleeve, then lifted her skirts and started down the stairs to the entryway without him.

He watched his sister run, then looked back into the hallway. "Jo."

Indecision ripped through him. He couldn't leave her. But he couldn't reach her in time and still hope to get Lauren safely away. He clenched his teeth, feeling something inside him twist. "Jo."

"Nathan!" Lauren cried from the foyer. "Hurry!"

He turned his back on the gallery, on Jo, and leaped down the stairs two at a time, damning himself with every step he took. He'd come back for her; he would. He'd come back.

Seventeen

The carriage was gone.

Nathan slid to a stop on the terrace and searched the courtyard for the horses he'd left tied in the front drive.

"What's wrong?" Lauren gripped his coatsleeve and looked back through the open doors behind them. In a voice breathless and panic-filled, she cried, "Nathan, I hear them. Where's your carriage? We've got to go!"

"It's gone."

Her fingers dug into his arm. "What do you mean, gone?"

He took her by the hand and hurried along the drive that circled the keep. Which direction were the stables? He looked from one dark vista to the other, where wind drove thin clouds across the setting moon, shadowing the land. Fulepet had to have a horse. But searching for the stables, then bridling a mount required time he didn't have.

"We'll have to make for the forest beyond the wall," he told her. "We can use the trees for cover."

Without another word, Lauren took off down the driveway, her skirts hiked up around her knees. Nathan caught up with her and pulled her off the main path and along the base of an outbuilding. He led the way, but slowed his strides to match his sister's labored gait. Wind whistled over the grounds and around corners, moaning over rooftops. Leaves and dirt swirled against their legs. His breath plumed like cold smoke ahead of him. With every step he expected to hear the sounds of men shouting, the report of a gun, the frantic bark of dogs being set loose on a hunt.

Reaching the gatehouse, he stopped to glance behind him. Lights flickered, then vanished in the second-floor windows, but as yet no one had emerged outside. Lauren fell against him, clinging, panting for each breath.

"We'll have to find a place to hide." Nathan held her close. "You'll never make it to the ship."

"I can," she said, gasping for air. "I don't care how far it is, I'm not staying near this place."

The fear in Lauren's voice made Nathan clench his jaw. The castle towered like a dark shadow against a darker sky. Jo was still inside, waiting for him to join her. What would she think when he didn't arrive? Would she hate him? Curse herself for trying to help him? Had they found her yet?

Nathan ran his hand through his hair, feeling a new kind of fear that eclipsed what he'd felt for Lauren. What would Fulepet do when he discovered Jo? *I can take care of myself.* He prayed that were so, but he knew her words were more bluff than truth. But knowing Jo, if Fulepet found her, she'd fight before being taken captive. And this time, without her crew to protect her back, she was sure to lose.

"I shouldn't have left her." Yet even as he said the words, he knew he'd had no choice. He had to get Lauren away first. He'd gather Jackson and the rest of the *Sea Witch* crew and return for their captain. But first he had to get away.

Taking Lauren's hand, he pushed away from the granite wall and led her through the arched stone gate. With nothing to stop the wind, icy, needlelike gusts stung their faces and necks. He veered off the main road, heading down an embankment for a line of bare, leafless trees. It wouldn't provide much cover, but it was all they had.

They pushed through clumps of nettles that tore at their clothes. Lauren stumbled, banging down hard on her knees. She cried out and tried to rise.

Nathan lifted her in his arms and felt the wound in his side threaten to tear. He started off again, only to pause when he heard the rattle of wood and metal and felt the ground rumble beneath his feet. *Horses!*

The trees were too far for him to reach. Fulepet would find them within moments. Nathan glanced back at the gate just as a team of horses pulling a carriage burst through at a dead run.

The driver in the high seat flicked the reins, her cape whipping behind her.

"Jo!" The wind slapped her name back into his face. He held tight to Lauren and pushed through the brush, heading for the embankment even as Jo darted past him. "Jo!"

Her head snapped around. She pulled back on the reins and stood up in the carriage, searching for him in the dark. The horses pranced, tugging at their bits as if they felt the urgency to be away. "Nathan? Where are you?"

"Here!"

There were shouts from the castle, and he saw torches dancing in the wind as men hurried about the yard.

He ran the last few feet to the carriage. Jo climbed down from her seat. Without a word she opened the passenger door, standing aside as he helped Lauren in.

"You ride with her," Jo ordered. "I'll drive."

"No, you stay with my sister."

"Nathan—"

"I don't know how you escaped, but I'm glad you did."

"I told you I could take care of myself." She quirked a brow. "You should have believed me."

He caught her by the shoulders, hauled her to him and planted a fast, hard kiss on her mouth, just as he swore he would. He still might wring her neck later, but for now all he felt was an outpouring of relief at the sight of her. "Get in the carriage."

"What was that for?"

"For being you." He turned her and shoved. "Now get in."

Nathan bolted into the high seat, while Jo did as she was told. Hearing the door click shut, he gathered the reins and spurred the horses into a run. The wind beat his face, but he hardly felt it. Lauren was safe.

And so was Jo. His chest squeezed with a pressure too foreign to name. By God, so was Jo.

The sounds of creaking wood of water lapping against the hull as it plowed through the ocean's swells comforted Jo like the voice of an old friend. The smells of sea spray and the open night air rushing through a nearby hatchway were just as welcome. The companionway where she stood outside Jackson's cabin might be tight, confining, but it was swept clean, and familiar, and hers. Never had she been so relieved to feel the lull of the deck beneath her feet, hear the crew's reassuring voices as they pulled lines, raised sails, stood watch for signs of trouble.

During the mad race from Fulepet's chateau, through the sleepy streets of Saint-Nazaire, Jo had reassured Lauren that all would be well, though she wasn't sure the girl had heard her. During their reckless drive through the dark, she'd seemed lost within herself, repeatedly looking out the window as the road vanished behind them, undoubtedly expecting to find Fulepet, or perhaps de Maurier, in close pursuit.

Reaching the harbor, Jo had sent one of the three crewmen she'd left behind with a dinghy to tell the others guarding the harbor that it was time to leave. As they rowed across the ink black cove toward the *Sea Witch* and safety, the girl hadn't uttered a word. She'd sat beside her brother, huddled in his coat, her face colorless in the moonlight.

Jo could only imagine how Fulepet and Philip had abused her. Anger, frustration, the sense of injustice—all familiar emotions—ran through Jo's mind, making her hands shake. She knew Lauren must feel lost, vulnerable, tainted, much as did the orphaned children Jo was trying to help. Lauren might not need food or clothing, but she undoubtedly needed a friend right now. Too well, Jo recalled Philip's taunt about Lauren not being a virgin any longer. If that were true . . . Jo drew a deep breath, determined to help the girl.

Dressed in her wool pants and shirt, with her hair in a braid down her back, Jo held a lit taper in one hand and knocked on Jackson's door, the cabin Lauren had been given during their return trip to England.

There was no answer, but Jo hadn't expected one. She lifted the latch, opened the door and stepped inside, bringing light into the narrow room. Still wearing her filthy gown and Nathan's coat, Lauren sat on Jackson's bunk, her knees drawn up to her chest as she stared out the small porthole.

"I prefer the dark, if you don't mind," Lauren said, giving Jo a cursory glance before turning once again to the window.

Shutting the door behind her, Jo blew out the candle. Darkness floated in, sealing the room, but it was a comforting dark, not the stifling blackness she'd experienced while inside Chateau de Noir Bois.

"When I reach Winstone Castle," Lauren said in a low, empty voice that bothered Jo, "I don't think I'll ever leave it again. Do you think Philip will come after me?"

"Unless he's a fool, he wouldn't dare set one toe in England for fear of having it chopped off."

A smile tweaked the girl's mouth. She ran her fingers

through her loose hair, the color much like her brother's—a shade darker than the shadowed room. "I'm ashamed to admit it, but I once imagined myself in love with him."

"You have nothing to be ashamed of."

"So Nathan has said."

Jo wanted to move closer, take the girl's hand and offer comfort—it was what Morgan would have done—but it had been so long since she'd consoled anyone, she wasn't sure how to go about it, so she stayed by the door. "Not all men are deceitful."

"No, my brother gives testament that some are indeed honorable." She glanced at Jo with eyes that held no trace of the naivete Nathan had claimed she possessed. Bathed in moonlight, they were eyes much like Grace's, soulful and world-weary, trapped in an angelic face.

"Your brother refused to rest until he'd found you."

Lauren smiled, yet there was a faint brittleness around her mouth. "I knew he would come, though it frightened me to think about him confronting Philip."

The tenderhearted shouldn't be forced to face the harsh realities of life, Jo thought. *Some people should be excluded from having their dreams ripped away.*

"Nathan told me you're a pirate."

"I am."

"And that you attacked his ship and stole his gold. Yet you helped him rescue me. Why would you do such a thing?"

Jo wondered if he'd left out the part about her nearly killing him. If he hadn't mentioned it, she certainly wasn't going to.

"When Nathan told me about de Maurier kidnapping you, I had to help. The way he described you, you sounded very much like one of my sisters."

"Whatever your reason, I'm grateful you did." Lauren faced the window again. There was barely a trace of moon left; the dawn would soon bring the sun, shedding light over everything that had happened.

Jo took a deep breath, not knowing how to phrase her next question. Tact had never been her strong point, so she decided to blurt out what worried her most. "Did de Maurier force himself on you?"

"What?" Lauren turned her dark, troubled eyes to Jo.

"Did he?" Jo's nerves bunched beneath her skin. If she was this concerned about a woman she hardly knew, she could only imagine the fury and guilt Nathan was suffering right now. "Philip said you were no longer . . . that is—"

"What does it matter? My reputation is ruined whether he . . . he . . ." Tightening her arms around her legs, she said, "Whether he did *that* or not."

"Your reputation?" Jo asked, frowning in confusion. "What does your reputation matter? You're alive."

"Alive." Lauren said the word as if it confused her. "I'll be shunned by my friends, doomed to be an outcast. What kind of life is that?"

"Only a few people know you were kidnapped." Jo thought about her brother-in-law, Daniel, and Mr. Fitzhugh, the banker. "I'm sure none of them will speak of this to anyone."

"A scandal like this is too delicious to keep secret for long." In the dim light, Lauren's features hardened as her anger took hold. "Besides, you and your crew know what happened to me."

Jo smiled, liking the fire she heard in the girl's voice. "But we're pirates. Who would we tell? And for that matter, who would listen?"

Lauren studied her for a moment. "You're not like any pirate I've ever heard about, except one. Morgan Tremayne. Lord Tremayne's wife. She was a pirate once. I've never met her, but I've heard she's rather unusual."

Jo stiffened at hearing herself so closely linked with

Morgan. If Lauren could tie the two of them together so easily, now that the danger was over she knew it wouldn't be long before Nathan made the connection, too.

Steering the conversation back to her original question, she asked, "Did de Maurier molest you?"

Lauren's expression turned rebellious. "I told you it doesn't matter."

"It does," Jo insisted. "Once you're safe in England, your brother intends to go after Philip."

"No! No, he can't. He could be hurt or killed." Lauren scooted off the bed. Even in the pale light Jo could see that sudden tears had replaced all signs of defiance. "I have to stop him. Philip's insane. There's no telling what he'll do now."

Jo couldn't agree with the girl more. She didn't want Nathan facing de Maurier again either. He had been lucky to escape with a bullet scratch for a wound; he might not be so lucky the next time, especially if Jo wasn't there to help him. He had his sister back—that should be enough, but she knew it wouldn't be, not for Nathan. *He'll want revenge, just as I did for Robby's death.*

Jo closed her eyes briefly and sighed, not wanting to question her own motives, but knowing she'd have to sooner or later. But first she had to stop Nathan from hunting down de Maurier. If Lauren hadn't been assaulted, perhaps she could persuade him to let the London magistrates handle the matter.

"Did de Maurier hurt you?" Jo asked again.

"Not in the way you mean." A sob caught in her chest. "He told me things, threatened to hurt me, but he never touched me. I promise you, he didn't. I couldn't stand it if Nathan thought he did."

Jo took the girl by her shoulders and urged her to sit on the bed. "Let me talk to him. Your tears will only upset him more."

Lauren wrapped her arms around her own waist, hugging herself tighter into Nathan's coat. "If . . . if you're sure you can convince him."

Jo nodded, though she wasn't sure of anything.

The sun crested the horizon, rising from the sea like a cool, white disk, shooting streaks of misty purple and gold into the night. Clouds raced overhead with the wind, heading south while the *Sea Witch* struggled to keep a northerly course.

Pacing the deck, hardly feeling the bracing cold, Nathan watched Jo's crew hoist endless yards of line, each man working in unison, hand over hand, backs bent into their task, their goal to gain as much speed as possible.

"Rise tack and sheets!" Jackson shouted from the forecastle, his blond hair blowing loose around his squared jaw.

As if his voice alone had willed it, the sails unfurled and slowly climbed the three towering masts. Cold wind filled the sails, snapping the fabric taut. The quarter-master spun the wheel, turning the bow so the worst of the gusts hit the larboard side before sweeping over deck and man alike. The hull groaned and keeled beneath Nathan's feet. Jackson issued another order, which sent smaller sails skimming up thick poles. The *Sea Witch* shifted into a steady position as she sped forward, taking the restless waves with ease.

Nathan faced the stern just as the shores of Saint-Nazaire faded from view. The knots tightening his muscles loosened, allowing him to draw a full breath. Lauren was alive and safe. He repeated the phrase over and over again in his mind until he could unclench his hands and release the last of his fury.

The first—and most important—part of his nightmare was over. Once Lauren was back at Winstone Castle, he'd return to France and complete his vow to bring his sister's kidnapper to justice.

In the meantime, though, there were other issues he intended to resolve, beginning with Jo, the Emerald of London.

He hadn't seen the pirate captain above deck since they'd sailed out of the cove, which surprised him. He'd come to know Jo well enough during the past two weeks to know she didn't leave the work to others. Nathan headed for the hatchway leading to her cabin. She'd had little rest during the past two days, and was probably asleep, but he'd waited long enough to question her.

Taking the ladder to the lower deck, Nathan paused on the bottom rail just as Jo came out of his sister's cabin. He descended the rest of the way, his body blocking the light and throwing her into shadow. "My sister is supposed to be resting."

Jo glanced at the closed door behind her. "I need to talk to you."

"I want to speak with you as well, though what I have to discuss might be better done in private." Frowning, he extended his arm. "After you."

He followed her down the companionway, each step a challenge to keep pace with the roll of the ship. Once they were closed inside her cabin, heat soaked into his clothes, warming his hands and face as if he were sitting before a fire. He spotted half a dozen buckets filled with cannonballs placed around the room. Holding his hand over one and feeling the rise of heat, he looked at Jo in surprise.

Her mouth quirked as if she were resisting a smile. "Not your typical bed warmers, but they work." Pouring them both a tumbler of brandy from the decanter she kept on a wire-bound shelf, she asked, "Do you want to go first, or should I?"

"Ladies first," he said, because he wanted to know why she'd been with Lauren.

Jo arched a russet brow and handed him his drink. "We both know I'm no lady."

You may not be a lady, Nathan thought, letting his gaze roam over her braided hair and men's clothing, but you're incredible all the same.

"I thought it important that I speak with your sister."

Nathan felt his muscles tighten. "She needs her rest."

"She needs a lot of things, but rest isn't one of them."

"What do you mean by that?"

"I mean your sister isn't as helpless as you think she is." Jo leaned against the desk, crossed her legs at the ankles and took a sip of her liquor. "Or at least she isn't any longer. She's strong. Given time, she'll recover."

"Once she's home she'll have all the time she needs."

"There are other things that concern her that I think you should know about."

"Her reputation. I know. I've been giving some thought to that."

"Bloody hell," Jo ground out, standing up to top off her drink. "The girl could have become a slave or died, and you're both worried about what people might say!"

"For myself, I don't give a damn what people think, but for Lauren . . ." Nathan placed his drink on the desk, then stared down at Jo. "I don't want her to suffer any more than she already has. If her peers learn de Maurier kidnapped her, I know how my sister will react. She'd never show her face in public again. She'd never visit her friends, or do her charity work, or even hope for marriage."

Jo sighed with disgust. "I suppose that's another difference between our classes. My peers wouldn't shun me; they'd hold a celebration because I'd returned home safely."

"Then I envy you your friends."

A smile softened her mouth as she returned his gaze.

The green of her eyes deepened with swirls of emotion. "There's something else you need to know."

A chill went down his spine. He'd wanted to question his sister about what had been done to her, but forcing her to relive the last few weeks so soon after her release seemed too cruel. "And that is?"

"She wasn't harmed . . . sexually."

Nathan's knees nearly gave out. He gripped the back of a chair. He'd been so afraid . . . not knowing how to help her if she'd been molested.

Jo didn't give him time to let the information sink in before adding, "She also doesn't want you to return for de Maurier."

Nathan glanced at the door, imagining Lauren huddled in a room down the hall. She'd been courageous while escaping the castle, but once in the dinghy she'd withdrawn, not speaking or meeting his gaze. He'd realized then that the artless girl he'd helped raise no longer existed.

If for no other reason, Nathan would make Philip pay for shattering Lauren's innocent view of the world. "She can't think I'll let him go unpunished."

"What she thinks is that you might get killed trying to bring him to justice." Jo held up her hand when he started to object. "If you're going to tell me it's a risk you have to take, I'm going to advise you to reconsider."

"You're going to *advise* me?"

"He isn't worth your life, Nathan."

On impulse, he reached for her necklace and pulled the toy soldier from inside her shirt. "But claiming revenge for your brother's death is worth *your* life?"

Jo reached for the toy, but he closed his fingers over it. Wrapping the leather rope around his fist, he drew her up against him. "Answer me, Jo. Do you lie awake at night wishing there were something you could do to right that wrong? Is that why you turned to piracy?"

"This isn't about me. It's about you and Lauren—"

"You became a part of this the day you attacked the *Lady's Luck.*"

"I already told Lauren that neither of you has to worry about my talking and jeopardizing her reputation. I'm a pirate, remember? It's not as if I mingle with your kind."

"No," he said, releasing her necklace. He drew a steadying breath, then ran his thumb across her cheek. "It isn't as if I'd meet you at a masked ball disguised as the Emerald of London, now, is it?"

She sucked in a breath. He waited for her to deny the assumption, tell him another lie, maybe even call for Jackson to lock him away now that he knew her secret.

She clamped her jaw and tilted her chin. "When did you realize who I am?"

"Before we left for Fulepet's estate."

Anger flared bright green in her eyes. "Why didn't you say something?"

"And ruin your charade? If I had mentioned my suspicions, you'd have tossed me overboard, then sailed away before I could learn who you really are."

"There's nothing more about me you need to know."

"I happen to disagree." Nathan took her drink and set it aside. He placed his hands on either side of her, trapping her against the desk. "You pretended to be a lady at Daniel Tremayne's mask, which is strange in itself. Daniel's wife is a pirate. Do you know her?"

"I've never met her."

"But you know Daniel. How interesting."

"Get out of my way, Nathan," she warned.

"Not until I have my answers. Somehow you learned I was to sail to France with a cache of gold; then you attacked the *Lady's Luck,* you stole my gold—"

"I saved your life."

"Only *after* you tried to take it."

"Stabbing you was wrong, but I made up for it by helping you rescue Lauren."

"Who are you, Jo? Joanna? You said Finn was your last name, but I think you lied about that as well."

"It is my name," she insisted, though something flared in her eyes that told him she lied.

"How did you fool Daniel Tremayne into allowing you into his home?"

"I'm warning you—"

"He knows who you are; he was going to introduce you to me. Only you interrupted him. Give me your real name, Jo. Tell me who you are!"

"No!"

"Tell me!" he insisted, tempted to shake her.

"Get out of my cabin, Nathan."

"All I have to do is ask Daniel about your true identity."

"Then ask him." She pushed against his chest, but he caught her around the waist, holding her stiffening body against his.

"I don't care to wait until we reach England. I want to know now."

"Let me go." She fisted her hands, and he half expected her to strike him.

"I will if you answer one question." Though now that he held her, felt the angry tremors rippling beneath her skin, he knew he couldn't release her. "Who are you?"

"You know all I'm going to tell you."

"Bloody hell, you're the most infuriating woman I've ever met."

"Believe me, my opinion of you is just as flattering."

"Is that so?" Nathan stared down at her, knowing this was how it would be between them—fire and temper and heat. With her he felt a wildness that defied logic or reason. For the past two weeks, he'd resisted her allure, had tried to deny his attraction to her, but he couldn't any longer. Before the day was out, he vowed, he would know her true name, where she came from, why she had turned to piracy. But more important, he would know *her,* every incredible inch of skin, every curve and scent and taste.

"I'll give you one last chance to tell me what I want to know," he warned.

"Or you'll do what?" Challenge blazed in her eyes, along with a portion of uncertainty.

"This." He covered her lips with his, a hard lesson of what would follow. He would have her, by God. There was no alternative.

Before the day was through, she would be his.

Eighteen

Sensations flooded Jo, so fast and furious they numbed her limbs, her mind, her ability to breathe. She could only taste Nathan, hot and rich, powerful, an overwhelming mixture of male and heated musk. His lips were hard and demanding, the growth of his beard a sensual scrape against her skin. She stiffened, tried to move, but his body was a forceful wall that prevented escape.

She turned her head, managing to break the kiss. "Nathan—"

"Tell me, Jo. Your name." He kissed her temple, her cheek, skimming down to the sensitive vein along her neck.

"Don't—" She clenched her jaw to hold back a gasp as his tongue circled over and over the vulnerable curve of her throat.

The heat that had fueled her anger now fanned a stronger fire inside her core, building, expanding, rising like a consuming tide. She clenched her fingers in his shirt, felt her heartbeat race against her chest. She had to stop him; he was moving too fast, not giving her time to think. This was dangerous, risky, ludicrous! Didn't he know what would happen if she let down her guard, if she gave in to the desire she'd fought to suppress?

Of course he does, she thought furiously, remembering the kisses they'd already shared. *And he intends to push me until I tell him what he wants to know.*

His hands were everywhere, never stopping, skillfully touching her back, her hips, smoothing over her thighs and up to her waist. She felt her skin tighten over her breasts, felt her nipples roughen against her shirt, making her want to give in, just this once.

She gasped, and shoved against him, forcing him back a step. "What do you think you're doing?"

"Giving you a choice." His chest heaved as if he were struggling to remain in control. Morning light streaked through the windows, coating the walls with shifting patterns of orange and yellow. His eyes seemed to absorb the light, making them burn with gray fire. "Either submit and tell me who you really are, or be prepared to submit in another way entirely."

"You arrogant bast—"

He caught her hand an instant before she slapped him. Hauling her to him, he said, "You want me, Jo."

"I don't!"

"You want me as much as I want you." He shook her. "Admit it."

Admit what? she wanted to scream. That her name wasn't Finn or that he was right, that she wanted him? She couldn't confess to either, knowing she'd lose what little advantage she had.

"Release me, Nathan, or I'll have you chained and thrown into the hold."

"You won't," he said, and she felt a shudder run through him. Whether it was from anger or desire, she couldn't have said. "If you really wanted to escape me, you would have called for Jackson by now. Or reached for your knife, or tried some other trick."

Meeting his confident stare, she wondered if he knew her better than she knew herself, because, God help her, having him bound in irons and locked below was the last thing she wanted. Reaching for the *Sea Queen* blade to stop him had never occurred to her; it was shut away in the desk drawer, safely out of her reach.

"Tell me, Jo," he coaxed, his voice lowering, rumbling, drawing her in. He shifted, aligning his chest to hers, bracing one thigh between her legs. He held her still with the heat of his body instead of the strength of his hands. "Which is the truth? Are you a lady pretending to be a pirate, or a pirate pretending to be a lady?"

She tilted her chin, struggling to hide the turmoil he caused in her body. "I told you before, I'm no lady."

"So you're a pirate who has access to one of the best homes in London. How is that possible?" He frowned, and his voice hardened with suspicion. "Morgan Tremayne used to be a pirate. Is she involved with this somehow? Are you working for her?"

Every nerve along Jo's spine clenched in alarm. "I've told you before, I don't know the woman."

"Two female pirates under the same roof? It's too much of a coincidence."

"Stranger things have happened."

His eyes roamed over her face, studying, calculating. "Like my meeting you?"

"Exactly." She glanced at the desk, the shelves of books and maps, searching for anything she could use to distract him, divert him from connecting her to Morgan. But there wasn't a bell to sound an alarm, or a way to reach a weapon, not that she could—or ever again would—use one against him.

Her gaze landed on her narrow bed with its tumbled blankets. Unless she gave him the answers he wanted, she knew he'd have her there, trapped beneath him, whether she consented or not. The way her body ached for his touch, for the feel of his skin flush against hers, she knew she wouldn't continue fighting him for long. She had to end this, get away, but how?

Exuding little effort, he held her pinned between his body and the desk, making escape impossible. She

tugged anyway, but he merely tightened his arms
around her, flattening her stomach against his, burying
his arousal into her core. Desire spiked, sizzling like
lightning through her veins. Nathan emitted a low growl
that made her skin ripple and warm.

"Move like that again," he said, his face so close to
hers that his breath swept into her mouth, "and I won't
care if you answer me or not."

"I'm warning you, Nathan, let me go."

"Why do it, Jo?" he demanded in a harsh whisper,
ignoring her order. "Why risk your life? I remember
the way you were at the ball, richly dressed, mingling
with the wealthy as if you were one of them. Did you
pursue me because I'm an aristocrat, and you'd wanted
revenge for the loss of your brother? Or is there another
reason you stole my gold?"

"It began as revenge, but—" She cut the words off
and shook her head. *I can't tell him. I can't!* "You
wouldn't understand."

"Then make me understand." He brushed a kiss over
her lips. "I want to know everything about you."

Her mind reeled, but she glared at him, furious that
she was tempted to concede and tell him all. She
wanted to trust him, wanted to stay in his arms, where
her guilt didn't weigh so heavily. She wanted to remove
the barrier between them so he would kiss her again.
She needed his mouth on hers, hard and demanding,
taking her until she could forget the gold and pirating,
forget her part in Sammy's and Robby's deaths.

Condemnation pushed in, making her back go rigid.
"Let it go, Nathan. I'll not tell you anything more."

Cupping her face in one hand, he forced her head
back so their gazes locked. "Stop being stubborn, Jo."
His eyes sharpening to points of gray steel, he lowered
his head, bringing his lips within inches of hers, teasing
her, tempting her with a bounty that couldn't compare
to gold. "You have nothing to fear from me."

Nothing to fear except losing my heart. And that is

something I can never do. Jo squeezed her eyes shut and silently cursed. Her heart didn't matter. It was her life and Morgan's that were in danger. Did she dare trust Nathan with the truth about her family? She wanted to, but couldn't—the risks were too great.

"Whether you answer me or not, I'm going to make love to you." He ran his hand down her neck and over her chest, coming so close to her breast she had to clamp her mouth shut to keep from moaning.

"No." The word shook through her.

His right hand skimmed down her side, cupped her bottom and lifted her against him. "Yes."

"Don't do this, Nathan." *Don't make me want you so much I'll betray myself, my sisters, the children I've sworn to help.*

"God, I want to kiss you and never stop."

"Damn it, Nathan. Stop this." She kept her hands fisted against his chest, fighting the desperate need to rub her palms up to his shoulders, over his neck, bury her fingers into the cool silkiness of his hair. If she gave in she'd take hold of him, force his mouth to hers and kiss him until she couldn't see or think. She wanted to feel the heat of his skin, the beat of his heart, taste the fire in his mouth.

She wanted to feel him, all of him. *Take what you want, Jo,* a voice urged from the back of her mind. *You always have. Take, and walk away.* And she'd have to walk away. He would never fit into her world, and she wanted no part of his.

Her limbs shook with the effort to remain still. Could she do it? Make love to him, then leave? She didn't know, couldn't see that far ahead. She could only think about now, feel the fierce desire begging for release.

She met the intensity of his gaze, saw his passion burning in the depths of his eyes, and knew that if she resisted, if she walked out of her cabin without touching him, tasting him, loving him in every way, she would regret it until her dying breath. She'd wanted him from the moment she'd spotted him at Morgan's ball. Denying it was foolhardy—and useless.

Perhaps it was meant to be. Perhaps just this once . . .

She opened her hands, pressing her palms into his chest, feeling his muscles flex and tighten beneath his shirt. Clenching her jaw, she made her decision. She wouldn't turn her back on her feelings for Nathan, or regret them. She wanted him, needed him, so much she thought she might splinter apart from her need. *Take what you want. Take and don't look back.*

Gripping the edges of his shirt, she jerked them apart. Buttons flew. Nathan sucked in a surprised breath. Jo ran her nails down his firm chest, following the contours to his stomach, stopping only because the waistband of his pants forced her to. He quivered against her. She trailed her fingers upward, burying them in the swirls of black hair that tickled her fingers like a seductive whisper. She skimmed her hands over his male nipples and felt him bead against her palms.

"Yes," she heard herself whisper. Her body tensed, growing warm, determined.

"Yes to what, Jo?" he asked in a tone that sounded as dangerous as it did intimate.

She pushed his shirt off his shoulders, working it down his arms, letting it drop to the floor. She grazed her hands over his lean chest, feeling his muscles ripple beneath her touch. His shoulders were broad and hard, his arms ropy with a strength he could use or contain at will. Right now they were knotted as if he were in a struggle for his life.

Never before had she thought a man beautiful—until now. Nathan was everything a man should be: caring, forceful, courageous. "This is what I want."

She heard the demanding tone of her voice, and wondered if he'd take offense. But it couldn't be helped. Touching him poured a strange kind of strength into her limbs, a willful power that made her feel taller, stronger, capable of any feat.

"Jo." Nathan gripped her face in one hand, searching her eyes. Whatever else he'd meant to say was left unsaid. With a muttered curse, he took her mouth in a kiss, deepening it with rough impatience.

She raked her hands into his hair, holding on, crying out when his tongue found hers, startling her with his taste of liquid heat. The edge of the desk pressed into her thighs as he bent her backward, towering over her, consuming her with his hands and mouth, enveloping her in a blanket of lust.

Jo felt as if she were drowning, as if the floor of the *Sea Witch* had opened up and plunged her into the depths of a blustering ocean. She was caught in a current, a violent riptide that swept her up and carried her away, twisting and turning her so she didn't know which way to go. She wrapped her arms around Nathan's neck, ground her body into the solid length of his, and let him take her wherever he would.

He tugged loose the strings that tied her shirt. "There's no turning back, Jo," he said, as if expecting her to object.

In answer, she lifted her shirt over her head, tossing it aside. Warm air brushed her bare skin, but that was nothing to the hot blush she felt under Nathan's stare.

"My God," he whispered. He touched the fingers of one hand to her collarbone, trailing them down over the mound of her breast, grazing her nipple. She felt herself harden, contract. Sensations too alive and raw to withstand speared beneath her skin. She gasped, but didn't move, afraid he'd take his hand away when she wanted more, so much more.

His cool fingers curved around the underside of her breast, holding her, lifting, flooding her with a dizzying light that pulled a moan from her throat. Her skin felt hot, searing, tight to the point of pain.

Then his fingers were fumbling with the strings of her pants. He pulled them off, her leather boots with them. Within a moment she stood before him naked, her breath caught in her throat, her heartbeat bursting against her chest. His gaze traveled over her, touching every part of her until her nerves strained, waiting for his touch. He didn't say another word, and kept his hands to himself. She didn't worry that he'd changed his mind; she recognized the hunger in his eyes, and understood that the fire burning in her raged in him as well.

She remained still, barely aware of the sunlight shining on her body, of the crew working above deck not far away. Everything narrowed down to this one moment. Nathan had been more right than he'd known when he'd said there was no going back. She'd never be the same after today. Just knowing him had changed her. His touch had brought a hidden part of her to life. What would making love to him do to her?

She waited, and still he didn't move, didn't raise a hand. "I've never done this before, Nathan, but I'm sure one of us has to do something."

"You've never?" A faint smile softened his eyes, making him more handsome than she'd thought possible.

Taking the initiative, she untied his pants. Her knuckles brushed him; he grunted, his stomach muscles flexing. Holding her breath, she slid her palms over his hips, pulling his trousers down as she did.

"Jo." He caught her wrist. "If you've never done this, perhaps I should warn you."

"I've seen you bare-skinned before, Nathan." It had been a sight she'd known she would never forget. Now she had the chance not only to see him, but to touch him, learn every texture, every smell, imbed him in her memory in a way she'd never forget.

With his pants barely lowered enough to free his swollen shaft, her first thought was that he was too large; they'd never fit. Nathan gripped her arms and hauled her up to him. She protested, wanting to touch

him, to learn whether he felt as hard as he looked, but
he didn't give her the chance.

"If you keep looking at me like that," he warned,
"this will be finished far too soon." Kissing her, taking
her like a wild animal driven to mate, he lifted her,
nearly dropping her onto the bed as he followed her
down.

He tugged off his boots, and his pants went next. He
slipped one leg between hers, nudging it upward to cup
the notch between her thighs. The startling pressure
forced a purring moan from deep in her throat. His
chest hair rasped her breasts. His hot, musky scent
filled her mind. Sensations she'd never known bom-
barded her one after the other, so fast she couldn't
grasp them all: shivers of pleasure, anticipation, a small
amount of fear—all fueled by an emptiness that pushed
through her in a growing ache.

Aching and empty, she realized, though only part of
her was capable of coherent thought. The rest of her was
twisting, tightening with the emptiness that branched out,
spreading into her limbs, making her body tense and
pulse, preparing for the moment he would make her complete.

Only one thing would stop the unbearable pressure,
feed it, satisfy it, and that was Nathan.

He nipped her neck with his teeth while molding her
breast, lifting it, rolling the nipple with the pad of his
thumb. She shuddered in near torture. Then he sent her
over the edge, replacing his thumb with his mouth. Jo
gasped, arching off the bed, stunned by the feel of his
hot, wet lips against her hotter dry skin. She burrowed
her hands into his hair, squirmed to get away even as
she held him to her. He laved her other breast, making
her agony complete. She wanted to tell him to stop or
do something more, but she could only whimper as her
pleasure-pain rose, tightened and built.

Nathan returned to her mouth, thrusting his tongue
deep, dueling, dancing, filling her with his taste. It was

too much. Her head spun. She couldn't take it all in, couldn't begin to control it, to guide her body or her thoughts.

"Nathan," she managed in a frustrated cry.

"I should go slowly," he said hoarsely, spreading her legs apart with his knee. It sounded like an apology to Jo, and she wanted none of it.

Warm air swept between her legs, whispering a faint touch against her sensitive core, making her feel exposed, reckless, out of control. She felt loose and twisted in knots all at once. She couldn't stop him even if she'd wanted to. She needed him inside her, deep inside, where he would fill her, bond with her.

"Now," she demanded. "Please, now."

Nathan levered himself on his elbows above her. His black hair framed his clenched jaw, shadowing the dark promise in his eyes. At that moment he seemed only half-tame, a man with no thought other than what he wanted from her.

The tip of his sex found her opening and pushed, adding pressure to her already unbearable ache. He rocked into her, then pulled away. He moved again, over and over, stretching her, preparing her a little at a time. She felt her body grow moist. Her muscles tightened around him, holding on, until she finally understood his rhythm and relaxed, letting him slide deeper, and deeper still. She shuddered, rubbing her hands over his sweat-slick back.

"Wrap your leg around me," Nathan said, straining with each move he made, his eyes never leaving her face.

She lifted one leg, draping it over his buttocks. She felt herself open wider, felt Nathan slip deeper inside. Jo arched her back and cried out in surprise and wonder, but no sound emerged from her throat.

Then he stopped.

"No." Jo gripped his hips, lifting herself to him, but he held himself still. Sweat beaded his brow.

"Damn it, Jo, I'm trying to make it easy for you."

"I don't want it easy!" She lifted her head and took him in an openmouthed kiss, drinking in the groan that roared from his throat.

He withdrew, then shoved into her, taking her cry of shock and pain. Searing white fire sliced through her center. She went rigid, her nails digging into his back.

"Shh, let it pass." His voice was tight, his breathing as labored and strained as her own. He soothed his hand over her brow and down her neck, making a sweep over her breast. "I'm sorry, Jo. I didn't want to hurt you."

She tried to speak, but there were too many emotions assailing her to manage a word.

"Breathe," he ordered. She obeyed, inhaling a lungful of air. She smelled sweat and heat, the spicy scent of sex. His hands moved over her, comforting like a healing cream, compelling her to ignore the pain that, to her surprise, had begun to fade. She focused on the raw sound of his voice, the hot, moist feel of his skin, the fullness between her thighs.

He shifted inside her, and the muscles in his jaw flexed. "God, you're as tight as a fist."

"Well, if you weren't so large—" He moved deeper, making her gasp.

"Large, am I?" he asked with a smile that abruptly faded. The veins pulsed at his temples, and a groan rumbled from deep in his chest. "I can't . . . Jesus, Jo, I can't. . . ."

He withdrew and pushed into her, filling her until he touched her womb. The desire she'd lost sight of moments ago returned with a fury. Her pleasure coiled, wrapping tighter, heating her skin, her blood. She held on to him, meeting his thrusts, wanting to cry out each time he impaled her, but the sounds wouldn't come.

She gripped his hips, urging him deeper, faster, meeting him halfway. Each thrust twisted the coil inside her, winding her tighter and tighter until she thought she would break apart. It had to end, she thought, yet it didn't, nor did it crest, but swept her higher and higher, spinning her out of control. When the first wave of pleasure broke through, she gasped. Her eyes flew open.

"Nathan—" She arched into him, straining, a ragged cry tearing from her lips. He pumped into her again and again, prolonging her release. The spasms flooded her limbs. Her muscles clenched around him, holding on, taking him deeper.

The shudders turned to tremors. Jo sighed, stunned, feeling as if gusts of warm wind were washing through her veins.

Then Nathan tensed. He bucked against her and threw his head back, baring his teeth in a feral growl. Jo gripped his slick arms and met his hips measure for measure.

With one last, vicious stroke, he buried himself inside her, his hoarse moan filling the cabin. Corded veins lined his neck as he burrowed even deeper, spending his lust in one shuddering groan after another.

Jo held Nathan's gaze, stunned by the fire in their gray depths. At that moment she thought she could fall into his eyes and become lost in the emotions he revealed. Possessiveness, need and overwhelming tenderness.

Take and walk away. She'd been a fool to believe she could do such a thing. A fool. She'd lied to herself, and now it was too late. Because she'd given him more than just her body; she'd given him her heart as well.

Nineteen

Nathan couldn't move. His body felt lethargic, heavy, but with a satisfying weight that made him want to smile. He could feel his heart beat in a slow, steady rhythm, a vast change compared to the last few hours. He didn't know how much time had passed since they'd first made love. They'd slept afterward, only to wake because neither of them had been able to keep their hands to themselves.

Wintry gray light filled the cabin with a dim glow, making him want to stay in Jo's bed and never leave. Billowing clouds, growing dark and brooding, swept past the square-paned windows, warning that a storm might be approaching, but at the moment he didn't care. Jo was curled into his side with one of her legs threaded between his. Her right hand was limp against his chest, her face tucked so close to his neck he could feel her breath against his skin. He could also feel her occasional shiver.

The buckets of heated cannonballs had long since lost their warmth, but Nathan had hardly noticed, and Jo hadn't complained. He pulled a blanket from the floor and spread it over them, careful not to disturb her.

She sighed nevertheless and scooted closer. He slipped his hand beneath the blanket and down her shoulder, tempted to explore the curve of her slim hip, the muscled length of her leg; he'd never imagined a woman could be as finely honed as Jo, lithe and graceful, yet strong.

But he forced himself to lie still. Their first loving had cooled the hot, forceful urgency that had nearly driven him insane. The following hours had been a slow exploration of each other's bodies, a torturous process he wanted to repeat again and again.

Nathan closed his eyes and concentrated on drawing one steadying breath after another, but it was useless. Just the thought of Jo's hands on him stirred the blood in his groin. He felt himself harden and grow warm, felt the pulsing tremors spread through his limbs. He'd never experienced anything so powerful in all his life— the sweeping, driving need to possess a woman, to bond with her, to make her a part of him. And every move Jo had made, every touch and kiss she'd lavished on his body had been just as possessive, just as demanding. There had been no embarrassment when she'd bared herself to him, no coy games; she'd faced him as if he were a bounty to claim.

And claim him she had, in every way possible.

He glanced down at her. Her long auburn lashes were lowered, shadowing the lingering traces of exhaustion. Her skin glowed with an inner strength, and he knew that if she opened her eyes, they'd glitter like emeralds left in the sun. He touched the stray curls that had escaped her braid, then lifted the end and did something he'd wanted to do since first meeting her.

He untied the string holding the plait, then combed his fingers through her thick russet hair. Cool satin molded to his hands. How had a willful, stubborn she-pirate come to mean so much to him? he wondered. He'd wanted nothing more than to wring her neck when she'd attacked the *Lady's Luck*. Now he wanted her in London, away from the *Sea Witch*, where she'd be safe and he could keep her from her reckless pursuit of revenge. The day she'd challenged him to a duel, he could have easily killed her; another man might have. The muscles in his chest clenched, compressing his heart.

He loosened the last of her braid and fanned her hair over the bedding. She stretched like a kitten stirring awake, arching her back, pressing her breasts into his side. Nathan cupped one and was rewarded with a purring moan.

"I love the feel of your hands on me," she said in a throaty whisper that made him harden all the more.

"I love having my hands on you." He urged her onto her back so he could touch her the way he'd earlier imagined, but she pushed his shoulder and slid her leg across his hip, sitting up to straddle him.

He gripped her waist and pressed his arousal against her, gritting his teeth. She was warm and moist, but he knew she was tender from their times before. Taking her again was out of the question. But still, he had only so much control to fight his insatiable desire.

"Woman, we'll be the death of each other if you aren't careful."

"There'll be time enough to rest once we return to England." She ran her hands over his chest, her eyes following their path as if she were touching him for the very first time. *Or the very last.* He tried pushing the thought away, but couldn't.

"How long do you think that will be?" Her hair slipped over her chest, draping her pale skin in a fiery veil. He cupped one satin-covered breast.

She spared a glance out the window, frowned, then returned to massaging him. "Two days, perhaps three."

For mere days he would have Jo all to himself. *And then what?* He would take Lauren to Winstone Castle, and Jo would go. . . . "Where do you live?"

"In England."

He knew she was being evasive on purpose, and he wanted none of it. Jo had secrets, and it was long past time she shared them with him. He circled his thumbs around her nipples, a light, feathery touch that made her shiver. "Where in England? The north, south? In London city itself?"

"What does it matter?" Her head dropped back on her shoulders and her nails dug into his chest. "Nathan—"

"I want to know."

She leaned forward, trying to force him to take her into his hands. He refused, teasing the pebbled orb, though it nearly killed him to restrain. He knew her taste and wanted it again.

Her eyelids lowered. "Make love to me."

He pressed against her, wanting to slide into her warmth. Grinding his jaw shut, he forced his desire under control. "You're too sore. Now tell me where you live."

She shifted, circling her hips, rubbing her cleft against him. "I live here, on the *Sea Witch.*"

His body clamped down, straining with the shuddering need to drive into her. Nathan drew a deep breath, and it took a moment for her words to penetrate his mind, but when they did, he gripped her hips to hold her still. "You live here. On this ship?"

"Yes."

He didn't believe her, and considered questioning her more, but he didn't think he'd survive. He might have resisted burying himself inside her so far, but at the moment she was the one in control. To prove it, she bent over him, kissing his neck, then grazing her teeth along his jaw before claiming his mouth in a draining kiss that went on and on and on. She was hot and sweet and demanding. Nathan struggled to retain his wits, but God help him, it was a losing battle.

"I love the way you taste," she whispered against his lips. "Like warm water on my tongue."

He groaned into her mouth and ran his hands up her back, pressing her to him. He loved the way *she* tasted, loved the feel of her skin, the way she smelled. He

even loved how her mind worked—sure and resolute.
She didn't waver in her beliefs or shy away from her
fears.

Which was what frightened him most about her.
She'd do whatever she thought was right, regardless of
the consequences. She was a pirate, who would be
hanged if she were caught.

A warning bell went off in Nathan's mind. He
gripped Jo's arms and forced her upright. "Tell me
about the Emerald of London."

The emotions swirling in her eyes shifted from passion to apprehension as she searched his face. She
straightened her back as if resigned that this time she
wouldn't be able to distract him from his questions.

"What do you want to know?" she asked, going so
still he couldn't tell if she was even breathing.

"The truth. All of it."

She arched a brow. "You don't ask for much."

"You can trust me, Jo." Then, because she looked
every bit a woman, and nothing like a pirate, he added,
"Joanna."

Frowning, she said, "No one calls me that."

"They should," he said, taking her hand and kissing
it. "Your name is as beautiful as you are."

Her frown turned skeptical, leading him to believe
that no one had ever told her how exquisite she truly
was. "Trust me, Joanna."

"I want to. . . ." She glanced away and pulled the
blanket up around her shoulders as if she needed armor
for protection. Slipping off of him, she leaned against
the wall.

He missed the feel of her wrapped around him, but
he let her go and waited for her to continue.

Moments passed, and he thought that if he wanted
any more information, he'd have to pry it out of her.
Finally she said, "I was born in a small fishing village
northeast of London."

"Where?"

"Don't be so mulish, Nathan," she scolded without any real bite to her tone. "The name doesn't matter."

He immediately wondered if she was hiding something important from him—or was she keeping the name a secret because she was protecting someone else?

"Our village was a poor one, even before the Seven Years' War, but we had all we needed. Then the war intensified and most of the young men left to serve in the king's army. Our small fields began to flounder, and what did grow was destroyed or taken by passing regiments." Her voice hardened and she stared at the facing wall as if witnessing a scene from the past. "Then a storm crushed our fishing boats and destroyed our homes, leaving us with no way to survive. We were facing starvation, certain death."

"I'm sorry," he said, imagining her as a young girl on the verge of womanhood struggling to exist from one day to the next. But as difficult as her life had obviously been, it didn't explain why she'd been in Daniel Tremayne's home disguised as a noble lady. "What does this have to do with your hating aristocrats?"

Her attention snapped to him. "What was the purpose behind the Seven Years' War?"

He realized her question was more of a test than a demand for an answer, so he kept silent.

"It wasn't a battle to keep an enemy from invading our country. It was a war over riches—aristocrats wanting to fill their purses with even more gold than they already possessed, not caring that they caused the poor to become desperate, unable to put a simple meal on their table, keep a roof over their heads. There was no money for food, Nathan. And medicine . . ."

She turned away, but not before he saw angry tears fill her eyes. Drawing a deep breath, she clenched her jaw, blinked away her tears and faced him. "Medicine could not be had at any price. Both my parents became ill and died within months of each other. Many in our village died that year when they shouldn't have, but we kept on, determined to survive."

She touched her bare chest, and he knew she was searching for the toy soldier, but it was on the desk, out of her reach.

"Then Robby became ill," she continued in a voice as cold and still as the room. "I tried to save him. Had there been no war . . ."

He didn't need her to finish to know that had there been no war, she would have been able to buy the medicine needed to save her brother, and perhaps her parents as well. But England's battle over valuable trading ports across the world had taken away all her hope, leaving her with nothing but anger and a deep-seated hatred for the people who'd not only started the war, but had benefited from it.

He wanted to pull her down to him, to comfort her in his arms, but he understood the source of her strength and knew that the time for consoling that little girl had long since passed. The woman she'd grown into had built a protective wall in order to carry on. "After you lost your brother, what did you do?"

A rueful smile lifted one corner of her mouth. "Why, I became a pirate."

There were a thousand questions he wanted to ask: how had she survived so many years at sea without being captured, how had she become captain of her own ship, why did she continue to risk her life?

But those questions would wait. Right now he wanted to know what had brought her to Daniel Tremayne's home and why she'd been so desperate to keep his gold. Was it for herself? He thought he knew her too well to believe that amassing her own wealth had been her motivation.

"How did you become the Emerald of London?" he asked.

She shrugged and looked away, a sure sign she was hiding something. "I have no title, and we both know how much the English covet their titles. So I became a lady of mystery instead, and the doors of the elite began to open."

"So you took your pirating into the drawing rooms of London?" He took her hand, which clenched one end of the blanket, and held it between his own. Her fingers were cold. He half expected her to pull away, but she gripped him instead.

"I . . ." She paused, and he could tell she was searching for something to say that wouldn't reveal the entire truth.

He wanted to shake her in frustration. *Trust me, Jo, damn it, trust me!* He decided on a different path of questioning instead. "You said you had plans for my gold. What are they?"

She looked at him, her expression troubled, and he sensed she was weighing her options. "You'll think it a waste of money."

"Perhaps." He pressed her hand flat against his chest, just over his heart. "Tell me and let me be the one to decide."

"My village wasn't the only one to suffer during the war."

"Don't tell me you're trying to save all the poor in England?"

An angry shimmer brightened her eyes. "Just the orphans."

Nathan's heart seemed to stop in midbeat. She risked her life to help orphans, the homeless waifs who roamed London's streets? He felt a tremor start in his limbs, and his hands clenched of their own accord.

He lurched from the bed and paced the small cabin, oblivious to his own nakedness. Spotting the toy soldier attached to a worn leather rope, he picked it up. Jo couldn't have been more than a young girl when her parents had died, leaving *her* an orphan with a sick baby brother to care for. Facing her, seeing the stubborn tilt of her chin, everything clicked into place.

She'd blamed the aristocrats for her brother's death, but she'd blamed herself as well. As her penance, she'd decided to care for every child the wealthy had forsaken.

"Bloody hell," he ground out between his teeth. "You can't save them, Jo."

A muscle pulsed in her jaw. "Perhaps not all, but with your gold I can give some of them a chance."

He joined her on the bed and held up the toy soldier. "Fifty thousand pounds is a great deal of money, but there must be hundreds, perhaps thousands of homeless children. You might feed and clothe some of them for a time, but what will you do when the money runs out? Raid another ship? Challenge another man to a duel in the hope of stealing his gold?"

He threw the soldier aside. "Or die trying?"

"Someone has to help them." She wrapped the blanket around her like a shield, but he saw her fear—and her stubborn determination to carry on, regardless of the price she might have to pay.

"I agree, but that someone doesn't have to be you." He cupped her face, running his thumb across her cheek. "Not when it means risking your life. There are agencies in place to help these children."

She laughed, the cynical sound warning him of what she was about to say. "Such as the Marine Society for Educating Poor Destitute Boys at Sea?"

"It's a worthy organization."

"It's England's way of legalizing slavery. The boys have no rights, no one to watch out for them. The ones who don't die from disease or a broken spirit become hard, soulless men."

"Not always," he argued. "Some boys find a good life."

She scoffed, her expression hardening with her rising temper. "Then there's the Foundling Hospital."

Nathan closed his eyes, sorry he'd taken her down this path. The Foundling Hospital had been established to bring children off the streets and give them a chance at life, when in fact it was an overcrowded hellhole where England placed—or rather hid—its unwanted bastards.

"Some of the children under my care I rescued from there," she said. "They were living worse than rats: filthy, sick, fighting for what little food there was to be had. These are the only options our orphans have, Nathan. Do you think they're good enough?"

He regarded her a moment then shook his head. "No."

"Helping them is a part of who I am." She searched his face. "I have to do this. Try to understand."

But she couldn't save them, not even a dozen, without risking her life. Didn't she see that?

"I understand more than you know. But it ends here. I won't let you endanger yourself any longer."

"You won't *let* me?"

He heard the controlled anger in her voice, but he ignored it. "You can do what you will with my gold, but once it's gone, your helping the children will end."

Her eyes flashed like crystal fire. "You have no say over what I do. I'll steal from the king himself if it means feeding one more child."

"You'll do no such thing. If I have to turn you over to the magistrate to save you from yourself, believe me, I will!" he threatened, knowing he'd do no such thing. But if it meant keeping her safe, he'd tie her up and lock her away at Winstone Castle.

For an instant her eyes widened and her jaw went slack; then she shoved against him and tried to leap from the bed. Nathan caught her around her waist and forced her onto her back.

"Let go of me, damn you!" She swung her right hand and would have knocked him senseless had he not seen it coming and caught her wrist inches from his head.

He caught her other hand and pinned them both to the mattress. "You're not going anywhere."

She bucked against him, but Nathan levered his body over hers, trapping her with his weight. "I'll never forgive you for this."

"For what? Trying to keep you alive? Jo . . ." Sighing, touching his forehead to hers, he let the anger and fear drain out of him. "I'll help you in any way I can, but you can't expect me to stand by while you continue to put yourself in danger."

"I can take care of myself."

He kissed her lips, relieved when she didn't turn away or try to bite him. "You don't have to do it alone."

He didn't know what his statement entailed, not to the fullest extent, at least. He and Jo were from two different worlds, as far apart as the earth from the moon, yet he wasn't about to let her out of his life. That much he knew without any doubt.

"You'll help me?" she asked, bewildered, as if not believing the words.

"Yes."

She swallowed and watched him with eyes that glistened with unshed tears. "We'll be partners? You, a nobleman?"

He released her hands so he could touch her face, bury his fingers into her hair. "Yes."

"You won't try to stop me?" she asked, the doubt in her voice stronger than he liked.

"I'll help you raise money and find a home for them," he reassured her. "Whatever you want."

Her jaw clenched, and he thought she was going to start arguing again, but she whispered, "Then kiss me."

Nathan did that and more, knowing he'd not only

committed himself to her; he'd also entrusted her with a part of his soul.

Nothing would ever be the same again.

Twenty

"Drop anchor." Jo gave the order in a hushed voice that the dark seemed to absorb. She fisted her hands behind her back and battled the urge to rescind the command.

Her first officer and best friend hesitated, his whiskey brown eyes flashing shards of gold in the lantern light. "Perhaps you should think this through, Jo."

"Are you questioning my decision?" Standing on the forward deck, she could see her crew working below in the predawn darkness, lowering and tying off the canvas sails. They moved like ghosts, quiet, their capable hands stopping all sound that could echo throughout the night and alert the sleeping port of Weymouth of their arrival.

"Someone has to question you. You've always been impulsive, but even this is unlike you." Jackson swiped a hand through his loose blond hair and muttered a curse that would have brought a blush even to Jo's cheeks if she weren't so numb inside. "Considering how determined you've been to help Lord Darvill and his sister, why are you doing this to them now?"

Lord Darvill. Nathan. Jo tensed her spine, making it as rigid as the wooden mast towering three stories above her. Jackson's question hung in the air, demanding an answer she couldn't give, at least not in any form that would make her friend understand. It would

mean revealing a part of herself that no one, not even
Jackson, was aware existed.

For the last two days she'd lost herself in Nathan's
arms, loving him in a way she'd never imagined herself
capable of. For two days she'd kept the future at bay,
focusing on nothing but every moment they'd shared,
every kiss, every word, every exhausted sigh.

But tonight, after sharing a meal with Nathan in her
cabin, then making love with a fierceness that stole her
breath even to think about, he'd fallen asleep beside
her, holding her to him as if he'd never let her go. *If
only things could have remained that way.* She'd run
her fingers over his cool skin, memorizing the shape
of his arms, the power in his hands. He no longer wore
Lauren's ring on his little finger, having given it back
to his sister soon after they'd boarded the *Sea Witch.*

But as hard as she'd tried, as much as she wanted
to, she couldn't ignore the future any longer. They were
less than a day's sail away from London. If she didn't
act now, she'd be tempted to reach for the impossible—
a life with Nathan.

Surrounded by his arms and the comforting dark, listening to the sound of his steady breathing that had
become as familiar and as cherished as the whispering
creaking of her ship, she'd made her decision. It had
been a hard choice, the hardest she'd ever made, though
in truth, there'd been only one option to choose from.

A choice that would irrevocably change the rest of
her life.

The rest of my life. The phrase ground a hole through
her chest, exactly where her heart was beating at a furious pace.

A life without Nathan. She tilted her head back,
wanting to scream at the starless sky. When she'd decided to make love to him, she'd known the risk to her
heart would be great. She just hadn't realized how
great, or how deeply the pain would go.

"Damn it, Jo," Jackson said. He gripped her arm

and forced her to look at him. "I know you care about
him. I'd even go so far as to say the man is half in
love with you."

"Don't." She raised a hand to stop him from saying
anything more. Love couldn't come into this; she
wouldn't be able to walk away from Nathan if she
thought either of them felt even a glimmer of love.

She didn't love him, she vowed, almost choking on
the lie. *I don't love him! I can't!* Turning her frustration
on Jackson, she argued, "You were the one who urged
me to part company with Nathan. Now I am."

"That was before he became your lover."

She heard no censure in Jackson's voice, only heart-
felt concern. Regardless, she had to ask, "Do you think
I was wrong?"

Jackson studied her, the harsh angles in his face unreadable in the flickering light. "If anyone deserves hap-
piness, Jo, it's you. But did I not warn you the man would
break your heart? After seeing you with him, seeing the
effect he's had on you, I imagine your heart is taking a
beating right now. But to leave him like this . . ." Jackson
scowled at the leeward side of the ship, where a dinghy
waited below. "It isn't right."

"It can't be helped. This is the way it has to be."
She could have explained her reasons, but voicing them
right now wasn't possible.

She was a pirate, a fisherman's daughter, and Nathan
was a nobleman, a product of England's elite; the two
weren't meant to associate any more than were dogs
and cats. But their social differences weren't the real
reason their relationship couldn't continue.

The children.

Nathan might sympathize with her need to help the
orphans, but he thought it was something she could do
for a time, then turn her back on and walk away from,
like a hobby she'd grown tired of. *How could a man
who makes me feel as if I've found the secret to life
know me so little?* An ache close to grief pushed

against her chest, filling her with the trembling need to cry.

She turned away from Jackson's prying gaze and went to the side railing, gripping it as she stared down at the empty dinghy below.

Nathan would demand she do things his way, she reasoned. He was a lord; commanding others came as naturally to him as blinking. And if she didn't agree, if she dared to balk, what would he do then? Would he shrug his shoulders and let her continue supporting the children? She thought the probability of that happening was as great as her reaching up and plucking a star from the sky.

Or would he wield his aristocratic power? Call the magistrate and have her arrested as he'd threatened? She'd have to stand trial for piracy, answer for her crimes against the Crown. Nathan had claimed he wanted to protect her, and she didn't truly believe he would hand her over to the authorities. But hoping he wouldn't do so and knowingly making herself vulnerable to such a risk were two different things.

Besides, too many lives were at stake for her to give Nathan so much power: her life, Morgan's and Grace's, Daniel's, the orphans'.

There was another reason to end this now. If Nathan even mentioned marriage, she'd be tempted to accept. And she couldn't, not ever. She might care for him— more deeply than she wanted to admit, more than she thought herself capable of—but she couldn't be his wife. She didn't belong in his world, didn't want any part of it. If she couldn't change—*refused* to change— then their feelings for each other would never endure. He'd come to hate her. She didn't intend to wait around for that to happen.

Squaring her shoulders, she turned to a passing crewman. "Dillon, wake Lady Darvill and bring her here at once. It's time for our guests to leave."

"Aye, Cap'n. Do ye want me tae bring her brother, as well?"

"No." She turned away and faced the darkness. Emptiness moved in like a shadow, cold and hollow, swallowing the last bit of her heart. "I'll see to Lord Darvill myself."

He smelled something spicy, like cinnamon warmed over a stove. The fragrance drifted through his head, stirring him from his sleep. Nathan breathed a deep sigh and turned onto his side, his only thought to burrow into the woman whose scent could follow him into his dreams. Sensuous Jo. Vibrant Jo. Joanna. His pirate. He reached out for her. Instead of touching a body he knew so well that he didn't need to open his eyes to see, he found her pillow and a crumple of cold sheets.

His eyelids flew open, and his mind came to alertness, every sense focusing on his surroundings. The cabin was as black as a tomb, the air as still and frigid. He could see dark shapes against the darker night—the silhouette of a desk and chair to his left, a trunk of clothes in a corner beside the door. Rising up on one elbow he listened to the soft lap of water against the outside hull, the tweak of settling wood, the muffled sound of footsteps aloft. He frowned.

The *Sea Witch* wasn't moving.

And Jo was gone.

A ripple of unease tightened his skin. Had they reached London already? Navigated the long stretch of the Thames? It didn't seem likely, but he had to admit that, with his sister safely aboard, his thoughts had been consumed by the *Sea Witch*'s captain, and even she had paid little attention to their daily progress.

He drew a relieved breath. He could finally take Lauren home, where she could begin putting Philip de Maurier and all he'd done behind her. But his relief was short-lived. Doing so meant leaving Jo's cabin and the private world they'd created. He wasn't ready to give up their time together. *Be honest,* he chided himself. *You're not ready to give her up yet.*

They hadn't discussed what would happen after reaching England. Given her past and his position, it was a conversation too complex to have when all they could think about was losing themselves in each other's arms.

There was no reason she couldn't accompany him and Lauren to Winstone Castle. In fact, he could think of no place else he'd want to take her. Jo would undoubtedly protest, claiming she had to help the orphans she'd assumed responsibility for. He wouldn't try to stop her, but surely she could wait a few more days.

Throwing his legs over the side of the bed frame, he rose and lit the lantern suspended from an overhead beam. Light flooded the cabin. He blinked against the sudden glare, but didn't wait for his vision to clear before he began to dress. Once his eyes adjusted, he paused long enough to notice that her toy soldier was gone from the desk, as well as her jeweled knife.

Minutes later, dressed in the pants and coat he'd borrowed from Jackson, he walked down a companionway as dark as coal, toward the steps leading above. A chill grazed his neck, not from the cold that seeped through the walls, but from something else. He hesitated and glanced down the corridor. It was empty and quiet, which was strange. Even in the dead of night, the crew on watch would be moving around the ship, completing one task or another. He shook off the sensation, attributing it to his own restlessness, the disturbing feel of waking and finding Jo gone, and climbed the ladder.

Reaching the deck, he frowned. No more than two lanterns had been lit, and those allowed only a faint glimmer of light. The layers of sails had been lowered and tied off. A few crewmen were busy coiling ropes, while the rest were standing at the ship's wheel with their hands deep in their pockets, or kneeling in the shadows, as if waiting . . . but waiting for what, Nathan couldn't begin to guess.

He searched the indistinct faces, and instinctively knew Jo wasn't among the crowd. He headed for the other lantern, which illuminated Jackson standing midship near the railing, his arms crossed over his chest as he watched something over the side.

Stopping beside him, scanning the darkness that seemed to push against the light, Nathan asked, "Where are we?"

The pirate looked up at him with cold disapproval, surprising Nathan. The first officer had seemed to relax during the last few days. Nathan wouldn't have gone so far as to say Jackson had become friendly—he was still highly protective of Jo—but the pirate had seemed to accept Nathan in Jo's life. Or so he had thought.

"We've reached Weymouth," Jackson said in a tone so hushed and grated that Nathan could barely make out the words.

He searched the night for some shape, or even a flicker of light, some indication a village or town lay close by. But there was nothing. If there had been any sliver of moon during the night, it was hidden behind a sky thick with clouds. Perhaps it was a trick of the eye, but he thought he could make out faint shapes of buildings in the distance.

"Why have we stopped here?" he asked, feeling the cold seep through his coat, though it wasn't only the chilled air that made the hair lift on the nape of his neck. Something was wrong. He couldn't put his finger on exactly what, but so much tension filled the air, Nathan thought he could hear it crackle.

"You'd better ask the captain."

Nathan met the man's unyielding stare, and felt sweat bead on his brow, only to turn icy in the wind. "Where is she?"

Jackson nodded toward the pitch-black waters below.

Frowning, Nathan leaned over the railing. "What . . . what in bloody hell?"

"I told you, you'd better ask the captain." With a muscle pulsing in his jaw, Jackson turned and walked away.

Far below in the still, dark water, a lamp barely illuminated a skiff filled with four people. Lauren looked up at him, her face ashen against her loose soot-colored hair. If she recognized Nathan it didn't show in her features; her expression was closed, resolved, as if nothing could ever surprise her again.

At the stern, two sailors sat with their backs rigid, each gripping the end of a thick oar. The fourth person was Jo. She said something to the men, then reached for the wooden steps fixed to the side of the ship that served as a ladder. She began climbing with a speed and agility that made Nathan's heart lodge in his throat. He stepped back, not knowing if he'd yell at her for placing Lauren in a skiff without his permission, or for risking her life by scaling seventy feet into the air.

As soon as she appeared at the railing, he gripped her arms and pulled her onto the deck. Only supreme control kept him from shaking her. "What the hell do you think you're doing? Why is Lauren out there?"

Jo twisted out of his hold and moved a pace away. Light washed her face, though it was the face of a stranger. Her green eyes were narrowed, as if she were looking at a sworn enemy instead of the man she'd spent the last three days making love to. With her hair pulled back in a braid, her cheeks seemed carved and unforgiving, her jaw a harsh, angry line of sheer determination. Never had he seen her so stern, so controlled, not even when he'd dueled with her aboard the *Lady's Luck*. Even then there had been fire in her eyes, a passion fueled by her contempt for aristocrats as much as by her love for adventure.

Nathan let his hands drop to his sides, realizing he didn't know the woman before him now. *Dear God, what has happened?* "Answer me, Jo. What is going on?"

"You're leaving."

"I'm . . ." He tensed, trying to decipher the coldness in her tone. Keeping his own voice level, he said, "I don't know what you're trying to do, but I want Lauren brought back up here immediately."

Jo took a leather pouch from her pocket and tossed it to him. He caught it and heard the clink of coins. "This should be enough gold to see you to London. Perhaps not in the style you're accustomed to, but I can't spare anything more."

He narrowed his gaze, stepping closer to her. "You expect me to leave? Now?"

She gave an abrupt nod of her head.

"Why are you doing this?"

She tilted her chin, matching him stare for stare. "It's time to part company."

"Why like this?" he demanded, waiving his hand to encompass the dark, the pouch of gold, the secrecy.

"This is the way it has to be." She turned away. "Eric and Theo will row you and your sister to shore. I suggest you hurry; I plan to be gone before sunrise."

Nathan gripped her arm before she'd taken two steps and forced her around to him. He saw a flare in her eyes—regret or pain—but it was gone before he could tell for sure which it had been. Aware of the crew nearby, all watching and quiet, he lowered his voice and asked, "We don't have to part this way. We can—"

"There is no *we*, Nathan. We were attracted to each other, but it's over now."

"Attra . . ." Disbelief tightened his chest like an iron band. "You call what is between us simple attraction? It's more than that, and you know it."

"Get off my ship, Nathan." Her icy tone raked over him. "Or I'll have you thrown overboard."

"Damn it, Jo." He had no idea what had caused her

to change, but he wasn't leaving until he found out. "You care about me; I know you do."

"Dillon, Mac," she called, "throw Lord Darvill over the side."

Nathan released her, staring down at her, not believing this could be happening. They'd made love only hours before; he'd held her warm body to his, had felt the depth of her feelings for him, even if she hadn't spoken them out loud. He felt the same about her. He adored her, cared about her, knew that she, above any other woman, had the power to steal his heart—or rip it to shreds, as she was doing now.

For a moment no one moved; then the two sailors rushed forward, each grabbing one of Nathan's arms. Two more men joined them, gripping his legs and hauling him up.

Enraged, Nathan struggled, demanding they release him. "Don't do this!" They carried him closer to the rail. "Damn it, Jo!"

He fought, but they pinned his arms and legs, holding on to him with a steel grip. He glared at her, thought of a thousand things he wanted to shout at her, but he didn't say another word. She watched him, her hands fisted at her sides, her face as hard as the knife she carried at her hip.

Frigid wind whipped over his body. The deck moved farther away as the crewmen lifted him higher. He waited for the brief tumble through darkness, then the plunge into the freezing cove.

How could she do this to him, after all they'd shared? How?

"Release him!" The barked command didn't come from Jo. The men paused. Nathan angled his head and saw Jackson striding forward.

He jerked Nathan out of the sailors' hands.

"Jack," Jo warned, "don't interfere."

The first officer ignored her. His face as stony as

his captain's, he said to Nathan, "I suggest you leave. Now."

Nathan shook with the need to stay and force Jo into telling him why she was pushing him away. Her crew quietly gathered around her, though he didn't think she needed their protection. She stood rigid, her shoulders as squared as he'd ever seen her. If she felt any remorse, it didn't reflect on her face or in her eyes.

Obviously she wanted him gone before they reached London. Nathan felt something tear loose inside him, the rip so strong and sudden it forced him to take a step back. He turned the unwanted pain into fury. If this was the way she wanted it, he'd be damned if he'd try to change her mind.

Crossing to the wooden ladder, he paused at the railing, turning when he told himself not to, to look at her one more time. He waited, watching her, still foolishly hoping she'd say she'd made a mistake. *Say it, Jo. For the love of God, say it!*

A muscle pulsed in her jaw, and she angled her chin a notch higher.

Cold wind blew over him. Touching his brow in a mock salute, he climbed over the railing and scaled down the ladder, vowing with each step to forget everything that had happened to him since he'd first laid eyes on Jo. He repeated the vow over and over again, furious that it rang hollow in his ears.

The lapping of oars against water was nothing more than muffled sound, too far away to distinguish, though Jo knew what each stroke meant. She couldn't see the skiff any longer, couldn't see much of anything with the dark pressing over her like a smothering hand. Yet even the darkness blurred.

"What now, Captain?" Jack asked in a reserved tone she'd never heard from him before.

"We sail for Chattenden," she answered in a voice she didn't recognize any more than she had Jackson's.

"Jo." He touched her arm. "You're crying."

"Don't be ridiculous." Yet she felt the hot streak of tears running down her face. Mindlessly she touched her fingers to her cheek, feeling the wetness she hadn't felt since the day of her brother's death. "I never cry."

"I know." Jackson put his arms around her shoulders and drew her close. "Tears are only for broken hearts."

Twenty-one

"Who would 'ave ever thought dirt could look so lovely?"

Sitting back on her heels, Jo stabbed her trowel into the ground and shielded the sun from her eyes with her hand. Mira Fenner stood over her, appraising Jo's progress. The plump woman's cheeks were two perfect spots of pink. Wiry yellow hair escaped her lopsided cap, and would have made her appear a bit crazed if not for the soft light sparkling in her brown eyes.

"Have you come to help me, then?" Jo asked, rotating her shoulders to ease the ache in her muscles. It was a pleasant ache, the kind that said she'd accomplished something worth doing.

" 'Elp ye?" Mira admonished, chuckling. "I'd be think'n ye have enough 'elp already."

Jo looked down the long rows of black soil, freshly turned into mounds that held newly sprouted buds of cabbage, carrots, peas and potatoes.

If only Morgan could see me now—a farmer, digging in the earth instead of running away to my ship, where I'd always vowed to live. But that was before I found them.

Spread out among the rows, attacking the weeds that had dared grow in her vegetable garden, were her children.

Peter, the self-appointed leader of the group, was patiently replanting the onion shoots his younger brother, Farley, had pulled up by mistake. Or perhaps on purpose; as mischievous as Farley could be, it was hard to tell. The ten-year-old twin girls, Lark and Robin, so named because when they'd been born they'd made a chirping noise instead of crying, had the largest pile of weeds between them. Each group of children had been assigned a vegetable row to take care of, but the twins took special affront when the invasive plants appeared in their row of carrots.

Chelsea, Darren, Elliot, Amy and a dozen more were elbow-deep in dirt, their faces smudged, their new clothes so soiled, they'd have to strip down to their undergarments before being allowed into the house. They might even need a bath, Jo thought, smiling, imagining the protests that that would invoke.

She couldn't care less if they ruined their clothes; it was worth a few stains to see the smiles on their faces, the color in their cheeks, hear the laughter that was slow in coming, but sounded like a gift when it did.

"It's a wonderful sight, is it not, Mira?" Jo asked, feeling the familiar tightness in her chest.

"That it is, Jo. You've done a fine job with 'em."

"But it's not enough," she said, more to herself than for the other woman's benefit. But Mira had the hearing of a guard dog.

"I'll be putt'n up with none of that now," the older woman scolded. She stooped to retrieve a pail, then began tossing plucked weeds into it. "You've done more than anyone else ever gave a thought to. Bought us a fine home, ye did."

Jo glanced over her shoulder at their "fine" home. The two-story farmhouse, built of timber and stone, had been constructed with a large family in mind, added onto over the years. It needed a new roof and fresh paint, and the chimney in the kitchen would likely collapse if she didn't have it replaced soon, but it was still a good place to live—large, yet warm, with character and room to grow. But above all, it was safe. The first time she'd seen it, she'd known it would be perfect for her diverse family.

"We're close to London," Mira continued the lecture Jo had heard a hundred times before. "Yet far enough away so folks leave us be. You've provided more clothes than a body needs. And food . . ." She patted her stomach and sighed. "I've never eaten so well in all my life. Neither has a single one of those babies. And now you're teaching us how to grow our own food so's we don't have to be reliant on anyone in case things go bad. And the good Lord knows, eventually things always go bad."

"But it's only twenty children, Mira." Jo wiped sweat from her brow with the back of her hand. "There are so many more who need our help."

"You can't save them all," Mira said quietly as she looked across the fields. With a pang of remorse, Jo knew Mira was thinking about the family she'd lost because of disease and war.

"But we have room for more." Pushing to her feet, Jo slapped dirt off of her pants. Whenever she was away from Morgan and London, she left her day dresses packed in a trunk. She wasn't on the *Sea Witch* any longer, and would probably never be again, though it hurt her to think about it. *But this is my home now.*

"Ye can't make children who've seen nothin' but bad believe in ye in a day."

"A day? It's been four months since I bought this farm." Five months since she'd returned to England. *Five months since the last time I saw Nathan, the night I forced him off my ship.* Jo gritted her teeth and forced the thought away, knowing it would return before the day was out, bringing with it an emptiness that now seemed as familiar as breathing.

"My advice is to give the ones we left in London some time." Mira's smile returned as she squared her rounded shoulders. "Word will get out. Once the other children realize you aren't like some of them evildoers who capture orphans for them slave ships, they'll come running, and kicking themselves for waiting so long. See if they don't."

"I hope you're right. Because I feel . . . I feel . . ."

"Frustrated?"

No, Jo thought to herself. *I feel lost. I've accomplished so much, yet it isn't enough. Even if I bring every orphaned child into my home, I'll still feel lost.* She squeezed her eyes closed and turned away so Mira couldn't read the emotions that had to be clear on her face. Unbidden, the questions she couldn't escape raced through her mind: Where was Nathan? Safe in his home at Winstone Castle with Lauren? Or in Saint-Nazaire seeking revenge against Philip de Maurier? Her heart pounded against her chest at the thought. He couldn't confront de Maurier, not alone. She wondered if Nathan ever thought about her. Or did he hate her so much he'd wiped her out of his life?

She stomped her foot and called herself a fool. *Forget him!* She'd told herself that a thousand times, too, yet her heart refused to listen.

"Are you all right, Jo?"

"What?" she snapped, regretting her angry tone the instant the word left her mouth. Gentling her voice, she said, "Yes, yes, I'm fine. It's as you said, I'm frustrated. Everything will come together; I just need to give it more time," Jo said, almost believing her convincing tone.

"Do the children know about their surprise?"

"What surprise?" Lark and Robin asked in unison. Each holding on to the handle of the same wooden pail, they stopped by Mira. Their high-pitched voices caught the other children's attention.

"Hey," Peter called out as he ran. "Miss Fisk has another surprise for us."

"Is it sweets?" Amy asked, hopping up and down. "I didn't like the lemon tarts, but Miss Fenner's roly-poly pudding is good. Are we having some? Oh, please say yes, please."

Jo listened to their excited chatter, and knew she'd done the right thing by taking Nathan's gold and building a new life for these kids. Leaving Nathan had been right, too. It didn't matter that she still felt as if her heart had been ripped out of her body and shredded beyond repair. A future with Nathan would have been as likely as reading a fairy tale and hoping it would come true. But these children, they were real, and so was the life she'd helped create for them.

"It isn't sweets, Amy," Jo said, feeling her gloomy mood lift and her smile return.

"It's a pistol, then," Peter announced, his thin chest puffing up. "I need a pistol, being as I'm the oldest man 'ere."

"Peter Aylwin, it most certainly is not a pistol." Jo propped her hands on her hips and studied the assortment of upturned faces, all eager, all hopeful. Whether they stayed so remained to be seen once they learned what their surprise really was.

"But—" he argued.

"Honey is doing a fine job keeping us safe."

"Honey? Honey's a bloom'n dog!"

Jo ignored the boy's language—one thing at a time, she told herself—and glanced at the dog. The wolfhound lay beneath a half-grown oak, watching everything around her and missing nothing. When she stood, her head topped Jo's waist. Her shaggy gray coat was more than a hand's-width in length, making her look wild and untamed. Her long muzzle concealed rows of teeth that could snap off a man's arm with little effort.

Jo had been alarmed when the hound had first wandered onto their farm half-starved. But to everyone's surprise, and against Jo's orders, shy, timid Elliot had coaxed the dog into the barn, where he'd cared for her. That had been nearly two months ago. Since then Honey had doubled in size and had taken her place among the assorted orphans, appointing herself their guardian. Jo felt confident that no one could trespass onto the property without Honey knowing.

"Stop interrupting 'er," Chelsea ordered with the authority of a seasoned seven-year-old. "And let 'er finish. Now what's our surprise, Miss Fisk?"

Jo hated to prolong the suspense any longer, so she blurted, "I've found you a teacher."

Their smiles vanished, and their mouths gaped as they stared at her in silence.

"Hmm," Mira mused. "Seems we've finally found a way to quiet this group."

"A teacher!" Peter spat. "We don't need no bloom'n teacher."

"We've done fine without one," Farley said, then echoed his brother. "We don't need no bloom'n teacher."

"Is that so?" Jo sighed. She'd known they wouldn't be thrilled with the idea of having lessons, but it was something they were going to have to accept. She didn't want to frighten them, but they had to face the truth. She still had a good portion of Nathan's gold left, but how long would that last? She had to make the farm and the children self-sufficient or else it would all be for nothing.

"What will you children do with yourselves when you're grown and leave the farm?"

"We don't want to leave," Amy said, gripping Jo's pant leg in her small fist.

Jo ran her hand over the girl's brown curls. "I don't want you to either, sweetheart. But if, or when, you do, I want to make sure you know how to read and write."

"But—" Peter tried interrupting again.

Jo held up her hand. "If you learn to read you'll never have to live in the streets again. You'll be able to find jobs."

"We can work 'ere," Farley added grudgingly. Wide-eyed, the others shook their heads in agreement.

Yet Jo continued. "Every one of you will eventually marry and want a home of your own, want to have a family of your own. How will you support them?"

"We could be farmers," Peter insisted. "You're teach'n us how."

"And how will you know if someone's trying to cheat you when you sell your food at market?" Jo asked.

Scowling, the boy said, "I'd know."

"You'll know because if you have some schooling, you'll be smarter than the other man."

Peter stubbornly held her stare, then nodded as if reluctantly accepting his fate. "I'd still rather have a pistol." He plucked at his brother's sleeve. "Come on, Farley. We got more weeds to pull."

As the children dispersed, Honey bolted to her feet and faced toward the front yard. Her ears flattened against her head, and her lips pulled back in a deep-throated growl.

"Someone's here." Jo didn't hear anyone approach, but she didn't doubt the wolfhound's instincts. "Stay with the children, Mira."

Jo hurried around the side of the house, alert to anything out of the ordinary. A warm breeze stirred the trees overhead, bringing the smells of grass and wild-flowers, the earthy scent of dirt that clung to her clothes. Then she heard it—the steady gallop of a horse's hooves. They'd had few visitors since they'd taken over the farm—three women from the nearby village and the priest, but no one else. She touched the *Sea Queen* blade sheathed at her side. As with her pants and boots, she hadn't been able to give up wearing her knife. Peter wanted a pistol, and though he didn't know it, Jo kept one in her room. She thought about retrieving it now, but realized she didn't have time. Blast it, she had to be better prepared than this!

She hurried to the front porch, where she could best

see the road. Honey came around the corner and waited beside her.

Through the line of trees, she caught a glimpse of a sorrel horse and a male rider. "Who . . . ?" Her mouth dropped open and she couldn't draw another breath. "It . . . it can't be him."

The man on the horse was tall, well built, and though she hadn't seen the color of his hair, her mind began to buzz. Without thinking, she crossed the yard, straining to catch another glimpse of the man. It couldn't be Nathan, she told herself. Only one person knew where she was, and he wouldn't tell. Not even Morgan or Grace knew about the farm. There was no way Nathan could find her. Yet her skin tightened and felt flushed. She hurried her steps, everything inside her pushing her forward when she knew she should turn and run. She pressed her hands to her stomach. How had he found her? What would she say? What did he want?

The horse rounded the last curve in the road and slowed to a trot, closing the distance between them. She saw the rider clearly for the first time, his squared shoulders, the reckless tilt of his chin.

"What are you doing here?" she demanded, crossing her arms over her chest to hide her sudden shaking. It was surprise she felt, not disappointment.

"Well, I'm glad to see you, too." Jackson reined to a halt and dismounted. He removed the hat that covered his blond hair and slapped it against his thigh, sending a puff of dust into the air. "Is that any way to greet me after I've half killed my horse to reach you?"

She glanced at the gelding. Sweat slicked his brown coat, and his sides heaved as he labored to breathe. It was obvious Jackson had pushed the animal. But why? She shifted her frown to his serviceable wool pants and shirt. They were as travel-worn as the expression on his face. Not even the bright noon sun could dispel the serious glint in his whiskey brown eyes.

Her stomach immediately tightened with dread. "What's happened? Is Morgan hurt? Is it Grace?"

"It's nothing like that, though you might want to do harm to Morgan once you read this." Jackson took an envelope out of his saddlebag and handed it to her. "She sent it to Dunmore, since that's where you're supposed to be."

Jo took the letter, noting the official Tremayne wax seal on the back. The ivory paper was thick and expensive, and looked out of place in Jo's dirty hand. Her name was scrawled in black ink. She shoved it back at Jackson. Knowing what event was to take place in another week, she didn't need to open it to know what it said. "I don't want it."

He raised a blond eyebrow. "You can't ignore it, Jo."

"Yes, I can."

"Your baby sister's birthday?" He gathered his reins and led his horse toward the barn. "Grace might forgive you for not coming to see her before she leaves for that bloody finishing school, but you can be sure Morgan won't. She'll come looking for you—in Dunmore, Jo."

"She won't. She's too busy." Though Jo didn't believe her own denial.

"And when she arrives in Dunmore and learns you haven't been there these past five months," he said over his shoulder, "she'll demand to know where you've been and what you've been doing."

Jo shuddered. If she didn't go to London, she'd have to answer questions she'd rather not face. Like where had she found the money to buy a farm? How could she support so many children? Why hadn't she told Morgan and Daniel about her plans? She hadn't confided in them because she hadn't been able to come up with a believable story. She couldn't fool Morgan. Her sister would suspect that she'd stolen the money, and then there'd be no end to Morgan's lecture. Never mind that Jo's actions had been for a good cause.

"We'll have to leave in the morning."

"You don't have to sound so cheery about it," Jo grumbled.

"You think I want to be a part of this?" Jackson asked, stopping just before he disappeared into the barn. "Watch Grace parade herself in front of all those men who are looking for a wife?"

"She's going away to school. She's not looking for a husband."

"She will be. Soon as she thinks she's a good and proper lady." Jackson shook his head and stared at Jo, though she didn't think he really saw her. In a voice lacking any emotion, he said, "It won't be so bad. It's to be a masked ball."

Jo closed her eyes and crushed the invitation in her fist. *A mask.* At the last ball she'd attended she'd been the Emerald of London, a woman of mystery and allure. She'd met Nathan that night and her life had been forever changed.

She stared at the crumpled envelope, but all she saw was the dirt beneath her nails and the calluses that scarred her palms. She belonged in the country with the children and Mira, not in London, where she'd have to pretend she was something she wasn't. But this was for Grace's birthday. She had to go.

What if Nathan is there? She'd be able to see him. . . .

She pressed her hand to her chest, where the empty ache still lingered, all the more powerful despite the passing months. "He can't be there," she whispered to the heavens, hoping the Lord would hear her this one time. "Please, please don't let him be there."

Twenty-two

"You've had your birthday, Grace." Jo peered through the curtained nook just off the ballroom floor. "Does the party have to go on all night?"

Seated in a padded, straight-backed chair with her legs crossed at the ankle and her arms folded over her chest, Grace frowned up at her. "Since you haven't actually been a part of the party yet, I don't see why you're fussing. You've either been in your room hiding, in the library with your nose in an agriculture book, in the kitchen bothering Cook, or in here. I didn't invite you to my birthday mask so you could hide like a mouse."

Jo glared at her sister over her shoulder, ready with a retort, but she kept her mouth shut. *A mouse, indeed.* She parted the drapes a slit once more, but she could see only the left side of the room. People twirled on the dance floor, or mingled along the edge, their heads bent in conversation. With all the masks and feathers and glittering beads, she couldn't tell who anyone was. More important, she couldn't tell if Nathan was among the guests.

At least Morgan and Daniel where nowhere to be seen. They still had no clue about her involvement with the *Lady's Luck*'s demise. When she'd arrived in London two days ago, she'd learned the ship had sunk off the coast of France. The crew had been rescued, but had evidently taken work aboard another trading vessel instead of returning to England. She forced thoughts of the *Lady's Luck* aside; she didn't want to consider what her actions had cost her sister and brother-in-law.

"I'm not hiding," Jo insisted, though the declaration sounded weak to her own ears.

"Then come out with me and join the party. Unless you're afraid," Grace urged with a dare. "There are a number of men who would love to dance with you."

"I'm not in the mood to dance. And I'm not afraid of anything." *Except running into Nathan.* Even Morgan's discovering the truth about Jo's pirating would be preferable. Though to see Nathan again, just one more time . . . Jo clenched her jaw. Was she really so reckless? Things were finally going the way she'd planned; meeting him now would risk everything she'd worked for.

"Then I could introduce you to some of my friends. Allyson Whitehall will be attending Wilmouth with me in the fall. She's younger than I, of course. All the girls will be much younger. But Allyson is very nice. I think you'd like her."

"Maybe another time."

"Is something wrong, Jo? You're acting as nervous as a chicken with a wolf at its door."

Jo released her stranglehold on the drapes and turned around, only to meet her sister's shrewd gaze. "You don't need to stay in here with me, Grace. You have guests to see to. Why don't you see to them? *Now!*"

"Unlike you," she said with as much sarcasm as she could manage, which wasn't much, "I'll admit that I'm trying to avoid a certain someone."

"Who?" Jo retrieved her mask from the opposite chair. "Some penniless ninny who wants the dowry Daniel will give to whomever you marry?"

Grace narrowed her eyes and her cheeks flushed, giv-

ing evidence that her temper was close to the surface.
Jo arched a brow in surprise. Of all the sisters, Grace
was the most self-restrained and tenderhearted. She
hadn't earned the nickname Angel for nothing.

"I'm not foolish enough to marry a man who could
love only money."

"Or who could love only the sea?" Jo returned.
Seeing her sister's eyes widen with shock, she wished
she could take the words back. There was a bond
between Grace and Jackson that didn't need any encouragement. But her sister wanted a stable home;
Jackson wanted to roam the sea—it was obvious their
paths would never meet. "I'm sorry, Grace. That was
uncalled-for."

Her sister rose and placed her half-mask over her
face, though the disguise couldn't hide the hurt in her
eyes. She tilted her chin and forced a smile. "Wish me
happy birthday. I'm about to start a new adventure."

Jo kissed her sister on the cheek. "Happy birthday,
Grace."

She watched her sister leave the nook, only to be
surrounded by a swarm of men before she'd taken
ten steps. Grace laughed at whatever one of the
young men said even as another one led her onto the
dance floor. Across the ballroom, wearing solid black
evening clothes and a scowl, Jackson leaned against
a marble pillar and watched as Grace was whisked
away.

Jo shook her head. Whatever Grace's adventure, she
knew it would be unlike either hers or Morgan's.

With a sigh of resignation, Jo secured her mask of
ivory feathers. At least Morgan's adventure had had a
happy ending. She had a loving husband. She had no
children as yet, but she would, undoubtedly someday
soon. Just because Jo didn't have what Morgan had
didn't mean . . .

Jo cursed, suddenly annoyed with herself. She batted
the curtain aside. What was wrong with her? Staying

close to the walls to avoid as much attention as possible, she left the ballroom. Perhaps she didn't have a man in her life, but what did that matter? She had something better: the children, Mira, a farm she could be proud of.

She smiled to herself, feeling her confidence return. Things were not as bad as she made them out. Even Grace's party wasn't the disaster it could have been. The hour was growing late and still nothing unforeseen had occurred. She hurried down a nearly deserted hallway toward the library. She'd seen a number of books on history and geography the new teacher might find useful. She'd have to ask Daniel if he'd mind her borrowing them.

Farming the Land, A History of Antiquity, and *The Transformation of England* were the ones she was most interested in. Perhaps she would include a novel or two to read to the children before bedtime—something fun, a tale of mystery that would hold their interest.

Entering the paneled room, she untied the string to her mask, cursing when it knotted. Fumbling to loosen it, she breathed in the scents of leather and dust, of wood and age. They weren't the smells of the sea, but they were comforting just the same. Whenever she stayed in London, she always enjoyed spending time in Daniel's library. The dark paneling and elegant furnishings gave it a masculine feel. It was warm and safe, a place she could spend hours without ever growing bored.

Finally the knot came loose. Pulling the mask free, she tossed it aside on a forest green velvet chair.

"Well, if it isn't Jo."

She froze, sucking in a breath before whipping around to where the voice had emerged. What she saw made her mouth go dry. *No.*

"Or perhaps I should call you the Emerald of London?"

A chill sped down her back, followed by a rush of heat. Seated on lush velvet settee, Morgan regarded her with eyes as sharp and silver as the point of the *Sea Queen* blade. Daniel sat beside her, his hard jaw no more relaxed than his wife's. But it was the third person who had spoken, catching her attention as surely as if she'd been trapped in a snare.

"Nathan, what . . . what are you doing here?" Her stomach flipped and waves of heat raced over her skin. He stood near the hearth, his hands clasped behind his back, his gaze as hard and unreadable as stone. And just as unforgiving.

Maybe he doesn't know who I really am. She discarded the worthless thought. Considering the three people facing her, their expressions equally furious, she was certain Nathan knew everything about her. Or almost everything.

They were going to demand answers. What she'd done might have been wrong, but she wasn't about to stand still while they scolded her like a child. She could always turn around and run, find her horse and leave. They wouldn't know where to look to find her.

Jo clenched her hands. What was she thinking? That she could scurry away like the mouse Grace accused her of being? She never ran.

Never. But hearing Nathan's voice, however cold and distant it might have been, made her head feel light and dizzy. And seeing him . . . He wore dark evening clothes perfectly tailored and pressed, the shade darker than the warning in his gray eyes. He seemed every bit as tall, as strong and commanding as she remembered. More so, she realized, as the air vibrated with his anger.

"Or perhaps," he continued in a voice as hard as steel, "I should call you Joanna Fisk, sister to Morgan and pirate captain of the *Sea Witch?*"

He knew the truth, all of it—she saw condemnation in his eyes. He hated her for what she was, who she was. Defeat sank through her body, leaving a staggering trail of grief.

Maybe she should have run after all.

Nathan held still, not trusting himself to move. If he moved, he'd touch her, and if he touched her he'd either wring her neck for the depth of her deceit or kiss her for finally having found her. The anger tightening the muscles in his limbs and the fact that he and Jo weren't alone made both options unacceptable. But heaven help him, she was even more beautiful than he remembered. Her ivory satin gown, with its curved neckline and fitted sleeves decorated with hundreds of seed pearls and vines of gold, flowed around every feminine curve she possessed. The pale color accented the healthy glow of her skin. His fingers flexed as he remembered the warm feel of her shoulders, the full weight of her breasts. His body heated and he cursed under his breath.

"It seems you've been busy, Jo," Morgan said, putting a bite into her words.

Jo's jaw firmed, and though she hadn't moved, Nathan pictured her as if she were a doe backed into a corner by a pack of wolves. "I had a good reason for what I did."

"The orphans." Daniel rose, leveling Jo with a glare that would have sent most men to their knees trembling. Jo narrowed her eyes.

"Why didn't you come to us?" Morgan bolted to her feet, her silver eyes flashing like steel. "We gave you money before when you asked. We would have again."

"I know you would have," Jo said, slightly relaxing her stance from aggressive to defensive. "But I had to do this myself."

"By sinking my ship!" Daniel crossed to her, and regardless of the internal warning not to interfere, Nathan took a step forward to place himself between them if need be. Only Daniel's next statement and the raw tone of his voice stopped him. "You could have been killed, Jo."

She dropped her willful gaze. "I hadn't meant for the attack to go so far. I'm sorry about the *Lady's Luck*, Daniel. But I couldn't continue coming to you for money."

"Yet you had no problem going after mine," Nathan said.

Her shoulders tensed again. "I did what I had to. Besides, Nathan, I earned the money I took from you."

"By sneaking into France to rescue his sister!" Morgan turned away to pace, her burgundy gown rustling with each step. "You've always been a risk taker, Jo. But this time you were irresponsible."

"You wouldn't say that if you were to meet the children I've saved."

Morgan sighed, and even Daniel's anger seemed to deflate. The older sister said, "I have met them, Jo, and I understand your need to help them." Clenching her jaw, she regarded her husband, and some silent message passed between them. "Promise us you'll never do anything so foolish again."

Nathan could see the defiance in Jo's eyes, the willfulness to do whatever she thought right, regardless of the consequences. Just when he thought Morgan would take Jo by the shoulders and shake her, the younger woman said, "I promise not to do anything that will risk you or Daniel again. It was foolish of me to return to pirating on the *Sea Witch*."

It wasn't the promise Nathan wanted to hear. A quick glance at Morgan and Daniel told him they weren't happy with Jo's response either, but they didn't demand anything more.

Daniel faced Nathan. "You know our family secret. What do you intend to do with it?"

"You mean, how do I think Jo should be punished?" She crossed her arms beneath her chest and glared at him. "I'm not going to stand here like a disobedient child while you three decide my fate."

"There's one thing I want," Nathan said, not moving from his place by the hearth.

Morgan clenched her hands at her sides. "We'll repay your money, Lord Darvill—"

"No."

Daniel visibly stiffened. "If you intend to go to the king, Nathan—"

"Surely there's something we can do to right what Jo has done." Morgan touched her hip, a move Nathan had seen Jo do a dozen times before. Was she looking for the *Sea Queen* blade? Did she think to protect her sister from him? As well she should, he thought, feeling his chest tighten with emotions that were too strong and too numerous to identify.

"There's only one thing I want right now," he said. The other three watched him as if they were holding their breath. "Leave me alone with Jo."

Of the three, Jo was the only one not to react.

"Why don't we let the ladies leave," Daniel suggested. "We can come to some agreeable terms."

"No." Nathan strode to the door and opened it. "Leave us."

Exchanging a wary look with his wife, Daniel took Morgan's arm and led her from the room. He stopped beside Nathan. "I would tell you to have a care with her, but I'm not sure you know what you're up against."

"Oh, I know," Nathan said. "I know very well."

Morgan arched a dark brow, her mouth almost curving into a smile as she urged her husband away.

Nathan closed the door behind them and took a slow step toward Jo.

"What are you up to, Nathan? We have nothing more to discuss." She clasped her hands at her waist as if she were a normal lady having a normal conversation.

Nathan scowled, knowing it was an act. He methodically closed the distance between them, his scowl threatening to twist into a grin when she held her ground instead of backing away. He had a sense of déjà vu from the time he'd stalked her in her cabin, only this time he was fully dressed and not weak from a stab wound.

Ten feet and a velvet settee still separated them, but he swore she wouldn't escape him again. If she tried, he'd chase her through the halls to stop her. Watching her, seeing the defiance sharpen her features, he realized the reason he hadn't been able to put her out of his mind.

Too much had been left unsaid. Too many questions and doubts still lay between them—such as the real reason she'd forced him off her ship.

"Now that I know your true identity, I believe that opens up an entire new line of discussion." He heard faint laughter out in the hall and the rustle of clothing, along with muffled footsteps, but he wasn't about to turn away from Jo to see who might be in the hallway. Who knew what she would try? "Morgan told me about your history with the *Sea Queen* and King George's warning never to sail the ship again."

"Then you know everything."

"Do I?"

Her eyes glittered with anger. "I had good reason for attacking your ship."

"Yes, I know. The orphans."

"It's the truth."

"Is it?" Nathan wanted to shake her so badly that the muscles in his arms knotted. After he'd talked with Morgan, the pieces of the puzzle he'd collected while with Jo had begun to fit together: the source of her anger, her determination. He understood Jo and the reason for her reckless behavior. Guilt. She was consumed by guilt over her brother's death, and thought helping a bunch of stray children would somehow make amends. He had to make her realize what she was do-ing, before she got herself killed.

Deciding on a tactic, he said, "You've lied so many times, I'm beginning to wonder if you know what the truth really is. Even your sister was surprised by the depth of your dedication for homeless children."

"I didn't want Morgan involved. She has enough to deal with since *your* peers refused to accept her. Be-sides, the only thing I lied about was my name." Her pulse beat frantically at the base of her throat. "I told you the truth about why I needed your gold. The chil-dren . . ."

He quirked a brow, which had the effect of cutting her off. He really didn't give a damn about what she'd done with his money. He wanted to know if she was still captaining her ship, risking her life. Because if she was, he intended to put a stop to it.

He shifted to his right, removing the settee as a bar-rier. She faced him, her shoulders squared, her chin tilted with the stubbornness he'd grown to love. The thought stopped him in midstep. *Love?* Five months ago he'd thought he'd been obsessed with her, thought it all too possible that he'd fallen in love with her. Now the only thing he knew for certain was that he wanted to kiss her *and* lock her in a cell, where he'd know she'd be safe.

"You didn't answer Daniel before. Do you intend to go to the king and tell him what I've done?"

Though she faced him as defiantly as she had while on the deck of the *Lady's Luck*, he saw the fear in her eyes. She should be afraid, he thought. She'd been a reckless fool to go against the king's order. She'd risked her life—and Morgan's—and for what? To take a hand-ful of children off the streets?

"I could go to the king," he said evenly.

The green of her eyes turned dark and turbulent. "Will you?"

"It's what you deserve."

"Don't come any closer, Nathan."

He took another step. Two more and he'd be within reach of her. He could smell her now, that unique, spicy scent that was all Jo. Memories and sensations flooded his mind. His blood heated, racing through his limbs. *Don't touch her. Don't. Not until you know if she's still playing the pirate.*

"I'm warning you, Nathan." She raised a trembling hand to ward him off.

"Do you realize how selfish you've been?"

"Selfish?" Her eyes widened with outrage. "Taking the *Sea Queen* out again, stealing the gold, none of it was ever about me."

"Damn it, Jo!" Without thinking he gripped the back of her neck and hauled her against him. "It was always about you. You and the demons you fight."

He closed his mouth over hers, taking her in a harsh, consuming kiss. She tensed and gasped, but he inhaled the sound and pulled her closer.

"Nathan, don't. I can't—"

"It's not over between us," he whispered against her mouth.

She stilled, her gaze searching his. With an agonized sound, she angled her head and kissed him, opening herself wider. Her taste flooded his mind. His head spun; the floor tilted beneath his feet. His limbs began to burn.

"Jo, my God, Jo." He burrowed his fingers into her hair, pins clattered onto the floor. He touched her face, her jaw, the length of her neck, grazing his palm down until it rested on the curve of her breast where her heart raced fast and hard. It had been so long since he'd felt her. So long.

He pulled back enough to see her eyes. "I swore I wouldn't touch you until you confessed everything."

"You know all my secrets, Nathan."

"Not the most important one."

She frowned, searching his face, obviously confused.

"Why did you force me off the *Sea Witch?*"

She briefly closed her eyes, then looked down. She tried pulling away, but Nathan wasn't about to let her go. "The answer should be obvious now that you know who I really am."

"Morgan's sister?"

She straightened in his arms as if trying to gain some distance. "A fisherman's daughter who hates aristocrats."

"You don't hate me, Jo."

"No, I don't," she admitted with a grimace. "But it would be easier if I did."

"Why easier?" Unable to stop himself, he released the remaining pins in her hair. The length fell down her back in a veil of fire and gold. Despite her incredible gown, she now looked more like the Jo in his dreams.

"I never thought you to be so thick-skulled, Nathan. We're from two different backgrounds."

"Morgan and Daniel—"

She shook her head, stopping him. "Don't say it; I've heard it all before. If they worked out their differences, then so can we. I'm not my sister, Nathan. She *wants* to fit into Daniel's world. I won't even try."

He fingered a strand of her hair, not wanting to admit she was right, but he'd known she would never be a woman of society and etiquette, who attended teas and shopped and pretended to love the opera. "No, I don't suppose you would try to fit in."

"That's why I made you leave." She stepped back, her shoulders rigid and her chin as tilted as ever, only now there was a shimmer of tears in her eyes. "You would have tried to turn our affair into something more, and I would have been tempted to let you. But it wouldn't have worked."

It can work, he wanted to tell her, but the words didn't come—partly because he knew she wouldn't listen, and partly because he wasn't sure she wasn't right.

There had to be a way to make it work, but he didn't see how, not yet.

"Now you know the truth." She pressed her hands to her stomach. He didn't know how she did it, but the simple move created a wall around her. He wanted to reach for her again, but something kept him from moving.

"So now I'm supposed to forget you?" he demanded. "Pretend you don't mean anything to me?"

"I told you I would help you rescue Lauren from Philip de Maurier, and I did. I fulfilled my part of the bargain."

"Your bargain," he said in a growl. "And now you think we should go our separate ways."

"You have your life, Nathan." She drew a steadying breath. "I have mine."

"With the children." For once he wished she weren't so damned strong, wished she would break down like a normal, emotionally overwrought woman and lean on him.

She nodded. "And your life is at Winstone Castle."

He clenched his jaw, wanting to argue, wanting to throw her over his shoulder and steal her away. He moved to do just that when she said, "I think it's time you left. There really isn't anything more for us to say."

He hesitated, watching her, wishing he could make her see reason. Theirs wasn't the perfect situation, but there had to be a solution. He couldn't accept that he'd never see her again, not now that he knew where she was, *who* she really was.

But considering the depth of her stubbornness, if he tried to convince her their relationship didn't have to end, she'd only fight him harder. Perhaps it would be best if he retreated for now, gave her time to think, and came back to fight another day.

With a plan already taking shape in his mind, he nodded to her, then did the hardest thing he'd ever done in his life: he turned and crossed to the door. At the threshold, he paused and said without turning, "I never would have gone to the king."

Not waiting for an answer, he stepped into the hall, but not before he heard her whisper, "I know."

Twenty-three

Jo pushed the gray mare through the dark, the sound of hooves a steady rhythm against the hard-packed dirt. Lather coated the mare's neck, and her breathing was labored, but she didn't slow her pace, as if she knew how desperate it was that they reach the farm. Except for shadowy trees and the glow from the waning moon, the road was empty. The birds had yet to stir awake, but even if they had, Jo wouldn't have heard them. Her mind felt numb, her body cold despite the heavy coat and wool pants she wore to keep out the chill. But this cold wasn't from the night air. This chill had started inside her, deep inside where the emptiness spread like a disease, emptying her of every emotion and leaving only pain.

A tear skimmed down her cheek, but she was too tired to wipe it away. The wind caught hold of it, dried it against her skin.

"Damn you, Nathan." She'd told him to leave, that they had nothing more to say. And he'd left! A small sound of protest escaped her. He'd just left. Because she'd been right. Well, she might have been right, she thought, urging the mare faster, but he could have argued, denied her reasoning. But he hadn't, evidently agreeing that they had no future.

So now it was over, she thought with resignation. Really and truly over. She could get on with her life, stop yearning for something she couldn't have. It would get easier, she swore, given time. She'd forget him eventually. Now that she knew how wonderful it was to be with a man, maybe she would meet someone one day, a man she could share her life with.

She laughed, the sound so raw and grating it hurt her throat. Her chest squeezed around her heart, forcing her to take a sobering breath. Reining the mare to a walk, she wiped another tear away with the back of her hand.

"There isn't another man who can compare to Nathan," she whispered, almost angry that it was so. No one could make her feel as he had, so alive, so complete. She wouldn't even bother trying to find someone else, knowing how fruitless it would be.

When the turnoff to her farm appeared up ahead, she urged the gray into a trot and focused on the day ahead. She'd cool the mare down and feed her, then start breakfast for the children. There was still no sign of the sun, but the blanket of stars overhead had begun to vanish and she knew daylight would appear within the hour. The children would be up soon after that, all chattering at once, wanting to know every detail about the ball. She'd have to make up a story for them, because the truth would never do.

Inside the barn, Jo lit a lantern. Light spread out in a three-foot circle, enough for her to find a brush and a bucket of oats. Removing the saddle, she set it aside, then began wiping down the mare's wet coat while she ate. She worked fast and methodically, her thoughts as dark as the night outside. A sound—the stirring of trees and a soft thud beyond the barn door—caught her attention. She turned, instinctively reaching for her knife, but it wasn't there. In her haste to leave for London with Jackson two days ago, she'd left it on her nightstand upstairs in her room.

She cursed under her breath, but when she heard a deep-throated bark, she sighed with relief. It was only

Honey. Hearing Jo in the barn had undoubtedly made the wolfhound anxious.

"I'm in here, girl," Jo called, turning back to the mare.

Honey growled, a long snarl of warning. The hairs on the back of Jo's neck stood on end. She spun around, but could see only the dark shapes of trees, bushes, a portion of the house in the clearing beyond the tall doors. "Honey?"

The wolfhound growled again. Jo heard the shuffle of gravel and the faint pounding of feet; then the dog yelped, the sound high-pitched and painful. The mare whinnied and shifted nervously. Then everything went quiet.

Jo reached for the pitchfork leaning against a stall gate. Clutching it in one hand, she doused the lantern with the other. She backed away to the other side of the barn, staying deep in the shadows as she neared the doorway. She held her breath, listening to the wind whistle through the cracks in the wood, the stir of tall grass in the yard, the beating of her heart in her ears.

Someone was out there. She was sure of it. But who? How could anyone have gotten past Honey? What had happened to her? A shutter at the house banged with a sudden gust of wind. Jo pushed her concern for the dog aside. She had to find the intruder; then she'd help the wolfhound.

At the barn door, she pressed her back against the wood and clenched the pitchfork in both hands. Sweat coated her skin, but her blood ran hot with anger. Whoever was out there would soon regret trespassing on her property. She was damn well going to make sure of it.

She peered around the doorway, into the yard. Shadows stirred with the wind, tricking her eyes and making men out of trees. Stepping into the opening, she kept her back to the wall. She had to get to her room. Her pistol was there, as well as her knife. Scanning the yard, seeing nothing out of the ordinary, she decided she couldn't delay any longer. Whoever was out there could be in the house already. She had no other choice. She had to make a run for it.

Jo took two leaping steps forward before sliding to a halt, her heart turning to stone in her chest. A man separated from the shadows in front of her. The moon cast a dull gleam off something he held in his hand. It was black and sleek—a gun, she realized, feeling the cold wind rush down her back. She angled the pitchfork, knowing it was as good as useless against a bullet.

"Who are you?" she demanded. "What do you want?"

"Don't you recognize me, Jo?" he asked, his voice flippant, taunting.

A chill sped over Jo's skin, jarring her with a shiver. "Oh, my God."

"I take it you're surprised to see me." He grunted as if amused. "That's good, because I do so love surprising people."

Jo gritted her teeth, her mind racing furiously for a way to stop him. "How did you find me?" *How does he even know who I am?*

"It wasn't difficult, I assure you." He moved forward with lazy arrogance, closing the gap between them. "I simply followed you from London."

From London? How was that possible?

"Your sister does give a lovely ball. A convenient one, too. I just love the anonymity a mask can give you."

He'd been at Morgan's? In her house, free to go where he wanted? Jo's heart beat against her chest with equal amounts of fury and fear. "What do you want?"

"I think that should be obvious, my dear woman." He sprang forward, startling Jo. She lifted the pitchfork, but he swung his arm, knocking it from her hands. It clattered at their feet. She reached for it, but he straightened his arm, aiming the pistol at the center of her head.

Lifting her hands out to her sides, she asked again, "What do you want?"

"I want the fifty thousand pounds you stole from me."

"I—"

The pistol's steel butt struck her temple with a crashing thud. Light exploded behind her eyes, but everything else went black, everything except the dark outline of Philip de Maurier's face.

The fire had long since burned low, leaving a glowing bed of embers that seemed to expand and ebb with a will of their own. The room was stuffy and dark, the heavy brocade drapes pulled tight against the sun outside, though some internal clock told Nathan it would be dark again sooner than he'd realized. He didn't care. He had no intention of leaving his study, or his town house, not until he knew for certain that when he left, he'd have a plan that would convince Jo to give them a chance.

When he approached her again—and he had every intention of sitting her down and forcing her to listen—he had to have a solid reason for them to stay together, one she couldn't punch holes through. Evidently their feelings for each other weren't enough, he thought, scowling into the dark.

Since returning from the Tremaynes' ball the night before, full of anger and frustration, he'd consumed a decanter of brandy. With each glass of the potent liquor he'd consumed, he'd thought of another idea of how to approach Jo, only to discard it and every other option he'd thought of.

He didn't care that she was of common birth; it was her uniqueness he'd fallen in love with, not her bloodline. No other woman had her strength and determination. When life was unjust, she took it upon herself to make it right. He couldn't help but love her for that quality alone.

"I love her," he said, his voice a faint whisper of awe in the dark. He loved her, and nothing was going to keep him from having her.

Nathan swept his hand through his hair. The muscles in his arms and legs tensed with anticipation when they should have been heavy with fatigue. He hadn't slept in two days, and thought he might not for another two, not until he had Jo with him, where she belonged.

He pushed out of his chair, clasped his hands behind his back and paced the room. A knock at the door made Nathan grind his teeth.

"What is it, Williams?"

His butler opened the door only enough for him to slip his rail-thin body through. "Pardon, my lord. I know you gave orders not to be disturbed, but you have a visitor."

Nathan's drew himself up. "A woman?"

"No, my lord." The older man pursed his lips. "A young boy. A scrappy thing. I told him to leave at once, but he slipped right past me and is now in the foyer. He refuses to leave, my lord. Shall I call the constable?"

Nathan sighed. "If he's hungry, take him to the kitchen."

"It's not food he wants, my lord. He wants to see you. Something about a man named Jo."

"Send him in," Nathan said, barely stopping himself from bolting to the foyer himself.

No more than a moment later the paneled door opened again. Only a flicker of light reached the far side of the room, but it was enough for Nathan to see the boy. He was thin and tall, reaching Nathan's chest. There were gaunt hollows in his cheeks, as if he'd missed more meals than he'd eaten. But it was his eyes that drew Nathan's attention. They were dark and solemn, and far older than any child's should have been.

Was this an example of the children Jo felt compelled to save? If so, he could understand her reasoning. Something about the boy made him want to reach out and help.

Remaining by the hearth, he asked, "Did Jo send you?"

The boy glanced from side to side as if expecting someone to jump out of the shadows and haul him to jail.

"You have nothing to fear." Forcing himself to remain calm, Nathan held out his hand to a nearby chair, when he really wanted to demand the reason for the boy's visit. "Have a seat."

He crossed the room, careful not to brush up against a table crowded with knickknacks. He reached the chair, but ignored it, regarding Nathan instead, as if he were taking his measure.

"What is your name?"

"Me name's Peter Aylwin," he said with an accent that placed him from near the docks. "I've brought ye a message."

Nathan took the scrap of paper Peter thrust out. It was wrinkled and smudged with dirt. Reaching into his pocket, he took out a shilling and tossed it to the lad. The coin hit the boy's chest, then landed on the carpet, bouncing at his feet. Peter didn't even glance down.

"I don't want your money, mister. I just want tae know what you're gonna do."

Frowning, his heart suddenly pounding against his chest, Nathan unfolded the letter. Something slipped out and fluttered to the ground, where it disappeared in the shadows.

"What . . . ?" He searched the floor, everything inside him going still and cold when he saw what he'd dropped.

"It's hers," Peter said as if he held Nathan responsible.

He picked up the lock of red hair. "No." Memories

of another letter he'd opened only to find a strand of
dark hair came flooding back. "Tell me. . . . No."

Jerking the letter open, Nathan angled it against the
fire in the hearth. He read the letter, but needn't have
bothered. He already knew what it would say.

> *I might have lost your sister, Alcott, but the
> game is far from over. The king frowns on those
> who associate with pirates. I wonder how he'll re-
> act when he learns what I know? The price for
> my silence is the fifty thousand pounds you still
> owe me.*
>
> 					*Philip*

"He . . ." The paper shook in Nathan's hands. A
cold, dead chill grazed over his skin. "He has her."

"What are ye gonna do about it?" the boy demanded.

He glanced up, wanting to strike out, to smash his
fist into a wall. *God, Jo.* "How are you involved in
this?"

"She's ours."

"Ours?" Then Nathan nodded, knowing without a
doubt that this was one of Jo's orphans.

"That's right." A tremor tore through the boy's thin
frame. His cheeks flushed and his jaw tightened with
anger. "And he's got 'er now."

Nathan gripped Peter's shoulder. "Where are they?"

"Get the money. I'm supposed to take ye to him."

Nathan looked away, afraid to breathe, afraid to give
the fears racing through his mind free rein. Philip had
Jo. He crushed the letter in his fist. Not again. He
wouldn't let Philip hurt someone he loved again.

"Ye can get the money, can't ye?"

Absently, Nathan nodded. The money. He had to con-
tact Byron Fitzhugh, arrange for another withdrawal.
And he had to hurry.

He started for the door, but the boy's voice stopped
him.

"This didn't have tae 'appen," Peter said, staring at the embers in the hearth. His bottom lip quivered. "She should have given me a bloody pistol. I could 'ave taken care of that no-good bloke. I would 'ave. Shot 'im right between the eyes."

Nathan went back to the boy and cupped his face in his hand, urging the lad's gaze up to his own.

"I'm the oldest," Peter said. "She should have given me a pistol."

Nathan drew a steadying breath. "It's all right. We're going to get her back."

He turned for the door, the boy close on his heels. He would get Jo back. He would; if it cost his own life, he'd save her. But he had to hurry. Jo wasn't like Lauren. She wouldn't sit back and wait for him to come for her. She would try to escape on her own.

And this time, she might not survive.

Twenty-four

Jo twisted her hands, only to suck in a breath. The hemp rope cut into her wrists. Welts circled her skin, decorating it with swollen red bracelets. Since regaining consciousness from de Maurier's blow to her head, only to find herself thrown into a corner of her parlor, bound like a trussed-up hog waiting for slaughter, she'd fought the bindings, growing more desperate with each passing moment.

The rope digging into her wrist also looped around her ankles. She could only sit with her knees tucked beneath her chin or lie on her side. She chose to sit, so she could glare at de Maurier whenever he came to check on her. She tugged the rough cords again, regardless that her efforts only caused the bindings to tighten that much more. The stinging heat in her wrists crept upward, creating a path of pulsing fire. She focused on the pain, using it to fuel her mind to think of a plan of action. She had to get free. *Damn it, Jo, think!* Being trapped in her own house and all because of her own carelessness . . . Her chest squeezed, nearly suffocating her with her bottled-up anger.

She dropped her head back and stared at the ceiling. Nearly an entire day had passed since Philip had captured her. How long would it be before he lost control? Who would he take his animosity out on? Her? The children? *Please, no . . .*

A water stain had spread in one corner of the sitting room. Jo stared at it, trying to empty her mind of fear. She had to concentrate, to think of a plan that would stop Philip. She needed to fix the leak, she thought distantly, before it ruined the plaster and the connecting wall. She shook her head, the insane urge to laugh filling her throat.

She'd fix the damn leak, she thought, if she survived—if any of them survived.

The little furniture Jo had managed to acquire—a worn settee, two ladder-backed chairs and a rough-hewn table—had been shoved to the side of the room, near the doorway. Mira and all the children but one sat lined against a wall opposite Jo, their knees pressed into their chests, their arms locked around their legs.

Philip had tied Mira's hands to her feet, the same as Jo. When he'd failed to find enough rope to bind the children, he'd warned them that if they tried to release the adults he'd punish them all. Just seeing Jo tied hand and foot and shoved into a corner, the cut at her temple still bleeding from where he'd hit her, had been enough to gain their cooperation.

"Peter's not comin'," Farley whispered, rocking back and forth, staring at the floor.

"Don't talk," Amy warned, pulling herself into a tighter ball as if trying to make herself invisible. "He'll hear you."

"And if 'e hears ye, 'e'll come back." Robin glared at the doorway. "I don't want 'im tae come back."

" 'E's not gonna show 'is bloody face until 'e's finished eat'n all our food." Farley licked his lips. "I'm hungry."

After dusk had fallen and night had sealed the room like a tomb, Philip de Maurier had lit an oil lamp on a nearby table. The faint light did little to brighten the room, but it was enough for Jo to see the fear in the children's eyes. Not that she needed to see it; she could hear it in their voices. A fire needed to be lit; they were shivering with cold, their thin nightclothes not enough to keep them warm.

But she felt their apprehension as well, saw the pensive set of their jaws, the grim calculation that had some of them staring at the window as if tempted to leap through the glass. Intermingled with her fear for them, she felt a renewed sense of pride that made her sit up as straight as she could. Her kids were stronger than they looked. They'd survived living on the streets with no one but themselves to look after them. They'd known starvation, had avoided the bands of thieves and cutthroats who thought nothing of harming an unwanted child.

They would survive this, too. *But only if I find a way out!*

She jerked her ropes again, harder this time. She'd promised to make a better life for them, yet look what she'd done. She'd brought Philip de Maurier right into their home.

"I should have shot him with my crossbow when I had the chance." Jo clenched her jaw, trying to control the ragged pace of her breath. If she ever had to do it over again, she swore she wouldn't hesitate. It didn't matter that she'd vowed never to harm another person ever again. Philip didn't deserve to live; not now, not after he endangered her children. She needed her pistol or her knife, but both were upstairs.

"Hush now," Mira soothed them. "Peter will be back. He's a good boy; he knows what he has tae do."

Mira met Jo's gaze as if seeking reassurance.

"Farley," Jo murmured, "how do you know the man's eating?" De Maurier had left them alone no more than fifteen minutes ago, disappearing into the back of the house. She hadn't seen him or heard a sound from him since.

"I can hear 'im, that's how." He scowled. "Probably finishing off the pork roast Miss Fenner made for us last night. It was real good, too."

"I'll be making ye another, Farley," Mira said. "Just see if I don't."

Jo glanced at the door. She had to do something. She hadn't tried anything desperate yet because of the risk to the children. But she couldn't wait any longer. If de Maurier was eating his supper, this might be her best chance to get free and retrieve her weapons. She bit down on her lip and looked at the nearly two dozen pairs of eyes watching her. But if she didn't make it, she might put them in even greater danger. *But can I sit and wait for Nathan to walk through the door with Philip's ransom?*

She knew he would come, and that terrified her as much as her inability to protect the children. Once again Philip would have the opportunity to exact his revenge on Nathan, killing him. She knew Nathan well enough to know he wouldn't defy Philip's demands, not if it meant jeopardizing her. She couldn't allow him to simply arrive, possibly unarmed, hoping that this time Philip would honor his word.

Nathan would walk into another trap, and this time she wouldn't be able to help. *I can't let that happen to him. I can't!* Her decision made, she whispered urgently, "Farley, come over here and untie me."

He leaped up without hesitation and began fumbling with the ropes, his small fingers shaking.

"What are ye think'n, Jo?" Mira asked with a gasp. " 'E could be back any minute."

"I have to get to my room. My pistol is there, and my knife."

Farley sat back. "I can get 'em, Miss Fisk."

"No, Farley—" Before she could say more, the boy darted from the room, his bare feet a whisper against the wooden floor. Seconds later she heard the stairs creak. She started to order him to return, but she pressed her lips together and locked the words inside. Lord, what had she done now?

She glanced at the remaining children. "Spread out

and fill his space." They did as instructed, looking up again as if nothing had happened.

And just in time. Philip sauntered into the room, licking his fingers and chewing what she assumed was the last bit of roast. He waved the gun at the row of children. "I thought I told you, no talking."

"They're hungry," Jo said, her skin crawling as she watched the lazy way he aimed the pistol.

"And they'll eat." He grinned, a cold pull of his lips that deadened his eyes. "After Nathan arrives with my gold."

"They need to go to the privy, de Maurier. They're children—"

"They need to stay where they are if they want to live another day," he said in a tone that warned he meant what he said.

Trying another tactic, she told him, "Nathan doesn't care about the children. He doesn't even know them."

"He'll care." The amused glint in his eyes sent a chill creeping down Jo's spine. "Or have you forgotten? I saw the two of you huddled in the library at your sister's home. I heard every word you said."

"How? The doors were closed."

"Are you really so naive? Walls have ears."

"But how did you know about us? Or were you at Marquess Fulepet's? Hiding like the rat you are?"

"If I were you, my dear, I'd learn to watch my tongue. Or you just might lose it." He drew the pistol down her temple, digging the cold barrel deeper as he skimmed it over her jaw. "I didn't know anything about you until last night. Imagine my surprise when I learned you were a pirate, and on thin ice with the king."

Jo strained against the rope, wanting to wrap her hands around Philip's neck, if only to wipe the dangerous sneer off his face.

"After I'm done with you, I think I'll pay your sister

Morgan a visit. I wonder how much she'll pay to keep me from spilling your secrets?"

"Leave her alone!" Jo lunged for him, but the ropes caught, forcing her to fall onto her side. She pushed herself back into a sitting position. *I can't let him harm Morgan. I have to stop him.*

He sighed, then chuckled to himself. "I wouldn't worry about your sister. You have your own troubles that should keep you occupied. As for Nathan? He will come. And knowing this pack of beggars are at my mercy will only make him arrive all the sooner."

"I'm telling you," Jo said, shivering with anger, "he won't care about them."

"He's a do-gooder, the kind who comes to the rescue of worthless children, while he ruins men who run legitimate businesses."

"If you can call selling people as slaves legitimate." Jo knew she risked sparking his temper, but she couldn't stay quiet.

"I've been thinking about going back into the trading business." He tilted his head, eyeing the length of her body. "If everything goes as planned, you and this bunch will be my first cargo in my new venture."

Jo yanked against her bindings. Her fingers curled with the need to scratch out his eyes, smash his face until he lay bloody at her feet. He wouldn't get away with this, she vowed. Somehow she'd stop him. She had to, or he'd kill Nathan. If he accomplished that . . . A shudder tore though her. If he killed Nathan she had no doubt he'd force the children onto a slave ship.

Philip faced the children lining the wall. He pursed his soft mouth, and she could almost hear him counting, his narrowed gaze touching each child. "Well, it seems someone didn't heed my warning about leaving this room. Where is he? The boy that was sitting there?"

Everyone tensed, looking straight ahead without saying a word.

Philip turned his icy glare on Jo. "I warned you that you would be the one to suffer!"

"No one has moved, de Maurier," Jo said, pulling on the ropes. Farley had loosened one end, but not enough for her to work it free.

Philip raised his arm to backhand her across the face. There was a creak of wood, and the twin girls, Lark and Robin, squeaked. Suddenly Philip stumbled forward, nearly falling on top of Jo.

"What—" He spun around. "What are you doing? Get off me!" Farley had launched himself onto de Maurier's back, clinging to the man's waist with his skinny legs. The boy held her pistol in one of his hands, her knife in the other. Philip jerked around, loosening the boy's tenuous hold. The dagger went soaring, striking the wall and landing with a clatter on the floor beside Amy, the deadly tip inches from her thigh. Philip reached back, gripping the boy by his shirt, and hauled him over his shoulder.

Farley stumbled, trying to pull free, but Philip held the slight boy inches off the ground. "Let go of me! You bleed'n—"

"I suppose I need to teach you a lesson first." De Maurier reached back, angling the pistol he still gripped, then brought it down.

"No!" Jo cried, but not loud enough to do any good or cover the sickening sound of the blow to Farley's head. Her pistol dropped from Farley's limp hand, clattering to the floor.

Darren leaped up and tackled Philip around the legs. Philip stumbled; his arm hit the lantern. The lamp toppled, then flipped off the table, shattering into a thousand needlelike shards. Oil splattered across the walls and the bare wooden floors. Fire burst out in a sucking whoosh. A gust of heated air blew against Jo's face. *Fire!* She had to get the children out. She futilely wrenched the ropes. Someone screamed. From the cor-

ner of her vision she saw a rush of movement as everyone scattered around her.

But she couldn't say who moved where.

She only saw Philip shove Darren, sending him skid-
ding across the floor as if he were a dirty rag. De
Maurier straightened and aimed the gun at Farley.

"No!" Jo surged forward. The ropes tightened
around her wrists and ankles, sending her face-first to
the floorboards. *"Farley!"*

She turned her head, trying to see. Fire licked up the
walls near the doorway. Heat burned her cheeks, dried
her eyes. The air seemed alive with a crackling roar.
Her gun lay abandoned three feet away. She had to stop
Philip. *God, help me! Farley!* Her pistol! She had to
reach it. She rolled onto her side, stretching her arms,
her fingers grazing over the handle.

A gun exploded. Jo flinched. Denial screamed
through her mind, but the only sound she made was a
ragged sob. *Farley!* Her limbs, her heart, the blood in
her veins went cold with an agonizing horror. *I'm too
late, God help me, I'm too late.*

Nathan tied his reins to a low-hanging branch and
studied Jo's farmhouse through the scattering of trees.
Wind skirted through the budding leaves, creating a
rustling so close to the sound of whispers, he had to
glance around to ensure he and the boy were alone.
Cold air snaked beneath his coat, chilling the sweat that
glazed his skin.

Stopping beside him, Peter dismounted and secured
his horse. He could barely see the boy in the dark, but
he didn't worry that Peter would falter or make any
unnecessary noise. The boy seemed familiar with moving without being seen or heard. He wanted to ask Peter
what had happened to his parents, what dire events had
caused the suspicious glint in his eyes, but now wasn't
the time. In too many ways, Peter reminded him of Jo:

wary yet strong, capable and unafraid. He imagined
they had both survived by living with the motto, Trust
no one.

The muscles along Nathan's back clenched into
knots; his legs ached with the need to run across the
open yard, barge into the house and find Jo. The
thought of her in Philip's hands, perhaps beaten or even
dying, wrenched some primal emotion loose inside of
Nathan. If de Maurier so much as bruised her, he
thought with a tremor of rage, he vowed the man would
die.

"For once, Jo," he whispered, "don't do anything
foolish." She had the children's safety to consider, not
just her own. Maybe, just maybe, she'd do the sensible
thing and wait for him to arrive.

"Jo do something sensible?" Nathan gritted his teeth
as fear pushed up through his chest. She'd sacrifice herself if it meant saving the children.

Touching the saddlebag loaded with gold coins as
well as paper money, Nathan decided to leave it behind
for the time being. He'd met Philip's demands to the
letter once before—he wouldn't be so foolish as to do
so again. When he'd arrived in Saint-Nazaire, he hadn't
wanted to believe de Maurier would try to kill him
outright, but this time he knew better. Philip wanted
him dead.

Only now Jo's life—and that of the children she
cared for—was at stake. The blood pouring through
Nathan's veins turned hot, nearly boiling with the need
for action. He understood how Jo's consuming anger
had driven her to take revenge against aristocrats. The
need for justice was a heady feeling, one that almost
blinded him to reason. Philip wouldn't walk away from
this unscathed, not this time. If it meant ending Philip's
miserable life, then he would make sure that happened—anything to keep de Maurier from harming
someone Nathan loved ever again. The intensity of his
conviction that he could take another man's life—the

almost savage taste of blood lust in his mouth—should have shocked him. But it didn't. Not when it meant possibly losing Jo for all time.

He retrieved his extra gun from his saddle and started through the trees, careful to keep to the shadows.

"What about one for me?" Peter asked, staying close to his side. "Don't go tell'n me I'm too young. 'E's got me brother in there and Miss Fisk and all the others."

Nathan glanced at the boy. Even in the dark, he could see Peter's angry defiance. "I only brought one," he lied. He had another gun tucked into his waistband beneath his coat, but he wasn't about to endanger the boy's life any more than it already was. "Besides, I need you to stay by the barn and keep a lookout."

"Lookout for what?" Peter demanded. "Owls? Ye can't go in there by yourself."

"De Maurier might have accomplices."

"I done told ye, it's only him. Calls 'imself Lord de Maurier. 'E might 'ave been a lord once, but looking at his clothes now, all ripped and dirty, it was a long time ago."

"I'm going alone, Peter. I want you to stay back where it's safe."

"I got a better idea." He touched Nathan's arm, stopping him. "You need a distraction."

"Peter, we don't have time for this."

" 'E's expect'n me. Let me go in first, tell 'im you're on your way. You can sneak in the back."

Nathan gritted his teeth, not liking what the boy was suggesting. But a delay would give him a better chance of catching Philip unaware. "All right. You go in the front. But don't do anything foolish. If anything happens to you, Jo will never forgive me."

Even in the murky light, Nathan could see Peter's cocky smile. "Don't worry 'bout me none. I can take care of myself."

Hearing an echo of Jo's words, Nathan nodded and

headed for the bulky shadow of the barn to his left. Hurrying to the front corner of the barn, they stayed in the dark, out of the light of moon that had topped the trees.

"When you're inside the house, Peter, find de Maurier and tell him I'm unloading the gold off my horse."

"What if 'e looks out the window and doesn't see you or no horse?"

"It won't matter." Reaching the front of the building, Nathan stopped and crouched low, knuckling sweat from his brow. Light shone through a front window of the farmhouse. *So this is the home Jo's made for her kids.* A knot formed in his throat. *I should have taken her more seriously, realized just what she was trying to accomplish.*

Shadows flickered off one wall, but he couldn't see anyone moving. The rest of the house was quiet and dark. "Philip won't have time to look out the window. I'll already be in the house, ready to deliver a surprise of my own."

Nathan motioned for Peter to go ahead while he started off to the left, taking no more than half a dozen steps when a scream from inside the house shattered the quiet night. Birds squawked in startled protest, taking flight from nearby trees. The hairs on the back of Nathan's neck rose in warning. He heard a crash, then more frantic shouts.

Peter glanced back at Nathan, his eyes wide, his mouth dropping open. A gunshot ricocheted through the night. Peter flinched, and Nathan felt his blood turn to ice.

"Jo."

Peter turned and bolted for the front porch.

"Stop!" Nathan called, going after him. "No!" He caught up with the boy, forcing him back. "Wait here," he ordered, not waiting to see whether Peter obeyed.

Leaping onto the porch, Nathan threw his weight

against the door. Old and partly rotted as it was, metal buckled and wood splintered. The door swung wide, banging against the opposite wall.

Smoke curled in a black stream along the ceiling, growing thicker at a doorway to his right. The smoke thinned closer to the floor, as if nothing more than a morning fog had invaded the room. But the orange glow of curling flames around the doorjamb made his heart freeze. Someone cried out, a wrenching sob—a child, judging by the high-pitched sound.

Bending low, he rushed forward, reaching the threshold just as three small bodies came darting out. They each gave a yelp, two boys and a girl, he thought as he gripped their arms and pushed them toward the exit. "Go!"

Behind him wood sizzled, an ominous crackling sound that told him to hurry.

Inside the room, he used his hand and arm to shield himself from the worst of the heat, but the air dried his lungs. He breathed in smoke, felt his chest constrict. Coughing, he bent closer to the floor. Flames leaped up the wall to his right; fire ate the floorboards in the corner beside him, spreading deeper into the room as he watched. Through layers of gray smoke and dancing yellow flames, he saw shapes, people moving.

"Jo!"

He heard coughing. Someone else was crying. He skirted to the left, away from the fire. His lungs tightened with the building heat and thickening smoke; he could barely breathe. He kept going, reaching out. "Jo, where are you?"

Ahead of him, glass shattered. A window, he thought, and would have felt relief if only he could see someone.

"Hurry out," someone cried—a woman, Nathan guessed, though the sound of her voice was too rough for it to be Jo.

"Stay where you are," a man ordered, his voice coming from somewhere directly ahead of Nathan, and low, as if he were stooping close to the floor.

"Let them go!" a woman ordered.

Jo. Just hearing her sent panic and relief through his mind. But he couldn't see her. There were shapes and figures, faint colors of clothing. He moved closer. He raised his gun, keeping the barrel pointed toward the ceiling. From the sounds of struggle, there were too many people in the room. Even if he could see Philip clearly, he might hit someone else.

"Jo!" he shouted.

"Don't come any closer, Nathan," Philip warned in a frantic shout that nearly drowned the roar of flames.

The smoke thinned as it shifted through the broken window, giving him a brief glimpse of Jo. Philip was kneeling on the floor behind her, his arm tight around her throat, forcing her head back, choking her as much as the smoke was. She watched him with eyes red-rimmed and full of anger and fear. She gripped Philip's arm with hands bound by the thick rope that also tied her ankles.

"Get the children out, Nathan," Jo pleaded in a wheezing cry.

Philip jerked his arm, causing her to straighten or suffer a broken neck. "Shut up!"

A handful of children and another woman huddled close to Philip, but they didn't move to escape. Nathan saw the reason why. Philip knelt between the children and the open window, blocking their path. Nathan glanced behind him. He could get them out through the front. . . . A wall of red flames and black smoke consumed the floor of the doorway and most of the flanking walls. Within minutes it would reach the ceiling, then spread to consume the entire room.

He spun back around, gripping the pistol in his sweaty palm, knowing he couldn't use it, not when de Maurier held Jo hostage. "Let them go, Philip. The gold's outside."

"I knew you'd come through," he shouted.

"Let Jo and the children go now!"

"Drop your gun first." Philip pressed the black barrel of his pistol against Jo's temple. "Drop it."

Nathan hesitated only a heartbeat, then tossed the gun aside. "Release her. We don't have much time."

"I agree," Philip said, shoving Jo toward him.

The ropes around her wrists and ankles caught, sending her to the floor. Nathan gripped her shoulders to help her upright. A gasp from the children brought his head up. His heart froze. Philip grinned, his eyes glowing like cold fire. He leveled the pistol and aimed it at Jo's back.

"No!" Nathan shoved Jo to the side, toward the other woman, and leaped for Philip, catching his wrist and forcing it back. Philip crashed into the wall with a thud that brought a shower of embers falling around their heads. Smoke burned Nathan's eyes, filling his lungs with the acrid taste of burning wood; scalding pricks of heat blistered his arms. He couldn't breathe, but he'd die before he released his hold.

"Get out," he shouted at the others behind him. He slammed Philip's hand against the wall, then did it again, trying to force him to drop the gun. He banged Philip's wrist once more, feeling bones grind beneath his fingers. Philip's eyes bulged, and his lips pulled back in a furious scowl.

"You're not going to win, Nathan," Philip said in a sneer as the pistol clattered to the floor. He swung his arm, landing a blow to Nathan's ribs. "It's time for you to pay."

Philip pushed him back, swinging his fists with a strength Nathan hadn't thought the man capable of, catching him in the jaw, the temple, a piercing blow to the stomach. Nathan doubled over, sucked in a lungful of smoke.

He heard the others rush for the window, the older woman in tears as she helped the younger children through. He didn't see Jo, but she had to be with them. The other woman would get her out. *I have to stop Philip.* If it meant keeping the miscreant inside the house until it fell, burning them both alive, he wasn't going to let Philip escape.

Nathan straightened, bringing up his fist, catching Philip beneath the chin. The man's head jerked back, his arms flailing to the sides, but he didn't go down. He rushed Nathan, grabbing him around the waist. Nathan twisted to break his hold, but not soon enough. Philip gripped the second pistol tucked into Nathan's pants, ripping it free. Nathan caught his arm and wrenched the gun high into the air.

He had to get the gun back. He had to.

He heard the whimpers of the children as they crawled through the window, heard their sobbing cries and hacking coughs. He couldn't see them, though. His eyes blurred with tears that stung and burned.

Philip, still holding the gun, yanked his arm down, bending so the barrel was aimed at Nathan. "It's time for you to die!"

Nathan twisted to the side, bringing Philip's arm around just as the gun exploded. The vibration shot up his arm. He went still; he felt the heat of the gun, smelled the acrid scent of gunpowder.

Philip's face was within inches of his. The man's eyes widened, his mouth thinning with a vicious grin. "I told you. It's time for you . . ." A muscle twitched in his cheek. His eyes glazed. ". . . to die."

Philip fell back, landing hard on the floor that had all but disappeared in the ground-eating smoke and flames. *I killed him.* Nathan tossed the gun aside, thinking he should feel remorse for killing a man, but he didn't.

He glanced behind him and saw that everyone else had left. Rushing to the window, he tripped and nearly fell. He looked down and saw a boy unconscious at his feet. Lifting him up over his shoulder, Nathan dove through the window, turning to take the brunt of the landing. He struck the wooden porch and heard the bones in his shoulder jar and crunch.

He felt hands on his arms, helping him up. Someone lifted the boy away. He struggled to his feet, coughing, drawing in clean air that hurt almost as much as the smoke. Sitting up, bracing himself with one hand, he ran the other through his hair, waiting for the moment when his vision would completely clear. It was over, finally over, he thought, feeling numb with relief. Philip wouldn't hurt anyone again.

"Where is she?" someone demanded. Peter, Nathan thought, from the sound of the voice.

He gritted his teeth against the pain in his lungs and the aching throb in his shoulder. "Who? Where is who?"

Nathan closed his eyes for a second, feeling their gritty dryness. But when the question finally registered, he looked at the children surrounding him, not needing them to respond. He didn't need to see their faces streaked with soot, vertical lines washed clean by their tears, to know the answer. He already knew.

Twenty-five

The floor was hot beneath her cheek, the wood pressing like heated splinters into her flesh. Her throat felt raw, as if she'd swallowed shattered glass. But it was the pressure in her head, the vise that squeezed her lungs, that she focused on. It hurt to breathe. She drew a shallow breath and winced. She couldn't survive much longer. The fire surrounded her, billowing closer with deadly speed. She could feel it, hear it, the hungry sound of destruction.

Get up! a sluggish voice urged in the back of her mind. When Philip had shoved her away, Nathan had caught her, only to let her go—to fight Philip, she knew. But she'd struck her head on the floor, becoming dazed. Mira hadn't seen; she'd been pushing the children toward safety, when it should have been Jo helping them escape.

Damn it, Jo, get up! She lifted her arm, but something held it down. The rope, she recalled distantly. She was still tied hand to foot. She couldn't move; she'd breathed too much smoke. She hadn't been able to help the children through the window. She hadn't even been able to stop Philip from carrying out his threats—Nathan had done that. She'd failed again. God, would she ever learn? No, she realized. It was too late now. And this time she couldn't take care of herself. But then Nathan had always known that—had always seen through her arrogance.

Nathan. She thought she moved her lips to say his name, but no sound emerged. She heard nothing but the sharp crackling of wood, the bellowing roar of flames, spreading, eating, destroying everything they touched.

She tried opening her eyes to see—maybe there was another way out—but she couldn't lift her eyelids; she was so tired, heavy and tired. *It will be over soon.* The fire was behind her, the heat so intense she thought her clothes would melt to her skin—if they didn't ignite first.

But the children were out, safe. That was all that mattered. And Nathan. She hadn't seen him leave through the window. A moment ago, or perhaps it had been longer—she had no way of knowing how much time had passed—the smoke had swirled around her, revealing Philip de Maurier's lifeless body. The memory made her want to smile, yet she felt a trickle of tears roll down her hot skin.

That was when she'd seen her knife, inches from her hands. She'd reached for the hilt, her fingers closing around the smooth handle. The three thumb-sized gems burned into her skin, but she didn't mind. If she was to die, she wanted to do it holding her knife.

But I have to see Nathan once more, make sure he's all right. Tell him I love him. Tell him— A sob wrenched her chest, turning into a hacking cough that seared her body like lightning.

She turned onto her back, or was pushed, she couldn't tell.

"Jo."

Hearing her name, she frowned, struggled to take another breath and curled into a tighter ball, her body shuddering with violent coughs. Her mind spun; the floor seemed to drop out from beneath her. She pressed

her bound hands to her mouth, trying not to breathe.
But not breathing hurt just as much.

"Jo, answer me! Damn it, open your eyes. I can't
untie the knots."

She forced her eyes open. "Nathan . . ." His name
came out so hoarsely, it sounded more like a moan.
"Leave . . ." He couldn't be here. He'd die. He had
to go. Now. But how to tell him?

He jarred her shoulders, as if preparing to lift her;
then he stopped. Taking the knife from her grip, he cut
the ropes.

"Put your arms around my neck."

She tried to do as he said, but she couldn't move.
Her hands, limp against her body, felt as if they were
made of stone. He lifted her in his arms; her head fell
back. She saw flames throw themselves toward the ceiling in bright spears of light. Smoke swirled in thickening layers the higher she looked, until all she saw
was a barrier of black, rolling clouds.

Then she felt a wash of cold air. Her body arched
instinctively, drawing in a fresh lungful, only to clench
in agony.

"Is she going tae be all right?"

Jo didn't know who had asked the question, but she
heard Nathan's response, and the quaver in his voice.
"Jo's too stubborn to quit. Let's move her into the
yard."

She felt herself being lifted once more, and wished
she could open her eyes, but she couldn't. She was
dizzy and weak, her whole body aching as if she'd
fought a bear and had lost.

"Miss Fisk told us we'd have to leave the farm one
day. It looks like we'll have to leave sooner than we
thought."

Jo heard Amy's voice, though it echoed, then faded,
as if it came from a great distance away. Little Amy,
a girl of eight with the insight of a thirty-year-old

woman. Only now her voice sounded small and lost, and so sad that it pained Jo to hear it.

"And we didn't get a chance tae learn how tae read," she added.

"Shh, now. We'll have none of that."

Mira. Jo wanted to smile at the unique mixture of severity and love the woman always managed. But it hurt to move. Something pressed onto her chest, a weight that suffocated and burned.

"Jo," Nathan urged, his voice torn and desperate. "Open your eyes. Please, Jo. Look at me!"

She felt his hand on her face, cupping her jaw. He was warm and solid. And here. God, she'd thought she'd never see him again. Tears pooled behind her closed lids, burning her eyes as much as they soothed.

Then she gasped, feeling her lungs contract. She lurched sideways, trying to sit up. Hands pushed her back down, though she thought it might have been barely a touch. She was tired, and she hurt. Her legs, her arms. Her skin felt hot and tender, as if she'd been in the sun too long.

"Jo?" Nathan whispered into her ear. She reached up and gripped his wrist, wanting to cry just from the feel of him.

"Nathan—" She blinked her eyes open. The first thing she saw was Mira's round face beside her. The woman was blurry at first; then she cleared. A frown dug deep lines into her brow and around her soot-smudged mouth.

"The children—" Her throat closed around the croaking words.

"They're fine. Your man got all of us out." She scowled, her face turning hard in the glow of reddish light. "Well, almost all of us."

Jo struggled to sit up, but Nathan forced her back down. Only then did she realize she wasn't lying flat on her back, but leaning against his chest, his arms wrapped around her in a possessive hold. He touched

her face, her neck, skimmed his hands down her arms
to her legs, as if ensuring that she wasn't injured.

Then he touched her temple where Philip had struck
her with the butt of his gun. She winced, squeezing her
eyes closed.

"Look at me," he urged. "Let me see you're all
right."

She worked her eyes open and saw Nathan above
her, his face streaked with soot, his gray eyes hard and
intent, his lips a thin line of worry.

She struggled to sit up, but he refused to let her
move. His fingers trembled against her cheek. He
clenched his jaw, but she saw the anger flare in his
eyes, the fear.

"I thought . . . I thought . . . God, Jo . . ." He
touched his forehead to hers and whispered above the
roaring blaze that filled the night air, "I almost lost
you."

She wanted to bury her face against his neck, to hold
on to him and never let go. After the ball she'd thought
she'd never see him again; then during the last few
moments of the fire . . . But he was here, with her.
"You came for me."

He held her gaze, ran his thumb along her jaw. "You
knew I would."

She nodded and fisted her hands in his shirt. "He
wanted to kill you."

"He won't hurt anyone ever again, Jo."

" 'E's dead, Miss Fisk," Peter said, kneeling beside
Mira. He handed Jo a dipper filled with water, telling
her as she drank, "Lord Darvill done took care of 'im."

Jo looked at Nathan and saw the grim look in his
eyes. She cupped his face, feeling the stubble of his
beard, a beard she loved so well. "I'm sorry. I should
have been able to stop him."

"Bloody hell!" His eyes flashed with anger. "I'm
the one who's sorry. If not for me, you and the children
never would have been in danger."

"But it's over now." Then she remembered the children. "Farley!"

" 'Ere, Miss Fisk." The boy was sitting beside her, his shirt bloody from the gash on his head that had to be almost identical to the one she felt at her temple. "I'll be all right, but Honey's been hurt."

"Where is she?"

"In the barn," Mira said. "Elliot found her and made her a pallet of straw. She's got a few broken ribs, I think. Nothing worse to worry over."

Behind Jo and the group surrounding her, wood popped, cutting off her reply. The air cracked, the sound loud and ominous. The yard flickered with red and orange light, swirls that built, growing as bright as a midday sun. She twisted in Nathan's arms just as the roof of her home caved in, filling the night with a surging roar of flames and ash. Walls crumbled; glass shattered. The blaze licked the sky, reaching higher and higher, as if it wanted to burn the stars as well.

"Oh, my God, Nathan. My house . . ." A sob broke through her chest, stopping her from saying more.

He hugged her to him. "It will be all right, Jo. I promise."

"It won't be all right. This was their home!" Every word was a torment to her throat, but she couldn't stop. "Everything I did—*everything*, Nathan—was so they'd have a place to live."

"I know."

"Then how can you say it will be all right?" She wanted to shout at him, but she could barely manage a hoarse squeak. She shoved against his chest, needing to stand.

Nathan gripped her hands and helped her to her feet. She was so weak she had no choice but to let him help her, but it angered her to do so. How could he be so blind? So uncaring?

"You can build another house." He frowned at her,

holding on to her hands regardless that she tried to tug them free.

"If I use the rest of the gold on another house, there will be nothing left. How will I get more? I can't return to pirating."

"You don't have to."

"Then how? How——"

He gripped her face between his hands, stopping her demands. "I love you, Jo. Have I ever told you that?"

She stared at him, afraid to breathe, afraid the fire had done more than hurt her throat, that it had also damaged her hearing.

"I love you," he said again, grinding out the words.

She shook her head. "Don't . . . don't do this. Not now. I have to think about the children. They need me."

"What about me?"

"What . . ." She had to swallow, but her throat was as dry as winter grass. "What about you?"

He glanced at the burning remains of her home. "I almost lost you tonight. I'm not going to let it happen again. No one is going to stop us from being together. Not this farm or these children or your fear that we can't bridge the social gap between us. I need you, Jo. In my life, and by my side."

"Don't be a fool, Nathan." She tugged her hands again, but he hauled her up against him

"You're going to be my wife, Jo. So accept it."

"Let me go." The words were no more than a whisper, but they were all she could manage. She wanted to believe him. She wanted to. . . .

"Never." He shook his head, the look in his eyes as grim as the day she'd first taken him prisoner. "We belong together."

"Is he asking her to marry him?" Amy asked, looking up at Peter.

"I think so." Peter stood beside Jo, grinning in a way she'd never seen him grin before.

"You're going to say yes, aren't you, Miss Fisk?" Lark asked, tugging Jo's shirt.

"He's not asking me to marry him."

"That's right, I'm not asking you; I'm telling you." His voice deepened with emotions that seemed to have been pulled from his soul. "Joanna Fisk, you're going to marry me."

"Nathan, I can't," she said, though it nearly killed her to say it. Not because it physically hurt to say the words, but because they were words that broke her heart. "I'm a pir—"

"You're an incredible woman who wears her heart on her sleeve, even though you think you've hidden it away." He lifted the leather strap that held the toy soldier and pulled it free of her shirt. He gripped it in his hand. "We belong together. You know we do."

"You can't pretend my past doesn't matter."

"I don't have to pretend, because it doesn't."

Jo clutched his shirt in her hands. She wanted to believe him, believe they would build a life together, but a marriage with Nathan would be like reaching for the stars. Regardless of what he said, she couldn't do it. But she wanted to; God help her, she wanted a life with him.

"It wouldn't be fair to you." She glanced down. "Or the children. I have to think about them."

"Then think about them, and what we can give them." He threaded his fingers into her hair, forcing her to meet his gaze, forcing her to feel the tremors that shook his body.

"When you told me about your orphans, I didn't take you seriously. But I understand now." He pressed a kiss to her lips. "I don't just want you to be a part of my life; I want to be a part of yours. I'm going to help you build a new house and raise these kids."

"But—"

"No buts, Miss Fisk," Amy ordered. "Just say yes."

"You've taken risks in your life, Jo. Take another one now."

"I didn't want to love you," she admitted grudgingly, tears filling her eyes. "But I do. So help me, I do."

The worried frown eased from Nathan's eyes, but he didn't say anything, seeming to be holding his breath. She wanted to laugh, but it turned into a quiet sob. Nathan wiped the tears from her cheeks with the pads of his thumbs.

"If I say yes," she warned, "you can't change your mind."

"I don't intend to."

"Once I say yes, Nathan, you're mine. Forever."

Smiling, he cupped her face. To the sounds of shouts and laughter, he kissed her, a deep, sealing kiss that made Jo realize one thing.

Loving Nathan was a risk, the greatest one she'd ever faced. But he was a risk she couldn't live without.

Epilogue

"I don't have time for this, Jo." Grace folded her arms over her chest, wrinkling the bodice of her royal blue traveling gown, and glared at the wooden deck beneath her feet.

"It won't take long." Jo paced to the railing and glanced over the side, relieved that her last passenger was climbing the last few feet of ladder. The cove below, the color of melted jade, was still and quiet, as was their childhood village of Dunmore.

"I'm leaving for the Wilmouth School for Girls in the morning," Grace continued to complain. "I still have to finish packing and—"

"I said it won't take long." Jo stepped back, giving her oldest sister, Morgan, room to board.

"What I wouldn't give for a pair of your pants, Jo," Morgan grumbled. Once on the deck, she untucked the hem of her skirts from her waistband and straightened her pleats. "Daniel and Nathan are waiting for us at the tavern. I suggest we hurry, or we'll end up staying the night in our old cottage."

"Would that be so bad?" Jo asked, wondering which couple would get the only bedroom and who would get the loft above stairs.

Morgan glanced up to answer, but caught her breath. She tilted her head back, smiling as she scanned the towering masts, the sails all neatly folded and tied off.

She took in every inch of the forward deck, the binnacle box and ship's wheel. She pressed her hand to her chest and sighed. "It's been too long since I've stepped foot on the *Sea Queen.*"

"*Sea Witch,*" Jo corrected, then wished she hadn't. Morgan still hadn't forgiven her for sinking the *Lady's Luck.*

Morgan pursed her lips. "Yes, well, it's still good to be back."

"Speak for yourself." Grace frowned at her sisters. "If I never set foot on this ship again, it would be too soon."

"How can you say such a thing?" Morgan asked, though in a tone meant to soothe instead of reprimand. "If not for this ship, I never would have met Daniel."

"And I wouldn't have married Nathan," Jo said, unable to stop the smile that spread over her face. She raised a brow at her young sister. "And you, Grace, wouldn't be able to attend Wilmouth so you can become a true lady of society. Though I still think it's a waste of time."

"Well," Grace conceded reluctantly, touching the railing before jerking her hand back. "I suppose she served her purpose. But I still don't know why we're here now."

Jo strode toward Grace. Unlike her sisters, she still wore her pants and boots, though her new ones were made of fine wool and soft, hand-tooled leather. Stopping before her youngest sister, she withdrew the knife sheath at her waist and held it out with both hands.

Grace tensed, her arms going down to her sides. Her gloved hands curled into fists. "What are you doing?"

"This is yours now. Neither Morgan nor I have a need for it any longer."

Her sister retreated a step. "You can keep it."

"Take it, Grace," Morgan said. Jo exchanged a glance with her older sister, and knew Morgan understood why Jo had called this meeting aboard the *Sea Queen*.

Four years ago Morgan had given the jeweled dagger to Jo for safekeeping. Now it was Jo's turn to hand it down to the youngest Fisk sister. Passing down the watch, as it were.

"I don't want it." Grace glared at the knife as if it were a coiled snake, ready to strike.

"It's yours," Jo said evenly. She understood her sister's aversion to the ship and the sea, but the dagger belonged with her now.

"I told you, I don't want it!" Grace spun away and rushed to the side of the ship, where the ladder would take her to the skiff waiting below.

Jo caught up with her, stopping her with a hand on her shoulder. She held up the knife. Cool afternoon sunlight reflected off the embedded gems, sending glittering sparks of color into the air. "This dagger and this ship saved us, Grace. You shouldn't resent them. I know you didn't like living on the *Sea Queen*—"

"Didn't like?" she interrupted, her face turning pale with disbelief. "I hated it, Jo. Every day I lived in fear that we'd attack a ship and one of you would die. Or both of you! Yes, this ship might have saved our village, and both of you were fortunate enough to find men who love you. But both of you could just as easily have died."

"Grace—" Morgan began.

"I want nothing to do with this ship or the knife. Do you understand me? Nothing! I want to be a lady. I want a husband and a home. Is that so much to ask?"

"No." Jo sighed. Perhaps she shouldn't have pushed Grace, but she'd thought her sister had understood that a tradition had begun with Morgan, and it needed to end with Grace.

"And I won't find a husband if I strap that dagger to my side."

"Then don't." Jo held out the knife, the hilt toward

her sister. "Just keep it as a reminder of where we've been and what we survived."

Grace tilted her chin, but something in her blue eyes made Jo think she might be wavering.

"You don't have to wear it," Morgan added.

"What about the ship? When you gave Jo the dagger, you gave her the ship to take care of, as well."

"Do you want the *Sea Witch?*" Jo asked, feeling her hope begin to build.

"No, I do not!" she said, her tone so appalled, Jo thought she might have asked her sister to strip naked in the center of Hyde Park.

"Then what do we do with it?" Morgan's brow furrowed as she studied the ship from stern to bow.

Jo knew her sister was thinking about adding it to Daniel's fleet. It would only be fair, since Jo had sunk the *Lady's Luck*, but she didn't want it used as a trading vessel—that was not what it had been built for. "Let's leave it here, in the cove at Dunmore."

"And let it go to waste?" Morgan tilted her head as if she were about to give an order.

"It won't be a waste, but a reminder." She held the dagger closer to her youngest sister. "Like the *Sea Queen* blade. It's only a reminder."

Grace eyed the dagger as she would an enemy. Then she closed her eyes and sighed. "Very well." She gripped the hilt, angling it, studying the polished steel blade. "I'll keep it, but I won't ever use it."

"Don't be so sure." Smiling, Jo led her sister toward the ladder. She was ready to leave the *Sea Witch;* Nathan was waiting for her, and Daniel for Morgan.

"You're looking for something, Grace," Jo said in a whisper, more for herself than for her youngest sister to hear. "This ship and the blade you're holding just might help you find it."

ABOUT THE AUTHOR

After selling the computer resale business she owned with her husband, Tammy Hilz left the corporate world to answer the creative voice that had been whispering to her for years. Thus began her new career in writing, a challenge she hasn't once regretted. Winner of the prestigious RWA Golden Heart award, she lives in McKinney, Texas, with her husband, Steve, her three children, John, Christi and Trevor, and two obstinate cats, Bonnie and Clyde. You can write to her at hilz_tammy@msn.com

We hope you've enjoyed ONCE A PIRATE and ONCE A REBEL. Now look for Tammy Hilz's next installment of the Jewels of the Sea series, ONCE AN ANGEL, available June 2001 in stores everywhere!

Having had a difficult childhood, an orphan and then a pirate, Grace Fisk has always desired the stability of a home. The transition from pirate to socialite wasn't easy, but having finished boarding school, she boards a ship headed for Boston . . . and her future husband. Jackson Brodie is surprised to discover Grace on the ship he's just commandeered. After having served Morgan and Jo, he's taken over what was once the *Sea Queen* and *Sea Witch* and renamed the ship *Sea Angel*—after Grace!—to aid the cause of the American Revolution. Five years have passed since he's last seen Grace, but the memory of their friendship still lives strong in his heart . . . and she's more beautiful than ever. So when he learns she's to marry another, Jackson does the only thing he can think of . . . he takes her captive!

Put a Little Romance in Your Life With
Betina Krahn

BOOK YOUR PLACE ON OUR WEBSITE
AND MAKE THE
READING CONNECTION!

We've created a customized website just for our very special readers, where you can get the inside scoop on everything that's going on with Zebra, Pinnacle and Kensington books.

When you come online, you'll have the exciting opportunity to:

- View covers of upcoming books
- Read sample chapters
- Learn about our future publishing schedule (listed by publication month *and author*)
- Find out when your favorite authors will be visiting a city near you
- Search for and order backlist books from our online catalog
- Check out author bios and background information
- Send e-mail to your favorite authors
- Meet the Kensington staff online
- Join us in weekly chats with authors, readers and other guests
- Get writing guidelines
- AND MUCH MORE!

Visit our website at
http://www.zebrabooks.com